KAR
KALIM

Tor Books by Deborah Christian

Mainline

Kar Kalim

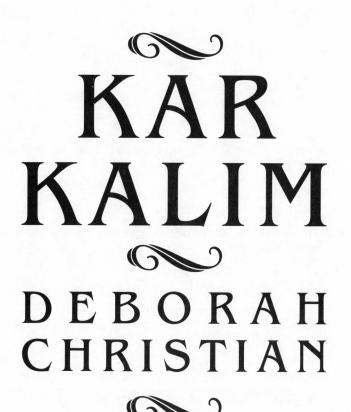

KAR KALIM

DEBORAH CHRISTIAN

TOR®

A TOM DOHERTY ASSOCIATES BOOK
NEW YORK

This is a work of fiction. All the characters and events portrayed in this novel are either fictitious or are used fictitiously.

KAR KALIM

This book is printed on acid-free paper.

A Tor Book
Published by Tom Doherty Associates, Inc.
175 Fifth Avenue
New York, NY 10010

Tor Books on the World Wide Web:
http://www.tor.com

Tor® is a registered trademark of Tom Doherty Associates, Inc.

Design by Basha Durand

Library of Congress Cataloging-in-Publication Data

Christian, Deborah.
    Kar Kalim / Deborah Christian. — 1st ed.
      p. cm.
    "A Tom Doherty Associates book."
    ISBN 0-312-86341-1 (acid-free paper)
    I. Title.
    PS3553.H7257K37 1997
    813'.54 — dc21   97-7599
                                                CIP

First Edition: August 1997

Printed in the United States of America

0 9 8 7 6 5 4 3 2 1

To Maria Isaacs, who enabled, informed, and helped shape this book. With great understanding of the wielding of power, she enhanced this work as she enhanced the author. I dedicate this to her with much love.

KAVRO ISLANDS

GRAELG

CARACK

MORIGAZ · Keshnazar

TOR MAK

City-States of ARGUENTA

1 Stavlia
2 Solente
3 Corvis
4 Gervaes
5 Burris
6 Vene
7 Caronne

Stavlia

Burris

Caronne

SALT COAST

Telemar

8 Egrania
9 Mardevis
10 Telemar
11 Pelestria
12 Selenus
13 Veredux
14 Nicosaria
15 Danistan
16 Singfa
17 Singut

18 Rajpor
19 Rajmana
20 Baremos
21 Caelos
22 Vorsevia
23 Evornia
24 Taelos
25 Aelius

△ Moontooth

G. Mitchell 1997

CHAPTER 1

Higher up in my tower, on a clear day, I can see the glitter of sun on water where Caronne sprawls before the sea. The lower hills, green and stalwart, stand between tower and ocean, and most days a haze dips the road in obscurity. When it rains, the air is fresh. Afterwards, I can see the ocean far distant, the tile rooftops of Caronne, and closer, the caravan trail where it twists among my hills. My tower rises from those hills like a fang tearing at the sky; Saahnmorsk, the hillmen call it: "Moontooth." It is better known as the Tower of the Midnight Rider. From that vantage I first glimpsed Amrey as he rode through the Ronde hills.

He came slowly, a lone rider, picking his way as if looking for something. I could make out no detail of the cloaked figure, but thought he must be overwarm in the early summer sun. He paused in a certain place and looked my way. I felt he was truly able to see—the tower, myself, and the path before him. He had stopped at a point where one of my hidden ways joined the trail. Most passed it by, unaware of its existence. As I watched, he turned his mount and set foot upon it.

I left the window and went downstairs, calling for Una. Together we made ready for our visitor, for at the tower all who come are greeted, although not all are made welcome. Una brought my robe of ceremony and I donned the gold-filigreed mask. With a sign I set the incense burning and arranged my gown and robe as I sat in the great chair. Witchfire began to glow about me as my waiting-woman darkened the hall. Young Corwin brought dates and cheeses, and was dismissed. Una had just poured the wine when Lesseth announced our visitor.

I can see Lesseth if I try. It is seldom worth the effort. To the normal eye he has no form, though voice and substance: it is unsettling to many. The cloaked traveler followed him into the hall, his expression ambiguous. Lesseth carried a lamp, which seemed to float through the air. The great hall is empty and ghost-ridden on such occasions. The only light was the yellow flicker of the lamp and the blue balefire about myself. It pleases me to have it so for first-time visitors.

I nodded and Lesseth set the lamp on the table and closed the door behind the young man. The traveler jumped, startled, and glanced over his shoulder at the door. Turning back to me, he drew himself together. Erasing his misgivings, he bowed, hat in hand.

"Lady, I am called Murl Amrey, of Burris. I would speak with the master of this place."

I smiled, the expression indiscernible behind my mask. I motioned to Lesseth, who placed a chair behind the fellow. "Sit, Master Amrey." He did so, hesitantly, as if he expected the chair to vanish. "Will you take refreshment?"

"Please."

Una brought what had already been prepared, setting it on the table near him. He murmured thanks, and refreshed himself. The silence grew heavy as I waited for him to speak. Now and then he would look at me, but I offered no word as I sat silent and motionless, acting the demigoddess I am rumored to be. It is a useful effect at times. The witchfire gives a foreboding cast to my presence and the mask lends a bit of inhumanity to my appearance. Those who find it disturbing need to be disturbed.

The blue glow limned my form and the lamp lit Amrey's face. He looked unruffled as he finished his wine, unmoved by the urgency of silence to fill the hall with words.

He replaced his empty cup on the table and stared at me as if he could see behind my mask. Glimmers of balefire seemed to dance around him where he sat. I gave no sign of my surprise. Was he trying to impress me? Perhaps he was adept enough to realize that I was merely trying to intimidate him. My efforts had no immediate effect. I don't really concern myself one way or the other. Still, this time I did something entirely unplanned. I broke our silence first.

"Why do you seek the Midnight Rider?" I asked.

Reassurance smoothed his brow. He leaned back in his chair and reached for the wine flask to refill his cup. As his fingers touched it, the flask rose and floated out of reach— Lesseth's work. He brooks no abuse of my hospitality and insists that when I ask a question, it is answered.

It takes some guests longer than others to realize this. Not so with Murl Amrey of Burris. He frowned at the interruption of his refreshment. Sitting more erect, his eyes narrowed as he replied.

"Tales are told. I've come to see if they are true. There are things I need to learn from the Master of the Tower."

"What do you know of the Master?"

Amrey shrugged. "Little. It was suggested that I come here, and so I have."

Suggested by whom, I wondered, but forbore to ask. Once again the pale flash of witchlight sparkled about him. What was he doing? Was he even aware of it? His expression remained unchanged as he confronted me. "I thank you for the food and drink, Lady, but you delay me overlong. You know with whom I have my business. Where is he?"

The man was haughty. His demands grated on me and I spoke more harshly than I had intended. "Things move here in my time, not yours. You would do well to remember that. You will not meet the Master of the Tower."

Temper glinted in his eye. "I must see him! My master said I would be made welcome."

"You master sounds as foolish as yourself." I stood, prepared to leave and end this interview. "You will not meet the master here. There is none. I am she who is called the Midnight Rider by some, the Dark Lady by others, and I weary of this conversation. I bid you good day."

"Wait!" Amrey leapt from his chair in a fresh blaze of balefire—and was abruptly shoved back into his seat by the invisible hand of my good servant Lesseth. Struggling to stand, he called after me, "I was to tell you Clavius Mericus sends his greetings!"

I froze. The witchlight left my form, washed away by my surprise. Slowly I walked to where Amrey sat, no longer struggling. "Do you claim your master to be Clavius Mericus?"

Eyes wide, he nodded, and his fingers fumbled around his neck. "This is his token." He drew out a medallion on a thong, held it out to me. It glowed with faeryfire, the source of the energy I had seen around his aura. I knew the medallion well.

Once it had been mine.

I turned away again, grateful for the mask I wore. "Una, show Master Amrey to chambers he may use. Lesseth, leave

him be. He is no threat to me." To Murl I said, "I will speak
with you after the evening meal."

I left the hall and went to my rooms.

I had been here long and long when Clavius first came to the
tower. I have few visitors who come unbidden: he was one
such. Always such arrivals surprise me. The hillmen note my
midnight forays and avoid Saahnmorsk out of fear and respect. Some few seers have known of my dealings with the
"gods" of this world; they have told tales and the talks have
grown. Some think me a god or goddess; all keep their distance. This is not unwelcome to me. I seek company when
and where I wish it, not at the whim of others.

Clavius was twenty-three, a young and ambitious alchemist,
searching for knowledge and mysterious ingredients he
thought only I could help him find. He loved bards and their
story-songs, and he had taken it into his head to see if the
songs about me were true.

He was surprised to see me. I was not the old and withered
crone he had expected, although I had been here at that time
for over three hundred years. He was clumsy, and polite, and
intriguingly innocent. I am less inclined to teach than I am to
learn, yet Clavius appealed to me, and I taught him. He was
with me for four years.

He became a traveling companion. I gave him a charm of
protection for his journeys through the portals which the tower
guards. Our companionship grew closer, and as his lover I
showed him places and times that I should perhaps have left
unseen. After a sojourn in a land of purple skies, nearly caught
in the cataclysmic downfall of the moibrin, I gifted him with
a medallion of greater power and significance. Later, as must
happen, he outgrew me, for I had taught him too well. We

fought. I made foolish threats to which he made foolish replies, and on that note he took his leave.

I wondered occasionally what had become of him, but spent little time on such thoughts. They are fruitless, and frustrating. What is done is done. I had known him more than forty years agone. I remained unchanged in my physical self: still, it was surprising to hear that Clavius yet lived, indeed now was the teacher and master I had been to him scant years before. I had never thought to see that medallion again, and now who should come bearing it but Clavius' own pupil.

I would give the man a hearing, for his master's sake.

I took supper in the study that night. It is a room of memories for me, sometimes unpleasant, more often not. Three quarters of the walls are covered with niches for the storage of tablets, books, and scrolls. Most of the niches are filled, and I am forced to make uncomfortable decisions about what to keep on hand and what to store, for I collect new tomes frequently.

Thick rugs cover the floor, and there is a fireplace in one wall. It is unnecessary, for there are other sources of heat here. Yet I like the light and the flames, and so there are fireplaces throughout the tower. My desk is near the hearth, facing the leaded window. From the desk I also have a view of the memorabilia that take up the remaining wall space in the study.

The map of Chernisylla is my only reminder of home. The rest are items collected in my travels: sunstones from Oursei, a wall hanging of pak root woven by the Burrowers of Zila, a small bronze urn from Grell. There are devices of science here, too: a particle screen from future Nimm, a holocube from Fornoy. I keep them, although they are useless. The art of "science" works here but imperfectly. Even so, they are all keepsakes. The wall displays many such items, reminders of other times and places—and often prompters to go there again.

In the evening I joined Amrey in an alcove off the dining hall. He busied himself, plucking the strings of the lyre I keep there. He stopped as I entered.

"Please continue," I said. "That was a pleasant tune."

He did not continue. His hand stilled the strings as he stared at me.

"Is something amiss?" I demanded.

He blinked, and turned to hang the instrument back on the wall. "I'm sorry, Lady. I do not always stare as if I had no tongue. You do not wear your mask now."

My fingers strayed to my face. No, I had decided not to wear the mask. Clavius, unseen, stood between us, a presence grown fond with my memories of him. It seemed the mask was unnecessary.

I came into the alcove, sat in a deep-cushioned armchair, and motioned him to the bench nearby. He studied me beneath lowered lashes. Outside the tower, people see me differently. Here I appear as I really am. My hair is black and wavy long, my eyes gray. I am light-skinned, for I seldom venture out under the sun—at least, under the sun of this world. As people here judge beauty, I am considered fair. I look thirty; young among my own people, who are long-lived. I do not age here, and so people invent reasons why that might be, never striking near the truth in all their tales of magic and gods.

"Did Clavius tell you so little about me that you are surprised at my appearance?" I asked. Indeed, I thought Clavius must have told him nothing, from Amrey's earlier demands. I was right.

"Lady, he told me only that I should journey to this tower, that who and what it held would help me. You know him?"

I nodded. ''But he never said anything about me?''

Amrey shrugged. ''We'd spoken of the Midnight Rider, and that Master Clavius had come here once. He told me what to look for to mark the path off the caravan road. But no—he never mentioned you, exactly. I have heard of the Dark Lady who dwells near here.'' He looked me over appraisingly. ''That is you?'' he asked boldly.

I inclined my head.

''Some of the hill people worship you. They say you are sister to the Goddess of the Moon.'' It sounded strange, half question and half challenge. Murl Amrey of Burris was prideful, and seemed to think everyone owed him answers. I, at least, did not.

''What do you want here? I speak to you now only because of the medallion you bear. No, I do not want it. Keep it, and return it to Clavius when you see him again.''

''But—I had hoped not to see him soon.'' He paused, judging my reaction. None showed, and he went on. ''I came to ask if you will teach me, take me on as apprentice.''

To that I had a reaction. He saw my eyebrow raise, my lips turn down. I did not know what to think of this. Had Clavius put him up to it, knowing that I might—*might*—take on a pupil once more? Was this his own idea? He claimed Clavius had said nothing of me.

I was inclined to say no at that moment and leave, but I reined my impatience instead. ''Tell me why you think you are suited, and why I should consider this thing.''

He nodded. ''I am a magician, a thaumaturgist. Master Clavius has taught me all he can. I am exceptionally talented, and I want to learn special things.''

''Is Clavius no longer an alchemist, then, that he has taught you to be a magician?''

''Oh, he's not been active in alchemy for decades. He went

on to other things—healing and magic. Now he is a thaumaturgist of the third rank.''

''And yourself?''

''I am of the fifth rank, Lady. The Master and I both agree
I should not continue with thaumaturgy; from here on the
knowledge merely becomes more specialized. I need to
broaden my experience.''

I looked him over. ''You seem terribly young to be an
accomplished thaumaturge.''

''I am that talented,'' he replied coolly.

Once again I raised an eyebrow. ''Demonstrate.''

He looked surprised, but stepped to the center of the alcove.
He reached into his pouch and drew forth something small
that fit into the palm of his hand. He worked it rapidly, looking not at it but at me all the while. He was not staring as he
had before, but rather was in a semitrance, concentrating intently. His eyes never left mine. I began to wonder what he
crafted here before me. In a moment he had finished with the
object. It appeared to be a lump of clay, and he held it now
between cupped palms.

I am warded and safe from harm in my tower, yet my natural caution awoke. A lump of clay fashioned after me? Was
this offensive magic? I grew alert to any sense of danger or
threat, but sensed none. Now, as I watched, Amrey's eyes
remained open yet distant. A glow began to form in and
around his hands—not the blue of Clavius' medallion, but a
white light, tinged faintly green. The light grew more intense
as I watched his hands. They parted slowly, revealing a ball
of scintillating energy formed around the clay he had worked
a moment before.

His hands stretched out before him, and the globe hovered
stationary. As he began to mutter the brief syllables of a spell,
I could see what the globe held: a miniature clay figure of

myself. The form had been shaped as he looked at me, the energy clothed in details. Hair, face, dress—all seemed reproduced in miniature, though obscured by the globe of light. I felt uneasy with this duplicate of myself. I knew only too well the magical laws "as above, so below", and "like unto like", the heart of the thaumaturge's art. I opened my mouth to protest—and found that I could not move.

No: I could move, barely. Bound, so quickly, with no warning! Had I been a lesser person, or less well protected, I would have been held immobile. With effort I began to stand, slowly, tortuously, as if mired in a pool of molasses. I rose, oh, so gradually, to my feet. I opened my mouth after an eternity, and croaked one word: "Stop."

He watched me for a minute, a minute I had no choice but to wait out. Then, in a gesture of negation, he canceled the spell. The globe of energy faded, and the clay figure fell to the floor.

Time and motion flowed normally for me once again. I staggered forward a step, surprised and more than a little angry. I flung out my arm and shouted a *word* of power, and Amrey was surrounded by a blaze of light.

Now he stood before me, as immobile as a fly in amber. When I cast a hold spell, I prepare for the strength of my target. He would stay there, englobed by the man-sized sphere of energy, until I was ready to deal with him.

I ordered Lesseth to leave our "guest" untouched, and to bring me wine. I returned to my rooms, for I had much to think about.

CHAPTER 2

I drank the wine Lesseth brought, then sent for more. In anger I paced back and forth before the study fireplace. Once, in a fit of rage, I smashed the goblet against the stone, and only dented the bronze for my trouble.

I was too agitated to think clearly about this evening's events. I prowled the study like a caged beast, furious at my surroundings and finding no release. This was not my wont. My eyes strayed to the sunstone on the mantelpiece, a casual solace when upset. Within the stone one can see sparkling landscapes, dazzling otherwheres soothing to mind and soul. I have lost myself in them for hours at a time—but not this night. Forcing myself to sit, I considered Amrey and the problem he had so suddenly become.

He had dared to ensorcel me—me, his better, so much the wiser and more powerful than this upstart apprentice of my former lover. I would leave him captive of the hold spell for weeks and months and years, a decorative centerpiece to my dining. I would chase him forth with hunting beasts freed from otherwhere, creatures whose tooth and claw caused indescribable agony and great festering wounds. Nay, best were to cast him through the topmost Gate, the secret portal over which even I retain only the most tenuous control. He would travel on the winds of time and fate like a leaf upon an icy torrent, beyond recall or hope.

No matter if he was a thaumaturgist of the fifth rank; it was a minor distinction compared to my own. Even though, I thought grimly, he was more powerful than I had expected, or been prepared for.

What had happened in the dining alcove tonight? I had invited him to demonstrate his powers, and he had. I had not specified what he might or might not do, although propriety set its own limits. He had grossly overstepped those bounds. Still, a voice nagged in my head; I should not be too harsh, for he had done only that which I had invited him to do. The fault was mine, for underestimating him.

No, I could not accept that! I had been insulted, virtually attacked in my own warded home, and my pride was sore wounded. I desired revenge, as a slighted child desires attention. I am a proud woman, and I know it. Fault it may be, but it is a fact from which I do not try to hide. And injured pride must be assuaged.

I rose late the next day, and took breakfast in the dining hall. My chair faced the alcove where Amrey stood, prisoner of my craft. My feelings were not the unruly tangle they had been the night before. I dislike hasty decisions, and although I did not regret my sudden spell casting of the evening past, such was not my custom. Now my anger had faded, and I was able to consider Amrey coldly, as he deserved.

Right would be mine if I refused to accept him as apprentice. The reasonable course would be to free him of the hold spell, and have Lesseth show him out. I could bar the pathway against his return and need never bother with him again.

It disturbed me that Clavius came to mind at this time, try though I would not to think on him. I owed Murl Amrey less than nothing, but I held Clavius Mericus in high regard, even after past unpleasantries between us. I pondered undecided long after my meal was done. I had my pride. I also had my honor, and it was this that moved me to treat Clavius' apprentice more kindly than he deserved.

After I freed him—what then? I could neither destroy him nor cast him out; neither could I agree to take him as apprentice. That were too kind, unsuited to my feelings towards him. In fact, I wanted something from him. An apology would not suffice. He must be made to know that I was his superior in things magical. He must make up to me the affront he had given.

I knew then what he should do. Amrey would perform a service for me, one I did not care to do for myself. I would teach him, oh yes—just enough so that he would be well prepared to accomplish the task I set him. Thus would Clavius be satisfied, and perhaps the youth as well.

I thought more on this dilemma, and I remembered something I had long forgotten. Through one of the gates of this tower lies a primitive land—primitive and dangerous. I journeyed there but seldom, yet I recalled what I had learned from the spirits of that plane. Hidden deep in the mines of that world are found the crystals of Styrcia—jewels of dream and illusion, useful in sorcery and scrying. The mines are worked by slaves, and only rarely does such a crystal come to light. Outside of the mines, the gems are found only in the strongholds of the rich and powerful.

Long had I desired such a jewel, yet to gain one was a perilous undertaking. The world where they are found is deeply and inherently magical—and shadowed by evil. I have much else to do than to risk life and soul merely to obtain a magical stone. Yet, I wanted one, and if another were to run the risk for me . . . yes. I would send Amrey there, to recover a Styrcian crystal for me. A simple geas, a compulsion to fulfill the quest for me, and he would serve me in penance for his insult.

To journey in that place, thaumaturge or no, he need must be trained. His knowledge was inadequate to face the dangers that abode there. I would teach him what he needed to know to pursue this quest, and no more. Then would I be done with him and my obligation to Clavius—small though it might be—forever.

The alcove was lit by the globe of power surrounding Amrey. A *word* had been needed to cast the spell; a motion of my hand sufficed to negate it. I drew a rune in midair. It flamed briefly, then it and the spell faded from the room.

Amrey must have been surprised as I caught him in my enchantment. His face showed startlement, and now, freed from that frozen moment of time, his eyes continued to widen. He threw out his arms, as if to catch himself, then noticed that I no longer stood before him. Glancing quickly about, he saw me standing in the dining hall. He turned, puzzlement and concern apparent in his expression.

He noted that my dress was different, and that daylight now came through the unshuttered windows. "What happened?" he asked.

"Half a day has passed," I replied, leaning against the table behind me. "I do not abide behavior like yours in my own house."

He bowed toward me, a brief movement. "No offense was intended, Lady."

How quickly he regained his composure! As if he had committed a simple gaffe at a dress ball! I drew myself up, standing taller than he, and his eyes had to look up to meet mine.

"Do you always conduct yourself so, when you are a guest in someone's house?"

"But—you asked me to demonstrate my powers. I thought—"

"You didn't think." Irritation crept into my voice. "Anyone who claims to be a master of magic must know not only how to use it, but when and where. You seem to be an exceptionally poor judge of those things. Is that what Clavius taught you?"

"Master Clavius has nought to do with this!" he retorted. "I thought you were so powerful—or did, for so said the folk who live nearby. I wanted to show you one of my best spells, to show you what I can really do. How could I know it would work so well?"

Yes, I had wondered about that, too. I had not given it the thought it deserved last night. I was not eager to arrive at the conclusions I thought I must come to. I avoided the subject and answered him with a question instead.

"Can you give me one reason why I should teach you anything at all?"

He stood silently, arms crossed on his chest. Finally he spoke. "I don't know that you *can* teach me anything. Certainly you're more powerful than I, but I don't know how much more." He looked closely at me, as if judging my reaction. "And pardon me for speaking out, but you react too extremely. You are guilty of the same failures in judgment of which you accuse me . . . Lady."

I bridled. This was not at all what I expected to hear from him. Not only did he accuse me, he did so in a tone I had not heard since the Guardians ordered me out of this tower in Chernisylla. I turned away, keeping tight hold on my temper. I deal with the people of this world seldom and I was not accustomed to encounters like this. I considered briefly that he might be right, that I did overreact—and dismissed that as soon as it came into my mind.

He was very brash, this man, or very confident of himself. Even as I fought my temper under control once again, admiration for his mettle flashed through my mind. My other reactions I could deal with later. Most urgent right now was the hint that he would leave. I still had plans for him, and I turned to face Amrey with new composure.

"Listen to me. You may remain here, under the following conditions. Firstly, magic shall not be done here without my permission. When you do have my permission for your efforts, I suggest you temper them with prudence."

Surprise showed on his face. After a moment he nodded agreement, and I continued. "Secondly, you shall follow my orders exactly, and do all that I bid you, as long as you are under my tutelage. Is that clear?"

"Then you take me on as apprentice?"

"No. You are not my apprentice—but I will teach you, as long as it pleases me. Are you agreed to my terms?"

"Certainly." Good; he had not heard all of my conditions, not yet—and it would be some time before he knew them all.

"Very well, then. Lesseth will show you to the study this afternoon. Your lessons begin then." That time would seem late night to him after his dalliance with the hold spell. No matter: his schedule would work to my convenience in this thing.

So began Amrey's instruction. He was an apt student; brilliant and quick to learn. He listened well; seldom did he ask questions, and those were concise and to the point. For a day or two he had little to do but listen to me, for I had to lay a groundwork upon which he could build. That same week, though, we began that which was to occupy us for several more: the mastery of the Power Within.

That Power is something shared by all, in varying degree.

Those with greater insight have it in greater measure. I am a master of the inner Power; Amrey, too, controlled a portion of it. A thaumaturge's art requires direction and single-mindedness of purpose; such powers of concentration are useful for more than that specialized art. There was much, much more for him to learn, though, than concentration alone. How to find the core of power within himself, and how to use it to shape form and function—there Amrey's lessons would begin.

We had been reviewing his knowledge for a week or two, trying simple magical exercises. Before we could build on what he knew, I had to discover exactly what the limits of his experience were. It was an exercise in the properties of colors that persuaded me to move our classes from the study to the workroom upstairs. I but wish the decision could have been made with less disruption to my household and personal life.

It began innocently enough. Colors have vibratory ranges, and magical effects and affinities that vary with the range. The better a magician can visualize a color, the more he is in tune with it and its capabilities. We had been working with colors in preparation for use of their various magical properties.

"Murl," I said, "what does green signify in auras?"

He ran his fingers through his hair, mussing it. He was tired of this drill and review, and eager to work again on visualization—the first step in tapping his inner reserves of power.

"Green . . . represents growth, nature, new experiences, learning, sometimes jealousy or envy—it depends on the context," he replied.

"If you see it in a child's aura?"

"In a young person, it usually means that person is learning something new, or is gathering experience, information."

"And in an old person's aura?"

Amrey shrugged. "It signifies a healer or someone close to nature."

"Any exceptions?"

"When that person is going through new experiences."

"How can one mark the difference?" I asked.

"By the secondary colors in the aura."

"Good." I nodded. "Enough review for now." Murl smiled his relief. "Try the experiment again, this time with the color green."

He had been working all morning on visualization. It still wasn't quite right—something was lacking in his mental picture. The colors he imagined were thin in quality and had the wrong texture to them. I knew that refreshing his memory on the sense and significance of colors would aid the visualization exercises. Now we would put it to the test.

I signed to him to begin. I waited as Murl got comfortable in the chair by the fireplace. He sighed and his body relaxed. Soon he was in trance.

Fine, I thought. He was quick at this. I reached out with the edges of consciousness, my mind brushing his. *Do you remember . . .*

. . . the format? he asked. *Of course.* Our thoughts were linked, as so often happens in that state of mind. Murl would try once again to visualize green, to make that color a tangible thing pervading the room—for without the most concrete and intense of thoughts, form and function drawn from Power cannot take on any real substance.

Think of Green, I thought at Murl. *Let it come alive for you.* Minds joined, I saw what Amrey saw. This time, finally, he became totally involved in the visualization, aware of the nature of *green* and all that it could mean.

The room began to change color about his relaxed form. He saw the hue, he breathed it, tasted it—Green was soft and

resilient, unlike sensations ought to be. He relaxed into a cocoon of nature, of growth and learning, pushing forth tiny
exploratory thoughts into the room around him.

Make it grow now, I thought at him. Tendrils of thought
began to take shape. I watched through Murl's consciousness
as greenery sprouted from his hands and arms. Feelers of
thought spread throughout the room, exploring and seeking
out places Murl had never been.

I could feel it in his approach—he had a better grasp of
this than I had judged. He had needed only to recall his subject, to remember it in detail. Now he thought *green*: nature,
growing, verdant and leafy. The room became a jungle even
as I watched, matter—illusion or not?—shaped and reformed
by Amrey himself.

I found it difficult to separate my consciousness from
Murl's; he held me close bound to him, as vines hold a fallen
branch to the ground. I felt him begin to invade my mind, a
creeping ivy probing mortared stone: persistent and irresistible. He did it unwittingly, for I perceived no evil intent in his
mind; it just happened, as weeds might overgrow and smother
a garden. I strove to break free, but I found myself caught to
him with sprays and leaflets of thought.

Murl, I protested, trapped close to his consciousness, *what
are you doing?* There came no reply: he was too involved in
his own mind, questing, growing, seeking things out like vegetation run rampant. Did he even notice what he did to me?
I could not tell.

I struggled to get away. It was a feeling not unlike falling
into quicksand—slowly, inevitably, one is grasped closer and
closer to the bosom of oblivion. Fronds flourished, vines
stretched and grew—and with them the danger that I would
lose myself among them.

Even as I fought against the pressure of Amrey's presence,

I felt the change in his attitude. His thoughts flowed in a new direction: he reflected now on experiences, the gaining of knowledge, the weathering of hardship, the rejection of love, the hurt.

No! Enmeshed in his daydream, I could not distance myself from it. I felt the hurt as he thought on an imagined rebuff, as he recalled with spite one who refused him the joy of requited love. Anger directed at others, resentments—the green turned to brambles and thorns, the leafy fronds to grasping underbrush.

I tried again to break free from this morass of emotion— and found that I was once more a prisoner of Amrey's. Caged in my own body, I discovered that my physical sight would not work. I was mired in the overworld in his mental vision of resentment and spite. Growing things died around me, and the green that had pervaded the room took on a sickly hue. I tried once more to sever the link between us. Echos of Amrey's passion for his lost love washed over me, and I thought fleetingly of Clavius.

Clavius had bedded me—or had I bedded him? No matter: yet even as I put that though out of my mind, I knew that another took it up. Amrey had penetrated my intimate imaginings. My heart and emotions lay open to him now, helpless against this creeping invasion. I felt assaulted by time and nature, the inexorable pressure of growing things choking out my life and integrity. I began to retreat from the vitality and intelligence that smothered my own, even as I rebelled against it. I was a person, not a thing, to be overrun by the unchecked imagination of my student! I had no idea what went through Amrey's mind. I only sensed his change of mood, slow at first, then swifter, in keeping with the withering and carnage in the visualization about me. He thought of loss, of hurt. I had no idea how greatly his mental image had changed—until I felt the shock of . . . rage? . . . anger?—*jealousy.*

The green Murl envisioned had become a more vile thing than I had ever wanted to see in my own home. The fancy of a lost love, the anger and resentment—and now, in my own heart and head, where did Amrey stop and I begin? I struggled to push him off; this accidental link had outlived its interest.

Even as I gathered my will for another try, I stopped, struck with the realization that I—no, he, Amrey—was jealous of Clavius!

He wanted me. Murl wanted to strike back at someone, somehow—me? Clavius? The lover who had jilted him? No matter who; I was the one caught up, bound to him with runners of thought. A torment of soul and agony of heart swept through me, or was it Amrey? Anything to cease this hurt! I wanted to cry—I sobbed—I tried again to break free, and felt only a flood of envy and mistrust and hurt.

The force of his emotions loosened my control, swept away my reservations. I thought that I—we—must stop soon, surely such intense emotion could not last long. My mind reached out to push against this overwhelming presence—and cringed from the wall of feeling that loomed before me. I despaired, I gave a mental cry of anguish. Was it my own pain? I thought not . . . yet *he* was too close, I was Murl, he was me . . . and he wanted me.

Green, green all around me. I struggled, openly now, pushing against him, against the green wall barrier, against the awful, gut-wrenching wave of spite and envy, lust and jealousy—

I think I screamed.

He can't have you . . .

No one has me—

Don't look at others!

I look at no one . . .

Plants are loyal, they cause no pain—

I am no plant, stop thinking plants, green, growing, your jealousy is growing—

With good reason. You're mine!

I'm no one's!

You're mine! Mine!

No! No one's!

MINE!

And Amrey reached for me, tendrils of thought and waves of willpower clutching me close to him. His intent swept over me, beat upon me like a wave. Who was I? Why was I so selfish? I hurt; there was no need for envy!

Another wave of anguish and desire flooded through me. I knew not if I cried or screamed. I remember only that I could not get free, and I knew of but one way to end this agony of heart and soul.

I gave in.

CHAPTER 3

The dream was long and restless. Emotions and warning voices plucked at me, pulling me awake even as I fought to sleep. A bower of springtime growth beckoned, the scent of wildflowers wafted on the breeze—yet the ground was rocky, and lumps pushed painfully into my back. A chill crept over me, and I shuddered awake.

I blinked, not certain where I was. It was dark, and still, and I ached in every muscle. I pushed myself upright and crushed a leather scroll case beneath my hand.

Scroll case? Yes—I was in the study. I glimpsed stars through the unshuttered casement; I lay on the furs near the chair where Amrey had done—what? Scenes flitted through my mind . . . had they been real, or the fabric of nightmare? I was uncertain. Unease swept through me as I stood and groped towards the lamp on the desk. I smelled once again the wildflower scent that had called me from my dreams— my hand touched the puddle of lamp oil, spilled over the desk and floor. Small things crunched beneath my feet as I searched blindly for the lightstick kept near the lamp. I went about my task mindlessly, my brain not yet reasoning, as if shying away from a thought too upsetting to acknowledge.

Marshaling my concentration, I found the lightstick. It flamed to life in my hand, and I faltered as I beheld the shambles of my desk. There was still some oil left in the overturned lamp. I righted it, wiped the excess from the edge, and lit the wick.

The lamp illuminated chaos.

For an eternity I stood there, lightstick dead in my hand. Surely this was still a dream, a dream verging on nightmare. A litter of scrolls and souvenirs met my eyes on every side. Desk and chairs were shoved awry; crushed rolls of vellum marked where I had lain on the floor. Hardly an item was in its rightful place, and everywhere, scattered as if by an autumn wind, dried leaves covered the floor. It was those that had crunched underfoot in the dark.

Dried leaves? Yes, and bits of creeper vine, and thorny bush, withered, but still rooted in stone and woodwork. Plants, once green, now dead . . . all signs of Amrey's work.

My knees went weak and I sat. I closed my eyes to shut out the disarray, and tried to gather my wits. Amrey's work. And where was he? Not here, though he had been here—I remembered more fully now, for all that had happened could not so easily be shut out of my mind. The burning in my loins told me more of what Amrey had done here, though I sought not for that memory. He had overrun my body even as his magic had overrun my home.

And how could he have done this thing? Again my wards had failed to protect me from his magic. I realized with a start that my safeguards were devised to keep harm outside my walls, and to protect me from physical harm within the tower itself. Such spells were of little use against a psychic on-slaught that began within these walls and that swept my will-power before it like a floodtide.

I looked up in the flickering lamplight and glanced at the door. It stood ajar, and a trail of shriveled greenery stretched through it and into the hallway beyond. Had he gone that way? His magic had. I rose, and quickly checked the secret door in a corner of the study. It was undisturbed; he had left as he had entered, then. I went through that door, following the runners and dried leaves, unanxious to see what I might find.

The trail of vegetation stretched both ways along the hall, yet one path was more overgrown than the other. It led down the passageway to the great central staircase, a spiral that reached most of the way up through Moontooth. Tendrils of plants lodged in cracked stonework, and I pulled some loose, fretfully, in passing. I followed the trail down, down to the great hall and kitchens. I heard movement there and looked in.

Corwin and Una were cleaning up the kitchen, as ravaged by Murl's "exercise" as the upper halls had been. As I watched, vines and creepers were pulled from the hearth and ironwork and borne through the air into a handcart already more than half filled with plant debris. I entered the kitchen.

"Where is Amrey?" I asked.

My servants looked up. The floating creepers stopped in midair: Lesseth held them. Corwin blushed and turned away. Una studied the ground at her feet. "Upstairs, Lady," she replied.

I began to say more, but the vines dropped and Lesseth came swiftly towards me, catching up a table linen as he did so. The cloth unfolded in the air before me. I frowned and drew back.

"Your robes, Lady," he said in his husky whisper.

I looked down, and stared in surprise. My robes, indeed!—or what was left of them, for they hung in tatters from my body. I stood, rather indecently to Corwin's mind, I'm sure, for he kept his back to me. I nodded curtly as Lesseth wrapped the table cloth about me and took the oil lamp from my hand.

I had not noticed in my earlier confusion, but my gown

looked as if it had lain on the forest floor and been weathered to shreds, then donned once again. Lesseth kept an arm protectively about me, and escorted me from the room. As I left, I heard a muttered remark from Corwin, to which Una scoldingly retorted, "... and none of your concern, I've said before!" Her voice followed us to the stairs. "Stranger things happened here before you came to comment on them. Mind, now!" Corwin had been with us but a few months. I was glad to note Una's loyalty, even through my haze of embarrassment and surprise.

Lesseth walked beside me up the stairs. "Are you well?" he inquired.

A simple question, but one I could not answer. I asked him one instead. "What happened below stairs?"

He deferred to me. I felt him shrug. "A season passed where there should have been none. All became overgrown in the afternoon, then shriveled and died into the evening. Una was trapped in the pantry: vines tied the door shut. Corwin tried to get to her, and became entangled himself."

My estimation of Corwin improved a bit.

"And you?" I asked.

"I tried to get to you, but the stairs were too blocked. And when they were clear . . . Amrey came down to us."

"What time was this?"

"Shortly after moonset."

I nodded and Lesseth continued. "He ordered that we clean up. He would be with you, he said, and you wished to be left alone." He paused. "Was that so?" he asked after a moment.

Few question me or what I do. Lesseth had that privilege through our long association and friendship. Still, a mixture of feelings raged within me, and I answered ambiguously. "Perhaps," I replied.

Lesseth knew better than to push me. He sighed. "I hope

all is in order. I do not trust him." I knew what he meant by
that: that I should not trust Murl, either. Again, a confusion
of emotion boiled within me. I had to find Amrey and confront
him. I recalled my mental and physical discomfort, so recently
past, then shied away from the memory, not yet ready to dwell
on that which had happened.

"Be not too concerned, Lesseth," I reassured my friend.
"I understand Murl better than he thinks." That comfort rang
hollow in my own ears, yet even as I spoke those words I
knew they held more truth than I had intended. "He won't
get out of hand. His magic just went further today than we
had thought it would." More than that I would not admit,
even to Lesseth.

I felt his eyes upon me. Lesseth was my first and truest
spirit companion, and he knew me well. He glanced knowingly at the evidence of Amrey's powers; we passed the study
now, on the way to my rooms, and the remains of dried vegetation littered the hall around us. I avoided his gaze and
stared straight ahead.

"You know best," he said, opening the door to my chambers. "But I haven't seen such an undisciplined display of
power within these walls since you were that age." That
brought me up short. I stood frowning while he placed the
lamp, badly flickering and almost out of oil, on the ledge near
the door. He bowed, his shadowy form dim before my eyes,
and left, closing the door behind him.

I let the linen fall from my shoulders. The lamp flame fluttered, was almost out. I reached for a nearby candle, lit it, and
blew out the smoking oil wick. I turned and walked about the
room, lighting candles and lamps. I could have done so with
a motion and a word, but one conserves power for serious
magic. This trivial task was a comfort in its way, and delayed
the time when I would have to think of weightier things.

I set the candle back in its sconce. Brocaded wall hangings gleamed with flecks of silver in the warm light. Scented wax filled the room with the smell of myrrh, and I glimpsed my reflection in the polished shine of a carved walnut sideboard. This was my anteroom and dining alcove when I desired privacy. A small fireplace gaped in the north wall, filled now with cold ashes and unburned wood. I went to the mantel, took down the flask of cordja that stood there. I poured and drank the dark, spicy liqueur. Then I poured another, and crossed to the wardrobes that lined the short passage into my sleeping chamber.

I sipped from my drink, and set it on the side table. I shed my gown and shift and pushed them aside with my foot. They were good now only for use as rags, and perhaps not even as those. Naked, I threw open the garderobe doors, and took an embroidered shift from those stacked within. I keep my plainer things in chests, of course, but these were special—marked for the quality of their weave, and for the spells worked into their fabric. I needed one such now, for before I located Amrey, I planned to call my magic to me. I would dress myself in the aura of the Goddess: not merely in mortal garb would I face him, for I needed the extra advantage of undisguised power. That much was clear to me, though I would say it to no other.

Yet as the shift slipped down over my head, a motion drew my eyes to the garderobe door. It swung farther back than I had pushed it, for a hand grasped its edge. I drew back, concealing my startlement, as Murl Amrey stepped in front of me. Before I could move farther, he was upon me. His arms held mine caught to my sides, and his lips pressed hungrily against mine.

I struggled and pushed back, yet he held me close. Almost I bit his tongue within my mouth, yet something warned me

against his anger, and I forbore. I know not what sped through
my mind. I was repelled, and yet, I was attracted. His manhood throbbed against me, and an answering rhythm pulsed
within my own body. I was shocked. What was happening to
me? Did he have me under a spell? Not possible, I protested
to myself—but I had seen what he could do to me. I was
shaken, and dared not let it show. I tried to twist my head
away. I could not. I found myself returning his kiss, pressing
against his body . . .

"No!" I exclaimed, jerking back. With an effort, I pulled
away, far enough to glower at him in the candlelight. His
nostrils flared, his breath came short. His desire was unmis-
takable, but I could not give in.

"Hold!" I commanded. Somehow the few threads of power
I grasped to me held strong. He stood, let me pull from his
embrace. Then he threw back his head and laughed.

I flushed with rage and embarrassment. "What do you here,
sirrah?"

He stood boldly before me, in the door to my own bedchamber. He wore only his undertunic and hose—he was
nearly as undressed as myself.

"Why, I needed a place to rest. I thought you would join
me soon."

I choked on a reply. Nothing was suitable, and I could force
no words past the tightness in my throat.

"I knew I would be welcome," he added. His eyes ran
over my body as if it belonged to him. My pulse hammered
in my throat. Welcome! In my rooms? I wanted to feel outraged, and almost succeeded.

"We must talk," I gritted. "Go. Await me in the anteroom." I turned to the wardrobe, but his hand on my arm
pulled me back to him.

"Yes, we must," he agreed. "Now. In here." And he dragged me into the bedchamber after him.

I hung back, yet he was stronger than I. My steps faltered. He drew me to the bed, pulled me down beside him. I pushed him away and sat up. He kept his grip on my arm, and I could go no farther. I steeled myself and frowned down at him.

"What do you imagine you do, Amrey of Burris? Are you as insensitive to hospitality and power as you seem?"

I accused him with my eyes. He smiled in the dim light from the doorway, and freed my arm.

"It would seem that the student is more powerful than the teacher," he observed. I listened for a hint of smugness in his voice, and found none. He merely stated a fact, one that my ears burned to hear. I began to speak, but he cut me off.

"No, Inya, look not so angry. Yes, I know your name. And much more about you, since this afternoon." I leaned back, startled at the sudden memories that welled up in my mind: Murl and his father Keshdar, spice merchant of Burris. Pack trains of spices and herbs. Lord Pelan of Burris, and his thaumaturge—Clavius Mericus. An apprenticeship, proposed by the youth. The rage of the father. Other bits and pieces flashed in my mind's eye as Murl spoke again.

"You are beautiful, and I wanted you. I could not control what you awoke in me—my power or my lust. It sprouted and grew and ran its course, and you were its cause." He met my eyes. "We were both lost in it."

Should I believe that? How lost had he been? He was the one who had remained conscious, had wandered about the tower while I lay entranced or aslumber in the study.

"Perhaps I need to learn safeguards other than those I know," he proposed. He stared at me intently. "I do not wish to hurt you."

It seemed he left something unsaid, but his fingers strayed

up my arm and over my breast, and I pushed his hand away, distracted.

"You have a rare talent," I said, trying to keep his mind off me. "Yes, there is more you can learn to control the power within you. But"—I swallowed—"I don't think I can be your teacher."

I recalled my original plan, to send him aquesting for me. It still appealed to me, but now it seemed the danger to myself might outstrip the benefits. Yes, I knew more than he, but I would have to be very careful about how I warded myself in the future. Should I send him away?

I looked down at him as he lay stretched out at my side. His eyes were like a deep pool, drawing me down . . . aye, I found him attractive, and even then, resentment burned inside me. He had worked his will on me, mentally and physically. Without my consent, he had made free with me—

Was I excusing my own weakness? I crushed a thought that suggested I had wanted him, too, even though the way of his taking had not been expected.

He looked at me, with anger, I thought. He said, rather harshly, "You can work with me. You must work with me. Only you can teach me what I must know." Was I so indispensable? It sounded not like a plea, but like an order. My anger rose even as he reached for my arm once more and jerked me prone beside him.

"We should learn from each other," he breathed in my ear. His hand was on my breast, his lips on my neck. I felt myself begin to melt, and refused to yield to him thus.

"Murl," I said, placing my hand on his mouth, "you have wronged me—"

"No!" he grated. "And if I have, I will make it up to you. So." He kissed me on the lips. "And so." His teeth nipped my neck, moved to my shoulder. "And so." His mouth moved to my breast, and his fingers slipped up beneath my shift. I sensed a change come over him. The anger was gone, and desire flooded in its place.

"Let me make it up to you," he whispered. His breath was warm and moist in my ear, and thrilled me in spite of myself. He felt my response beneath his touch, and his lips joined with mine once more.

For the second time, I surrendered myself to Murl Amrey. This time I knew full well what I did, and there could be no accusation afterward.

I lay awake that night long after Murl had fallen asleep. He had called me "Inya" again in the height of his passion. None here but Lesseth knew my real name; it had been long since any other had called me by it. I remembered what Murl had said: that he knew my name, and much else about me. I thought of the memories I had gained, and realized how intimately we must know each other.

I thought of Murl, how he had once been a hopeful elder son, dutiful, the protégé of his father, Keshdar. The elder Amrey was the only spice merchant in Burris: his pack trains were the marvel of the town, and himself the only merchant summoned with frequency to an audience with the autarch, Lord Pel.

At the age of nine, Murl began to accompany his father to the knight's stronghold, and there delivered rare herbs in carved boxes to the knight's thaumaturge, Clavius Mericus.

Mericus was tall and dark, imposing of appearance. The boy was fascinated by him, and it was Murl himself who one day gathered his courage and privately asked Mericus to accept him as his apprentice. To the boy's surprise, Mericus agreed, and interceded with Lord Pel. At the request of his lord, Keshdar had little choice but to comply. Murl, the bright

hope of the house of Amrey, was swept away from his father
and into the arms of the arts magical.

Forced to smile before his liege, Keshdar was under no such
obligation at home. Murl was cursed and disinherited by his
ranting parent. He was turned from his house, sent packing to
Mericus—"That fraud who's beglamoured your wits!"—and
loudly informed that brother Kevlin was now and would remain the only heir to Keshdar's "few and hard-gained sil-
vers."

Of injured pride there was no shortage; I ground my teeth
as I shared the memory of rejection with Murl. He turned his
back on his family willingly after his father's abuse, and im-
mersed himself in Mericus' work and teachings.

That he had excelled in his education was self-evident. I
knew much more about him—his pride, his righteousness, his
anger—than I wanted to know. It was helpful to understand
him in some small degree. And yet, how much did he understand about me?

I cast my thoughts back, searching for that which he might
use against me. Understanding was one thing, leverage to be
used for ill was quite another. Just how much did he know
about me?

Obviously Murl knew my name: R'Inyalushni d'aal. In my
own tongue, it meant "eldest daughter of Ushni, and Lady of
her clan." My mother had passed on but six years before I
came to this land of Drakmil, and so I had become clan matriarch in her stead. Well might that honorific d'aal be rather
ond'aal: *dishonored* Lady of her clan.

Rarely did I contemplate the circumstances that had forced
me from my home. I did not want to think on them now. But
if Murl knew, could the knowing be a weapon in his hand?
Reluctantly I called to mind all that he might have garnered

from my memories, searching for something that could give him a hold over me.

What he might have learned of other planes was not important to me. That he may have learned such was entirely possible, for travel in different realities is the privilege of those who guard the Towers of Chernisylla. The fabric of space and time is weak there, rent in places by stress and ill-wrought magic of old. The Towers hold the portals that guard those weaknesses in our defenses, and the Guardians watch over the Towers.

Ushniyalna was Guardian in Moontooth before me. The duty falls from mother to eldest daughter; I would be Guardian and head of our clan after her. Oh, how I dreaded that day! To be Guardian was a task much better suited to my sorceress-sister Belyin, or even to Lanla, the youngest and already married. They would be content to stay, aloof and dutiful, watchdogs on the frontiers of hazard. They had no desire to explore, to wander—and a Guardian alone was not permitted this, for always one must remain in the Tower if another chose to travel through the portals. Safeguards, they claimed.

Safeguards against what? I had asked. I worked well and often with elementals and spirits on other planes. What harm was there in them? Mother spoke of fears and possibilities, and yet it had been generations since there had been trouble with any of the Tower portals.

I, in my wisdom as clan head and Tower Guardian, chose to continue my travels, even though none other with Power remained in the Tower as safeguard.

And so it happened that the only unguarded Tower in Chernisylla fell one day to forces that pushed through a portal in my absence. I was beyond reach; other Guardians fought and saved my Tower and my people.

Eventually I returned. I saw the carnage in and around my Tower, and went outside in shock. Many of my clansmen and the Guardian Mertalluki d'aal were dead, and the Council had gathered before the gate.

I looked past the burned houses, the crying children. Cousins and aunts stared at me accusingly; I stared instead at those who confronted me. My sister Belyin had been recalled from her apprenticeship; she stood beside Vayanallini d'aal, head of the Council of Guardians.

Vaya stepped forward, for all her age and gray hairs still a commanding figure. She fixed me with her green eyes, dark now with ire. I could not look away.

"You left the Tower unguarded." It was a statement, not a question. "Your servants told us why—those that survived." Her tone was distant. Never before had any voice chilled me so.

"The Council approves of Guardians upon their inheritance," she continued. "It raises them up, and it can cast them down."

I took half a step back as I realized what she intended to say. She motioned Belyin forward. My sister looked anguished, but stood by Vaya's side.

"Tomorrow you will leave this Tower. It is yours to guard no longer." Vaya placed a hand on Belyin's shoulder. "Your sister will discharge the duties of Guardian, since you cannot.

"Where you go, what you do, is your own concern and that of your clan. You are no longer welcome on the Council.

"That is all."

She gave me a last, hard look, then turned and left with the Council. Belyin stood a moment, as if she struggled to say something. Tears came to her eyes, then she, too, left.

I was in turmoil. For a timeless while I raged and cried alone in my room. That did little to change the facts. I was

Lady of this Tower, not my sister. It was mine by rights and inheritance, and all I cared for was here. I had seen the looks of hate from my own relatives: how could I live among them now?

I laughed as I saw the solution to my plight. They wanted me gone? Very well, then: I would go, and the Tower with me! They could build another Tower, if they wanted to guard this rent in the fabric of reality. Anything can be moved, with enough energy. I had the Power, and I had the elementals; together we could push the Tower through the very rift it guarded.

Lesseth and the elementals aided me. That night, when the moon was high, the task was done. Thus had I come to Drakmil so many years before, and near dead with the effort.

I brought my thoughts back to the present. If these memories were all that Murl had picked from my mind, then no harm was done. But I recalled again why I avoided dwelling on Chernisylla and those I had left behind: always these unpleasant emotions curled within me, little dimmed with time. I refused to spend tears and regrets on people and events centuries behind me, by the scale of this world. Done was done. Of important matters, Murl could only have learned hints of what I would teach him in due course.

With a sigh, I pulled the feather quilt over my shoulders. However much we knew of each other, I could alter nothing now. I resigned myself to it, and fell restlessly asleep as the sky grew light.

CHAPTER 4

Murl's lessons moved thereafter to my workroom. He apologized, in his fashion, for the destruction his unharnessed power had caused earlier. He could not dissemble, however—I read in his face his interest in the other levels of this tower, and pleasure in his progression beyond the boundaries of the study.

His first visit to the upper levels evoked a strange reaction in myself. We walked along the hall leading from my chambers, past the study—set in order by Lesseth during the night—and on to the spiral staircase. The litter of the day before had been cleared away, though subtle evidence of Murl's powers could still be glimpsed in cracked stone and split woodwork.

On the stairs I turned left, to go upwards. I waited for Murl to join me on the landing, and felt silent turmoil as he stood expectantly beside me.

In all the years since my mother's death, only two people had passed this way besides myself: Lesseth, and the Guardian Paralanysha. Now, for the first time, I was about to show someone how to negate my own lock-spell—and someone, at that, whom I did not especially trust.

There is no help for it, I thought. I have more spells than this one to protect me, and it is necessary that he know how this one works.

"Attend," I said to Murl. "See you aught of significance here?"

He looked about. We stood on a square landing, of no evident purpose. Stairs stretched away behind us and ahead of us. The stonework was uniform, lit at intervals by oil lamps.

Murl shook his head. "Why do we stand here, then?" he asked.

"Try to proceed."

He look askance at me, then moved to set foot on the upward winding spiral. He halted abruptly, foot in midstep. His hands extended, stopped in midair. He turned back to me.

"The way is blocked!"

"Of course. This is a simple warding spell, preventing intruders from exploring further. Now, look at the air, about here . . ." I gestured. "What do you see?"

Murl concentrated, let his eyes unfocus slightly as he stared where I had pointed. "Ahh . . . a slight haze—and in it glows a rune."

"A glyph," I corrected. "It is written so." I retraced the pattern in the air. Lines glowed briefly, then faded once more from normal sight. "To allow passage, one must trace it in reverse, and visualize the erasing of the glyph as your finger traces over it. Thus."

I demonstrated. Murl watched as the glyph faded beneath my moving finger. I walked forward, up a few steps, and the glyph slowly reformed behind me.

He stretched out a hand, found the invisible barrier once more in place. "It returns," he said, stating the obvious.

I nodded. "There is a spell of permanency on it. It is like a door that always closes, unless it is held open."

He drew a breath. "Then I'll try it now," he invited himself.

Murl did it correctly the first time. The glyph disappeared

once more beneath his finger, and reformed to bar the way behind us. He followed me up the stairs to the next level and the workroom there.

I showed him how to unlock the workroom door, which bore a similar glyph. This one, however, also required a minor word of power. Centuries of secrecy kept a strong hold on my tongue, and it was with difficulty that I divulged that word to Amrey. I reminded myself that there were more safeguards in this one room than anywhere else in the tower, save for the portals and Gates on other levels. I had little to fear from him in these places where I was so well guarded.

Murl viewed the workroom in a sweeping glance. The eastern side of the chamber is partitioned off from the rest of the room: it is there that I do rites and rituals requiring a magic circle. I led Murl past an orderly clutter of jars and vials, candles and alembics and the other miscellany of my craft. At the partition I stopped, and drew aside the curtain that hung there.

Before us gleamed a magic circle, inlaid in the flagstones in a pattern worked of silver and iron. In the center stood the altar, decked with the accouterments of ritual magic. The power here was an almost tangible thing: when so much magic has been worked for so long in the same place, it cannot help but leave its mark on the ether there.

"We will work here," I told Murl. "It is safer so."

He regarded me with an expression I could not read, then swept the room with his eyes once more. "Well established, Inya," he said. "I'm sure I'll feel quite at home here."

I thought he referred to the similarities this room bore to one where a thaumaturge would practice his art—the Star of Shemm and the Triangle of Invocation were certainly symbols he would recognize. They were set into the floor nearby, of the same work as the circle that dominated the room. Yet, there was something in his voice that gave me a different message—one I chose to ignore.

Lessons began once again. The first few were the most difficult for me: Murl continued to practice visualization, and the first time in the circle I had to squelch a warning voice that reminded me of what had happened before. I pushed timidity from my mind, and watched as he continued his magical exercises.

Now, properly warded, I found my courage rewarded—his imaginings had all the texture of reality, but only within the narrow confines of the circle that I controlled. I remained untouched throughout. I thought that now Murl's illusions were directed less intently towards myself; now that he shared my bed at night, his actions had lost something of the urgency they had had about them. But whether or not that was so, I had made a wise decision. In using the workroom I remained unharmed, and Murl's powers were safely confined therein.

It was within that circle that Amrey truly began to learn. As a thaumaturge his powers of concentration and willpower had been honed fine; still, he accomplished by brute force what I could teach him to do with ease and finesse.

Thaumaturgy, by its very nature, concentrates on physical manipulations on the material plane. Murl had forced his great natural Power to obey the demands of his will: he had thrown boulders through the air without benefit of a catapult, and caused fire to burn where there was naught to spark the flame. He had no sense of the greater Powers—practitioners of his ilk seldom do—and appreciated ritual only so far as it forged a bond between his will and its object.

We had already reviewed theory and principle, and refreshed his memory of magical premises. Our early exercises

in the circle were simple ones. I sat before Murl to demonstrate.

We had centered our energies and lightly entranced ourselves. Power glowed around us in a perceptible nimbus, a
blue-white glow from myself mingling with the green
radiance of my student.

"This first effort will be a simple one," I said. "I will teach
you how to create light, or, in another form, balefire. Witchfire, if you will.

"You perceive the energy around us?"

Murl nodded. "Our auras, expanded with power, is it not?"
he asked.

"Yes. That power comes from within yourself. We each
have an innate amount of such energy to tap—as if each of
us were a living battery."

He looked at me blankly.

I searched for an analogy or word he would understand.
"Consider, then, that we are each of us a living well, that a
natural spring keeps us filled to a certain level. The water may
be depleted, but, in time, the spring will return it to its original
level."

He nodded his understanding.

"Very well. You may use this natural energy as you will,
within limits. The greater the feat, the more energy required
to accomplish it. If you drain your 'well' of power, you may
inadvertently draw on the reserves kept for your bodily func-
tions. If that comes to pass, you may die."

He raised his eyebrows. "A time or two, I've come nigh
unto collapse. Did I—?"

"Yes. You overtaxed your limits. But now, for this exercise." I held out my hand, took a breath and funneled my
energy into my cupped palm. A glowing light, blue-white in

color, sprang to life in my hand. The light seemed to have no source, yet burned as brightly as a lantern.

"You see?" Closing my fingers, I let the light in my hand extinguish and extended the glow up my arm and along the outline of my body. I sat, outlined with that aura of power that I use in my audience chamber, that some call faeryfire.

I let the coruscation fade. "Now you try," I said to Murl.

His brow furrowed in concentration and he stretched out his hand. With my other Sight I could see the energy shift in his aura, yet nothing flamed to life in his palm. He tried again, fruitlessly.

I laughed, and he looked up at me coldly.

I smiled then, to soothe his ruffled feelings. "You try too hard, Murl. You mustn't force it."

"I'm not."

"You are. To use this power, you must let it flow from you, not order it forth. It is the difference between coaxing a mule forward with hay, and driving it forward with a stick."

He frowned.

I held my own hand out. "I will describe this as I do it. Follow along."

He extended his hand once more, and I began.

"First, a deep breath, to relax, and center your energy. Good. Now, feel the energy in your aura—all you've tapped of your own resources. Glowing. Warm. Filling the air about you."

His eyes closed, visualizing what I described.

"Let all that energy flow along your arm and down to your hand. Feel it collect there, a ball of light, kindling from within until it glows like a flame. Visualize it, burning without heat in the palm of your hand."

His eyes opened—and the room grew bright with the light from a small globe of witchfire.

Murl smiled and the flame in his hand expired. I started to chide him for his lack of concentration, but before I could do so, his eyes closed and suddenly his body was outlined with a brilliant green radiance of faeryfire.

"Good!" I exclaimed.

"Show me more," he replied eagerly.

I did. I taught him how to cast a light spell, which is really just the act of binding the glowing energy to an object. Murl surprised me then by going a step further and animating globes of light so that they danced and swirled within the circle, finally marching around the circumference, seemingly of their own accord. At the end of that demonstration, though, he was pale and a fine sheen of sweat covered his face.

"Enough," I ordered. "You need to rest."

He did not resist, and we left together, to take dinner and retire.

Murl progressed rapidly, from manipulation of physical objects—levitation and the like—to scrying and minor telepathy.

Yet when the full of the moon came upon us, I had to excuse myself. Lessons were canceled that day and the following. The first time Murl took it with ill grace. The second time, he leaned forward, riveting me with his eyes.

"Why? I can understand that no lessons are held during Lahmasrad each week—that, after all, is a holy day—"

"It is Lady Day, and holy to that goddess," I corrected him.

He snorted and continued. "—but what has the full of the moon to do with my lessons? This interferes with my study. Why?"

I clenched my fists. Was he then so ignorant that he knew nothing of the moon cycles? Then I realized that he must not! And his ignorance was twofold, for neither did he know what it was that I did on the night of the full moon. Well, then: I must at least teach him about the moon, that he understand more of the source of his powers, and be the wiser for it.

"You are no ritual magician yet, Murl. There is that which I must do on those nights. The details need not trouble you."

Then he said something very revealing.

"Am I then to be a ritual magician?"

I opened my mouth to speak, then closed it. I had not really thought of him in those terms. In this plane, a confusion of deities disguises the true nature of the world-spirits that are one with life. Few men here know of the God; even fewer are called to serve him, just as women who serve the Goddess are rare. More often, persons are drawn to ritual for the plain power it exerts in their physical world. They style themselves ritual magicians, and exercise magic shorn of the spiritual understanding that gives it balance. To the uninformed eye my methods and their methods would look the same.

It was not a goal I had planned to offer Murl, but I also had no desire to share with him the spiritual insights that made me so powerful on this plane. If the title of ritual magician would keep him learning what he needed to survive on his quest, he could think that was the intent of this training. At least it would reduce his understanding to the forms alone, and leave untouched the underlying philosophies of power.

And if that were to be so . . . I changed the refusal that was on my tongue. "You might learn what one needs to master ritual. How far you progress remains to be seen. As for the full moon tonight—it means more than you know. You may join me, as an observer only. Is that clear?"

His eyes lit up. "Certainly!" he agreed.

I turned to leave, a wry smile on my face. Aye: he would learn somewhat that night, of that I was certain.

* * *

Horsetail clouds layered the night sky. It was crisp, too chill for this time of year. The moon cast a foggy half-crown halo over the nearby ridge-tops.

I had bathed and annointed myself, and the scent of patchouli filled the night air around me. I wore the requisite shift and silken over-robe, but felt no chill: the magical preparations warmed my blood, and I was oblivious to the night air. Amrey climbed the tower stairs behind me. He had glanced oddly at me as he had joined me outside my chambers. Now, though, he seemed to take all in stride, as if he were used to this monthly event.

We passed through several doors. I hid the signs that unlocked the glyphs of warding; Murl was discreet and did not press to know what my motions meant at each portal. On the landing before the roof we paused next that most difficult of doors; we had no business with it, but Murl was too sensitive not to notice the chill that poured forth from it, even through its wood and iron bindings. I passed it by, and asked Murl to open the trap to the roof. He nodded obligingly, but eyed that door as peculiar sounds echoed through it and into the hallway where we stood.

"What lies through there, Inya?" he asked, before ascending the ladder to the roof.

I shook my head. "Nothing, Murl. A void, a dangerous void. You cannot open the door. It is just as well."

A brief expression, almost one of disappointment, shadowed his face. Then he turned back to the ladder, and climbed to the tower roof.

We stood on the topmost platform of Moontooth; had it been daylight, we would have seen a breathtaking panorama of distant ocean and inland mountains. The tower peaked above us, a decorative crenelation of granite and obsidian. But it was late; the moon lurked, obscured behind clouds, and naught could be seen distinctly. The hour was near midnight, yet I knew there was time enough to see us to our goal, and back again.

Murl looked about curiously. The tower roof was bare, though wide; he saw little reason why we should be there, and in his hasty manner began to question me. Unheeding, I turned to the moon, a luminescent glow behind banks of cloud. I raised my arms—and in that moment, Amrey was stilled.

The clouds swept through the sky, moved by my summons. The words of power that I spoke went unheard or misunderstood by him. They blended with the freshening wind, an otherworldly undercurrent of sound. Murl stood by my side, gazing into the rampart of mist overhead, aware of its change, yet not certain what the effect had to do with us.

I spoke the final invocation, and my words echoed through distant planes. My friend and ally heard my call, and responded again as he had so often before. The night-dragon Reydjik gathered himself from condensation and mist; he mingled clouds with form and played illusory games of presence. He was a daydream of vapor, and a nightmare of solidity. He swooped down upon the tower in his fashion, scraps of moisture wafting ahead and around his person. He snorted at me; a billowing cloud of moisture roiled over battlements and obscured our selves in chill fog.

Murl recoiled. "What is that—that—"

Expression failed him. I supplied a description. "—that draft from the seven icy hells? Reydjik comes."

I looked expectantly upward, and indeed, boiling out of the night-cloaked sky, shouldering clouds aside, the night-dragon descended and settled atop Moontooth. I spared Amrey scrutiny of his expression; instead I grasped the vaporous bulk of Reydjik, and swung up onto his back. "Come," I ordered, extending a hand. I would not humor an awestruck youth. Murl would learn to respond quickly, or not at all.

I wasn't disappointed. Without comment, he scrambled to sit behind me, hands clasped about my waist. I murmured to the skybeast, and we lifted and swooped from the tower. I smiled to note my student clung to me as an anchor, and not as a lover.

The flight seems always longer than it is, yet is never so long as it ought to be. Winds that would chill normal mortals flowed past unnoted; their currents hindered or helped, but the effects of cold and wind could not pass the cocoon of magic within which we rode. I know not what Murl saw or watched: surely it was different from my perceptions, for I held brief converse with elemental friends, and paced old companions through the heavens, while he cast about, bewildered, and clutched at me whenever we flew into a cloud. I laughed aloud when Reydjik finally plunged earthward. I remembered well my early flights—I had grown to enjoy the heart-stopping dip towards the earth below, but Murl must feel as I once had, long ago. The motion caused him to groan; I laughed anew, and patted his hand in reassurance.

Below us spread a valley caught close between forest and mountain. Here, near Morigaz and the western jungles, the cloud cover was broken by the sudden rise of hills. The moon shone full and silver on the walled city of Tor Mak, its tile-roofed buildings of stone and brick in stark relief against the backdrop of bright cobbles, well lit even at this hour. Marble towers rose high above the city—the wall towers lofty, those of the citizens loftier yet. It was towards the greatest of those private towers that we angled: the refuge of Cendurhil, Master of the Mage Guild, foremost of wealthy citizens in a town known for its riches.

Torchlight limned the tower platform. Several figures

waited there, for this was my usual time of arrival, and I was
expected. Murl, however, was not. Reydjik settled his amor-
phous bulk upon the stonework; Cendurhil stepped forward to
help me down, but paused by the night-dragon's side, looking
askance at my companion.

"Who might this be, Lady?" he asked, even as he extended
his hand to me.

His question smacked of disrespect. Ignoring his hand, I
drew myself up and frowned down at him in my turn. "This
is Master Amrey, my guest and companion," I said shortly.

Cendurhil exchanged a look with me; the torchlight shone
off his stark elvish features, and it was clear that he marshaled
his tongue before he spoke. "Umm . . . this is a Conclave . . ." he began apologetically.

I cut him off. "I knew that before I came, Magemaster.
Amrey has a purpose here, as do I."

I saw he was not convinced. To forestall further argument,
I called power to me, and grew taller in my saddle. Murl's
breath caught short: his hands, still resting around my waist,
told him my form had not changed, but his other senses dis-
agreed.

The effect had an impact on Cendurhil, as well. "Who summons the Powers at the Conclave?" I demanded. "Who com-
munes with the gods and spirits, and becomes one with
them?"

To that he had no answer. Cendurhil avoided my eyes, and
ducked his head.

"Your judgment is not in question, Lady," he apologized.
The tone of his voice changed with his concession; sing-song,
he spoke in a pitch which carried to the gathered mages. "Join
us: you are welcome. Grace us, drink with us, feast with us
tonight. Blessed be." He completed the ritual formula, and I

dismounted. Sweeping into the midst of the mages of Tor Mak, I left Murl to fend for himself. He scurried after with what dignity he could maintain, and shadowed me throughout our stay.

CHAPTER 5

The four high wizards of Tor Mak gathered round their battlemented workplace, myself in their midst. Storm-wracked skies hung turbulent overhead, but no errant breeze dared sweep this warded place. The Circle of Convocation gleamed in smooth-grained granite before me, the inner compass inlaid with silver and mother of pearl, the gold and iron of the outer ring ignorant now of sun's warmth, unresponsive at this midnight hour.

Without the circle, four triangles of invocation marked the points of the compass. They were warding points, places to invoke guardians of the circle—or focal points at which to summon entities native to other spheres of existence. The granite here held hard-incised lines set with cold-forged iron and electrum, scribed round about with sigils and talismans of protection and confinement.

Preparations had been made before my arrival; it but remained for me to draw the circle with the crystal-tipped rod of power, and to lead the invocations that would ward our four elemental gates and gain the watchful aid of the guardians who dwell there. Cendurhil took up the invocation, his slender height facing the east, lilting baritone enjoining the air elementals that gathered there, unseen. Then grey-haired Berengar invoked fire to the south; soft-spoken Gaelis called water to the west; stern Liuthwe called earth to the north, her

voice ringing into the night fallen strangely silent as the circle
flared to completion around us, a hemisphere of light and energies I perceived with my other-sight, shimmering like an
aurora in the night around us.

Amrey stood behind me, out of my path; Cendurhil and the
others remained by their stations at compass points. I presided
in the center of the circle, near the altar where the trappings
of high magic lay ready for my use. I reached for incense,
cast a handful upon the tripod-clasped brazier that stood
alight. As fragrant smoke filled the spellbound air, the real
work of the evening began.

I faced the south, where the triangle of invocation was dou-
bly secure tonight, ringed round with salt and diamond dust
for restraint. Within those bounds stood a bottle of polished
agate, striations glistening like wet marble in the wash of
moonlight. It was there that I focused my intent and my powers, seeing the southern wardpoint as more than a beacon for
the watchfulness of friendly guardian entities. I *looked,* and
saw the glow of unearthly flames through that gate, a portal
to the Elemental Sphere of Fire, a pathway there and yet not
there, not until it should be more firmly called into being.
Devoid of visitor or elemental life until such should be invited
or summoned forth. The work of a few minutes . . .

Amrey observed carefully in the background, a watchful
Cendurhil eyeing him in turn, ready lest an unthinking move
betray our intent and ruin the working I had begun. For this
was a summmoning of the kind the forest-loving elves rarely
do and feel little kinship with: the elemental of fire is ill-
bidden and hard to control. Invoking the names of the Guardians of Power, of the higher forces of order and creation that
even the masters of that sphere must hearken to, wielding that
authority like invitation and quiet threat in one, thus did I
summon forth Ri'ush, Elemental Lord of Fire.

The wizards of Tor Mak knew it was not the Fire Lord in his own person that came through this small portal to the chill planes of earth—nay, for such a conjuring in full form would we must needs meet within the heart of a volcano, or as near as mortal form could bear, and use Words of Power that would deafen lesser sorcerors than myself. Here atop the Tower of the Stars in verdant Tor Mak it were but an avatar of the Fire Lord that stepped through that small gateway made by my bending of power to my will.

Murl did not know this, though, and when upon the heels of Ri'ush's name, a molten glow filled the stone bottle and spilled forth from the mouth of that container, then did my student gasp in surprise behind me. I quirked a smile he could not see from where he stood, then put the young man out of my thoughts. For Ri'ush filled the southern triangle with his presence, and the agate jar melted in that moment, slumping into a puddle of molten stone that smoked and steamed, pouring from the focal point that had become a gateway direct from the Sphere of Fire to this our native human realm.

Such heat, such elemental force should have melted the granite where the triangle was inlaid—but such was the warding, that it did not. What had begun as small point of warmth grew to fill the point of invocation, filling the form to its every border until naught remained in that triangle but a sultry light, a fiery heat like a pool of molten lava, halting only at the very edge of the iron-set lines that formed what had become a triangle of summoning.

Then did I call his name three times, the inevitable summons that no truly named creature can resist, and out of that volcanic pit came a steam, a boiling roil pulsing upwards, like lava flowing over the ground. The air writhed in protest above it as molten sludge poured in impossible volume from that smallish triangle, mounting higher and higher until a manlike form stood there. A form that stirred, like a monolith come to life, and trod our way with one heavy, molten foot, patches of black crusting over where this elemental figure cooled now in the earth-chill air. That foot halted just at the edge of the triangle of restraint. Eyes like smoldering embers cracked open and glared at me where I stood in the southern point of the circle.

"Warding against fire serves you naught, Dark Lady."

A voice like the pour of ashes from a bucket; a susurrus underlaid with the crackle of muted flames. The slate flagstones smoked beyond the triangle, but the metals of the warding there stayed cool and safe next that inferno, giving the lie to the Fire Lord's bold statement. He could perhaps break these bonds, if he chose. But then he would anger others who are my allies and it was all, perhaps, not worth the trouble . . .

Easier to hear what I had to say instead. "Why do you call me?" the avatar asked impatiently. "It is too cold to linger."

I took a breath, weighing the words I was about to speak. "You stir the earth with your grumblings, Lord of Fire," I said. "Maka'tange, Father of Ashes, stirs to life after these two centuries of slumber."

An indecipherable expression rippled across the elemental's molten visage. "And if it does?"

That volcano overshadowed Morigaz, lifeblood and port city on this western coast of Drakmil. Should Morigaz vanish in a paroxysm of the mountain's fury, then would Tor Mak wither and die. And all the other towns that relied for trade and food and commerce on the Morigaz-based shipping. Oh, other ports there were, small fishing villages, but none so well suited on this rock-cliffed and overgrown coastline as that city. The Father of Ashes had slept soundly for ages, and could yet for ages more. No need for eruption when there were other outlets for the Fire Lord's spite . . .

"Maka'tange is overdue for awakening." Ri'ush breathed, a smoky volume that stank of scorched rock. "It is easiest to work there." I sensed an image then, from Liuthwe, I thought, her glimpse of the smoking peak southwards of Morigaz, from her last scrying. Unbidden imagery, almost an intrusion, worthy of later reprimand—but useful for now.

"Ashfall has already spattered the city, hot muds have buried two villages. The ground trembles. You plan more." A statement, not a question.

"And if I do?" Ri'ush snorted. "No business of yours, Lady."

Our eyes locked, smoldering orbs unblinking in the glare of his form. "It is my affair, now. It does not suit my purposes for Morigaz to be destroyed because you must stretch out your fist through the earth's crust just so. I—"

"It is my prerogative. To explore."

"To intrude, you mean." Elemental outbursts, seething across the thin borders of the multiverse, not easily stopped, nor easily squelched. Ri'ush was not alone in that proclivity. All elementals are of like manner: fascinated by this playground of mixed elements, testing its boundaries as they strive to expand their own borders, push past their own limitations. For it is not in the nature of an elemental to abide limitations gladly.

"You would stretch yourself, then?" I demanded. "Try new territory?"

Ri'ush shrugged.

"Then let me suggest the Kavro Islands." Off the western coast, far enough seaward that explosion there would harm no land-based resources.

"No," grated the Lord of Fire. "Too difficult."

"Why?" I challenged him. "I thought you could thrust

magma to the surface of the land where and however you chose.''

"Be not coy with me, Rider," he growled. "You know that takes effort, to push past the barriers of Earth that lie between the firey realms and the surface of the land. Maka'tange is ready and convenient, vent holes and firespouts in place, a steamy cauldron awaiting a nudge—''

"And if I told you the way to Kavro could be eased? That is virgin territory, a place you have not yet touched. Surely, something more challenging, as befits the Lord of Fire . . .''

He paused then, and his form seemed to dim as the elemental divinity left the avatar for a moment, or withdrew its attention, looking perhaps to see if my words were true. As I knew they were. Back he came, moments later, the molten form glowing hotter with renewed vigor. "How could this way be eased?" he grumbled. "This place you name is of interest.''

As I thought it would be. A chance to throw up undersea islands, rising quickly through the shallows, challenging Water all the way and leaving a firebrand mark upon new-raised ground. Far more challenging than simply belching forth fire and rock from an old reliable source . . .

"Then who would owe whom a debt of honor?" he asked in his blunt elemental manner—as well he might. Would I owe him, for sparing Morigaz? Or he, me, for helping him to gain another toehold upon the earthly sphere, in a place not previously explored or touched by the Fire Lord's kiss?

"Let us say we will have had a fair exchange.''

He pondered, as I already had. I would be even with Yamaro, Lord of Earth, no debt owed or pending; but the wizards of Tor Mak would be indebted to me, and through them the port masters of Morigaz, and Jonkile, lord of that city . . . a worthwhile indebtedness to have, by any accounting.

There were other ways to persuade, yet more inticements to offer, a threat or two I could make—and carry through with, should I have need—but it was not necessary. Ri'ush considered where his interest lay, and the molten head nodded, once. "Very well. I shall look elsewhere for my contest. I am ready to joust with Water. It promises more conflict, as you say. You will have Yamaro clear a path for me, immediately."

"I will. Tomorrow will be soon enough. Thank you for speaking with me."

A false politeness, for bound and summoned he had no choice. As we both knew.

"Some day, Lady," Ri'ush remarked, "you will step false and you will be *my* guest, for a time. We shall see how you like my hospitality."

I smiled wryly. Always the threats and desire for contention with this elemental lord. Predictably so. "Some day, that may come to pass," I said. "But not this day. You may leave us, Ri'ush. It grows chill here."

Cold air crusted his molten form with black where rock cooled, dropped in smoking flakes to the ground with each movement. He inclined his head in my direction. "Until later," he growled, and his form melted in upon itself, pouring like hot syrup back into the magical rift from whence it had come. The glow of fire dimmed in his wake and then he was gone, untouched granite intact within the triangle, though heat-seared and blackened in turn.

An outrush of breath behind me spoke to Amrey's relief at the elemental's departure. I kept amusement from my face as I directed my companions about the last of their tasks, the dismissal of the guardians, the grounding of the power we had raised. Amrey watched all in silence. But afterwards, there were not the questions I had expected of his ever-inquisitive mind. Instead, there was reserve. My student's introspection

lasted longer than I had thought possible—through the repast
served by Cendurhil's people, through the ride back to Moontooth perched aback Reydjik's mist-wrapt form, through what
remained of the night as we returned to the bed we shared in
the still-black hours before dawn.

It was not the first time I had experienced this odd habit of
his, of sudden introspection and extended silence. But in the
coming hours it was the first time I saw it for what it was. A
time of calculation and spinning of ideas and an uncanny intuition that read uncomfortably close between the lines. And
it was the first time, for that matter, that he unsettled me most
profoundly with words rather than deeds. Though not the
last . . .

We respect that which we hold in awe. A body can hardly
feel the latter emotion without the former; even if it is not
conscious, or in the forefront of the mind, the respect, the
deference, the honoring will be there. This, I have observed,
is human nature, whether in Chernisylla or here in Astareth,
or in some nameless plane beyond.

I had thought with my elemental demonstration to make
Amrey more compliant, to put myself in a light which would
inspire awe, and thus bolster the deference rendered unto me,
increasing his willingness to bow to my will. How unexpected, then, his response when finally we awoke, and I
reached for him in the bed—and he did not return my touch,
but raised his head upon his hand, and looked at me with pale
blue eyes narrowed with calculating thought.

"How often do you deal with elemental lords?" he asked,
a question I would have expected the prior eve, but unwanted
now, here in my bed.

"Oft enough," I answered curtly, and reached again for
him.

He caught my wrist in one hand, but his words, not his
touch, halted my motion. "How many know that you barter
and dicker terms between them like a fishmonger buying at
wharfside?"

My mouth fell open. Before anger could flare, while surprise at his brazen rudeness held me in its grip, he said yet
more.

"I won't say you cheapen yourself, Inya, for only you have
the measure of your worth. But one day they will realize you
play them one against the other, favors given for favors owed,
and then you lose your grip upon them. Compel them to answer a summoning, you can, but command them to greater
workings at your behest alone? I rather doubt they will want
to continue that game when it is discovered."

I lay unmoving for a moment, his warm fingers pinioning
my wrist, and me not even fighting that constraint. My mind
was awhirl. What was he saying? For Murl had struck a nerve
too close to my heart. Always there is a careful balance of
favors done and favors owed, for coercion of forces so primal,
so powerful, is a game played with the greatest of delicacy,
surpassing the dance that keeps one alive in the courts of the
Empire of Korribee. And a part of that delicate balance was
to appear to have that which no one else could offer. In this
way, it seemed I could order Yamaro, Lord of Earth, to make
Ri'ush's passage to the Kavro Islands easier. But that was not
my real power; in fact, I would bargain with Yamaro to accomplish that feat. Either call in a favor, or offer a new one,
until I had the concession I wanted, and Earth split wide to
allow Fire egress in a place of my choosing.

Clearly, this son of a spice merchant had divined the strategy behind the negotiations I carried on with Ri'ush, a strategy the blunt-spoken, unsubtle elementals did not really grasp
on its most basic level. Yet I heard something else in his

words . . . a threat, if you will. *One day they will realize you play them one against the other.*

If they had not grasped this fact in centuries, why would they awaken to it now? Unless someone planned to alert them. To say, Wait, you need not let the Midnight Rider call the tune to which you dance. Cooperate or fight amongst yourselves, but the Dark Lady has no real power aside from that which you grant her over you . . .

It could happen. Had happened, once, on a world of water and ice, where sophisticated nature spirits realized I could really do very little for them that they could not do themselves. And so had my influence drained away like water through a sieve. It is a place I no longer visit.

Elemental lords are not subtle, but they are not stupid either. If someone were to point out the details of the game, demonstrate how their childlike directness was wielded by my own cynical, convoluted schemes, they would think they had been used. And the resentment at such a thing . . .

It was not to be imagined, how that would hinder my activities in this place. I scowled at Murl and wrenched my arm from his grip. "How dare you threaten me like that!" I spat.

He raised an eyebrow, a gesture copied from me. "Threaten?" he asked innocently.

"They won't know what you don't tell them." I sat up, was out of bed in a heart's beat.

"I had not planned on telling anyone anything." Was there a lingering emphasis on the word *planned*? Was this a threat within a threat: Don't pressure me, or I will talk out of turn after all?

I took a deep breath. What could he hope to accomplish by ruffling me in such a manner? Time to discover the answer to that, post haste.

"Speak frankly," I told him. "Why do you comment on my workings with the elementals in this way?"

Both eyebrows crept up his forehead this time. "It's obvious, isn't it? How you manage to be so persuasive with them? But I was only thinking to caution you. I was simply wondering . . . how is it that an elemental comes to owe you a favor in the first place? Where do you get that first bargaining chip that lets you parley one favor owed into many?"

Again, he intuited the strategy by which I wielded influence amongst the entities of this place. And best to leave that unanswered, to take control again of the drift of this conversation.

"What is it to you, what favors are owed to whom? You will not be working with elementals any time soon." I said it in a final tone.

"Ah, but I beg to differ," Murl replied. "I already am."

For the second time in the space of minutes, my mouth fell open. What new impertinence was this? With an effort I controlled myself and did not sputter or shout. "What do you mean?"

"A little air elemental, a conjuration of recent making. I was experimenting, and it came out of nowhere. It wishes direct bribery, incense smoke and airborne fragrances, but I want another way to command it. You are, after all, using a time-proven tactic. I simply wish to know the details of how you apply this to work with an elemental."

That set my teeth on edge. He simply wanted to know. And again, unguarded and unwarded experiments in magic and control here, in my home, yet something so minor my wardings were not triggered.

Ridiculous, and untenable. Awe? Of that, there was none inspired by last night's events, that was clear. Oh, perhaps a frisson of fear, of anticipation of the unexpected or unknown. But no reverence, no elevation of myself in his esteem. If anything, he fancied he understood me better, had seen through to the heart of my activities and scried me out as some common wharf vendor!

I flushed with anger, and kept my voice level with a practiced chill. "Listen to me, Murl Amrey. You wish to work with elementals? You wish to know ways to influence them short of outright bribery and paying for services? There are such." There are such that I will never teach you, I promised myself. "But you have much more learning yet before you can do so in safety."

Not that I was overly concerned about his safety. He saw too clearly things I did not wish seen. At times I enjoyed him, but trust him? No more than I must, and that was too little to allow him so close.

Then why was he here, after all? I had to ask myself anew. Not for fun between the sheets, though that was pleasant enough. He was here as a favor to an old friend, a favor I deemed I had near as full discharged. And because he would serve me, in spite of himself, for earlier affronts. And for current ones as well. Threaten to inform elementals of my manipulations, would he? No one would destroy out of hand the alliances I had spent so long constructing.

It was in that moment that I truly resolved to send him after the crystal, that power stone that I coveted so from the mines of Styrcia. The order disguised as invitation was easily made.

"I think . . . that it is time for an excursion. To take your skills afield, and see how it is one needs must treat with elementals. You can perform a small task for me, and in the process test your skills, and perhaps learn some new ones. Does that sound agreeable?"

He blinked, startled at the seeming change in subject. "And this will teach me more about elementals?"

I smiled, the meager expression I reserve for unworthy supplicants and those with whom I am not pleased. "Oh, yes. Much more than you had thought to know, I dare say." Only so much would I teach him, I did not say aloud—but the rest, the rest would come as he dealt with the hazards of Styrcia and suceeded—or failed—based upon how rapidly he learned when put to the test. It was, after all, the same testing I had faced many times over—there and elsewhere—and survived. He could do the same, or he was no worthy student of mine. And if worthy, it spared me instruction and rewarded me with a Styrcian crystal, all the same.

An intrigued look passed across his face. He sat up, ran a hand through rumpled red hair. "This sounds interesting," he offered. "What is it you would have me do?"

I wrapped a dressing gown about me, and smiled at him over a shoulder covered in blue brocade. This time the expression was sincere. "Come with me down to breakfast, and I will tell you about the power gems of Styrcia."

I swept from the room. He was quick to follow.

CHAPTER 6

I need something," I told Murl. "Will you do a task for me?"

He looked expectant, and I continued. "I would have you demonstrate your prowess, your inventiveness. Your competence . . ." A smile tugged at his lips; no modesty there, he was certain he held those traits. So. That set my hook; now to pull him in.

I stretched out one hand to cup his cheek, and held his eyes with mine. "I would send you to a place, Murl, where you can show your mettle. Find the people who call themselves the emek, and bring me back a kind of crystal from their mines. A *shia* they call it. A wizard-stone." Carefully I refrained from the name he might, in his eclectic learning, recognize. Who knew what tales floated through this world's cultures about the crystals of Styrcia? Better not to risk than to reveal too much. Even the name of that place I did not say.

"How will I know this stone?"

"Crystalline, blue-white, with a glow you will perceive with your other-sight."

"And what does a *shia* do?"

I smiled. "It is of use to me. That is sufficient for you to know."

Indeed, it was all I would say, for to mention the least thing about a wizard-stone was to say too much already. The fundamentals of its usefulness Murl would instantly grasp, for he already knew of the Power Within, that part of the body and heart and mind and soul which, if used for too long a span, drains one like a sponge wrung dry of water. And he knew of the Power Without, that force which is channeled like water through an aqueduct, directed by the medium, yet not a vital part of the medium. That is the manner in which the truly great magics are performed: the spellcaster becomes a conduit for greater forces, the flux and flow of cosmic tides pulsing through the channel, directed by will and intention. Yet to achieve this takes years of training. Each adept develops this talent only insofar as innate ability allows. Some are more talented than others. For all, it is an acquired ability, honed only with many long years of practice.

And then there were the crystals of Styrcia. Crystals of structure so fine, of prismatic quality so congruent with the elements of the universe that one stone resonates like a bell, affecting the multiverse around it as a magnet reorders the pattern of filings on a tabletop. It is a focal point of energy, of the raw stuff of creation; a primeval element, I sometimes think, akin to that used in the power crystals of Nesteferon, or Atalantis, or other wonder-working times and places.

Whatever their elemental nature, the fact is that a Styrcian crystal is a conduit for the forces of magic, an amplifier of intention, a supreme tool for manifestation and focus and the transmutation of will into results on the material plane. To the untalented, such a gem appears to be a quartzlike crystal, fogged lightly with casts of bluish-white. To those who see with other-sight, it is a glowing nexus of odd energies, a thing that sparkles in the hand and tortures space round about as it pulls the flux and flow of universal tides to itself. Adepts know that these forces, concentrated thus, can be shaped with a whim or a wish. Dangerous is such a stone for those who would use it unguarded. Precious beyond the value of worlds, to those who have mastered its secrets.

I had heard of Styrcian crystals long and long ago, ere ever I came to the hills of Caronne . . . but then it was a fairy tale, a reference to power that corrupted and wishes and treasures that were never used wisely. Surely if I had such a thing, I knew I would make wise use of it. No squandering of the power—or the wish magical—should I ever put hand to a wizard-stone. I remembered that childhood tale of the grieko-tamers, man and wife, who helped the injured watsel and thereby gained three wishes. And wasted them, on their sorry starving selves, conjuring a sausage and a curse and removal of same. Styrcian crystals, known by that name on Chernisylla, crossroad of rifts, remained the stuff of legend and cautionary tales.

It was on my unguarded, perhaps a bit careless explorations, that I came to realize that one of Moontooth's portals opened into that very same place where such gemstones of fame were said to originate. Styrcia.

A drear place it was, I thought, and so at first did not tarry long enough to learn its name. A land of sere brown steppes, wind-whipped grasses with razor-sharp edges; of low rolling foothills frosted by perpetual ice, interrupted by ravines and white-faced alabaster cliffs, and the sky, always leaden overcast and lowering, too close over head. The rains were grey in that place, laden with dirt or soot from far northern volcanos . . . the weather ever too chill. The tales of the Styrcia I had heard of depicted an idyllic place, but whether that were wishful thinking or the reflection of this land before elemental mishaps, I could not say.

Regardless, in my time and place it mattered not one whit to me, for idyllic Styrcia was famed also for its less-than-idyllic inhabitants: the long-fanged karzdagi, muscular, dog-faced creatures of fierce brutish nature, who hunted in packs and baying brought their enemy down, snarling like the worst of bloodthirsty beasts squabbling over living victims and fighting one another to the death amongst blood-warm, still-twitching limbs. This was a gruesomeness I did not recall from childhood stories but witnessed firsthand when I strayed there, and lost the leyline back to the rift-gate which my tower guarded.

I am not easily hunted by beast-men, not then, as Ushni's daughter, even less so now, as Lady of the Dark Tower. Yet did they give me a fright, truth be told, for I was surprised by them and chased until I found a defensible spot, a place with a rocky precipice to my back, where they could not surround me. Thinking to rush me and collect my broken body from the ravine below, perhaps, they ringed me half about and stalked forward, moving in for the kill. Spell-summoned lightning flared then, and three fell dead; again, and two more were singed. The pack turned and fled. But one was wounded badly and could not flee; from that creature I asked my questions and got my answers.

Much had he to tell of squalid living and contentious tribes, ever roaming for food and shelter. Of the emek, the mannish village dwellers, scraping out meager existence in their fortified settlements, guarding against karzdag raiders but never too proud to take slaves and force the dog-men to labor in the fields or in the mines. The tales of karzdag woe in the mines of Styrcia, gloomier even than the cold, cloudy nights upon the steppe, were nearly moving, had not the beast-men been so despicable in their own right. It were a living death for the karzdagi sentenced to work there, never released until their rotting corpses were tossed upon a carnal heap and left for scavengers and other karzdagi to reclaim.

It was then, during that conversation, that I realized the

nature of the treasure that these bestial slaves must mine. My prisoner's references were few and fleet—of stones that glowed blue-white in the dark, of the rare and terrible sorcerer who sought them out, and the manifestations that seemed so impossible they were dismissed as illusion or fantasy. Such a thing could not be, in this beast-man's simple brain, for he knew only the magics of shamans. The greater craftings of the rare dimensional traveler seemed the impossible stuff of legend. But such legends had I already heard, elsewhere. With a sudden pang I realized where I found myself, and in the next breath craved such a power crystal for my own.

Yet these were not to be sold or bartered, nor smuggled from the mines, which were guarded as closely as any source of royal diamonds in far Urshad. Nay, my informant knew what he knew only through rumor and word of mouth, but certain he was that the rare perfect gemstone recovered from the mines went promptly into the safekeeping of a patron, usually never again to leave that individual's hand.

Why then, in a land so barren, yet with sources of amplified magic to hand, were there no grandiosities? No burgeoning cities, no air ships, no transformation of the inhospitable climate? And it became clear that wizard-stones were thought mere decorations, baubles treasured by tribal chieftains for their beauty, their magical powers left untapped. Or rather, unrecognized, in this spell-ignorant place. Now and then, a traveler between dimensions would stumble across this location, and might divine the meaning of the crystals mined here, but such wayfarers were transient and very rare. I knew how difficult it was to cross dimensions reliably and return to the same time and place once visited. I could not do the same, were I not aided by the natural rifts that Moontooth controls. No surprise then that errant wizards had not yet returned to dominate or plunder this tedious sphere.

Such at least was my logical supposition, but I was unable to confirm all I would have liked. My informant perished as I questioned him, and I cursed his inconsideration for doing so.

After that, I did not linger. Not because I saw no way to claim a crystal for my own, but because I had not the time at my disposal for a possibly lengthy stay. I thought at some point to return, and see what I might discover that would help me towards my ends. But shortly later I was exiled from Chernisylla, and then my life changed so drastically I put aside my plans to gain a crystal. With time, it became an ambitious project toyed with late nights over a glass of brandy by the fireside, or reconsidered when a conjuration proved difficult. It was not a goal I had yet firmly resolved myself to—until Murl Amrey was mine to direct, and his ambitions and my needs were conjunct.

Of course he agreed. He readied himself, according to his judgment and my best advice. Once through the portal, he would have two weeks of time before I would reopen the passage to Styrcia, and two more beyond that should he need it. Time flowed differently there: one week's sojourn amounted to a mere day within Moontooth. So in a handful of days I would have my crystal, were it anything an eager and resourceful person could recover. Or not, and Amrey would have failed in the testing profoundly.

I did not think he would fail this task, though I did consider: what if the karzdagi caught him? For he was not yet master of lightning spells or greater offensive magics, not at all. Yet he had stealth and cunning, and shifty means of his own devising and which I had taught him: invisibility, silent passage, the means to step here and reappear there, a slight but important transposition in distance, and the magical mastery of tongues—thus could he meet and mix and talk, and see what he could see. As for the how of it . . . well, that was as much the test as anything else. If he could not devise a way to recover the prize I desired, then was he far less resourceful than I had thought, and indeed required of a student of mine.

Up the winding stairs we went, past the lower portals, past the midlevels, and close to the rarer spheres, the chancier gateways higher up amongst the tower's rifts. Just short of that topmost void did we halt, and stand without a plain oaken door, locked and warded and innocent to the unsuspecting eye.

Murl stood easy, a pack upon one shoulder, his traveling clothes mended and donned once more. "You will meet me here, in time?" he confirmed.

"In due time. Send the messenger if you need to." The messenger was a birdlike figment, an enchanted fancy that would home on this place of transposition and deliver his spoken words to me.

He nodded obediently enough, but regarded me with a strange expression in his eye. "There wouldn't be anything you're not telling me about this place, would there be?" he asked.

About the place? No. He knew of the karzdagi, the emek, the barren plains, the cold mountains. The close-kept mines. In this land, where magic of our ilk is barely known, he should have a hard but not impossible time of his reconnoiter.

But about the crystal? Aye, there was the omission. And one I would not correct now. "I've told you all that I have learned on my sojourns there." I said it firmly, to lay doubt to rest. "I'll await you on this spot, two weeks hence."

He seemed reassured, and so turned from me, threw the portal wide, and walked through to the other side.

That gateway from the vista of my tower looks out upon the same wasteland of yellow-brown grass that I recalled from before. In the hills, a speck of white shone bright even from these many measures distant. "At the base of those cliffs lies a valley, I am told." I pointed yonder. "There is one of the emek villages. If there is a mine there, or not, I do not know . . . but you will discover, I'm sure. We leave this here, so"— I placed a globe of blue glass in his hand, and Murl in turn set it in the grass at his feet, near the threshold of the gateway—" 'Twill resonate with your messenger and let you find this spot again," I explained. It was a precaution I wished I had had for myself, that earlier time.

"Well then." He locked eyes with me, stood there upon an alien landscape, the wind tugging at the hair curling out from beneath his hood. "I will be back with this *shia* soon enough," he said jauntily. "And then I expect my reward."

I kept my expression neutral. Rewarded he would be. With a thank you, and a fare-thee-well, fair return for his impertinances and petty irritations and major trespasses—none of which I counted offset by the fact that I allowed him in my bed at night. There are the pleasures of the body, and then there are the honors due the self. I see them as separate ledgers; only the latter weighed truly in the balance between us.

So he turned his back upon me, and set off through the waist-high grass, fading soon into the twilight distance in his hood and cloak of forest brown, pack awaver in the wind-tossed sea of vegetation. Too long, perhaps, did I hold watch there, from within the doorway of my secure place. Not once did he look back.

At last I shut the door, and did my best to put Murl Amrey from my mind.

Two days passed—two weeks in Styrcia—and I had heard no unexpected word or early recall from my absent student. At the appointed time I returned to that doorway and unwarded it and cast it open. No man awaited me on the other side. The

globe lay just where it had been left, intact, a shimmer of
arcane energies soft aglow around its form, if I focused just
so . . . Well then. A messenger flown home to roost.

I stepped forward, touched the globe briefly, and spoke a
word, then returned to the security of my threshold. A ghostly
flit of energy ascended, like a hummingbird on the wing, and
from its beak Amrey's voice spoke out in the wind-whipped
air.

"I fear I cannot rejoin you yet, Lady," came his disembodied words. "I have persuaded the emek I am a buyer of
crystals, and soon they will show me their mine. I must stay
a while yet. I'll see you in two weeks' time."

It was disappointing, but a thread of tension eased in my
stomach as his words sank in. He was not harmed, he was
worming his way slowly closer to our goal. Nor yet was he
in danger. Soon enough, a crystal would be mine.

Two more days crept past, days filled with aimless tasks and
pointless waiting, books that could not hold my attention and
servants scurrying out of my path, to avoid the thunderous
look I bore about with me. On that second day I awaited word,
the summoning I had crafted that would trickle through the
rift, through locked gate, and whisper in my ear that Murl
Amrey was ready to return.

The day wore on and no call came, and I grew tired of
waiting. I went to that gateway instead, and cast it open, thinking to pass time there, in the threshold, in the swift-flowing
timeways of Styrcia. With luck, I would soon see Murl in the
distance, returning as he had gone, a smallish figure growing
larger as he marched through the tall brown grasses of the
plains . . .

It was a colder day than before, the promise of snow in the
air, grey-white clouds hanging so low above the ground that

mist trailed in pockets and tendrils over the grassy earth. The distance was veiled from my eyes. I conjured an air spirit with a word, a friendly breath born of the storm clouds above, and sent it forth to scour the land between here and the vill whence I had directed Amrey. I bided upon the doorstep, wrapped in a cloak lined with soft grey kid fur, bundled against the icy winds that probed from that realm into mine.

I sensed the airy sprite return before I felt its fog-damp caress against my cheek. *Many come,* it told me, words whispered more into my thoughts than into my ear.

"Many?" I asked.

Many, the elemental confirmed. *There is the one, and far behind, the many follow. Slow moving, as flesh does . . . I could be there and back again many times over before they were here with you, they are so slow—*

I interrupted its chaotic ramblings. "They are coming here, you think?" Was it Murl and chance companions, or a hunting party of emek, come out onto the steppes for food, or yet again, karzdagi seeking prey?

As straight a line as two legs on earth can travel, yes.

Then its tone went pleading. *I'm bored,* it whined, mercurial of mood. It shot away, towards the nearest wind-roiled storm cloud, then swooped back down again, not yet released of my summoning.

Let me play, it demanded.

I ignored its plea. "Those who come," I queried, "are they men? Or beast-men?" No need for words to clarify: I pictured Amrey, and a karzdag—snouted, hunched, befurred—and the difference in mental images portrayed itself clearly enough to the sprite. Speech with elementals is not solely composed of words, unless one wishes to stay confined to such a medium.

The mist-wraith moved off some distance, as if to peer through the intervening cloud. Had it noted such details when it was distant? That is not the sort of concentration one can expect of an air spirit, especially the smaller, less focused ones.

The one alone—it looks like you. The others . . . furry. I think, beasts.

Sudden tension prickled my skin. One that looked like me—meaning, I sensed, without fur on the face—that would be clean-shaven Murl, or yet again, perhaps a woman . . . I doubted the sprite was capable of telling human gender apart, but with this timing, it must be my returning student. Had Murl traveled here in company with karzdagi? If so, how did such a perverse alliance come about? Or did he journey alone, ignorant of those upon his heels? Was he in danger?

Fruitless supposition chased heels upon self until I put such chaos from my mind. Better to watch and observe, and see what would come in sight soon enough. I thanked the sprite for its aid and released it. As it left, I summoned Lesseth with a word, a power-charged phrase that echoed along halls and stairways, destined for my companion's ears alone wherever he should find himself within the tower.

Momentarily I felt his cool and shadowy presence by my side, sharing my vigil as he had often done before. His eyes were only as keen as mine in the physical sphere; we noticed Murl at the same time, a speck moving through waist-high grasses where a moment before there had been nothing but pale blades wind-ruffled between cloud and earth.

The air sprite passed him unnoticed, skimming on the wind to reconnoiter what came behind him. A hand raised in greeting when he saw me. Still, he was two long bow casts distant when the sprite returned.

Stopped, they have, it reported. *They camp.*

I raised an eyebrow. Camped? This warranted a closer look, and more detail than this least of elementals could give me. I dismissed my summoning and the sprite fled promptly on the breeze. Unbidden, Lesseth rose to take its place, and passed into the airy spaces of Styrcia, fading on the winds before my eyes.

When Murl came near, I stood alone upon the threshold of the tower, bordered by the doorframe that was all that was physically present on this plane. I held the cloak against my chest in one hand, the other touching the smooth oaken door that opened into the stone hallway behind me. One foot on stone, in Astareth. The other on the wooden doorsill, in Styrcia. When standing between dimensions it was always so—I felt keenly aware of the impossible gulf that I spanned with one foot. It was only intellect that could make that distinction, for there was no gut-wrenching stir of displacement, as occurs during certain spells of transit. No, this rift was buffered by the tower's binding and the enchantments that made it stable. As long as the door was open, and I so near the gateway, I moved through time as it flows in Styrcia. Step back a few paces, and I would see the passage of clouds and sun in hurried motion, as Astareth's native time pace hurtled me fast forward in contrast to Styrcia's plodding rhythms.

Yet I saved that visual amusement for a later occasion. Here, now, I stood so that I matched my timeflow to Styrcia, to Murl Amrey's subjective experience. At his own pace I watched him draw nearer, a long-striding yet comfortable walk over slightly broken ground. I observed quietly, as I have so often from these portals, as if he were an object or an animal on an alien landscape—until he stood before me. Then I saw no humanoid or distant matter for my observation, but the man who had sought what I had commanded him to find.

His face was stubbled, his cloak and boots the worse for wear. He braced the strap of his pack with one hand, and gripped a walking staff in the other. He met my questioning gaze, then freed one hand to fish inside his shirt. The small leather pouch he removed sat heavy on his palm, and he extended it to me.

"Lady," he said somberly. "Your *shia.*"

My hand twitched in reflex to snatch it from him—yet I dared not squander the time, when in but a heartbeat it could be better handled safe within the tower. My prize was at hand and I was loathe to dawdle in this open gateway, my student in this far place followed by unknown creatures, and Lesseth not yet returned.

"Come through," I ordered him with an abrupt gesture.

He did as I bade, stepping past me into the hallway, pouch in hand. I let him pass, then faced out onto the plains again and sent a call to Lesseth, biding him return post haste. Murl's touch upon my shoulder turned me back around.

"Here, Inya," he said softly. "For you."

With a last look over my shoulder—no karzdagi in sight, nor yet Lesseth—I took the pouch from his hand. A faint blue light seeped forth as I unlaced the top—then I had it open, and the wizard-stone tumbled out onto my palm.

It was nearly the size of a walnut, yet elongated, and multifaceted, like a healing quartz. It had the same smoky, translucent quality of quartz, though touched with an oddity of hue and an ambient light from within, a greater heft than seemed should be . . .

I thought I heard a faint sound, like a discordant musical chime, when it rolled into my hand. *Shian,* singers they were called, for their resonant qualities—and now I heard for myself just how resonant.

"They become attuned through use, and touch," Murl said. "That one is not yet in harmony with a person."

I looked up at him, a smile pulling at my lips. "I can remedy that soon enough." I wanted to gaze into it, run energies through it, experiment, but did none of these things in that moment. With great self-control, I slipped it back into the pouch, and looked out across the steppes. What kept Lesseth? I wondered irritably, for I wanted this portal secured before I could spend the time that I desired with the wizard-stone . . .

I thought to summon my spirit friend once again, but before the word could leave my mouth, I sensed, then saw him, aflit upon the currents of that place, speeding like a stone from the sling back to the gateway he had so recently parted.

"Karzdagi?" I asked, as he settled in the portal.

"No. Men." Could an air spirit sound breathless, so would he have in his haste. "In furs, bearded, unkempt—the emek?" That last a question, directed at Murl, poised behind me in the tower hallway.

"Emek?" my student echoed, surprise evident in his tone. He rejoined me on the threshold, looked back along his trail as if to peer through cloud and distance, to see what had dogged his footsteps.

"Twelve of them," said Lesseth. "Stalking like hunters, but now making camp. One stands wary guard along your path of travel, as if he expected your return."

Murl's eyebrows crept up and then furrowed as he studied his backtrail. "I had no idea . . ." His voice trailed off, and then he faced me with a scowl.

"Seal and guard your gate once more, Inya. They are not wielders of magic, these vill dwellers, but they do marshal an esoteric kind of force. They believe it the gift of their degenerate gods. Be that as it may, it can kill at a distance and spy through the fog. Let us give them nothing to remember, nothing to draw their eye." For he knew that once the gateway was closed there would be no more sign that we had ever bridged this gap between dimensions.

"Why have they followed you?" I demanded.

Murl shrugged. "I told them I was a crystal trader from the south. Told them I journeyed back to my people with what I had bought from their mines . . . Perhaps they did not believe. Or perhaps they followed, to kill me and take their *shia* back. It cost a fortune."

He meant the coins of electrum he had spent, a modest sum to us but the wealth of princes in that metal-poor realm. Well had I supplied Murl for his errand.

"Why camp, if they seek to reclaim their treasure?"

Murl shook his head, as mystified as I. I cast warily out on to the steppes, attempting to feel magic, the gathering of reins of power, that primordial stirring that heralded an on-slaught. . . . Naught was there. Only the busy silence of nature, the background susurrus of earth and air and growing things.

"No matter, now." I motioned Lesseth and Murl back into the safety of the tower. "They may spy out your trail for years, for what it serves them. We won't be back there again."

Murl shot me a knowing look, and glanced to the pouch he yet held.

"I have what I want," I replied to his unspoken question. "Styrcia can rest behind closed doors, for all of me."

That easily did I close and seal that gateway, locking it against all intruders. Murl watched my actions, then stood back and followed me up the stairs, to the more esoteric of my workrooms where I could properly examine the crystal he had delivered. Already my mind was twining around the puzzle of the Styrcian wizard-stone, and I gave no more thought to the portal locked and left behind.

Luster of blue light on black velvet. That and a lone candle, the only illumination in my darkened chamber. I sat on one side of the worktable studying the crystal I had placed there. Murl stood opposite me, silent, outside the circle of candlelight. I paid him no mind, for the *shia* claimed all my attention in that moment.

Even at rest on the tabletop, its internal lights shimmered and danced contrary to the flicker of the taper. It drew my eye until I ceased trying to look away and studied what was there instead. There yawned a great depth, pools of distance and of substance undefined. The confines of this tiny stone held the coruscation of distant galaxies ashine in the night sky. There was a tone half heard by the ear, of a note chiming or about to chime—yet the air was still, unmoved by the near-cacaphony of the unattuned stone.

The use of a Styrcian crystal was the stuff of legend and folklore. No grimoire offered reliable instructions for one who would wield its power. Here must I rely upon my skills and intuition, my knowledge of arcane systems and objects that channel power. I was well grounded in such knowledge, and thus was it evident to me that this stone would respond to one user only, a person psychically linked to the *shia*. A likely process of attunement suggested itself as well: it seemed a directed focus of one's personal energies would be needed to blend and link with the wizard-stone. The same technique, perhaps, that served to harmonize with a plant in order to speak to its nurturing devas, or to connect with a brook to sense and direct its waters. A crystal in many ways was easier to grasp in such wise. Its vibrations were stronger, more distinctive; solid, in a way, even with these volatile energies aswirl around the gem.

I relaxed into training and instinct, and rested my hands a mere finger-span above the stone itself.

The power around it was tangible, a charged atmosphere that tingled the fingertips and roiled the stomach with anticipation of forces reined. With extended senses I tasted the weave of primal energy around the stone, heard again that dissonant chime as thought forms or will impinged on this power point beneath my hands. I stared at the lambent gem, facets drawing my eye down a long crystalline passageway into its heart, and beyond.

I felt the spirit of the stone.

Like pushing against the wall, only to have a door open unexpectedly against the shove of a shoulder—I tumbled through, a bodily lurch marking my surrender to the universe contained within the Styrcian crystal. Power was there, orderly, harnessed, something I could tap and wield as an extension of my own. Petty grievances were there too—local memories, impressions left like finger marks on glass from persons who had handled the stone on its journey to me. The heartbreak of a miner, whose infant daughter had just died of milk fever . . . skepticism and scheming from a patriarch who had briefly owned the gem . . . the impressions fled as rapidly as they came into focus, as the terrain shifted psychically and I gained a feel for the forces contained therein.

It seemed to me, whose bloodline was attuned to such things, that the Styrcian crystal felt like a dimensional rift in miniature: a nexus where the fabric of time and space could be stretched and warped; where points of probability melded in a curve slewed by the wielder's intent. This was a tool one could hold and say "I wish," and fulfill any folly with it. Intent steered its might, and skittish it was, like a half-broken horse. I would need to be clear of focus, to merge my will into the *shia*'s energy field, if I were to marshal this unruly medium . . .

Intent as I was on the wizard-stone, still I knew that Murl observed, and so could learn. "Like sharing our thoughts," I breathed, recalling earlier training sessions. He strained forward to catch my words. "A mental link," I mused out loud. "An intuitive understanding is what you need here."

"How does it work?" he asked in voice pitched equally low.

I shrugged, the movement of one shoulder. "Will." That much I felt, clearly. "Directed intention should do it, thus . . ."

In the workings of power, will and visualization are the tools that create what the heart and mind desire. With the *shia,* any intention would be amplifed, for such was the wizard-stone's nature. It seemed wise, then, to attempt only a simple effect with it, something easily imagined and achieved with the smallest of whims. Not a great working, that would require a strong bond with the stone, but a minor fancy, that this surface rapport seemed sufficient to enhance.

I relaxed further into that rapport, felt for those tendrils of power, and pictured the witchlight that I could so easily summon. I let the faery fire run over me, silhouetting my form with unnatural light—

The explosion occurred without forewarning. Light flared high and blue; the *shia* cracked with an ear-torturing report. The near-musical tone of the gem screeched like nails upon slate as the crystal burst and shards pierced the air.

The force of it hurtled me back against the wall and there I slumped, stunned. The room was dark, the candle snuffed in the blast. Lights danced before my eyes, an overlay like a galaxy of stars burst asunder. I sat in a strange cocoon of silence, and realized through the ringing in my ears that I was deafened. I thought I should move, but was unable for the nonce to move at all.

On the far side of the room, a sudden witchfire blazed, a greenish light that outlined Murl's hand. By that conjuring I saw him collect himself from the floor beyond the table. He spoke to me, I thought, made an obeisance . . . and left.

I blinked and Lesseth was there, the candle relit, then a

lamp. Where had Murl gone? I heard his words come muffled to my ear; we linked mind to mind, and I learned what he knew. Murl had passed Lesseth in the hall, pointed urgently to the workroom, and ordered my companion to aid me. While Murl strode purposefully—where?

Lesseth wanted to fuss over the cuts upon my face and hands, now oozing blood from the chance shards that had hit me. His touch made me aware of the stinging in my palms, which had shielded me from most of the shrapnel. I glanced down and winced at what I saw.

"Lucky you're not blinded, Lady . . ." I heard his admonishment through the ringing in my ears, but I pulled from his grasp after he had helped me to my feet, and stumbled into the hallway upon the trail of my student.

Why in that moment I should sense something amiss with Murl Amrey, I did not know, but the feeling was undeniable. "Find him," I ordered Lesseth. I leaned shakily against a wall until Lesseth's hasty return moments later.

"Treachery! He opens the Styrcian gate!"

My eyes widened in shock. "Stop him if you can!" I ordered Lesseth up the stairs. "Don't wait for me!" The spirit sped on, while I conjured a warding, a snake of power that would bind and hold intruders, and sent it to guard the Styrcian gate. Thus would I be effective before my injured body could reach that portal—a hasty-slow progress that soon reduced to a painful lurching walk.

My hands were torn; I was bruised, bleeding, and my clothing partly shredded, yet I stumbled on, intent only on halting Murl's treachery. Opening that gateway, was he? Then he had spied me out, and observed far more of my wards and precautions than I had given him credit for. The more fool I . . .

But why would Amrey leave me injured, to cast open the gate? I remembered the emek camped not far from the tower threshold on that sphere, wondered if he had planned all along to let them through and into my stronghold?

I set foot upon the stairs, and felt the gateway open in that moment. Realized he had thwarted my snake-guardian, or I had dispatched it too late, and Lesseth had not halted him either. It seemed it were too late to delay my traitorous student. By time I came in sight of the door, my fears were confirmed—it stood open, an invitation to intrusion from across the dimensions.

Lesseth hovered upon the threshold, guarding, the emerald snake of power coiled translucent beside him. I stepped beside him, on the lookout for invaders.

There were none.

Murl was already a bowcast distant, trotting at speed along the path he had previously traveled, his cloak and pack proclaiming his readiness for this departure. Back to the emek he went, with never a look behind him.

I could strike him down, or force him back. Send elementals to harry or waylay him, or scathing words upon a message-wind. But what would that accomplish, besides venting my wrath? And what rage I had was numbed with shock at this betrayal and my recent injuries. What did Murl hope to accomplish by fleeing? Was it mere accident, that I had survived the destruction of the crystal? Had he hoped for my death?

No, I refused to believe that, and besides, he had been in danger as well. No doubt the dramatic end of the *shia* had come as much a surprise to him as to me . . .

"*Fe'shia,*" said Lesseth, reading my thoughts. "*Fe'shia,* false *shia*. One emek bore the word in mind, in their camp."

I saw the anguish on his face, more perfect and less substantial than a man's. "There was so much to sort through, I didn't think it meaningful at the time." What stone could they have meant but the Styrcian crystal so flawed it could not be used in any real working? Had Murl known?

Curiosity burned within me, but so did rabid caution. My blood ran cold at his betrayal, so far beyond hurt or anger had it put me. I had done only good for him, asked of him a simple thing. Had he knowingly brought me a dangerously flawed wizard-stone? Or was it chance? And what did he hope to gain by this sudden defection?

The answers retreated before me as my student disappeared into the tall grasses of the steppes. The moment to pursue was passing as I stood locked in indecision. I could send Lesseth to fetch him back, make him account for what had just passed—

And what would I hear but excuses and smooth words of persuasion? Murl was a merchant's son, such speech his stock in trade. With that realization, a great bitterness welled up inside me. Better to cut my losses. He was in Styrcia, no threat to me. Did he hurry beyond my grasp, well, then—let him. And let him stay there.

"Let him remain," I advised myself aloud. Lesseth looked askance, and my pride felt stung. "He risks my life so readily with this unsafe thing," I declared, "and now he scurries back to his louse-ridden friends. I wish him joy of this desert. He cannot cross the spheres without my aid. He has it no more."

So lightly did I sever that tie.

I turned my back on the Styrcian gateway, and Lesseth shut the door behind me. The conjure-snake that guarded it I left upon the other side, a precaution to keep Amrey or other snoopers away from that rift point. All doorways once again secure, I retired to my chamber. I dismissed Una to the kitchens when she cried out at my bloodied state and would have tended my wounds. Lesseth, too, I sent away. I would see to my cuts and injuries myself, for the sake of the reminder they would be. And there was my rage and hurt to drink into numbness before I slept that night.

So did I close my heart to Murl Amrey, once student, once lover, in the same way I had closed the gateway to Styrcia: simply, and finally, never to be opened again.

CHAPTER 7

A mrey's flight disturbed me more than I thought it would.
Heartsoreness distracted like a festering wound, growing
more painful with neglect but promising agony if attended to.
Did I prefer the subtler ache to the acute pain? No, better
were the sudden sharp cut, and have it over with, to heal
cleanly afterwards—yet betrayal and abandonment leave no
room for closure. With Murl Amrey there would be no de-
nouement, no rendering of issues, no discussion or fight or
curses hurtled. Nothing to lessen the soreness of heart but
time.

I could only put the bold face on things. Unable to dress
the wound in any other way, I closed the door upon it and he
who had caused it. Corwin in his lighthearted manner had the
audacity to ask the next day about our late visitor, if he would
be returning, so as to order household chores and service accordingly.

"We have no guests with us at this time, Corwin." I spoke
harshly, dismissing the subject out of hand. "I will tell you
if you need to be prepared for one."

Weeks passed, offering far too much time and leisure in
which to dwell on the betrayal Amrey had dealt me. Oft would
I calculate how long a span had passed in Styrcia, and realized
my former student had no intention of returning, or surely he
would have attempted this long since. I felt surprised as that

realization dawned, and then bitter with resentment at my misplaced trust, for how dare he on the one hand infer devotion and service, and then turn his back upon me so? With nary a word or contact to bridge the gap between us? Not that I would deign to heed him, but my portal wards would have alerted me to his effort, had one been made.

An abandonment, it was, a desertion compounded, and I hardened my heart against him in his continuing absence. I spoke of him thus one day to Lesseth, naming him traitor.

"How so, traitor?" inquired the spirit.

I was shocked he could ask such a question. "He betrayed me! Used what he was not permitted to use, went where he was not given leave to go!" I responded heatedly.

"He considered himself a free man," Lesseth said dryly.

"He spied out knowledge about the workings of Moontooth, and used it to go where he was not permitted!"

"He saw a door he could open and had the will to walk through."

I frowned at my argumentative companion, who sometimes took the other side of an issue I held strong opinion on. It was his way to challenge me, and make me think things through. This time, though, I did not joust in good spirit. My hurt and anger lay too near the surface.

"He took the chance while I lay injured," I retorted sharply. "What he did was wrong."

"Perhaps. But he took nothing. He touched not one thing of ours but returned to Styrcia with only the clothes upon his back."

"And for that small favor I should be grateful?" My words dripped sarcasm, for I was heartily tired of hearing Lesseth's good sense. My right hand and my conscience he is at times, daring to tell me that which I do not care to hear. Part of me recognized the truth in what my companion said, but it was no truth I wished to acknowledge amidst the nurturing of my hurts.

Amrey had so lightly cast my trust aside and turned his back upon me. Why? It was the question that gave me no rest. Was I so horrid, then, that he could not bear to continue on with me? Were the offerings of Styrcia so great he needs must flee there, discontent to remain where his learning might have continued?

Or might not have. There must I halt and be honest with self. I had been ready to send him forth with barely a thank-you for his services. It was not Amrey's company that I pined over, for I had wanted to rid myself of his overweaning pride and manipulative ways soon enough. But that was to be done on my terms, in my time—not his. And therein was the hurt of it, the affront to my pride and my ability to exert control.

Or so I told myself, when I woke nights and wished he were still in my bed.

After some months, I scried no longer, to see what fate befell him. I kept the Styrcian gate well locked. When blue eyes and a face framed in red curls intruded in my thoughts, I calculated his likely life span, and the time that must pass here in Astareth, before his decades on Styrcia should be lived through and come to an end. Near five years, I thought, for him to become an old man in that altered time flow, and die. Five years before I could continue my quest for a crystal, and not by my mere presence there chance contact with the man who had betrayed me.

I put his image forcefully from my thoughts, and turned my attentions elsewhere with singlemindedness of purpose.

I do not frequent the halls of ruling lords and councils, nor yet am I a stranger to them. Often enough do envoys find me, beseech my attendance to solve a dispute, or to facilitate a decision of state. The first time, such a request took me greatly by surprise. Only later did I realize that one who consorts with dragons and elementals is commonly held to have higher knowledge and greater understanding than the ordinary man. A perception I thought I could turn to my advantage, over time . . . and subtly did.

Now and then I would indeed grace a lord's hall or regents' dispute with my presence and my insight. Was I wiser than the common man? I would scorn myself did I take such pomposity to heart. But a different perspective, there is no doubt I held: one based on awareness of many times and places, many different ways of doing things, the understandings I had gleaned of human nature, through my long span of years. For these reasons, I was able now and then to avert a declaration of war, to urge—and betimes, enforce—a diplomatic solution to problems, or to foster a strike against ill-doers who would otherwise eat at the body politic like a rotting wound.

That is how I found myself at the Autarchs' Council, a convocation of the lordlings and masters of the many city-states of the Salt Coast and their neighboring allies. Some years after I had put Amrey from my thoughts, this body came together to discuss alliance and argue disputes, and regulate trade along the warm southeastern seaboard. It was a body ruled in principle by an oligarchy of peers, or so the autarchs believed. In practice, the council was dominated by the most powerful amongst them: Valerian, lord of the great port of Telemar, shining gem of the coast, source of indigo dye and pearl oysters, and the gateway to overland trade from the heart of the island-continent of Drakmil.

I sat in imposing form, masked and dweomer-clad, upon the dais at the head of the council chambers. Here normally would sit Aruvic, priest of the ocean deity Saricos—a seer and moderator, a supposedly neutral voice who orchestrated this convocation of "equals." Aruvic reposed now upon the steps to the right of my feet. Lesseth, immaterial, hovered to my left, close enough to whisper advisings in my ear, of overheard snippets and noncorporeal observations I could not readily gain from my own vantage. Before me, the lords of the Salt Coast, arrayed at tables flanking the hall, a gallery of impatient faces glowering one at the other, but taking issue most with the man who had just shoved back his chair with a grate upon the flagstones.

Lord Valerian came to his feet and stepped back from the marble-topped table. "Not now nor later will you put me in such a grip," he growled. "Telemar is not yours to leverage as you wish, my lords. All your paltry armies and sling-armed rabble of goatherds is as naught to us. If you think you can persuade by force, then try it! Otherwise waste not my time with your useless posturings. Blustering I hear aplenty from fishwives who resent my fifth-pence tax upon their wares. I had expected better from my peers."

He weighted that last word nicely, calculated to provoke umbrage from his audience. Then he turned on well-booted heel and strode from the chamber, leaving an outraged clamor echoing off the marble pillars. I regarded the red-faced assembly, turning to egg each other on to action in the aftermath of the Telemar lord's sudden withdrawal.

Like children in a mort-ground, they were, vying for the puck and the right to shoot the goal. Yet none dared grasp at the disc, swift-flying and hazardous to fingers . . . so they snatched their hands back from Lord Valerian, the risky and unsteerable object set upon his own course—and that the reason for my presence at this time.

I raised one hand; the room fell silent and eyes turned my way.

"Let be for now," I said. "You knew he was not like to listen to your entreaties."

This was more frank than they cared to hear; eyes turned uneasily away from my masked visage. Only Caethon was bold enough to speak out, the gray-haired lord of Stavlia, one of the least affected by Telemar's wide-cast net.

"When Istanian pirates would have wiped Telemar from the sea, we came to his aid," he declared. "How quickly he's forgotten his allies! His stranglehold on overland trade threatens to break us. Now this unholy alliance with Ursbach hulls, inviting the same invader amongst us that our fathers repelled at such cost a generation ago. Telemar leaves us no trade and opens wide the door to those who have long coveted our lands!"

Caethon spat the accusation and others nodded in agreement. The words were nothing new to these halls, where autarchs had come to wrest control of trade back from their ally, and to shut their ports to the Ursbach shipping that carried Telemar goods far and wide. It was an argument well rehearsed, and now ignored by Valerian. He would reap the profits in his well-placed port as he saw fit, and hang those who suffered in consequence. Once-allies had grown resentful and their anger had boiled to the surface this day, couched in half-veiled threats and open recrimination. This negotiation upon Telemar's own ground was the last they had resolved upon before more desperate measures should be chosen. War amongst the city-states of the coast was imminent, a war that Ursbach would be all too glad to join, and it was the hope of many that my mediation could forestall such events.

But the most powerful of the Salt Coast lords enjoyed his near-monopoly and saw no cause to abandon it. Did neighbors close their ports, then would he sell to Istania or Ursbach. His

greed was surpassed only by his arrogance, and my words fell
on deaf ears, as had theirs.

A war would throw the coast into chaos, upheaval that
would wash up to the foundations of Moontooth, and hurt
many innocents as well. Warfare is especially bitter amongst
the city-states and bred feuds that lasted generations. I was
not anxious to witness yet another, or deal with the aftermath
as I would no doubt have to do. Valerian controlled the dyes
and pearl-bearing wealth of the Salt Coast; he alone had the
finances for an army well-manned by mercenaries and surpassed by none. With the aid of Ursbach shipping he could
deliver that force anywhere along the Salt Coast he chose.
Telemar's grasp equalled its greed, and the autarchs of the
city-states regarded it with well-founded hostility.

The chamber murmured in counterpoint to Caethon's rant,
and a gentle whisper filled my left ear. ''Marus tells his sec-
retary to seek a private audience with Valerian.'' Lesseth
sounded amused at the man's dim hope of success. ''Pelan
predicts to his coterie that you will aid Telemar, that he could
not stay so powerful with all his former allies arrayed against
him, did you not secretly support his maneuvers.''

Pelan was a fool, speaking out of hotheadedness. Opinions
from the autarch of Burris could be discounted two for one.
But his hangers-on were readier than that to believe the char-
ismatic lordling, and such rumors could sow dissent and dis-
affection. Best to disperse this assemblage now before feelings
could polarize in the heat of the moment. There were ways
and ways to deal with Valerian, but it must be done neatly,
if war were to be averted. He was no altruist, was the Telemar
lord. We had sparred with heated words behind closed doors,
he one of the few who viewed me cautiously, unawed and
cynical, daring to challenge my advice and my warnings. How

to handle him was a puzzle requiring all my talents of diplomacy and persuasion.

I rose abruptly, and the assembly rose with me. "We shall recess, my lords. I shall be taking council upon this matter before we proceed further." A ploy, that; while the autarchs assumed I would seek the wisdom of otherworldly forces, I knew I needed to retreat from the public eye, speak with Lesseth, give quiet thought to this conundrum. Let them imagine what they would. I would see them again when I had a solution to propose. Meanwhile they could enjoy the pleasures of Telemar while I contemplated how best to proceed.

Had I stayed in the Autarchs' Palace, it would have appeared that I could be influenced by, or at least be accessible to, courtiers' ploys and midnight visitations. It was more politic, with Reydjik at my command, to transport myself in the breath of moments back to Moontooth. There I could think quietly away from the influence of Salt Coast factions, petitioners and enemies alike. I departed that evening, set to return in a day or two, when the council should reconvene in calmer atmosphere.

Corwin greeted me with hot tchai and a fur wrap, the mild winter of this latitude turned biting with a spate of southerly storms. I dismounted atop the flagstones of the roof, accepted the wrap about my shoulders and drank the tchai as I descended into the tower. This was a night well suited to divination, I thought, the world asleep in the dormancy of winter and so all the better to listen to inner voice, higher voices, and scry out what path were best to follow.

I prepared my table. A casting of rune-wands, I thought, would give the right feel to read the nuance of Valerian's obstinacy. I needs must discover what crack might exist where his pride and sense of benefit to self could best be exploited. Somewhere there was an offer that could be made, a proposal that would wring concession from him. While autarchs muttered plans for war, as Lesseth told me, there might yet be a way to avert disaster.

I settled at the desk in my study, old familiar niche for those quick intuitive readings that were often my best. I pulled the bundle of yarrow rods from the ivory tube that held them, laid out paper and ink, pen and wands. I centered myself with a meditative time that would make me more receptive to unseen currents in the multiverse . . .

Perhaps that is why I felt the stirrings of something not right. My eyelids fluttered open and I looked about the room, empty but for myself. Yet I searched the chamber as if I would see or hear something tangible, a solid clue as to what had disturbed me. There was nothing. I closed my eyes again— and that is when the very foundations of Moontooth rocked as something vast and mighty shook the tower, a thunderous assault that ripped a ward-locked gate asunder. I felt it give and reacted physically as if I had been struck a blow that winded me.

I struggled for breath, near thrown from my chair, as dust and old mortar sifted down from rafters and walls. The sudden haze in the air tickled my nose. This heralded intrusion—and more than that. I had the kenning of these indicators from the Guardians of Chernisylla; they meant only one thing. Attack.

Who could? Who would *dare* attack this keep in violent wise? Nearly I suspected Valerian, knowing his hostility towards me, wondering how he could possibly have gained the means. I staggered to my feet, my breath not yet fully recovered, and moved to the door. Lesseth was in the hall already. Like the pull of tidal currents we both could sense the origin of the disturbance that we felt.

Up the stairs, higher in the tower, was the source of this

intrusion. It was a tear in the threads of magic that structure and guard this rift-spanning construct, and as I tasted the nature of what was wrong, I knew with a heart-sickening certainty: the Styrcian gate was opened once again.

The portal I had thought to leave sealed until Amrey's demise had been forced. Nay, more than forced: it had been reft from its casement, shuddering the very cross-dimensional fabric of the tower's underlying substance, and damaging the superstructure as well. Alarmed, Lesseth and I both dashed for the stairs.

My wardings, my spells, all should be engaged now, every defense of the tower should be actively directed at dealing with this intrusion. So had I orchestrated things, since that one time I had left the tower unguarded in Chernisylla, and invaders stumbled upon an open portal, and wreaked their havoc unhindered by the tower's Guardian. Myself. That was the first and last time I had ever been delinquent in my duties, a happenstance I had sworn would never repeat itself. Hence the protections, the safeguards, my almost constant presence in Moontooth, doing that which my family was bred and born to do.

And now? It availed naught! The guardian snakes that could halt a single intruder, the wards that guarded against many, the holding fields that immobilized trespassers, illusion that cloaked and confused the ways—none of these things felt active, none flared to life, invoked by the very trigger event they had been created to stymie. Only one person had had opportunity to study these things and knew of their existence.

I knew from the center of my being that Murl Amrey was at the root of this. How could he have come through the door unaided? How past the wards that seal these portals? What had he done, that Moontooth felt rocked to its foundations?

Lesseth followed me up the staircase at the same moment

that a blast of dust and ice-laden wind blew down it, whipping my gown about my legs, dampening my garments, and touching me with chill. I raised a hand unthinking, blinking against the onslaught—and the trampling and scampering that racketed down my stairs raised the small hairs at the back of my neck.

I raised a hand to invoke my personal defenses, to set barriers in place against this threat I heard, and now could smell: a musty, beasty scent I knew well from a time before. Karzdagi.

Here. In my tower. Burst through from Styrcia.

Sparked by anger, I cried out a *word* of power, enough to shake the walls around us and refill the hall with dust blown by that Styrcian wind. A blaze of blue light filled the stairs above, a stasis that would trap intruders like flies in amber, hold them until I could work my way to them, shrinking the barrier foot by foot, at my leisure—

In the next instant the blue flared white, and then was gone. Wiped away as it if had never been, by some other power than my own.

The air cleared with a crack like skies in a thunderstorm. The repercussion caught me, tossed me back—I would have tumbled down the stairs, had Lesseth not braced me back upright in that moment. He, beyond the influence of earthly winds.

"Who intrudes?" I exclaimed.

"I shall look," he offered hurriedly.

"You shall not," boomed out a louder voice. A disembodied voice, but one I recognized, nearly.

Murl. Deeper. More commanding. But Murl.

I gestured, prepared to invoke yet greater defenses—and froze in that position, a firm, invisble grasp holding me immobilized on the stairs. Like the stasis spell he had cast when first I tested him, but stronger, intractable. Unable to struggle in its iron grip, I trembled with sudden rage.

It was a pointless fury, holding me as captive as Amrey's spell, fueled by the sight of him descending the stairs as a king enters his own banquet hall. First I saw soft black boots with pointed toes, red felt trousers, white tunic covered with vest of fine black fur, the whole covered in beadwork and silver thread in barbaric patterns. Above it was a beard of medium length, thick red and unkempt, streaked with grey. A face I had known in relative youth, aged now to middle-late years and manly maturity, tanned and weathered. This man was muscular, grim, with the scent of horses and sweat and campfires about him. There was a gleam of triumph in his eyes as he saw me, his captive, and stalked me down where I stood helpless and fuming in his magical grip.

Not again. Not yet again. In a blaze of anger I felt vindicated that I had left him to his fate and not wasted my time and effort on helping this upstart so he could return for more effrontery.

Yet he had returned on his own, had he not? And he walked now with a power even I must deem formiddable.

He came to the step just above me, stared down into my face. His garb was wild, barbaric, grease-and smoke-stained, and worn too long, though he walked in it as if it were regal finery. He reached out one calloused hand and took me by the nape of the neck, his movement unhindered by what seemed stone-thick air about me. His fingers twined through my hair and bent my head back, his touch freeing that part of me to move at his command. I could not take my eyes off of him, my student become a different man. The full-blown presence of him was palpable, an aura of power and authority around him as I had seldom encountered in this world or any other.

''And so I find you again, my teacher.'' He forced me to

look at him. "My lover." He said the word with a twisted sneer, scorn dripping from his words. "Are you not glad to see me home once more?" His eyes were riveting, bluer than before, crueler than before, piercing me to the heart with a well-chosen arrow of guilt. Then his lips were upon mine, a demanding urgency to them.

When I did not kiss him back, his teeth sank into my lip and bit me in parting. I gave an exclamation and tried to jerk my head away, but his hand and magic held me fast.

"You'll take that, and anything else I care to give you," he said grimly. "This tower is mine now, Inya. You are mine, as long as you amuse me. Soon, your world will be mine, as well."

A special emphasis on that, *world*, as if he really meant it. Anger, shock, frustration at my sudden powerlessness—all were replaced in a flash by an inkling of what he could mean, of how he punched so effortlessly through dimensions and my wardings, of how he worked his will here as if I had left no mark upon this place at all.

My eye caught the glimmer of a blue-white gem about his neck, suspended from a chain, and my breath caught in my throat.

A Styrcian crystal. And I, fool that I was, had as good as invited him to them. To it. To the one he wore, for it took only one, and since when had Murl Amrey ever lacked for cleverness in things magical?

Karzdagi clustered behind him on the staircase. One, bigger and more muscled than the others, clad in mannish garb, stepped forward with a box of chased silver, handing to his master the bracelets of gold and iron that lay therein. Amrey took the ornaments, set them about my unmoving wrists. A shock like electricity jolted me as the second settled into place and secured with a snick.

The air about me dissolved into its vaporous state, and I was free to move once more. Free to clutch at a thread of my magic, for if I could stem the tide here, there was a chance that I could avert the disaster I had somehow unleashed or invited into our midst.

But such a thing was not possible. There was my power, and here was I separated from it by some unbreachable barrier. I could sense it, curling latent within me, but like a paralytic was unable to make it respond to my command. Radiant chill washed up my arms as I reached with senses trained to the purpose . . . and Amrey laughed at me, deriding my pitiful attempts to gather power to me.

"No use," he said. "You're bound, Inya, well and truly, and will be as long as I desire it to be so. Now follow me."

My eyes strayed down to the bracelets, locked snug around my wrists, simple bands of gold worked through with iron— and there a wisp of silver or platinum, worked in the sigils of talismanic magic, a style and type I did not recognize but whose purpose was evident. And then I was stumbling down the stairs, shoved along by the karzdagi escort, whose beastly stench already clogged my nostrils over the cold Styrcian winds that whipped in gusts through these stairs and hallways.

Before I could gather my scattered wits I was thrust into the kitchen where the rest of my household awaited the invaders' unkind attentions. The only absence was Lesseth and I hoped for a wild moment that he could effect escape or rescue, unseen by those around us. Yet Murl knew of his existence, surely had planned to deal with that spirit as well as he had planned the breach of my defenses.

I looked to Una and Corwin, huddled nervous and cowed at the table. Beside them—ah, there was Lesseth after all, a vague form made more corporeal by some enchantment of Amrey's, no doubt, for his manlike figure hung visibly—

albeit transparently—between two karzdagi who had managed to lay hands upon him. His captors shoved him towards the others, then joined their fellows, grim dog-men in leather armor standing on crooked hind legs to guard the doors, snarling at us when we moved about or tried to speak.

"Leave it, Lady," my spirit friend breathed to me before karzdagi came forward to separate us. But not before he touched a hand to mine, and gentled me where I was picking, plucking at the infernal wristband that constrained my magic. I looked down, unaware of my nervous actions until that moment.

"This will not serve," boomed Amrey again. He spoke from the door in a voice pitched to battlefield volume. It seemed to be his normal tone, and he used it handily to intimidate. Karzdagi bowed and scraped out of his way, then ringed him half about in a guardful semicircle, fangs bared and spears at the ready.

I knew I must somehow gain back the initiative. I and my people were prisoners in my home, and fear twisted in my gut as I realized abruptly that I had no power, for the nonce, with which to halt these events. No power, that was, unless I could slip away somehow to study or workroom, places where enough objects of power lay that something would come to hand, some lever to use against this rock.

"Let me explain your status," Murl said, this stranger, this older version of one I had known, hair just starting to thin, distinguished grey at temples, brow heavier, shoulders wider. A fine-looking man in spite of his barbaric airs, had we met under other circumstances . . .

"You are my property." His eyes swept over us all. "I claim you as spoils of war."

"Nonsense," I retorted. "We are not chattel, and there is no war."

He raised one brow, amusement in his eye. "To the contrary. There is the war I have declared, and it is our custom to take slaves. You, Lady, are my first prize. A trinket I will keep, as long as you please me."

He scowled at the others, Corwin, Una, Lesseth. "These others serve no purpose to me. They remain alive on sufferance, as long as you remain . . . biddable."

So that was his game. Treating my household like bargaining counters, like the merchant's son he was. "They are surety for my good behavior? You act like a common brigand, Murl." I spoke as haughtily as I might, for it seemed my dignity was all I had to cling to in this moment.

Amrey responded to that jibe with a muffled snort and a glare that I met as an equal. "My name has changed since you left me to my fate, Inya," he declared flatly. "It is Kar Kalim, now."

A ripple went through the assembled karzdagi, recognizing those words from a tongue native to their world. Heads bobbed in unthinking obeisance, a few hands gestured in a ritual of greeting or blessing upon hearing that term.

I refused to acknowledge the awe they clearly felt for this man. "What is that supposed to mean?" I asked, disdain in every word.

"Loosely translated?" He curled a lip at me. "I suppose you would render it, *Conqueror of the world.*"

I gaped at that. It was the last thing I could have been prepared to hear. Was it empty boasting? Could he possibly have left such a mark on Styrcia? After all, the accelerated time flow there was clear to see in his advanced years. And here he intruded against all protections with a small army of karzdagi and a power stone about his neck. I felt its elemental tug from where I sat, now that I knew what forces were being dealt with here . . .

And yet, a small horde of beast-men and the power to push across dimensional borders does not make one a world conqueror. He saw the doubt on my face and merely smiled, a gentle smirk that spoke chapters more than protests or claims could have done. My blood ran cold at the certainty in his demeanor.

"You shall see," was all he said. He turned on his heel and left us.

CHAPTER 8

When the karzdagi were done securing the tower, locking us under guard in the kitchen, ensuring Murl's orders of silence with brutal blows that knocked Una sprawling and bruised my shoulder—when they were done, then did our captor return to us a last time.

He ordered food served for his minions in the tower, thirty of them. "You needn't worry about the army," he added casually. "They know how to forage."

He studied my face in vain for a reaction to that last. I had gathered my dignity around me, and no posturing of Amrey's would dispel it. If he had brought more with him than a handful of scruffy dog-men, that would doubtless come clear in time.

The karzdagi were fed by Una, she white-faced in the kitchen with Corwin uneasy by her side. Later Amrey returned and took me out of the room with him, pulling me behind him by the wrist. I saw no point in struggling against him. We ascended the stairs and my heart beat anxiously as I saw which chamber he brought me to.

"Long have I waited for this," he growled, and motioned to my bed—his bed now, as was clear from his proprietary actions in this, my bedchamber.

I sniffed. "And if you think I'll go to bed with you under these circumstances, sirrah, then are you sadly mistaken."

"Ah, but you would under other circumstances?"

I hesitated. I would have, once, and had dreamed of him often enough since. But that was neither here nor there. I thought of my people, prisoners below, and wondered if my body must be the price for their well-being. I thought not, thought Murl not that coldhearted, or not the Murl I had known, at any rate.

"No matter," he said to my seeming silence. "It is this simple. You will sleep with me willingly, or you will be raped. But have you, I will. Be it willing, then you can perchance enjoy it as well. Be it rape, well . . . mutual pleasure is perhaps better than one-sided." He turned a knowing look on me. "Unless of course you *like* to be violated . . ."

His words stung, striking too close to fantasies and the rough lovemaking we had enjoyed before he had abandoned me for Styrcia. I was attracted to him, of course, even more in his maturity than before. But that fleeting bit of mindless physical lust weighed nothing against the turmoil that near overwhelmed me at what he was about. I still could not grasp how he had penetrated my defenses, come in, and made himself free of the place, and these bindings that would not come off, that held me from my power . . .

I needed to lash out and I did: with a scream, I threw myself at him. It was the purest of outrage, an unthinking moment set off by that last look he had given me or that tone of voice or the proprietary way he ran his eyes over me—to think I would cooperate in any way with this brigand! I saw red, and leapt, thinking perhaps the right blow, the right touch of a nerve nexus and I would lay him out and then he would be the one in bonds, and his miserable dog-men blasted from this place, and his laughable threats of an army made clear for what they were—

The thunderclap that followed staggered me to hands and

knees, leaving me stunned. He busied himself in casual ways while I collected myself too slowly, numbed and chastised by his display of deadly power. The truth came home to me in that moment. He was far, far more powerful than I. And he was demanding that I bow before that power. Did I not comply, then he would compel it. There was no way I could defy him, not in that moment. Not if it meant losing what little freedom I still retained, or perhaps my life, if he held a grudge that demanded vengeance. There was only one path clear to see, the path of cooperation with a superior force—a path that roiled my stomach and set my teeth on edge. Would he know it was pretense? Would he suspect that my true heart waited concealed, seeking a chance to reveal my colors at a moment of weakness, when he was lulled? Of course he must, he was no fool even in his youth, that short, too short time agone. . . . How much more canny must he be now.

I came to him leery, he regarding me with frank appraisal all the while.

"For now, Murl Amrey," the words came out of me with slow consideration, "I will do as you bid." I stopped there, before threats or anger should follow, before I could say too much.

"Well that you see it so, Inya." He smiled at me from a chair. "You needn't call me Murl, though. My title will do."

What hubris. Kar Kalim, indeed. I nearly laughed in his face, but wrestled that suicidal whim down deep inside. That was a title I would never give him. In a controlled voice, I laid a different bait. "Rather would I call you by the name I knew." I inclined my head. "It reminds me of a man . . . whom I have missed."

There was some small truth in that. I can be as needs must

be, for I had missed him in my bed, though not the least in other ways. Would he sense that nuance? Did he sit even now with truth-spell detecting of my intention and heart?

Apparently not. Vain enough he was to be nearly flattered by that last. I read that in the unguarded expression my words surprised from him.

He motioned to the bed across from him. I sat there, perched warily on the edge. Too eager I could not seem, nor yet too reluctant. My anger must stay hidden completely, from myself as well, lest it color my actions detectably and ruin my pretense of cooperation. So in that moment, like all folk must betimes learn to do, I put aside the outrage, the fury, even the revulsion that threatened to well up as he drew near, and resolved myself to play the role of his reluctant leman, brought round by his charm and the history between us.

I hated that there was more truth in that guise than I wanted to see in myself. My resentment warred with my lust until I could decide and chose no more, but only succumb to his will, and do as he bid me beneath the blankets. At the end my surrender was no pretense, but afterwards, hot tears came to my eyes. Dawn lightened the sky before I found refuge in uneasy sleep.

A tremor woke me, a soundless motion that shook the bed and then turned to a grumbling in the heart of the earth. Moontooth shook from its very foundation. Windows rattled in their high, narrow casements and one cracked; a wardrobe door flung itself open and vials and combs tumbled off a dressing table with an alarming clatter and crash.

Murl came fully alert before I did. He flung one arm over me and clasped me to him until the trembling subsided, the earth settling with a receding roar. My heart raced, for that

was a quake of such violence as I had never experienced before.

"Finally!" declared Amrey.

"What do you mean?" I asked, puzzled.

"There will be no more where that came from," he said
dryly.

I looked at him in the morning light, not taking his meaning. "Surely you weren't expecting that?"

"A quake?" He shrugged. "I expected something. Now it
is passed, that will be the last of it."

How could he know that? Was he also an elementalist,
privy to the secrets of the earth? Before I could question further, he stretched, reveling as it were in the release of some
unspoken tension, or satisfied with an expectation fulfilled. He
didn't take his arm away, but instead drew me closer, then
silenced me with his mouth. He took me in a rough manner,
a continuation of the night before, then left me, tired and
aching, with a guard outside the door.

I did not waste the time in sleep. I thought fast and furi-
ously, in those precious moments by myself, without one
nearby who could conceivably dip inside my thoughts and spy
out my process through canny arts or intuition.

And what thoughts went round though my head . . . the self-
pity, the distress, the anger, I put aside. The mystery of this
quake he had expected, I must save for later. For now I must
know, as soon as possible, what I could accomplish with this
man. Kar Kalim, he styled himself. Not the nearly tractable
student of years before, but a headstrong and mighty wizard
of the highest order, whose Styrcian crystal was always
around his neck, even in the heat of passion. And, apparently,
a man of at least some military might. I had heard martial
sounds through the night, heavy tramping in the hallways of

Moontooth, the noise of an armed force from outside the high casement, and this morn I had no need to spy the landscape out: outside, men shouting in a foreign tongue, the clink of armor and buckles, the tramp of booted feet were unmistakeable. This force must have been moving through the opened portal all night, to be present in such noisy numbers now.

Meanwhile, what was I to do? Slip into this new role Amrey envisioned for me, of consort and lover, tidily putting aside my own concerns? He had stripped me of power, or muzzled it for the time being, that much was undeniable. Did he plan on keeping me hobbled forever? For a moment my heart sank in utter despair, for if he never removed these bracelets, if I never found the means to do so, when would I be able to tap and use my powers? It was beyond disheartening. I pulled myself from the brink of that abyss, turned my thoughts otherwise . . .

Suppose I seemed to cooperate, and earned his trust? Would he at some time release me from these bonds, thinking I would use my powers benignly to aid him? Perhaps. Or I could seem an earnest ally, one whose own schemes he could well apply in his own interests. I knew Murl's overreaching ego, his eagerness to grasp at a tool and set it to hand. Should I seem such a tool, then surely he would want to use me. Truth be told, I would rather be employed in such wise, than exist only to be used by him as he had night and morn. I must make him come to think of me in other ways.

For now my powers were as good as nonexistent, but they were something to be reckoned with, else he had not spent such care to rein them in. And my fund of knowledge and learning was still there. I wondered how he would respond to me should I do that which came most naturally: refuse to accept his overlordship. I could proceed as if I were my own person, with my own affairs to tend to—for such was certainly the case, and I have found that when a body proceeds in such wise, others bow before it. Thus can deference be compelled, with force of will alone.

I did not think that I would sway Amrey to deference, but it seemed that continuing as if I were independent would open more doors than it would shut. I did not think he would want to see that spirit entirely squelched, even as he tried to bring me to heel.

For that matter, there was no other option I could stomach. To be his tame geierhawk would not give me the room I needed to counter this man and his machinations. For Amrey to force his way into this sphere, to neutralize the Guardian of Moontooth so neatly, to establish a military bridgehead, all in the course of one evening . . . his stated ambition to conquer the world might not be hollow boast, much as I wished to dismiss it as such, but it was no plan I could countenance.

So resolved, I rose and dressed, and confronted the karzdag at my door. The foul-smelling creature curled a lip back from long yellowed fangs when I spoke to it. He blinked at my words, ignorant of their meaning, and when I tried by reflex to invoke a spell that would let me comprehend tongues so we could converse, I drew up short. Touching fingers to the bracelet on my left wrist, I shivered from the chill that ran up my arm when I had tried the working of magic.

Well. If we could not converse, there was at least one phrase the dog-man must know the meaning of. "Kar Kalim," I said. "Bring me to Kar Kalim."

Canine eyes widened in recognition, and brow furrowed as the karzdag visibly decided how to deal with me. He hefted his spear, then, barring me inside the door of my bedchamber, turned his head to the stairs and gave a howl that broke into a high-pitched series of yips. A howling yip echoed in response, and soon an escort of beast-men came to take me from my rooms and down to the audience chamber, where Amrey had ensconced himself upon my throne.

I think he sat there simply for effect, to see what might shake me, to bring home the fact that I no longer ruled here. Karzdag and human warriors flanked the hall on either side, arrayed in little clusters intent on conversation, one group about a table with maps spread upon it, elsewhere a few armored warriors in debate over a row of tally sticks. The humans were dressed in a style similar to Amrey's own, in felted trousers and pointed-toed boots, fur vests over hauberks of scale mail. Faces dark-weathered and rough-bearded; the scent of horse and smoke and sweat mingled over all and gave an unwonted pungency to my hall.

Talk ceased as I drew near. I refused to let my reaction show upon my face. Instead I made the shallowest of courtesies, bending one knee and dipping my chin, the same recognition I might offer a peer in magic or the Emperor of Koribee, or someone similarly placed. One karzdag in my escort stepped forward, clawed hand raised to shove me to my knees, when Amrey shook his head and forestalled the movement.

"Ah, so you join us at last," he said in a nearly courtly tone. "No need for your presence, however; we fare well enough without your supervision." A sneer tinged his words, but the soldiers gathered about did not react to his statement in the least. I realized then that they spoke another tongue and did not understand Arguente, the language of the Salt Coast; therefore our words and veiled insults would pass unattended by those roundabout. It was just as well, for Amrey would play differently to an audience, I sensed, than to me in private speech.

"I fear I am not accustomed to aiding invaders who make camp in my home," I said.

He frowned. "There is much more than that which you will have to adjust to, Inya. Come here."

He beckoned me to his side as one would a dog. I held my ground, then stepped slowly closer, obeying his command but in my own time. He rose from my throne and met me at the foot of the dais, dismissing the karzdag escort with a gesture. Then he turned to the left, one hand at the small of my back, gesturing broad with the other arm as he took me on a tour of my own hall.

"Vanye, my commander of horse," he nodded to a gray-haired warrior, blind in one eye, who affixed me with a challenging scowl over his bristling beard. Amrey moved on, motioning to the group pouring over maps that I recognized as plundered from my study. "Strategists, and leaders of scout troops, learning the lay of the land. Here, my provisioners calculating logistics." I studied the trio with the tally sticks, wondered how wooden counters could suffice to track the needs of an entire army, if that is indeed the size force he had brought with him. "Scouts are out already," he added, "and foragers seeing to supplies."

I cocked my head at him. "Just how large a force do you have here, this army of yours?"

He quirked his mouth in half a smile, and rather than answer, turned his steps to the doorway. I followed by his side, willing myself not to pull away from the proprietary guiding hand on my elbow, until we emerged at the doorway of the tower. There, on the flagstones of the landing, overlooking the slopes of grassy meadow dotted with bristlepine and black oak . . . there did I halt and take in an unwelcome vista.

The slope was black with the figures of men and horses, countless numbers of them. Already what had been my private parkland and scratching for Una's chickens and geese was obliterated, tramped into a muddy morass by men and mounts. Where had they all come from?

"They come through the gate," Murl said as if reading my thoughts. "This is the Lodanya-previtsch'ch, my strike force. When the Eshmiak-previtsch'ch are ready in place, they will move through the gate later this morning. Then the Kalimat, the elite guards—" He laughed aloud at the look on my face. "Yes, did you not hear them? These horses all trooped through your hallways and down your stairs. My stairs, now."

I had not realized such a flood of men and material and animals transited Moontooth, nor sensed it as I should have. I gripped the cold metal on my wrist, not warmed by my body's heat, persistantly dulling my senses. Amrey ignored me and spoke into the air. "It is an inconvenience," he remarked, "but not for long. Perhaps later you will help me readjust the gate's location and open a portal more convenient to military needs. Something wider, and closer to the ground outside."

He laughed at the expression on my face, aghast as I was. I would be sooner dead, than cooperate with you in that way, I yearned to say, but dared not be so foolish. With effort I composed myself and turned to him.

"You really do command an army."

"Oh, yes." It was the offhand tone of one who took something for granted. "Much more than a rag-tag collection of karzdagi, although they are some of my best stealthy raiders. Even so . . ." He extended an arm, as if presenting the camp abuilding to me. "I give you the horse tribes of Styrcia. The Breo'la. Outlawed from emek vills, feared by the settlements, the bane of the steppes and the wastelands between . . . once scorned and ignored, until brought by me to greatness."

"You?"

He smiled grimly. "I have indeed conquered the world, you see. All of civilized Styrcia is under my sway—or all of it that counts, the vills and the steppes between ice and ice. But that is very little, in such an unfertile, sparsely populated land. And yet my armies are hungry, and grow restive without new territories to challenge them. They have great ambitions, as do I. This country will do for now, don't you think?"

In that moment I realized how I could use him. His pride was as ever beyond measure, his ego vast, and with ambitions of this sort, I saw how he might be nudged, subtly steered, in a direction more of my choosing than his own. It would take the most delicate byplay, the most light-handed of misdirection, and there was no time to lose about it. Now, while the situation was fluid, before he had committed to plans of action, this was the time to influence him as well as I might . . .

"If that is your true ambition, Murl, then we have much to talk about. The Salt Coast is on the verge of warfare at this moment."

He glanced at me sharply, and I nodded. "It is so, and I am in a position to sway events one way or the other. Let us go within, and I will tell you something of the troubles on the Coast. At least you should be informed what broil you are stepping into here."

There. That was nicely calculated to sound as if I cooperated in his schemes, and yet, angled so that he would be the lever I had sought against Valerian. I saw by his look that the hook was baited. Time to see if this fish would swallow the lure.

"The Autarchs' Council presently seeks an argument that Telemar will heed, one that will bring Lord Valerian round to recognizing their interests. Even united against him, the resources of the lesser autarchs cannot match Valerian's might, not with Ursbach in naval alliance with him. Your horse-army—"

"Breo'la."

"The Breo'la could tip the scale in their favor. Be the iron fist that Telemar cannot ignore, help force him to come to terms at the Autarchs' Council, and the lords of the Salt Coast will owe you a great debt. If your force is superior to Valerian's, there may not even be need of bloodshed. At least in combination with Arguentan city-states, you stand to neutralize Telemar's present clear advantage."

My words were nearly spontaneous, neat but true. I faltered for a moment in spite of myself—the mention that bloodshed could be avoided caused Amrey's eyes to narrow, and methoughts promise of peace did not, after all, have special appeal to him. Had he become so brutal, then, or was it his barbaric horse tribes that required battle and blood?

No matter; it was true that he could be the irrefutable argument that could force Valerian to concessions, and thereby would power play into his hands. Power he would enjoy only so long as I was bound in the use of my magic, of course . . .

His words pulled me back to the moment.

"What need to ally with one faction or the other?" he asked. "I can take either of them unawares as they fight each other. They do not look to hostilities from this horde magically manifest upon their doorstep." He waved a hand gateward, and laughed.

He angered me. "Do you know how fragile a situation is here?" I said sharply. "You can come in with your conquering Breo'la, but there will be little for you to conquer if war breaks out for true."

"Bah. I have the superior force and the advantage of surprise—"

"Leave aside for now the question of how your steppe riders will adapt to this warm climate, the hilly, tree-filled terrain, the heavily fortified cities and strongholds about the countryside. If you encourage war between the autarchs, then you will be heir to a wasteland. Have you forgotten how they ravage the land here in battle? And so ruin the wherewithal of the cities in times of peace? Well you should recall, Keshdar's son of Burris. You know the tales from your youth. Those ways have not changed. And do you take neither side, but attack either faction alone, then will they unite quickly to face the common foe. They have done it before, against Ursbach and Istania."

"Wasting the fallen enemy is our way," he said dismissively. "It is no great loss to me to have torched farmlands and slaughtered vill dwellers. That is as it should be. In future battles, you see, those who do not die will surrender outright for terror of their likely fate, should they resist.

"This other, though . . ." He chewed his lip. "Alliance against a common foe. You are right in that much: if I am seen as outside invader, that is likely to happen. I can only take one or two city-states by surprise before the entire Coast is alerted to my presence. There are better ways to fight than against massed resistance."

His musings trailed off, but not before I was struck by the coldheartedness of his calculations, by the scorched-earth tactic he so blithely assumed was proper.

"What would you recommend, oh manipulator of masses and power behind thrones?" His question was half sarcasm and half humor; I quelled the retort that sprang to my lips and answered him frankly instead.

"I would say there are ways and ways to conquer. Ally with the weaker faction against the stronger. The majority of Arguenta's lords will be on your side, for you would be the key to victory by their terms, victory in negotiation and trade. It puts you in a politically powerful position. What you do after Valerian is made to dance to your tune, is something you can decide later.'' Or a decision I could sway him in at that time, I thought, if I had not yet won my freedom from his control.

"Hm." He rose from the desk in my study, leaving me standing before him without so much as the courtesy of a chair. I remained in seeming good graces as he paced, restless with thought and calculations. ''Valerian,'' he muttered. ''Haughty and rich as I recall. It would suit me to challenge him, and to gain the indebtedness of these lesser lords. As you say—obligation and influence is invaluable in building an empire.''

A smile broke out upon his face, the ghost of that boyish charm I had once been fond of. ''Thank you for the suggestion. It offers promise.''

I repeated my courtesy of acknowledgement. ''There is a convocation at the Autarchs' Palace, then, that you should attend. I am expected there—''

He cut me off with a wave of the hand, and the look on his face changed to one of cold appraisal.

''Now, Inya: why does the Midnight Rider choose to help me?''

His tone was cold and cutting and I sensed a dangerous abyss yawning at my feet. He suspected my motives. Why should I help him, indeed? It must look suspicious, and there was truth to that, that I served my own ends. Of course; when did I not? When did any wielder of power not take action with an eye to the final goal? All points that would not further my cause with him the least whit. I sensed this was a man would bridle did he think for an instant that he was being used. It remained to explain in neutral manner what my in-

terest was here. I am buying time, defining a purpose for myself and keeping you to the path of least damage in the
interim, I thought but dared not voice. How to say what he
would believe . . .

Well. It is possible to tell the truth, and have it be con-
vincing, even if it is not all of the truth. "You, sir, have
neutralized me quite neatly." I spread my arms, hands bent
to reveal braceleted wrists. "I am at your mercy. It does not
serve me to be enemies with you, upon whom my welfare
now must depend. That is common sense."

"Hm."

"Who rules and how is of little consequence to me. I have
been here for centuries, and seen lordlings come and go. Do
you have ambitions to build empire—well, it will be a new
thing, born on the Salt Coast, but not necessarily a bad thing.
I have one interest only: to remain Guardian of this tower,
and guard the rifts and the warp of time and space in this
fragile place. What passes outside my walls is of interest to
me in only a few instances."

"This quarrel between the city-states being one such?"

I inclined my head. "They sought me out, not the other
way around. So it goes, at times." I shrugged. "I am not
adverse to lending aid when I am asked."

The coldness left his weathered visage. My interest in the
tower he knew was sincere; that I could help where asked was
doubtless something he had hoped to use to his own advantage. My words struck home, and all of them truthful, as far
as that one facet of truth extended.

Amrey smiled full upon me then. "I am glad to hear that,
Inya. It does not free you from the leash that tames you"—
his voice became stern for that moment—"but perhaps you
need not be stictly imprisoned as I had imagined, either. We
shall see what accord we come to, you and I. You will come

with me to this convocation, and be my sponsor." He laughed, a short, sharp bark. "Indeed. You may speak for me to the lords of the Salt Coast. Until I am ready to speak for myself!"

He left me then in fair high spirits. I sat at my desk, no longer caring that a karzdag stood guard at my door. Relief washed over me. My words were plausible and I had won some measure of credence with Amrey in the last few moments, given him more reason than bed-sport to keep me to hand and work with me.

Still, a self-proclaimed conqueror of the world gives one pause. I did not want to aid him too much or too overtly. Even sponsoring him to the Autarchs' Council presented a problem, for with my introduction the lords would believe Amrey to be a suitable alternative to their present dilemma. I was not convinced of that, for the man's lack of ethics and readiness to harm were abundantly clear, and I was like to be dyed the same color when Kar Kalim should begin to act true to his nature. All the more reason, then, for me to stay close by his side, to become indispensable in his councils, so that I could forestall what I might and influence where I could.

Did bloodlust truly drive him, this man I had once known and who now seemed so different? I thought not; he harbored more the desire for power and control, it seemed. If that were so, he might be willing to reach for power by more temporal means, not rely solely on military exercises intended to keep his battle-hordes engaged in carnage. Or blatant displays of *shia* power, as he had done in the penetration of the Styrcian gate.

I remembered the merchant's son who in odd moments had charmed me, and saw that person still in this mature man so long unlooked for. I did not think him a bloodthirsty butcher. He would do this the subtle way. If he were clever as before, he would follow my lead and learn from how I juggled the nuances of this situation. And with my own conscience could I rest clear: from my viewpoint I was protecting my own interests, guarding those I cared for, preventing greater bloodshed by moderating the use of force.

Ah, yes. The Autarchs' Council would have a surprise or two on hand, when next they convened.

CHAPTER 9

"No," Amrey said flatly. "We have no need of your mist-dragon."

I faltered, completely taken aback by his words. I had counted on using Reydjik to travel to Telemar, never thought twice that this necessity would be questioned, much less denied. "It is needful," I protested. "It is the most rapid way to traverse—"

"No." His tone was biting; I fell silent, warily taking his measure. How did he think to get us there, without the dragon's aid?

"I'll not loosen your bonds even that little bit, that you may call and command your spirit friends." He shook his head once, emphatically. My heart sank. That had been exactly my goal, of course, to gain a little freedom, as well as to be the one in control of our transport, to get him used to relying on me in such little ways . . .

He crushed any such hope with his next declaration. "I will see us there, and back again. Vanye comes with us, and Elyek, my Master of Supply—they can gain what estimate they can of the forces that might be arrayed against us. Best to do that while we appear to be on a mission of diplomacy in the enemy's city."

Vanye the eye-blind eldster who had looked so grimly upon me in the great hall, and Elyek, one of those who had been so engaged with the tally sticks. I had thought to be by myself with Amrey, to have the opportunity to deal with him away from his officers and guards. I adjusted with difficulty to this revised framework of events. How did he think he would transport us all? Telemar was a ten-day journey overland by swift horse—

"You say Lesseth spies for you." His statement interrupted my calculations. I shook my head.

"He is no spy," I corrected him. "He shares what he gleans, what comes to his senses, that is all."

Amrey curled a lip. "Makes for a fine spy, whatever you call it. He comes with us. I want to hear his observations, not about the council, as you squandered his talents before, but about Valerian, and his plans for hostilities with the autarchs."

"Perhaps there are no plans for hostilities."

I said it out of petulance. I did not enjoy being ordered to order my companion. Lesseth was more than a servant and I had no wish to compel his aid in Amrey's unsavory ventures.

"Of course there are plans for hostilities," he said confidently. "At least as contingencies. We will spy that out. If Lesseth fails, Corwin will be punished. If he deserts, the boy will be killed."

There struck a true blow, so casually made but clearly no jest. From his time with us before, Murl no doubt remembered the personal interest I took in my young charge. Blue-eyed, blond-haired Corwin was so different from the Salt Coast natives, the old Arguentan bloodlines predominantly dark-haired, dark-eyed, and olive complected. He had come to me as an orphan from far Sabyt, found starveling on the plains after the death of his parents in their frontier homestead. Helfings, the diminutive near-men of that region, took him in and raised him.

When the Tinmoots were being held, I attended, and was captivated by the man-child already a head taller than the helfing chieftain he served as page. He was full of questions then, just awakening to his human heritage, coming to realize how different he was from the people he called family. I saw he had a bright mind, and a good skill with his hands; already trained to service, he was attentive, hungry to learn, and seemed so out of place in that environment. When asked if I might find a way to bring Corwin back into the society of humans, I agreed, and brought him with me to Moontooth. One day I had planned for him to grow beyond the borders of the tower and its surrounding lands. We did lessons weekly; one day he would go to Caronne for further education, or Telemar for the arts, or, if he showed magical aptitude, even Tor Mak was a possibility.

I who have no family here have made something of a clan of my servants and friends, those few I trust inside my inner circle. Corwin was one such. So did Murl Amrey up the stakes, holding people I cared for as bargaining chips and surety against the behavior he wished to see. It was a weapon that could be used against me only if I bowed to that hold, only if I conceded that Corwin's health or life was fair exchanged for my cooperation. I had guessed he would try such a ploy sooner or later; now we would see if and how I would accede to coercion. I thought I already knew how I would decide . . . how I *must* decide.

"How do you propose to get us to Telemar," I asked, changing the unpleasant subject, "if I am not to invoke Reydjik's aid in our travels?"

Amrey accepted the segue without comment, merely raising one finger and touching the blue-gleaming crystal trapped in a framework of silver filigree at his throat. "This shall tend to our needs," he said with finality.

I should have known. The wizard-stone that could breach a dimensional rift was more than fit to warp physical space in a single sphere of existence. I bowed my head before him, a gesture of obedience that I hoped would lull. "As you say. We shall be ready within the hour."

Gray clouds hung low, blackening early evening to the semblance of a later hour. A heavy cold drizzle dampened the military encampment before the white granite spire of Moontooth. The Kalimat, Amrey's elite guards, had taken pride of place and ranged their camp closest to the tower entrance. Low, round felt tents huddled in groups about central clearings where equipment and supplies were arrayed for storage and use.

The clusters of tents were *shivetu*, Murl informed me: warriors related by blood in family groupings, arranged by sept, and then by clan, within the military unit they formed. In this weather, at this hour, the troops that normally lounged about were snug inside their tents, except for those posted as guards and those whose business drove them outside in their wet horsehide cloaks. Their mounts were left to browse under the watchful eye of herdmasters, in the grassy meadows to the north and east of the tower, but Bronye and Vabronye—chieftains and clan chiefs—were allowed their personal mounts in camp. Torches hissed and guttered in the rain, pocking the darkness with light, marking the soggy horsetail and cloth banners of the leading warriors' tents.

It all seemed a dirty and disorderly way to run a military garrison to me, with more troops coming through the portal hourly, a constant distant hubbub of tents abuilding and gear being stored. The arrangement seemed to suit Amrey's rough horsemen, though, and their encampment spread now in a series of banner-flagged *shivetu* all about the hills and under the trees surrounding Moontooth.

Our departure to Telemar was done in plain sight of the tents and horse pickets of the Kalimat. Amrey led the way down the steps of the tower, to the clearing between Moontooth and the nearest *shivet.* For this occasion he wore the most elegant of his Breo'la finery: a blood-red tunic caught to the wrists by bracers of ornately worked silver; a short-furred vest worked in silver and semiprecious stones; trousers of a light wool, red and black striped; with a plain-hilted saber by his hip. Over all a cloak lined with a luxurious fine black fur he called *semyet,* which reminded me of mink. He had gone so far as to trim his beard and hair, exciting some small comment amongst onlookers. He kept the barbaric cast of his horse tribesmen, while making concession to the well-groomed standards of courtly circles. It was the first time he had washed it free of grease, I thought, in many long weeks, but the battle-braid remained, forward of his left ear, a shoulder-length strand intertwined with beads of stone, three blue, four red, two black. Each red agate represented a general and an army vanquished, he had told me; each turquoise, a people subjugated. The first onyx, to honor his deed of uniting the horse tribes of Styrcia; the second, to mark his overlordship of all they had conquered.

Lesseth and I followed him, as we had been directed to. Vanye, Elyek, and five guards armed with bow and saber came as well, in cleaner garb than the sweat-stained gear I had first met them in, but just as crudely martial in appearance. Seeing that we were all present, Amrey paused first to cast a spell of tongues upon his comrades, so they were fluent in Arguente and could understand what would transpire on our journey. Then he turned his back on us and placed one hand on the *shia* around his neck.

After a moment of concentration he raised a hand and gestured as if wiping a looking glass clear, one swipe from left to right. As his palm moved through the air, a rift opened before us, alight with the same blue-white glow that poured out from his fingers that grasped the wizard-stone. Stars or small bursts of light sparkled in that opening, like dust motes igniting and flaring to sudden death; beyond that coruscation lay only velvet darkness.

The few karzdagi and Breo'la who were about in the weather halted in their passing, keeping a respectful, nearly reverential distance from our party, some bowing in obeisance to Kar Kalim, as he was named in whispered tones from here and there. Amrey ignored that adoration, taking it as his due, and turned to us, blue eyes crinkling at the corners at the expression on my face. He pointed towards the portal he had opened. "Through."

Vanye drew his saber and started forward, the first to obey. Then Elyek and two guards, while the rest lingered to see that Lesseth and I should go as directed. Amrey cordially linked his arm in mine, as if we were the dearest of companions. He walked to the portal and I sensed Lesseth close behind us, loath to let me from his sight through the rift that had already swallowed four bodies whole from sight. This was not the kind of gateway we were used to, with a clear transition from one dimension into another. Did he know where this led, where we would step out? Even in a teleport spell, he would need to have a clear mental picture of the destination, lest the magic be inaccurate and deposit him and others too far above solid ground, or embedded in stone—

My concerns were groundless, I discovered in the next moment. What seemed blackness upon the entering turned in the next step into a new surrounding, perfectly real, perfectly lit with the silver light of half-moon and stars overhead. I smelled salt on the air and heard the ocean on the breeze, not far distant.

"Telemar," confirmed Amrey, releasing my arm to point to high walls on the hillcrest near the horizon.

We found ourselves upon a road, dusty in this warmer clime where winter's hold was loosened. "How do you move so accurately?" I asked, unable to hide my amazement. "Surely that is not possible with an ordinary spell?"

"Nor is it an ordinary spell." Amrey chuckled. "You were right in your workroom, those years ago, Inya: with these stones, intention is everything. I desire to arrive at a safe place, near an inn near Telemar—and here we are."

His light speaking of the matter raised the hairs on my neck. This was the kind of magic every sorcerer dreamed of wielding, literally a wish come true.

He led us to the inn, set back behind a courtyard at the side of the road. We sped our pace to avoid the wetting of a sudden cloudburst that had blown up, darkening the stars overhead. As we ducked to shelter, the next question came to my mind in a flash. If *shian* were so powerful, if Styrcian magic so amenable, why did he not simply wish himself ruler of the world? Surely the stone would make it so?

Or if not: what were the limits of the wizard-stone, that Amrey did not care to discuss?

It was something to consider, but such probing questions must await later contemplation. For the nonce I was this man's supposed ally, and I needs must attend while he instructed me to invite faction leaders to a meeting in confidence, an occasion to sound them out and introduce them to him.

To my surprise, Murl agreed to free Lesseth from the spell of half-manifestation that was upon him, leaving him able to move in spirit wise and speed my invitation to the necessary autarchs. "It is more natural, so," he remarked. "They will know Lesseth comes directly from you, and will not suspect anything amiss.''

Was there to be something amiss? I tested him on that point. "Attend to your persuasive words, Inya, and do not trouble yourself with my plans. All you need to do is encourage these lordlings to let me champion their cause. Nothing else is your concern.''

That was calculated to unsettle, and was a success on that score. I frowned at his closemouthedness. Was there anything Lesseth could do while out and about? Amrey's threats to Corwin ran through my mind, and I knew, now that Lesseth was free to move again, how I must play out this cast of the dice. Resigned to unpleasant realities, I accepted the room offered me and Amrey's presence in it, and prepared myself for the meeting with the autarchs that lay ahead.

Caethon of Stavlia was gentle spoken except when his principles were involved. Known as one to take the middle road through tangled affairs, his moderate and level-headed attitudes—outspokenly defended—had made him unofficial leader of the Open Port faction, those city-states of old Arguenta that demanded more than crumbs from Valerian's plate. The autarchs of the Salt Coast let Caethon speak for them, and so came that gray-haired lord to join me in secret conference in the back room of a traveler's inn outside Telemar.

Caethon did not come unescorted, of course. With him was Halvericus of Caronne, a tall, lean man with modest fighting skills but deft at husbanding his fertile lands. He was present, I supposed, because Moontooth stood at the edge of his domain, and he was more experienced in dealing with me than most. Pelan of Burris I could only presume attended as gadfly, for the florid portly man was the voice of contrariness, and seemed to speak for the malcontents amongst the Open Port faction and the neutral city-states as well.

That they had expected to find me alone was evident from the open surprise on their faces. Entering the room where I sat, masked, glamour-clad only by Amrey's working—a cantrip that lent me greater presence, so that my appearance should be what they were used to—still did they halt like a cluster of guilty schoolboys in the doorway, looking from myself to Amrey and his commanders and guards.

"Please." I extended a hand, the gold-and-iron bracelet slipping down my wrist to glitter in the lamp light. "Sit."

They took places at the opposite side of the table. I read Caethon's questioning look clearly, and answered it with introductions, remembering the instructions Amrey had given me on our way here.

"Allow me to present to you Murl Amrey, called Kar Kalim. He is a mighty general in a land far distant from here. He comes to us with his armies and considerable magic, and will fight to champion your cause. He has no reason to love Valerian."

Pelan of Burris started, as well he might. "Amrey?" he echoed, confused by hearing the name of his favorite spice merchant.

"Just so." Murl inclined his head. "Son of Keshdar, once student to Clavius Mericus at your court."

"But . . . but . . ." Pelan sputtered, ogling the man's appearance, "Amrey is a mere child!"

"No more. I have seen a quarter score more winters than you, fought and ruled far longer than any of you here. Listen to the Lady, she will tell you what you need to know."

Clever, that, to let me speak for him and thus lend him credence with my seeming endorsement. I did not name Styrcia, though I outlined his exploits as he had related them to me, of generaling a vast force to victory, of remarkable battles fought against great odds, aided by unique magic . . . downplaying the fact that he destroyed or conquered whatever opposed him or whatever caught his fancy. That would raise questions he did not care for at this time. In the end, my speech was like the flowery circumlocutions of epic poetry, more evocative than definitive. While lacking specifics, Caethon and the others were left with a sense that this was a hero out of legend, come to aid them.

When they wavered, and Pelan pressed to know how young Amrey could have become this graying master of wonderous forces, I began to speak. "Time flows differently where he rules—"

Murl cut me off with a sideways slash of his hand. "The hows and whys of my aging and my accomplishments matter little," he said in his rumbling baritone. "What is important is that I control the tools that can aid you now. I understand you are at the mercy of Valerian and are hard-pressed to persuade him to your way of thinking. I am here to offer you the force that will carry that argument."

There. It was out on the table, in plain language none could quibble over. Amrey's former association with Burris seemed to account for his personal interest in this affair. That he had great forces to command they took for granted, because I said it was so. And the fact that he spoke over me was not lost on them either. The autarchs' faces became veiled as they considered the significance of one whom I let overrule me in conversation and who spoke with authority in my place.

"So you are proposing an alliance with us, is that it?" Caethon asked after some hushed discussion with his peers.

"That is so." Amrey dipped his chin.

"At what price to ourselves?" Halvericus asked bluntly.

A smile creased Amrey's beard. "Let me be an autarch among your numbers," he said. "My holdings can be whatever I wrest from Telemar's control and manage to keep."

Vanye, sitting to his right, smiled ever so slightly at that remark, phrased so nicely to imply that it would be difficult to hold ground under Telemar's very walls. It was a territory the Salt Coast lords could easily cede as the price of a new autarchy, since it cost them nothing and the risk would be borne by he who was ambitious to join their number. Yet with the Styrcian crystal on the side of the conqueror and his forces, it would be surprising if he did not hold his chosen ground—and all the rest of Telemar, for that matter. I saw where Amrey must be going with this; soon enough, he might be the prime autarch the others must bow before.

I sighed but kept my council. If these lords did not correctly assess Amrey's ambitions and capabilities, then there was nothing I could do for them, far less warn them in open talk before the conqueror himself. I did all that I could by working close to the enemy of our common good.

The nuance of my position was completely lost on the autarchs; it was clear they took my presence—and my silence— to be endorsement of my companion. Halvericus looked reassured; Pelan nodded reservedly in agreement. Caethon was the first to stand and thrust his hand out. "Very well, then. We shall speak with the others, and when you come before the Council, you will have a warm reception from us, sir."

"Kar Kalim," Vanye interrupted gruffly. "It is his title."

Caethon looked apologetic. "As you say. Kar Kalim. We look forward to making our demands of Telemar with you beside us."

A fine sentiment for now. I wondered how long it would stay that way.

* * *

Valerian did not deign to attend the last of the Council meetings held in his city. He had said his piece, marked out the line, and dared his peers to step across it. No doubt he had expected the lesser lords to slink away, cowed by his seemingly unassailable position. The introduction of Amrey had irrevocably altered that formula, however. The last meeting was simply a public formality endorsing the private understandings Caethon and others had come to outside the walls of the Autarchs' Palace.

The appeal to the lords of the Salt Coast was irresistible: Amrey would tweak the griffon's tail for them, freeing them of the need to seem too bold or too offensive. Kar Kalim the newcomer could defy Telemar all he liked. Did he seem successful, no doubt the autarchs would rally by his side, to press home their demands on Valerian. Did he fail in his challenge, then were they poised to disavow any connection with the upstart.

They thought their interests and their backs well protected. I saw only that Amrey had clear field to move as he liked, with the tacit support of the city-states. I could tell by their ambiguous speech that some, like Halvericus, thought it would be easy to deny supplies and aid to Kar Kalim's seemingly vast army, should such demand seem too taxing to fulfill. I supposed we would all see in due time how Amrey would deal with recalcitrance. In the meanwhile, emboldened by this new weapon in their arsenal, Caethon and a delegation of autarchs delivered a last ultimatum to Valerian in his own hall.

The words fell on deaf ears, the threats airily dismissed by the lord of Telemar.

The autarchs withdrew, satisfied that they had done all that was honorably necessary to come to a peaceful resolution.

That having failed, they were prepared to let Amrey proceed as he wished. The only real concern, that outsiders like Ursbach would enter on the heels of internal strife, was pacified by myself at Amrey's insistence. With the aid of the *shia,* he could absolutely prevent such interference, he swore to me privately. Only upon his utmost solemn assurances did I guarantee to the council that they need fear no threat from that quarter.

The autarchs began to take their leave of Telemar, returning without ceremony to their various domains along the coast and inland.

Amrey and his escort remained with me at a private lodging I sometimes used, a discreet house at the edge of the merchant district set back from the street behind a verdant forecourt and walled off from neighbors, with secret entrances to ease needful comings and goings. Many last-minute conferences were held there with incognito lords and their delegates. Before the last discussions had been had, the support agreements and rights of passage negotiated, the terms concluded for sharing spoils in combined actions, should any occur—before such business was full embarked upon, while autarchs still haunted Telemar in low profile, Amrey spared attention to Lesseth and the mission I hoped he had forgotten.

"As to intelligence," he said to me, "it is time for Lesseth to be vigilant on our behalf."

I regarded him attentively, wearing the look of mild interest and focus I had been cultivating. It saved me the effort of asking disingenuous questions, and gave something of the appearance that I hung on his words, awaiting direction or instruction. It was flattering to his ego, it seemed; Amrey never failed to open up and speak at length when listened to so invitingly.

"I want him to spend most of his time spying on Valerian's private councils. From other sources we have count of militia and mercenaries, of naval reserves and fortifications . . . there are some points Lesseth can clarify, though. For instance, does he perceive spell effects beyond the physical sphere that would be due to defensive enchantments on Telemar's walls? And Vanye desires to know about armaments . . ."

I nodded and took note with half a mind, my face schooled to a complacency I did not feel. If he were so anxious to scout out these unseen factors and overheard whispers, why did he not conjure up a scrying device or spirit beings that would be his own to command? Clear it was that these demands upon Lesseth, and thus upon myself, were an exercise in control. Did I bow to this pressure, make concession to Amrey's requirements in this way, then would I be yet easier to command in others.

That is where it must stop. I would cooperate in general, for to some extent I *must* do so, were I to remain in a position to affect this man's headstrong path. But I would render that aid where it seemed most benign to me—not in this backdoor manner, treating a friend as if he were a mere conjured servant, and gleaning intelligence that truly stood to aid Amrey's bid for power. I did not mind if a long and harrowing road stood before him. Better he should bog down in the vagaries of warfare, than speed to triumph and be in a better position to usurp power to himself. Once he had power, would he need me anymore? I doubted it.

Holding that viewpoint, there was but one way I could handle this situation. When Murl dismissed me to confer with Lesseth, I knew I could delay my chosen course no longer.

"He wearies you," Lesseth observed when I joined him in a private room.

I shrugged. "He is demanding. Now he demands that you help him by spying on Valerian and Telemar."

Lesseth came more manifest, so I could see his more than human face and the look of concern he wore there. "You know I'll do whatever I must to help you—"

"What he asks is of no concern to me," I cut him off. "That only plays into his hands. No, while you are still free to move, here is what you must do."

My voice trailed off, and my thoughts became more intense, more focused. We dropped into rapport together, that telepathic communion we shared at times. Conveying my thoughts and feelings in that manner, I expressed what would have taken many minutes to put into words.

Lesseth disengaged from our connection. "I see." He backed off physically, a little way distant. "And if I do this thing, you think he will not take retribution, as he has threatened?"

I swallowed and gave words to the thought I had hated to formulate. "Corwin's one life cannot weigh more in the scale than the lives of innocents that Amrey will endanger." The words sounded so cold, but true they were, so true. "We can't give him what he asks—"

"—and this insurance against his aggression is vital. Yes, I see that." Lesseth spoke softly, respectful of my tears. I had kept them inside so long, why did they well up now, just when I needed to seem cool and composed for my captor?

"Are you sure you are not at equal risk, Inya?" My friend touched my arm, the sensation barely noticeable.

"I can only take the chance that he needs me yet, or desires me yet, and that will offset the consequences of this defiance. I will do what I can to get Corwin and Una away from his malignant attentions. But do you speed now, Lesseth. It is a long journey to Tor Mak, even for you between the spheres.''

He bowed to me deeply. ''I will find you again, when I have the assurances you seek.'' Then he faded from sight, and I was left alone in the company of my enemies.

CHAPTER 10

O ur return to the tower was sped by another *shia*-forged rift, a quick transit through starry blackness to emerge before the Kalimat *shivet*. We stepped into a cutting wind that mixed rain with sleet, then gave over completely to snow flurries rarely seen at this latitude. Amrey gave me to an escort of karzdagi to usher me within Moontooth. We made a slippery dash across grass tramped into sodden muck, and thence up the stair-stepped entrance to the tower. Behind us, Amrey disappeared into the military camp, barking orders through the worsening weather as he gathered his war leaders to him.

I saw little of him in the following days. Horse troops from Styrcia continued to move hourly through that gate, down the halls and stairways of the tower, and out into the sprawling camp of their fellows. They left a trail of filth and mud and scored flagstones that Una despaired of ever restoring to a state of cleanliness. Let her fret about such a simple thing, I reflected; it was a welcome distraction from the menace collecting outside our doors. By time we returned from Telemar, an army of twelve thousand huddled in rain-wet *shivetu* outside Moontooth.

The conquering hordes of Kar Kalim, I was told, amounted to one hundred thousand horsemen, and near that same number again of supply hostlers, armorers, cooks, camp followers, and the related flotsam that accumulates around an army on campaign. Amrey planned to bring at least half that number through the gateway into my domain. I gathered that there was need in Styrcia for the force that remained behind, but massed cavalry fifty thousand strong was a force far greater than the five or ten thousand soldiers the typical city-state could muster when hard pressed. Even city-states in full alliance for war could not answer the Breo'la for mobility and speed.

This formidable army collected at a slow but steady pace; in only a few weeks they would be fully assembled and ready to march. Already the six previtsch'ch, or banners, that were present strained the resources of the countryside to feed them. I gleaned this and more from Murl's casual remarks when he returned to my bed at night, though that information was limited: it was not until much later that I learned of entire villages stripped bare then burned to the ground, others abandoned before Breo'la foragers could torture and kill the inhabitants in their quest for loot as well as food. From Murl's lips I heard only that it was time to move the army out. His horse tribes longed to be on the move, to see new territory, to freshen foodstuffs in short supply. Caronne was the only logical destination, so close at hand, a well-stocked city with grain silos and food supplies warehoused for the winter. Halvericus had committed the city to help Kar Kalim's cavalry force, and it was aid Murl wished to lose no time in claiming.

"Breo'la will continue to come through from Styrcia, gathering here in stages, then advance to join my banner. After they are on the march, you will be left with one previtsch'ch, a garrison camp of twenty-five hundred horsemen. That is not too many to guard this strategic point, and besides, I will be a mere summons-spell distant, should I be needed here. It's important to keep you and the tower safe and accessible to my needs. Who knows what reinforcements I may have to bring through from Styrcia in the future?'' He asked the rhetorical question with an easy smile that chilled my blood.

Without magic to command I was powerless to open or close this gate to Styrcia; could not, for that matter, unlock the doorway to my upper workroom or unseal the locked cupboards and secret cubbyholes where I kept the only weapons and tools that might have given me the surprise advantage over my captor. When Amrey braceleted me, he snuffed my ability to channel the Power Within, that small but essential spark of impetus that worked or unworked locking spells and minor wards. Without it, I could not hope to pry open the greater seals that guarded the rift-spanning portals of the tower, much less my own, magically secured belongings. I was like a visitor to the tower, unable to go where the Dark Lady did not wish the visitor to go. The irony was, I knew what I had locked myself out from—and for a great deal of it, Amrey could reach what I could not, for where he did not know specifics, he at least knew in principle how I had warded things, and what techniques to use to unlock my protections about the tower.

No, *I* would not be opening or closing the Styrcian or any other gateway. Murl Amrey could do as he chose in that regard and I was powerless to hinder him.

I listened to his plans with an acid stomach stirred by the resentment I kept checked inside. This was not the time to explode, to speak my mind. This was a time to listen with that disingenuous expression I had practiced, to encourage him to talk, to confide ever more of his plans and schemes to me. Over the next days our lovemaking grew fiery. Did he fall for my ruse, or did I fall for it myself? Did I subvert my anger into passion? Impossible to say . . . yet in the aftermath of our nightly encounters, I asked the leading questions and lent the sympathetic ear that encouraged revelations. I did what I could to gather intelligence against Amrey, and thought myself quite successful for a time.

For several days Kar Kalim busied himself in council with his commanders and chieftains, planning the movement of his forces. I busied myself with other things, what I could do on the sly in front of a constant guard of stinking karzdagi bespelled with the gift of tongues so they could monitor my speech. The written words of Sabytan, however, I was certain they could not decipher. It was a script only Corwin would understand, and he knew to destroy the note I passed him under pretense of inspecting the larder, newly stocked from plundered foodstuffs.

At night I continued to draw Amrey out about his plans. He spoke guardedly, but I gathered that soon he would be on the road with what was assembled of his army. The rest would follow later and I would be left behind, a prisoner in Moontooth whom he could return and fetch if and when needed. My magical fangs drawn, he felt I was harmless enough to leave in his rear. My use was as mouthpiece to the Salt Coast lords, and he had already forged his alliance with them, had the appearance of legitimacy through his association with me and the speculation that surely must be rife about the nature of our relationship. Irritating as such public perception might be, that was a frontier I could not allow myself to study too closely. There were more pressing issues, more personal ones, to attend to first.

Freeing myself of his binding seemed an urgent matter, albeit one that had me stymied. Even so, I dared not let the solving of this riddle fall by the wayside in the tense monotony of my days as housebound prisoner. On my own there seemed nothing I could do about this predicament: the bracelets were impervious to knife, to heat, to the pressure of a fierce grip, and were not so much as scratched by a smashing

stone, semblance of soft gold to the contrary. There was no
visible latch or lock in the fine-scribed filigree of the wrist
bands. The talismanic sigils worked in iron were enough to
tell me that a command word or spell were the only thing
these devices would respond to. With my adept senses dulled
I could not intuit what that might be, and the working of such
a spell was, for the time, completely beyond me.

In frustration I quit testing the bracelets, this enigma at my
wrists, and tried at such times to ban the echo of words long
past from my mind. Proud Vayanallini had confronted me on
the steps of this very tower that long time agone in Chernisylla, her words standing for the sentiments of the others who
had accompanied her ready to banish me from the charge I
had neglected. *"The Council approves of Guardians upon
their inheritance. It raises them up and it can cast them
down . . ."* A fate no Guardian in my time or my mother's
had suffered, but now Vaya's pronouncement upon me had
been fulfilled. Did my kinfolk know of this perfidious trick?
Would they be as outraged as I? It was a temptation I nearly
played with, a scheme for returning to my home world to be
freed of this curse—but thus was the Council's sentence upon
me fulfilled, and why would they care to free me from it? The
Guardians would no doubt be pleased to see this my fate.

No, Chernisylla held no answers for me. Cendurhil and the
wizards of Tor Mak seemed a likely alternative, magically
adept, allied and able to help me. Surely they would render
what aid they could, especially after Lesseth carried word
from me . . .

Such thoughts occupied my dreams on the fourth morning
after our return from Telemar, when Amrey awakened me in
the predawn grayness with his ardor. I felt disjoint, my mind
seeking solution to my dilemmas in dream-state wanderings,
my body caught up in stirring desire that roused me fully and

rooted me in the physical. Afterwards he lay more alert than dozing, as did I—both our minds occupied with greater matters than bedsport, that much was plain to see. I leaned my head on one hand, looking at him in the half-light as he toyed with a strand of my long black hair. At times like this he was most nearly like the lover I had once had a budding fondness for, seemingly harmless, affectionate, present in the moment yet with aspirations just beneath the surface. Age and maturity sat well upon his face, I thought. How to seduce an older man into trust, a trust that would take these golden shackles from my wrists?

He interrupted that line of thought with words spoken very casually.

"Lesseth has not returned," he remarked, twisting that strand of hair tighter around his finger.

My heart skipped a beat. My face must have gone blank for a moment, for he read some expression there that caused him to purse his bearded lips. "But I think that is no surprise to you, is it?" he said in a droll tone.

I opened my mouth to reply; he pressed a finger to my lips, that finger with my hair twined about it. "Don't compound your crime by lying to me. Lesseth would not abandon you, I think. If he has fled, it was by your order, not his own idea." His lips curled down. "Interesting where your loyalties lie. That a bodiless elemental should matter more to you than a flesh-and-blood child who looks to you for so much . . . Was Lesseth your demon lover, hm?"

His words had a jealous bite to them, and in that moment his calloused hand slipped along the side of my face, his fingers winding back into my hair. He clenched a fist, pulling my head back, turning me to face him as he pressed me down and loomed over me. "When you do as you are told, you will be rewarded," he said in a low, threatening tone. "When you disobey, you will be punished. And those around you will be punished. Weigh these things before you take action in haste."

His hand moved before I expected it, a slap that left my ears ringing and stunned me with the shock of it. He released me then and was out of bed. "You stay in this room this morning. Dress at noon. You attend our festivities then, as my, hm . . . consort, let us say. The Breo'la think of you that way, my dear. They do not see you as a powerful magical creature at all—merely as a woman who relies on me for her well-being, who should be grateful she isn't thrown to the *shivetu* for their entertainment. That is something you should think on."

He left and I collapsed back into the pillows. Corwin, he could only mean that he intended to harm Corwin, as he had threatened. And this barb, about how he might otherwise treat me . . . this was not the Murl I knew, but Kar Kalim, the rough man who spoke the crude language of the Breo'la and thought in their way as well: a fiercer, coarser way than I had ever had to live with before. I remembered my reassurances to Lesseth, that Amrey must still need me or the appearance of my aid for the sake of the Arguentan lords. I hoped that assessment was correct. There was little I could do if I was wrong; for all intents and purposes now, I was an ordinary mortal of this sphere. Except perhaps for lifespan I had no special protection but what Amrey might choose to give me.

And how long that would last when he discovered Corwin and Una were missing, I did not dare to guess.

There are ways out of Moontooth, secret passages in the storage cellars and through the foundation levels of the keep, intended for sly comings and goings or unforeseen emergency. For eons an integral part of the tower, I had never heard of their use but once in my grandmother's time, when they were thoroughly explored and mapped. I had studied those maps often as a child, planning how I would one day sound the depths of the tower, imagining what route I would take should ever I need to flee my home. Later, when I was free to roam the rifts, my attention turned elsewhere and those childish dreams of adventure and exploration were forgotten.

Not, however, the layout of those tunnels and passageways. Some I remembered, at least the route I had envisioned myself using. Even without access to the maps, magically locked away, that was the one I had sketched from memory for Corwin and annotated in the curling script of Sabyt.

The passage led from larder to storage cellar, down through the wall of a water well, into a crevasse, a split in the earth that ran tunnel-like beneath and beyond the foundations of the tower, thence into a series of small natural caverns. Like the other terrain immediately around Moontooth, I assumed that this groundwork, too, had come with the tower from Chernisylla, for on walks in the surrounding countryside, I recognize the hills and gullies identical to those I have known all my life, overlaid in some strange kinship across dimensions with local trees and shrubs. The terrain, though, was the same. I prayed it was so on underlying strata as well, or Corwin and Una would be trapped or lost underground with no exit to the outside world, and there might perish.

I had warned them of that possibility, although the maps showed this passage emerging into a ravine one valley distant and out of sight of the tower itself. "It does not matter, Lady," Una reassured me. "We must try it, wherever it leads. We cannot remain to be Amrey's tool against you, and sure it is we will not be free to walk out the front door!"

Indeed, that was the very reason I urged them to flight, to remove them from his grasp and to free myself from coercion.

Yet to send them off, into the unknown, was far harder than
I thought it would be. Una had come to me two decades before, at a time when she was so distraught over the death of
a daughter and grandchild that she sought what she mistakenly
thought was divine intervention in the person of myself. Desperation led her footsteps to me, across all the dweomer and
obfuscation that conceals my doorstep from strangers. Carefully, oh so carefully, did I disillusion her in her quest, but
made her welcome through those difficult days. Somehow she
began to cook and clean for me, and somehow I allowed this,
until she came to fit naturally into the household, a quiet comfort to me and something like the mother-care I had lost long
ago. To send her and Corwin forth was as hard as casting
family members to their uncertain fate.

Still, I was honored by their willingness to risk, and could
not argue with Una's sentiments. I entrusted them with the
map, told them all I knew of the route that lay ahead of them,
gave them funds for travel, and urged them, like Lesseth, to
seek refuge in distant Tor Mak, far from danger and in the
safekeeping of friends.

Those ancient bolt-holes remained accessible to us because
they were so mundane. There was nothing magical about
them: simple catch plates in stone, levers near frozen into
decrepitude, a simple mechanical working, and damp, mold-
reeking passageway beyond. Access my friends could operate
without my assistance.

We orchestrated their escape carefully, creating a moment
of confusion when food was being stored in the larder, after
Una had served the karzdagi who lurked as messengers and
sometimes household guard. A strange contingent for Kar
Kalim to have always at hand, I thought, but in some ways it
seemed Amrey trusted the dog-men more than he did the
Breo'la. The humans tried to read his moods and though loyal,

seemed cautious or fearful of the man. The karzdagi in contrast offered slavish obedience and were overawed by his might. They were the more easily cowed, the more fanatically devoted, and so, I thought, he kept them close in his personal guard.

As usual the beast-men ate in a frenzy, scuffling over the food, one or more going unfed when they were unable to press home their claim to sustenance. It was during a furor of nips and yelps that Una followed Corwin into the larder. I stepped in, loudly demanding an end to the conflict. Eyes turned to my end of the room, distracted by my sharp-uttered commands on the edge of their affray. They spent time snarling at me, trying to drive me from the area, yet were reluctant to put paw to me directly, unless Amrey ordered it. And Murl was with his council of war, in his banner-camp beyond the Kalimat *shivetu,* I knew.

By time the growls subsided and the remains of the haunch were more peaceably divided amongst the karzdagi, by time that confusion had passed, no one noticed if Una was on hand to clean up the mess, or Corwin there to carry food to Amrey's room, my room. After their meal I tidied up, so no one would question the cook's tardiness, and I carried a tray up myself, so appearances would be maintained as long as possible.

The wine keg that moved from the wall in the larder and the stone trap beneath it were things I did not dare to investigate after their usage, lest my interest in such an out-of-the-way chamber be noted. Una and Corwin did not return. As the evening wore on, I could only assume their escape had succeeded. Somewhere now they were in the long tunnel that led to a cave and keeping left, always left, would emerge some time near dawn one valley southward from the tower, near a goatherd's path that led to the Caronne road. There they stood fair to blend in with peddlers and pilgrims and whatever way-

farers traveled this region. To that end they had taken with
them red woolen pilgrim's shawls, the sort that in this weather
served as headwrap and short cloak. Fit disguise for Corwin's
tell-tale blondness, and Una's matronly form; together they
could pass as seekers bound for Arudevi's healing shrine in
the neighboring city-state of mountainous Singfa. It was
planned as well as it could be planned; the rest was up to
Lashana, Drakmili goddess of luck.

The karzdag most often keeping watch on me was a brindle
creature with a broken lower left canine. I had named him
Crookfang in my thoughts. He came chin-high to me with his
slinking hunched posture, but he was broad in the shoulder
and not one I would care to contest physically. When a cry
and stir began midmorning outside the tower, it was my long-
muzzled keeper who opened the door of my bedchamber, gave
me a meaningful leer, then hooked clawed fingers into my
arm and pulled me summarily down the hall behind him. Clad
only in my bed-gown, hair astray and bare-footed—this was
his version, I thought, of prodding me to a summons by Kar
Kalim. It was more contact with me than Amrey normally
permitted, but it was allowed to Crookfang, I thought, by his
apparent seniority amongst the karzdagi. I went, unwilling but
not hanging back, to see what Amrey wanted of me now.

To my surprise I was not taken to any chamber within the
tower, but to the broad flagstoned terrace that fronts the entrance instead. Grit and cold stone punished my bare feet as
Crookfang maneuvered me to the waist-high balustrade. The
karzdag did not attempt to move me any farther but stood
close beside me, to observe the scene unfolding before us. I
did not relish being on display in such undress before the
Breo'la; I clasped my gown to me, arms crossed on chest, and
tossed hair clear of my face in the gusting wind. Before me

was a vantage of the horse troops' mud-churned assembly field, the empty ground between Moontooth and the closest encampments. Pole-torches marked the edges of the field here and there, though they were not lit in this early hour. Men and horses milled about this place, and a trickle of the curious from nearby tents grew rapidly into a flood of onlookers streaming towards the assembly ground. It took me long moments to sort out the confusion. When I did, my blood ran cold.

Leather-clad tribesmen made way as a hand of scouts and a hand of heavily armed horse warriors rode into the square, a prisoner in their midst. The blond hair that drew my eye to that youth was unmistakeable. Corwin.

He sat on a mount I had never seen—not one of the Breo'la's short, sturdy beasts, but a dappled mare of ordinary pace and speed bearing saddlery of local design. So he had procured a mount for himself, and doubtless Una rode as well. I searched the guard troop for a womanly figure but saw none. Had she escaped their grasp? I hoped so, though my heart sank that Corwin had not. He was tied into his saddle, arms secured behind his back. His frightened eyes swept mine imploringly as they drove him past the terrace, to the Breo'la gathering on the far side.

I looked about for Amrey, whom I knew would not let this chance for public display pass unremarked. I did not see him and realized he must still be in council in his war tent, the largest in the camp a bowcast distant, marked with a blood-red banner easily visible at this remove. My eye lingered on the wind-blown banner for a moment, so different from the primitive Breo'la symbols: a stylized starburst in silver on a field of black and red. Amrey's heraldry was clearly informed by his heritage on the Salt Coast, in a style popular with Arguentan lords. I would not mind the presumption so much if he had cleaved also to the ethics and conduct of civilized lords, yet the mob of warriors before me gave the lie to that pretension quickly. Long-haired horsemen gathered in a motley assortment of riding leathers, vests, furred cloaks, and horseskins, some armored, most not, all with sabers by their sides or lances in hand, or bows clipped casually to backstraps. In moments they ringed the field round as if awaiting an exhibition. Their rough humor mingled with an eerie blood-thirsty enthusiasm, marked by growls and threatening gestures towards Corwin.

The youth shied from saber blades and lance tips flourished casually near his face. This amusement continued as a group of men formed up before Amrey's banner, and moved up through the crowd. As their presence was recognized warriors gave way before the newcomers, until a space cleared around Corwin, the warrior who led his horse, and Kar Kalim himself, come face to face with his captive.

Even on foot, Amrey seemed of greater stature than the mounted figures before him. Was it dweomer, to enhance how he was perceived? Mayhap, though with my powers fettered I was unable to detect it. Resentment of that loss twisted like a dagger within me. Were I empowered I would have freed Corwin in that moment, whisked him to safety, destroyed those who would be his captors—

Amrey's words interrupted my flight of fancy, the more startling because they sounded as if spoken in my ear, not from the far side of the muddy field that lay between us. A spell of his own, for my benefit no doubt. Or my unease.

Vanye and lesser commanders stood close escort behind their leader. A long-bearded man with black hair held the reins of Corwin's mount, steadying the boy in the saddle with a grip on the bonds that held him. The youth trembled visibly where he sat, but seemed to meet Amrey's eye.

The master of the Breo'la hordes looked dispassionately upon the boy, and spoke in Arguente as if in light conversation. "It is a sad thing to have to end a life," he said. "I would have done anything but this, but R'Inyalushni d'aal would not have it so. She decided that you would be forfeit to her schemes. She had it in her power to prevent your death, Corwin, and chose not to do so."

They both glanced my way, Corwin involuntarily, Amrey to gauge the effect of his words on me. I was stricken; oblivious to the cold wind that was chilling me to the bone, I locked eyes with my young ward, and he looked as appalled as I. Surely he did not believe that I *chose* his death? I had done what I could to see him to safety!

There was no way to share my sentiments with Corwin. Amrey gave me a somber look and returned to his conversation. He spoke the swift guttural patter of the Styrcian tongue, and Corwin's guard cut the boy free from the saddle, lifted him down to the ground. Several karzdagi came forward with spades and went to work in the center of the field with a will, digging at the sodden ground, and not for the first time did I heartily wish I understood Styrcian. It was something I must learn, no time to lose—

The musical rhythms of Arguente brought my eye back to Corwin. "I am not a pawn to you," he spoke bravely, a defiant voice that quavered in spite of himself. "You cannot force my Lady's behavior with threats to me."

Amrey smiled and shook his head, a wiser man marveling at a child who is self-deceived. "Her sin is compounded by your ignorance. You chose poorly, and now you will suffer the consequences of your ill-made choice. Run from me, indeed. Better you had run *to* me, instead." He snorted. "I make no threats. I speak fact: those who help me will be rewarded."

He raised his head, looked straight at me as he spoke to his prisoner. "Those who defy me will die, and those they care for will perish as well."

There was another flurry of Styrcian, and spectators moved back to ring the field. The scrubby dog-men cleared the hoof-churned muck from something I only now noticed in the center of the field: a pit, recently dug, the size of a well mouth and covered with planks. Those planks were moved aside now and karzdagi emptied the excavation of ooze with leather buckets and spades. It was not a deep hole, for when a dog-man stood inside his head was visible above the ground. Soon the worst of the muck was cleared away. Corwin was marched to that spot and lowered into the pit. Karzdagi spades worked fast to pack the mud and earth back into the hole they had just emptied, and my horrified gasp brought a chuckle from Crookfang beside me. They were burying Corwin alive, leaving only his head protruding above the ground.

Ten horsemen came forward then, from various parts of the field, walking mounts or having reins handed them by their fellows. Five wore leather trousers and short horse-fur tunics, all of a heavy-browed look that spoke of close kinship with each other. The second hand of warriors wore felted trousers and ring-armored leather, moving with the discipline of a unit long comfortable together. All sprang ahorseback without needing to use their stirrups—a common manner of mounting these barbarians practiced, to show off their agility, I took it—and each held a lance tossed to him by a fellow on the ground.

At first I thought they had meant to leave Corwin there to die a slow death by starvation; now I saw they intended nothing so simple. The same ugly thoughts took Corwin, too, it was plain to see, for his blond head moved and I heard an outcry of dismay from him. A last karzdag packed the ground nearby with his spade; he moved abruptly at the youth's panicked exclamation, swinging a leg. The kick stifled Corwin instantly. When the karzdag moved away I saw the boy, dazed and bloody-mouthed, chin resting on the muddy earth. In moments the field was empty but for the two hands of horsemen already mounted, and Amrey presiding in a cluster of officers on the far side facing me.

He gave me a last glance before he raised his hand and lowered it.

From one end of the field the horsemen started to ride, passing a stone's thow distant from their earthbound target. As each drew near, an arm raised and a lance flew to skewer the ground nearby. After each cast a clanmate ran forward and pulled the spear from the ground so as not to hinder the aim of the others. Another lance cast, and a near miss, three hands distant from the boy's head. Corwin jerked and his eyes widened but any cry he made was inaudible over the cheers of the gathered crowd.

More Breo'la streamed out from the camp until the field was ringed thick with onlookers. Many came to stand on the steps of Moontooth until the tower stairs were full of unwashed, greasy-haired horsemen jostling for position. Crookfang and other karzdagi kept them away from me, and so I had a cursedly unhindered view while the game continued. When I looked down, unwilling to watch this torturous event any longer, Amrey's voice spoke in my ear. "Observe and take note. Or I will compel you to observe. This is not something I want you to forget. There are other Arguentans close within our grasp—villagers, travelers—more fodder for our field sports, if you think there is no one else who can suffer for your intransigence."

Heartsick, I watched. Another lance was cast, passing so close by Corwin that blood started down the side of his head. Then a cast that took off the tip of his nose and that shriek I heard clearly even at distance.

I looked down, blinded by tears. "Oh, *do* keep watching," a silken voice purred in my ear. "I insist upon it."

An invisible hand gripped my face, tilted my chin up until my head was held rigidly, my eyes directed at the field before me. I glimpsed Amrey at the far side of the marshalling field, one hand grasping the crystal at his throat, staring at me intently. "You could have prevented this, Inya. Now reap what you have sown."

The tears dried magically from my eyes, leaving me blinking as if I had been exposed to a desert sirocco. A compulsion came over me to look, to watch, to observe Corwin's agonies in minutest detail. So clear it seemed to me, so slow in the playing out, it was as if I studied the scene up close from another time and place. Indelibly the images seared themselves into my mind.

Spear cast after spear cast. Each an injury, a nick that carried away part of his face or flesh. None fatal, none piercing the skull, which would have been a mercy. And then the horse races, the sprints in pairs back and forth over the patch of ground where the boy was buried, Corwin wincing away from oncoming hooves but the first that clipped him stunned him, and the second and third, I think, caved his skull in. The others battered him until brains oozed and a lifeless lump remained.

But that was not the end of the exhibition. Only then did the horsemen's games really begin, with the beheading of the corpse and a game played where the head was kicked and shoved by spear butt back and forth across the field, to score points in some crazed game of goal and guard. I was nauseous but bound by Amrey's cruel compulsion, unable, truly, to tear my eyes away. Their vile amusement was over soon enough, only a few points scored, and the winner—a lithe young rider from the dark-browed contingent—received his bloody, filth-covered prize, no longer recognizable as anything human. He busied himself at his saddle for a few moments and then dropped the head to the ground—washing his hands of it, I thought, until he held something aloft, and was applauded with cheers and handclaps. I thought it a dirty scrap, until he wheeled his horse about, and the tell-tale color of Corwin's hair showed beneath the filth that besmeared the scalp.

The victor rode off with his prize. The karzdagi collected the head for what purposes I did not care to imagine, and packed down the hole where the body lay buried until there was no trace that that was Corwin's grave.

Amrey let his compulsion off me and my body became my own to control. Under a compulsion of a different sort, I spun and ran up the stairs, back within the tower, fighting down bile and weeping with no regard for appearances. I dashed into my room, still mine for all Amrey's claims upon it, and threw myself in tears upon the bed.

Barely noticing the sound of the lock being turned behind me, I gave myself over to my grief.

CHAPTER 11

My good faith in Murl Amrey died that day. Gone was that inner voice that reassured me he could not really be as raw to humanity as his adopted brethren of the steppes. Part of me drew back, an emotional retreat as I floundered to make sense of this, of his threats fulfilled and the reality of my circumstances. He came to me again that night, as he did every night, but my withdrawal had a strange effect on him: he took me lustfully, with greater abandon and force than ever before, proving a point upon my body to demonstrate who was in control. I was unresponsive, but his point must be made nonethless. He left me crumpled on the bed, used and cold of heart.

"Now you have more to think about," he said matter-of-factly, pulling his trousers on. "I will have what I want of you, as I do of everyone." He was going to his war tent where he would sleep this one night, spurning my mood and leaving me to myself. "Next time, you will not be distant with me." He spoke sternly as he pulled a tunic over his head. "Find some pleasure in this closeness, Inya, find some joy in it somehow, or I will know that you do not. You will be with me willingly, or someone else will suffer a punishment in your stead."

The dichotomy of that was torturous. I did not want to be with him, as he could tell by this night's encounter. I could pretend it was a pleasure, of course, but he could sense the pretense, and he had magic to aid him in that detection as well. Did I not find some trick, some way to take delight in my time with him, then he would know it and someone would be hurt in consequence. No matter who—the most innocent villager would suffice to drive his point home. And that was an impossible alternative: there would be no more Corwins sacrificed to Breo'la bloodsport, I vowed.

So I found myself recalling things he had done of favor, seeking the good to outweigh the bad: reliving touch that had sparked my passion, remembering humor and curiousity and quirks of nature that I had liked about him . . . even the attractiveness of face and appealing muscular build . . . I held those thoughts to me like precious emeralds, bright colored bits in contrast to the darkness all around. I found things that brought small joy to my heart, that let me remember the person who was here, not Kar Karlim the cruel warlord, but Murl whom I would gladly have as my lover . . .

I began to think of him as two people, the behaviors of the worthy one at odds with the cruel willfulness of the other. It worked, it seemed. I found some sincerity in my heart the next time I was with him, and responded to his touch in a way that brought a smile to his face. How I tailored my memory to permit that freedom in his company! There was much that I put from my mind, simply absent from my thoughts, waking and even sleeping. Murl became a man I could relate to; Kar Kalim, a stranger rarely present by my side. Only sometimes did an insistent memory wake me from my dreams or make me inexplicably emotional for a minute, to the point of tears. Corwin's face coming into mind could spark such a mood, a mood I dared not embody—and soon enough, his face was one I could not conjure to mind even when I tried.

Self-preservation will be served, one way or another. When

Amrey demanded to know how Una and Corwin had escaped, I bowed to the inevitable and showed him. He scowled in frustration, for my serving woman had long since slipped his grasp. Amrey set a lock to the trap in the larder that gave way to that passage. He demanded of me whether there were other passages and there I stumbled: unwilling to admit that there were, or to mention the maps to the hidden pathways of Moontooth, yet unwilling to lie and be caught out in the lie. He saw my hesitation, assumed I was covering something up, and then the thing I had been dreading happened: he cast a truth-spell, to read my thoughts and check the veracity of my words.

This was a spell woven of his own power, no Styrcian enchantment, this: it was, in fact, a variant on a cantrip of detection I had been teaching him when he abandoned me those years ago. And because I recognized his gestures and his words, I had time enough to prepare my thoughts in the only way that is sometimes proof against a spell of truth discernment.

There is a knack for perceiving the questioner's words in such a way that answers are not a blatant falsehood, nor do they give too much away. To nurture this perspective, I needs must focus strictly on the interpretation that suited me, intentionally misapprehending the underlying intent of the question. It was not an easy task, but then, Murl Amrey had given me recent practice in lying to myself. I had far more experience with this spell, and this ambiguity of thought, than he did.

In the end I dwelt on my failing memory of the tunnels beneath Moontooth and could say—truthfully, as far as it went—that I did not know of other routes out of the tower. No routes in their entirety, I qualified silently to myself; no routes I can be certain of, that would definitely lead one to surface ground at a safe remove. The mental image of maps drawn in my younger hand was something I buried far in the back of my mind. By the time his interrogation was done, Amrey was convinced that the one passage I had mapped out for my servants was the only passageway I knew of. Was certain I held nothing back from him in this regard.

I thanked various powers that his concern at this moment was his safety and avenues by which attack might infiltrate unseen. Did he quiz me about secret hiding places or secrets locked away, there my misdirection might have been revealed. But he did not, this time. I was glad when he let the subject drop, fearing the next occasion when he might interview me under such an aegis of truth. It was an experience to be avoided at all costs, and all the same, one I sensed must inevitably draw nigh.

But that trial lay somewhen in the future. For now, I watched him prepare his horse tribes for campaign, keeping long council with his commanders and the Bronye who lead their kinsmen into battle; saw elements of the Breo'la start to break camp and marshal horse herds as they prepared to march. I held myself in readiness for his departure, calculating in my most secret thoughts how I might strive for my freedom when he was gone. It was either that—succeed in flight—or angle to be taken with him, for left behind in my stronghold, I would be as useless as a gilded orthop, pulled from its cage only when Kar Kalim desired. I was not lulled by the fact that he treated me with a tender reserve—a new manner born of the tension between us, a hollow composure that was the result of my distancing from Amrey and then my enforced contact with him.

Yet it was difficult to gauge appropriate response to the man. As I saw him as two people, so had I become two persons as well. The one, the surface shell, was what he required her to be; the me that lay behind that mask was the one at war with necessity, biding my time, scheming. That part reminded that I dare not become too distant, too alienated from this power-thirsty man, or there would be no way to lure him into a disarming position with me. Such a choice I was confronted with: to scorn that which was so clearly despicable, or be close to it for the chance of fulfilling greater purposes— gaining my freedom, thwarting his plans, protecting others from his cruel vengefulness.

When regarded in such wise, the choice was clear. I did not wish to see the Salt Coast or greater Drakmil or any other part of this world fall to Amrey's grasp, but I also did not wish to see unneccesary death and bloodshed. The reign of men comes and goes; one is much like unto the other, and seen that way, Kar Kalim's governance would matter little in the longer view of things.

In the shorter view, his ruthlessness was evident, and it was that which I desired most to mitigate. A man raised with the values and sensitivities of civilized culture, yet so readily assimilated into the mores of his adopted folk that he made bloodsport of a murder meant to punish me . . . I might choose to see him as two men for the need of the moment, but I recognized that he was the single person, with many contrasts wrapped in one mind and heart. There was such an alienness to his manner of thought—or a cultural distance grown so great—that the gap between us would be difficult to bridge. Yet bridge it I must. I must come to understand my enemy clearly, with no illusion about his behaviors or inclinations, or I would be severely handicapped in this subtle game of mouse influence cat.

I warred mightily with myself, sunk in deep contemplation over those next several days. How to separate the natural response of any war chief of that culture from the vindictive

manipulation that I sensed underlaid Amrey's revenge upon
me? How much was the man and how much the culture? At
what could I properly take umbrage? I was offended by the
totality, but seen one way, these crude steppe warriors merely
followed custom and a rough-hewn battle code that had
evolved for good reason on their home world. No doubt they
would seem beyond the pale of civility to the sophisticates of
the city-states, but by their own standards, this was simply
another campaign, carried out in the ordinary manner.

Our ways were very, very different—and could I hate them
for that? No. I was saddened by their lack of humanity, yes,
and their devaluation of human life. But find them inherently
hateful, I did not.

What was hateful was Kar Kalim's intentional use of
Breo'la mores to make his point with me. It was a lever to
compel me, a way to underscore his control of the situation,
of me, of the way things would unfold or the consequences
that would be reckoned. It was calculating beyond all measure. "This I can do," he had said the night after he had
Corwin killed. "This and much more that is repugnant to you.
Do not force me to such measures. I do not want to do them
and that is not the first thing I grasp to. You can help me
avoid needless pain and bloodshed; help me as I ask and such
things will never be necessary. It is up to you, Inya . . ."

Luring, insidious words. Righteous as I wanted to be, he
spoke with a logic that echoed thoughts of my own. I had
adhered to my high principles, for no immediate gain, and
seen miserable suffering done virtually at my own hands. Corwin's battered face haunted my dreams, the widening of his
eyes as the first hoof struck him in the temple . . .

If it had not been for me, he would never have been in such
a position. And for what gain? I reviewed my decisions and
found them wanting in wisdom. I had gambled with a life so

that Lesseth could warn allies of the existence of the conqueror from Styrcia, in the faint hope that that warning would
buy time to prepare against the machinations of Kar Kalim.
The wizards of Tor Mak would have heard news of Kar Kalim
anyway, in due time. Was it an advantage that was worth
Corwin's life?

The principles that had seemed so clear to me before were
muddy reasoning now. Now I saw only that Kar Kalim was
right: I did have the power to stop him from excess, but only
if I worked with him, hand in glove. It was a reality that galled
me but the truth of it was unavoidable.

In part he must have thought my spirit broken, that I was
subdued by his superior position and force of will. I did not
disillusion him. I would do as he said and lull him with my
compliance, for it seemed what he asked of me and what I
wanted lay upon the same path for now. I would be his lover,
his apparent companion. Let the lords of the Salt Coast think
him my consort, think his endeavors had my blessing, for then
they would not resist this unstoppable force, but cooperate
instead. Would Arguenta subordinate itself to his demands?
His eventual rule? Would he carry out his designs to greater
Drakmil as well? My mind skittered away from the prospect,
knowing I could not divine the answer at this time. I could
only resolve to push for peaceful resolution to problems, to
urge compromise where it would serve Amrey and avoid unneccesary bloodshed. For I appreciated as perhaps no other
could, that Murl's threats were not threats. He commanded
the means to level entire cities, and Kar Kalim would not
scruple against doing so. I heard his casual mention of vills
razed and pyramids made of the skulls of every man, woman,
and child that had lived therein, all because a demand to surrender had been defied. If I could cause such atrocities to be
avoided here, I would do so, whether by working with Amrey

or persuading Salt Coast lords with all of my influence and reputation.

The cold metal at my wrists reminded me of other things I wished to work towards as well. Not forgotten, that quest; but it was a goal delayed. First I must reassure Kar Kalim of my ardent support before I could be concerned with seeking my freedom.

An Arguentan army is an elaborate creature to get on the move, slowed by baggage trains, oxcarts, clerical adornments and portable shrines, camp followers who tend to the comforts of soldiers, and not least the soldiers themselves, sturdy warriors traveling on foot. Their steady tramp carries them eventually from border to border of their lord's domain and not often far beyond it. When they move across a greater distance than one city-state, they supply themselves from the bounty of allied villages and towns, or bring sufficient supplies with them from their home city, to see to their limited needs in the field.

How different the Breo'la. Mobile, swift-moving, traveling lightly, and supplying their needs in wide-ranging foraging and hunting sweeps in the lands they traveled through—this strategy, well suited to the steppes and vills of Styrcia, had one great flaw in it. Should these troops feed themselves exclusively off the land, as was their habit, they risked angering the very city-states that Kar Kalim wanted aid from as allies. Left to their own the warriors would take every last chicken and piece of jewelry or portable valuable they could lay their hand to.

This would not do in the territories of the Salt Coast lords, who had sworn to support Kar Kalim's army with supplies adequate for a lengthy march. It was high time for the horsemen to be underway, to stock themselves for the road

ahead of them, and guarantee that they would not be a nui-
sance to friendly allies along the way.

In surprisingly short order, Vanye had marshalled the horse
tribes for their trek. They assembled in the gray dawn of a
foggy morning, the clink of buckles and creak of tack carrying
easily in the still air. I heard the assembly through the window
of my chambers, awakening to it at the same time that Crookfang entered in his rude manner and pulled me from my bed.

There was no avoiding this summons. We paused only long
enough for me to don a robe, and the karzdag led me to the
steps before Moontooth. Soon a group of horsemen rode up,
Kalimat guards around their leader who sat a mincing, spirited
steed, coal black with sweeping mane and tail. No short-
legged steppe horse this; it was a blooded Guerian, the fast,
clean-lined mount of nobility—no doubt booty taken by
foragers from a horse breeder or hapless aristocrat. Kar Kalim
sat the horse as if born to it, and he reined up before the
terrace where I stood. His *semyet* cloak ruffled in the wind as
he fixed me with an appraising look. Without a word, he extended an arm to gesture where a riderless mare stamped restless by his side. I recognized the horse: a dapple with striking
black stockings, long-legged and deep-chested enough—not
as fine as the Guerian, but well enough for days of long riding.
Corwin's horse.

Unsettled by that recognition, I did not at first take his
meaning. Crookfang's hand around my arm prodded me down
the steps before his intent sank in. Amrey meant me to accompany him.

"I am not ready for this journey," I protested, only to flinch
as he lifted his hand to me. But it was not threat, merely a
caution to silence.

"You will be tended to along the way," he said. "There
is nothing here you need bring with you, Lady." That gentle

smile creased his lips; nearly laughing at me, he was, but only I could see that. "I will provide all that you could need."

I began to protest again, then thought better of it. I was in fact eager to go, and what, indeed, would I want to take with me? There was no device magical, no tome of use to me in my present condition. Only clothing, money, items of jewelry or scent—things he could conjure with the wave of a hand. The tools of divination would have been nice council, but were not essential. There is more than one way to consult the wisdom of spirit in the camp of the enemy than with objects that can be observed by another.

I ignored the proffered hand of a Kalimat guard, and raised myself into the saddle. "If you would have me ride with you," I told Amrey, "I would like some warmth against the wind. Winter is not past, yet." Chill bumps on my arms were testament to that, but he had already anticipated this need. He snapped his fingers, and a guard rode forward, unfolding the cloak at his saddle crown. A cloak of *semyet,* like Amrey's own, a garment fit for a queen. I accepted it laid about my shoulders and realized with this token that I was not to be treated as his prisoner, but as his companion.

He gave me an enigmatic look. He stroked his gray-touched beard thoughtfully, caution evident in his blue eyes. Assessing me, he was. He did not trust me to remain behind, where I might follow Una's footsteps and somehow slip out of Moontooth and away from his control. I squelched a guilty start, for I had played with that possibility again and again, even planned it out, for although I was not certain of alternative routes I thought I would be willing to take the chance exploring one . . .

Well. It were better that I accompany him, after all. By his side I could have contact with the lords of the Salt Coast and be present at the events that would shape our course in the coming days. Far better that than to be locked away in desolate isolation, surrounded only by dog-men and a banner of horse soldiers, cut off from all chance of monitoring Amrey or influencing his decisions.

The thought gave me strange comfort. Indeed, he would get no complaint from me. Crookfang handed up a package to a guard, a bundle I recognized from my wardrobe: masks of gold and silver-chased ebony, items I used in ceremony and magic, and for audience where my presence was intended to awe. The only things of all my needs, it seemed, that Amrey did not care to leave to chance in a conjuration. With the aid of a dweomer of presence, they were the faces by which I am known.

Obviously Kar Kalim had a purpose for me on this march. I looked from the bundle to the wizard-general beside me, and bowed my head formally. It could be taken as compliment, mayhap; as obeisance, if naught else. Regarding my appearance to others, we thought the same, and I treasured what common ground I could find with him. He spoke a word to his guards, and we joined the column of horsemen leaving the field, wending into the hills that led down to the sea and the coast road. Soon we rode at their head, Kar Kalim and I, bringing a fate kind or cruel—I could not determine which—to our allies and enemies unsuspecting before us.

The journey was rapid, a pace I was not used to, and me without magic to ease my way. We changed mounts twice in that day and kept a speedier rate of travel than I was accustomed to. At the rear of our lengthy column were reserves of horse and pack animals carrying supplies far swifter than carts could bear. Behind them lumbered a baggage train that could carry loot, bulkier supplies, and the great campaign tent that seemed a permanent centerpiece of any Breo'la war camp.

That rearguard would trail leisurely behind Kar Kalim's army, an entity unto itself. Before twilight the fast-moving part of the column was far ahead and topping the last ridge that separates the Caronne hills from the city of that name, high-walled and perched on a cliff overlooking the sea.

Travelers fled the road before us, or gawked far off to one side or the other. Mouths hung open in shock at the sheer numbers of the army: near twenty thousand horse troops were on the march, here, the remainder of the Styrcian army to follow when they had assembled in mass again at the tower. It was a force vaster than any that Caronne had fielded in its history, larger than most armies ever collected amongst the city-states. No wonder folk stared, torn between awe, amazement, and the common-sense caution to get far away from the path of fierce armed warriors.

Before the sun sank in the west, Kar Kalim halted the column's progress. Camp was pitched in meadows belonging to some unseen farmer, the cattle in his valley rounded up and slaughtered for the evening fires of the army.

I dismounted stiffly, sore from my unwonted exercise in the saddle. Amrey graced me with a half smile and touched a finger to the crystal at his throat. A moment later, pain melted from me, gone as if nary a muscle had been strained the whole day long. I felt renewed, refreshed, and taken quite by surprise.

"What—?"

"It serves no purpose for you to be exhausted now. You have more to do, before I am done with you today."

"How can I help you?"

It was a phrasing certain to appeal to him, and it did. "I and my guard will ride ahead to Caronne and seek a word with Halvericus. I want you to be there, too, but it would never do to have you ride up on a horse like any mundane

creature.'' He laughed under his breath, whether sneering at
me or truly amused I could not tell. "No, you will arrive
aback a mist-dragon, or the semblance of one, I should say.
It is how they expect to see you, after all. You can command
Halvericus to entertain me—us—for the evening. No need to
concern them with the sight of this army outside their very
doorstep; not yet, at any rate. Let us talk with this lordling
first, see what hospitality he is truly ready to offer. I care to
see if he will honor his promises made in Telemar. In the
morning the Breo'la will advance and resupply from Caronne's generous coffers. And then we will march to Telemar.''

I was silent for a moment, startled at this turn of events.
All day as we had traveled he had kept me by his side but
had had little to say to me, caught up in conversation with his
war leaders in indecipherable Styrcian, or pointing out features of terrain and commenting on farmland and orchards
through which we passed. Now he expected me to make a
grand entrance as if I traveled with Reydjik—but certain it
was this would be no mist-dragon of my own summoning.
Did Amrey even know how to call forth such elementals? It
was nothing I had taught him. I looked askance at him, and
soon enough his own boastfulness revealed his plans.

"You won't be aback a real dragon," he clarified. "I will
create a simulacrum—it will look close enough like Reydjik
that only you would know the difference. I command it. It
will take you thence, deposit you, and vanish. That is all that
is necessary. Oh, and your appearance, of course. Wear your
mask and I shall clothe you in dweomer and robes of white
and gold. You will be every bit as impressive as when you
sat at the Autarchs' Council, or greeted me when I first stumbled into your lair.''

He said it factually yet with a hint of sarcasm, and I perceived for the first time that Murl Amrey resented me. He resented the theater I put on, thinking it perhaps a show, an obfuscation . . . well, it was that, but no mean trickery was intended thereby. Such appearances were a protection, and a custom amongst my people who counted seers, speakers for deity, and sorcerers of great power amongst their numbers. To be seen as a symbol of imposing grandeur was the rule for us: it lent authority to our pronouncements and allowed us to pass unrecognized among common folk when we so chose.

I could not go into that now and it bothered me that I felt the need to explain myself and my motives to Amrey. I did not need to justify to him the public appearance of the Guardians of Chernisylla. He saw the private me, a knowledge privileged to few. Now he compelled me to appear in mundane wise to his troops and so had demystified the Midnight Rider to the Breo'la. At least he saw the value of maintaining my mystique before the power elite of the Salt Coast. They believed the Dark Lady to be other than an earthly woman. That perception was part of my power in this place, and it was one shred of power I gladly embraced when he offered it to me.

When darkness was full upon us, and the moon rose above thin scattered clouds beyond the northeastern headlands, I became the Midnight Rider once again—and not ungratefully, for all that the semblance was of another's making.

Kar Kalim, guards, and the highest-ranking of his commanders set off towards the lights of Caronne. I waited at the edge of the camp, clad in faery fire and regal robes, masked, my black hair piled high upon my head, an enchantment keeping me from the chill of the night. Time passed and yet more time; suddenly, in the clearing before me, the pseudomist-dragon came manifest, just as Amrey had warned it would. Breo'la muttered and moved back from the roiling cloud, some gesturing in warding at the hulking form mist-cloaked

within. I stepped forward to the fog made manifest, climbed
to insubstantial shoulder, and thence to straddle a back. It was
not my Reydjik, nor anything alive, and I felt that absence in
my gut. I took my seat and the making rose without a command from me, following the will of Kar Kalim to deliver me
before the gates of Caronne.

The walls and tiled roofs of the city slid past beneath me
as I descended from cloud-height to the group of horsemen
before the gates. Kar Kalim and the Breo'la reined their
mounts made nervous by the conjuration, prancing aside from
the manifestation I rode to the ground. The city gates were
closed for the night and every guard at that side of the walls,
it seemed, had gathered at that portal, made wary by the
Breo'las foreign appearance. The captain of the guard had
come forward, was speaking with Amrey as I appeared, but I
was a presence whose description was known, and the man's
widening eyes showed that he recognized me instantly. Only
one entity travels in such wise, in these parts. I dismounted
in one fluid motion and strode to Amrey's side, where the
mare was held ready for me, then turned to face the officer.
He bowed, as guards behind him drew themselves up to respectful attention.

In that moment, the ground began to shake beneath our feet.

The temblor was brief, barely enough to cause me to side-
step to keep balance. Horses snorted and neighed; soldiers and
Breo'la alike stirred in consternation. Somewhere close beyond the gate a loose tile slid from a roof to shatter with a
crash against the flagstones of the road.

I heard Amrey curse under his breath as he reined his mount
in. "Shel'a take it! Not now!" he hissed.

Those words struck a passing strange chord with me. Like
the previous quake, when it had been clear he expected something—had he expected this one?

With a flash of insight, I knew that he had. Suddenly I saw so clearly that I bit my lip to keep from exclaiming about it. The earth temblors were connected, somehow, to his use of the Styrcian crystal. The consequences of his use, perhaps? Unplanned side effects from the unruly, rift-related powers of the wizard-stone? Certainly he could not predict exactly when such a thing would happen, but his expectation that something *would* happen was clear.

Large *shia* effect, large quake. Small *shia* effect, small temblor.

The revelation had so many implications, my mind was awhirl with the possibilities. I spoke to the guard captain with the reflex of long years while my mind engaged elsewhere, hoping my distracted state was not too evident. Imperious orders flowed automatically from my lips, demanding as high-handedly as if I sat in my own hall that Halvericus attend us. Amrey and his strange warriors were a caution to the guards of Caronne, but I was a personage whom they did not hesitate to obey. They threw open the gates and let our entourage pass into the city.

Through the walls we went, across the great square, up the terraced way to the lofty castle, well appointed, with long galleries and marble colonnades and tinkling fountains. "This is a pleasure palace," snorted Amrey, "no proper fortress at all." Indeed, it was not intended for rigorous defense: it was the luxurious residence for the wealthy ruler of a prosperous land. Comfort and beauty were on every hand, in sculpture, in tilework and marble frieze, in lush flowering plants arranged solely to please the eye and nose.

No surprise that Halvericus lived so. Though the man himself had no reputation as a sybarite, his inheritance would have permitted such excess had he been so inclined. Temperate

climate, fertile fields, export specialities of wine and cloth
woven in elaborate patterns—upon such things was his wealth
founded. Caronne faces the sea at the Istanian Straits and
straddles the Rising Land, a plate of shifting ground that forms
shallows and sometimes a land bridge to Istania at unpredictable times of the year. The location was sheltered, and difficult
for ships of draft to reach, therefore safe from most vessels,
naval or piratical, that would ever pose a threat from the sea.
Small craft plying the coast had no difficulty reaching Caronne's bay-sheltered harbor, though, and the local market
was well stocked with regional specialities of the Arguentan
city-states.

Overland, Caronne was protected by close-allied neighbors
to each side and high mountain passes far inland, offering a
protected and idyllic existence to the city-state. Yet even Halvericus had begun to feel the bite of Telemar's monopolies
and stranglehold on overland trade. This had not affected the
produce of his farms and tithe-lands though, and it was that
abundance of grain and wine and oil, of flour and preserved
meats, that the Breo'la had need of. Of all the city-states,
Caronne's larders were fuller than most, the benefit of growing season, good husbandry, and the mild seasons in this part
of Drakmil. Some said Epernia, goddess of birth, farm, and
field, especially smiled upon Halvericus. I could not speak to
the truth of that, but knew that devas and elementals seemed
as content in this realm as one could hope to find.

Lord Halvericus' bounty was extended to us openhandedly,
with no dismay or niggardliness shown because of our unexpected arrival. He greeted us in his hall and we made stately
progress to join him at his dais. I walked as Amrey's equal,
him standing clear of my aura of power—and it was then that
I realized that he had bespelled himself similarly. He seemed
taller, more commanding of stature, and although unmasked,

nearly on a par with myself. So had he elevated himself to share my mystique, and all Caronnians assembled would think, naturally, that it were the other way around: that it were I needs must have imbued him with a special glamour, raising his status above that of the common man. What a signal sign of favor from the Dark Lady that would be! I admired the ploy at the same time that I resented it, and again was glad for the mask that concealed expressions on my face.

Halvericus sat over the remains of a meal, quickly cleared away, and ordered refreshment brought for us and our guard. He was gracious enough but seemed a bit nervous at our presence, for he was perhaps overconscious of our combined magnificence. Just as well, I thought; he would yield up what he had promised all the more readily, were he nonplussed by us. The autarch seated me to his right hand and Amrey at his left. He sent for his privy councillors and others to come and make us welcome. Nevertheless, Kar Kalim and his entourage were an astonishment, no less than my own self. Aristocratic Caronnians in bright-colored hose and carefully draped robes stared openly at the heavy trousers and furred clothing, the bone and bronze-scaled armor worn by the horsemen. Tanned, clean-shaven faces exchanged assessing looks with dark-bearded visages; of a similar height, the tribesmen were sturdier, more muscular with their rough life and lack of city living, quicker of movement than folk bred to the temperament of this languid climate. Their scent of horse and sweat and smoke, which I had nearly grown accustomed to, was in stark contrast to the perfumed bodies and flower-scented air of this autarch's court.

The Breo'la looked upon their surroundings with suspicion. They clearly did not know quite what to make of the overclean, underdressed, unarmed men around them, but they took their cue from Kar Kalim. Their leader sat confidently in Lord

Halvericus' marbled halls as if he had spent every day of his life in such a setting. Perhaps he had, somewhere in Styrcia, though I knew marble was seldom quarried there, and great halls in the Arguentan atrium style were a thing unheard of.

Halvericus allowed Kar Kalim's escort to keep their weapons, to the evident unease of his guards and murmured comment of the courtiers who soon thronged the hall. Ceremonial salt and bread were offered, and accepted by Amrey. I declined food and drink as I always did when garbed for ceremony but my abstinence was barely noticed as the Breo'la set to their food with gusto. They adapted readily enough to chairs—like unto camp stools they sometimes used on muddy ground—but they scorned the two-pronged forks beside each plate, and ignored goblets in favor of drinking directly out of pitchers set before them. Fine Edaeni wine was swilled by Vanye, then spat with disgust upon the ground, splashing on a nearby nobleman's sandaled feet.

"My men do not care for wine." Amrey dismissed the gaff with a laugh. "They drink fermented mare's milk, or plain milk or water. Have you water?"

With water before them, their fingers, knives, and *shivet* manners served well enough for dining, but I could see the amusement or scorn in some onlookers' eyes. The Caronnians thought the barbaric display entertaining. Amrey caught the nuance as well.

"These are the Breo'la." He gestured to his men as if introducing them, pitching his voice to carry. Although he addressed Halvericus, everyone in the hall heard him. "They are nomads who have made the horse their brother. Their land is cruel and harsh. They have no place for the niceties we have the leisure to cultivate in civilization." He spoke in an open aside to Halvericus. "There exists no finer horseman in the world. No more efficient dealer of death."

He glanced at his guards, the Kalimat of elite service, then swept his eye over the disdainful perfumed gentlemen and the spear-bearing guards of the autarch's household. "These are the forces that will be at Telemar like the wolves amongst your herds. Looking for the weakness, tearing out the throat in Valerian's moment of indecision." His smile was mirthless, cold humor on his lips. "Do not mistake table manners for a measure of battle prowess."

The crowd stirred self-consciously. Never was social disapproval confronted publicly in polite society. At their muttering, Plevak, leader of the Kalimat guard, looked up. He spoke in flawless Arguente, the benefit of Amrey's spell of tongues. "Do not scorn the dagger in your hand for its nature. The blade may slice your palm do you grip it wrong."

With such outlandish appearances, and hearing the Styrcian language spoken between them, no Caronnian present had expected Kar Kalim's warriors to be fluent in their tongue. An uncomfortable hush fell over the crowd as each courtier wondered which whispered criticisms had been overheard and understood.

Halvericus responded gracefully, ignoring the flustered members of his court. "We shall heed that advice," he said, inclining his head to Plevak. Then he turned to Kar Kalim, forging on as if they had spoken only of state matters all along.

Diplomatic affairs move slowly in Arguenta, given the opportunity, but Kar Kalim played a different tune. He would have supplies and an escort of nobles—a mere handful, a political token only—whose sole function would be to show Caronne's support of the Breo'la show of strength. "Messengers carry the summons north and east already," he told Halvericus in private conference after the public meal. "Spokesmen from Stavlia, Burris, and other distant courts

will travel to join us. But I will collect your representatives
and others personally as I travel the coast road to Telemar.''

This was no more or less than what they had agreed to
during our clandestine meetings at the close of the Autarchs'
Council, but now that the moment to deliver was here, Halvericus hesitated. He had seen now the type of men who
would be the mailed fist at Valerian's throat: coarse fighters
of a type completely unknown to him. Men who did not impress with highly shined armor and parade-field neatness and
disciplined airs. And the request to empty his winter reserves
into the supply wagons of this army and send officials with it
to boot—it would be unmistakeable proof that Caronne was
foremost amongst the resisters to Telemar's dictates. It
seemed in the end a bit more forward than he had really
wanted to appear. And of course it would be difficult to bring
wheat from the silos; the heavy carts would bog down on rain-
sodden roads. Andronicus, his premier ambassador long experienced at the Telemar court, was ill with ague—

Kar Kalim's back stiffened, broadening his shoulders with
that tension I recognized as prelude to an outburst. Clever
Amrey might be, but for effective diplomacy, he lacked the
patience, and temper was not the solution to this small im-
passe. ''The longer you delay supplying the army,'' I inter-
jected, ''the longer the Breo'la will have to feed themselves
by foraging. One hundred head of cattle were taken from a
field for this evening's dinner pots. Let them stay another
night and another, short of food, and wait until they decide to
supply for this long march directly from the farmers upon
whose lands they camp . . . is this the alternative you are prepared to face?''

A wince creased the high brow of Lord Halvericus as he
pictured thousands more bearded, burly foreigners ruining
fields, stripping provender from country homes.

"Of course we will give you what you need," he reassured Kar Kalim. "It is just that it will be difficult—"

"I appreciate your difficulties, of all sorts," Amrey said drily. "In the morning my supply train will be outside your gates."

"And the representative you choose in place of Andronicus will be ready to ride the following morning, I take it?" I prodded.

"Yes, Lady." The autarch offered a half bow from his chair. "Someone will be ready to speak for Caronne in your embassy."

Embassy. I bit back a laugh. Did he truly believe this pretense that Kar Kalim intended to knock politely on Valerian's door, settle into diplomatic negotiations, repeat at table the protests and claims so often rehearsed in the Autarchs' Council? I would not mind such a path at all, myself, for that way lay delay and the quagmire of endless talks—but I knew in my gut that Amrey would have none of it. I had witnessed fierce martial drills upon the assembly field, and the testy mood amongst the Breo'la, who seemed to yearn for conflict like blood-fed war dogs too long restrained from carnage.

Perhaps that was a mood that Halvericus could not afford to let himself recognize, for it never comforts a man to realize the snake he has innocently picked up is a deadly one. This autarch—and all the rest, I would warrant—had vested reason to act as if Kar Kalim and the representatives he collected along the way were a special body, a political embassy dispatched to handle this delicate task.

And so they were, in a manner of speaking, though I misdoubted me that Amrey would converse overmuch with the lord of Telemar. Let Halvericus call it what he would, as long as he was represented, and the other interested Salt Coast lords as well. This challenge from Kar Kalim required the legiti-

macy of their endorsement so he could be seen to be acting
in the interests of the greater good. As long as that need was
met, the master of Caronne and all the other city-states could
think of their delegations as benignly as they cared to.

Content with that affirmation of commitment, Kar Kalim
declined the invitation to lodgings, and left with myself and
his escort in the late night. Courtiers lined halls and townsmen
in unusual number looked from windows to see us leave their
city. They got as good a look as in broad day, too, for Amrey
scorned linkboys and lit our way with a spell that enveloped
our path in noon light. It was a working he took care to perform with open word and gesture at the gate to Halvericus'
palace, so that all could see he commanded magic of his own,
was not dependent on the legendary figure by his side for his
gifts.

Thus conspicuous we left the city, and Kar Kalim's light
did not fade until we were well out of sight of the city's walls
and high tiled roofs.

Once supplied and moving along the coast road, the pace of
travel picked up considerably. The banners spread out in a
column miles long, followed by pack horses carrying the bulk
of food needed for night camps, followed in turn by the wagons that carried the rest. There were no halts for supply, no
detours to call upon the autarchs of Egrania or Mardevis
through which we passed. Amrey dispatched Plevak and a
shivet of warriors to command the attendance of the autarchs'
representatives, monitoring their progress with messenger
spells lest they should balk at this invitation as Halvericus
had.

"But did you not wish to make a display of force to these
Salt Coast lords?" I asked.

"And bring the horse tribes to camp massed at their

gates?'' He shrugged. ''Why bother? To impress them? I care not for their opinion of my forces.''

''The sight of what they send against Telemar can keep their allegiance square behind you.''

''So can their common sense,'' he replied. ''If they do not exercise it, I want to know that, and I will remedy that error in leadership in my own time.''

So cryptic a statement that was not. I knew from other conversations that Kar Kalim had plans for any allies who might think to move against him in some unprotected moment. It did not seem likely, to me: after all, the Arguentan lords saw this general of my sponsorship as the answer to their problems with Lord Valerian. Years of intrigue and guarding his back in Styrcia, though, had shaped his attitudes. Spy birds and message spells and various precautions he set here and there to alert him to suspicious activities at his rear. He would not hesitate to crush any lordling who attempted to break alliance and threaten him. That was such a certainty, he gave it no more thought, but focused squarely on his objective instead: Telemar and Lord Valerian.

''We cannot move speedily enough,'' he said when I remarked on our relentless pace. ''If it did not mean we would be slowed by foraging, we would outstrip even the pack horses.''

''Why such haste?''

''Rest assured, Valerian must know already of our approach. At least some fly-spy has told him, some word from paid eyes at Halvericus' court perhaps, or in some group of merchants we have long since bypassed. Whether he believes the reports remains to be seen, and he probably does not know exactly how much support we have from the autarchs. But there is a difference between rumor and the reality of our might upon his doorstep. I wish to be there before he can set aside his doubts and respond to us militarily.''

''If haste is so needful, why not let us pass through a rift to Telemar, as you did that night?'' I took pains to ask that in seeming innocence; it was of course a natural question, given my prior experience with his powers.

He shot me a sideways glance and shook his head curtly. ''No. There are prices to be paid with the use of power. Better I save it against greater need, does Valerian not heed reason.''

Was there a limit to the use of the wizard-stone, I wondered? Did it marshal only a finite amount of power? Or did he refer to those quakes of the ground, that earthly protest at the exercise of dimension-warping powers upon its crust? I recalled no temblor the nights we had gone to and from Telemar . . . but there had been weather, sudden severe, unseasonable weather. Was that the fly in the amber? That *shian* affected the forces of nature in random ways great or small, depending on the magnitude of their use? I occupied myself with speculation, and forebore to stare at his neck where the filigreed cage held its gleaming treasure captive.

We journeyed southwestwards as rapidly as we might, collecting the representatives of rebellious autarchs as we went. Andronicus from Caronne recovered suddenly from his ague, and set out with us. On the road we were joined by Marius of Egrania, Otavian of Mardevis and their escorts, and others. The officials from Burris, Rajpor, Singut, Stavlia were all behind us, following in our wake in response to Kar Kalim's summons. Soon enough they would catch up with us when we were outside the walls of Telemar.

As we traveled, Amrey saw to it always that I was fine-robed, garbed in luxurious silks and furs and warm fine woolens as we traveled to the colder climes of the southwest. Gold glittered at neck and ear to compliment the hated bands that adorned my wrists; although a mask was not part of my everyday wear, he saw to it that a constant glamour was upon me which gave me an aura of unearthly presence and greater stature. The Arguentans among us treated me with greatest respect, awe-touched to be in my presence. The Breo'la, who had seen me first as mere captive and stifled adept, were less reverential, but behaved respectfully under Amrey's watchful eye. Even the karzdagi who traveled with us—including Crookfang, who had become my personal guard—treated me, if not with respect, then with crude courtesy.

This treatment from my captors, as if I were an honored dignitary, or indeed the mysterious and powerful Midnight Rider of reputation—this place of regard was only underscored by Kar Kalim's use of me as showpiece every time an autarch's spokesman joined us on the march. Never did he miss the chance to display power, or the trappings of power, and I was not the least amongst his set pieces for that purpose. Each ambassador from an autarch's court was introduced formally—first to me, as if this entire campaign were a project under my direction and authority, then to the red-haired man constantly by my side, who, it seemed, issued orders and directives under my command. It was made clear to them that the Dark Lady was not to be bothered with petty details of the march or the Salt Coast politics involved; Kar Kalim himself would handle such matters and consult with her personally, as she had directed him to.

I laughed to myself the first time I heard Murl say that—such a transparent lie, I thought—but the abassadors believed it, and the Breo'la did not care what tales their leader told. My enforced companionship to Kar Kalim became increasingly insular: deferred to by the horsemen, avoided by hesitant Arguentans, accompanied by karzdagi skulking at a distance, keeping me always in their sight but never addressing me. Only Amrey engaged me in conversation. Words with him became interaction I welcomed in spite of myself.

I wondered if I could find a way to play a bigger role in his contact with outsiders, or if I must resign myself to having Murl's ear only at private times, late at night or early morning in his tent. Such calculations occupied me as we rode on, through wooded, near-mountainous hills, down to rolling coastal plains, and into the valley where rich Telemar was situated on the bank of the Sevian River delta.

We reached that golden port midmorning on the fifteenth day of our travels, having outstripped the supply train, moving swiftly ahead the last day or two with seven banners of warriors and the Kalimat guard. Valerian's city loomed on the crest of Casian Hill, rising on the north bank of the broad Sevian, lifeblood of this famous sea and river port. As Amrey had rightly predicted, word of our approach had flown before us. The roads were free of merchants, of peddlers and travelers; farmsteads and homes near the roadside were abandoned the closer we got to the city. Oared ships of commerce moored far out in the bay at the river's mouth, not in the city's sheltered harbor. Only small craft, and precious few of them, were tied up at the waterfront quays. Uncertain what he was really dealing with, and cautious at reports of the size of Kar Kalim's army, Valerian had tucked up inside his city like a turtle in its shell.

We studied that city from a hillside as they must be studying us in turn. I sat with power, as did Kar Kalim, for the benefit of spying eyes and the inspiration of the Breo'la. Vanye sat horse beside his master and sneered at the enemy's defensive posture. "Valerian will sit inside until we burn him out," he spat. "He has no taste for battle, the coward."

"He is no coward," I corrected him. "He has fought his

share of pirates and raiders farther down coast, and cleared his realm and others of bandits and mercenary rovers. Overcautious he appears, until he sees an opportunity. Then he makes a sudden, unexpected strike from behind his defensive facade. When he spies his opening, he will show his hand.''

"And we have seen from Council that he scorns to negotiate," Amrey remarked. "Valerian thinks he holds the upper hand. Even with an army outside his gates?''

It was a musing that invited my opinion. "Even so," I ventured. "The advantage is his, in the defensive position. He will have his militia and mercenaries on hand for defense, and his Ursbach allies available by sea as soon as a message-spell can summon them. They are likely already on their way.''

We regarded the city again, a place we might not have the time to threaten with leisurely siege. Telemar had great, high walls of thick yellow sandstone, enforced with legendary spells that made them proof to magical attack. Wardings shimmered faintly in the air over the city, another precaution against airborne missiles or flying creatures that might threaten from above. Catapults rested atop lofty towers, permanent emplacements calculated to bombard enemy forces at considerable range, given the height of the engine stations. Secret sally ports were said to exist in the walls, though no one could say where, so that defenders could flank an enemy and attack unexpectedly from various quarters. The autarch of Telemar could muster a defensive force numbering at least ten thousand: five thousand militia, well drilled in city defense, and the same number again of mercenaries, the elite Sorex Command whose golden eagle standards winked atop the battlements.

It was clear Valerian need only sit snug within his walls until he had taken our measure, and then react to us—or not—in his own time. Meanwhile, our time outside his walls was limited, for when his allies came they could raise our siege, or at least cause sufficient distraction that a sally from Telemar might have a chance against us.

We faced classic problems in siege warfare, I thought—but so static a situation would never satisfy the Breo'la, nor Kar Kalim, who would not wait to dance to another's tune. Amrey spoke with Vanye in Styrcian, beginning a talk I was not privy to. They were soon joined by Plevak, Elyek, and other ranking war leaders of the tribes. Their discussion was animated, and now and then punctuated with a laugh. I was forgotten as they evolved their plans, inspired by the city's waiting stance and the deserted countryside around us.

Soon the command party left the winter-brown hillside and rode north to a safe remove from catapult fire. There, a sprawling encampment was taking shape. In the center of those lines stood Kar Kalim's personal tent, distinguished by its red and black banner and starburst. We retired there for more discussion. The camp bustled around us, as tents were raised and horsemen settled into their *shivetu,* sharpening their swords and gathering their battle gear.

In the command tent, we ate early, and for once I was included in the council of war that only a handful of select officers attended. Amrey bade me sit beside him. I knelt on a bear fur, my midnight-blue robes pooling around me. Others squatted on their haunches to study the map Murl unfolded before us.

It was a detailed hand sketch of the Emprelor, Valerian's palace, and the portion of the battlements that looked north towards our camp. "Pelan's spies were helpful," he explained, "when last we were in Telemar. Here are the autarch's living quarters, and here, the parts of the wall giving best view of our forces."

A flurry of Styrcian was exchanged, gutterals and sibilants

flowing in rapid succession, and not for the first time I regretted that I had not learned that tongue. Too much passed beyond my kenning while I was with Amrey for my lack of ability in that speech. I tried in vain to decipher his meaning as Vanye pointed to the place between city walls and our camp—a place where our visual reconnoiter showed outbuildings, cottages, and small villas clustering like chicks around a mother hen's skirts.

Amrey nodded in agreement and turned to me. "We have a bold plan afoot tonight. I want you to watch me, with magical means I will provide."

I was surprised at the request. "What will I be observing?"

He looked smug. "I will be having a little talk with Lord Valerian, and I want you to observe. Since you know these folk better than I, I want your feelings about his true reaction, his likely response to what I have to say. You will be another pair of eyes and an opinion I wish to hear afterwards."

"You will be confronting him in his palace?" I asked, shocked.

"Of course."

I absorbed that in silence. I had not thought Murl was inclined to parley after all I had heard of his martial ways, and knowing that the Breo'la so badly wanted to engage in battle. But his desire to try reason before argument spoke well for him, I thought.

"As you wish," I responded warmly. "When will you need me?"

"After sunset and before moonrise, when the fields between us and the walls are in darkness."

Well enough. Glad to be out of a saddle for most of the day, I slept until nightfall, when I was summoned again to Kar Karlim's side. Together we left his tent. I heard the stamp of horses in the dark, nearby. Vanye growled an order, and one after the other, torches were lit, until a long string of riders were illuminated in the night. They moved off towards Telemar, approaching the north-facing walls in best view from Valerian's palace.

"Inya." I heard my name and went to Amrey's side. "Watch and wait," he murmured, an air of expectancy about him, and faced the city in the distance.

Telemar's position could be seen by houselights gleaming off the occasional tower or gable that peeked over the great walls. In the darkness, the fields between our camp and the walls seemed a great abyss, threaded now by a string of pearls, each pearl a smoking, bright-burning torch carried by a horseman in the long line of Breo'la raiders moving through the night.

The horsemen rode amongst deserted buildings, setting the torch to them left and right, igniting orchard trees and heaps of straw, anything that burned. What started as a methodical, orderly progression grew into a fire-loving frenzy until it was a joyous fest of arson, riders galloping from target to target, their whoops carrying on the cold air as wooden shutters were kicked open and torches thrust into cottages and small homes. Some archers from the walls shot at the figures silhouetted in firelight, but missed their fast-dashing targets. Soon the abandoned buildings outside the city walls were an inferno lighting up the night like a giant's bonfire. More arrows flew at the escaping horsemen, who draped themselves low across their horses' necks and rode swiftly out of danger. One rider was struck and dropped from his mount, his fall clearly silhouetted by the fires at his back. Others collected him, two riders leaning quick from the saddle to grip an arm each, carrying their fellow like baggage as they rode close together beyond the range of arrows. Soon the Breo'la were back in the safety of the camp.

All that I could see from our hillside vantage. As the buildings burned higher, Amrey turned to me. "Now is the time," he said. Laying one hand upon the crystal at his neck, he made a pass over me with the other, moving his hand from crown of head to toe, a handspan out from my flesh, then tapped me on the brow with one finger. My earthly sight blurred and I saw a confused image in my mind's eye, as if I envisioned something on the verge of vivid memory.

I was oblivious to Amrey in that moment and so missed his gesture as he opened a rift, a black, starry gateway of the type that had carried us to and from Telemar in the past. Moments later he walked through that portal, alone, and the image in my mind's eye came clear.

Amrey stepped into a marbled room with high ceilings and latticed windows shuttered now and draped against the winter cold. One shutter was cracked open, though, and a tall man stood there in the curtains. Broad-shouldered, black-haired, robed in magenta serge and brocade silk—it was Valerian, watching the fires that blossomed beyond the walls of his city stronghold.

Kar Kalim appeared at his back with no warning. In that moment a thin shriek pierced the air, an alarming outcry—I recognized it as an enchantment upon the autarch's robes, a vigil-keeper of some sort to warn of an assassin's approach. Had Amrey meant to slay his enemy outright?

Then Murl gestured a spell and I saw the autarch entrapped in a blue-glowing stasis field of the same sort I had experienced more than once. His eyes were wide, arrogant face frozen in an expression more startled than frightened, and tinged with anger.

Helpless he was, and surprised by the man who had stepped thus boldly into his private chamber. It was no great challenge for Amrey, that: like wishing us to an inn on a road outside

Telemar, he had wished himself to Valerian in a private place, having made a display that drew his attention first. There was after all no telling exactly what sorts of magical resources Valerian might have at his command, so to surprise him was the wisest move. Surely he had some special protections, as did all autarchs with the wealth to afford them; the vigil-cloak was a fine example of this. But Amrey was also fully defended, cloaked in both his own power and the might of the wizard-stone about his neck. He walked up to Valerian, a man I knew was taller than him, but glamour-clad, Kar Kalim met the autarch eye to eye; indeed, seemed to be even greater in stature than the lord of Telemar.

"Tomorrow morning, you will come out and surrender yourself to me," Kar Kalim spoke sharply to him. "You will come alone, without an escort. Do you give yourself over to me, and surrender Telemar, then will your city be spared. Make us fight to take it, and your people will be butchered till your streets run red, and everyone you care for will be gutted before you. Then your eyes will be put out with a hot iron. You will be chained like an animal and sent on display to all the city-states your greed has cheated of their just due.

"Can I expect you in the morning?"

The nimbus that held Valerian in its grip altered in strength, and his head was released so he could speak. Anger swept over his face, and disbelief that he could be so accosted in his own palace. "My guards will slay you where you stand!" he raged, and Amrey locked up his mouth once more.

"Do not waste your breath with empty threats. No one moves freely in these halls right now but myself. You do not appreciate my strength, I think." He smiled bitterly. "But you will. You will be the key that willingly unlocks your city to me, or you will be the example of Telemar fallen in blood. Either way, your reign here has ended. Reckon with that, Valerian. And one way or another, I will see you in the morning.''

It was not at all a parley, as I had expected, but an ultimatum, cold and clear. When he had delivered it, Kar Kalim stepped back to the rift that sparkled night-dark in the autarch's chamber. He walked through at the same moment he released the man from the spell of binding. I saw Valerian stagger as he regained control over himself, saw the fury ignite his face—then the image was gone as Murl returned to the Breo'la camp in one stride.

The rift closed behind him. In that moment chill enveloped us, and the first flakes of snow whipped past, driven by a cutting wind not present before.

''Now join me,'' he said in passing, ''and tell me what you think. Will he fight, or will he surrender?''

I turned to follow him as a sudden winter storm unleashed its fury. A *shia*-born storm, now, I had no doubt, localized in the horsemen's camp. Within the hour we were near snowbound, with powdery drifts blown high against the southern sides of tents.

The fringes of the storm did not touch the fire-taken buildings outside the walls of Telemar. They burned hotly well past moonrise, then fell into embers and smoked in glowing ruin throughout the night.

CHAPTER 12

C ome morning, Valerian did not capitulate. His gates remained sealed and guarded, his defenders in great number stalwart upon the battlements.

Kar Kalim faced those walls sitting upon a camp stool with his commanders squatting round about. His *semyet* cloak lay wind-ruffled over silver-stitched black tunic and silver wrist bracers, eye-catching ornaments as he gestured now and then in discussion with his men. They breakfasted and studied the city defenses, and even told jokes, to judge by the laughter. I watched them from the tent, a cluster of men in horse leathers and scale armor on the slope of a south-facing hill. A long time they waited, seemingly at leisure, until finally the sun had climbed to the midmorning mark. Then a messenger ran into the camp, and soon Crookfang came to herd me to Amrey's side.

I was shown to a stool draped in yellow panther fur as was Kar Kalim's own, and soon enough saw why. Summoned by other runners, the ambassadors from the various city-states presented themselves in one assemblage before us, three Arguentan aristocrats brought from the camp in their draped robes and city finery, their leather-and-bronze-armored guards in close escort behind them. Andronicus took the lead for the others, offered a fine courtier's bow to myself, and then to

Kar Kalim. He addressed his words to us both, as if I had a say in things; for all I could tell, he believed it was so.

"We await the negotiations, Lady, Lord," he said, ducking his head to each of us. "We have copies of our claims and demands—"

Kar Kalim lifted one hand to halt the man's speech. "That won't be needful. All the words that are necessary have already been exchanged with Lord Valerian. We found him less than cooperative."

Andronicus raised one dark eyebrow. News of Kar Kalim's nighttime visitation had been shared with no one outside the command staff, and they would not likely have passed word to the Arguentans. "Oh? Then you move rapidly, my lord." He rustled the papers in his hand unhappily. "But there are certain concessions, certain points we must be quite clear on, conditions that Telemar will need to comply with after you have forced their cooperation. You at least should be aware of—"

Amrey's eyes narrowed. "Telemar has made its choice already, Ambassador. The time for talk is passed. In fact, it passed this morning, when Lord Valerian did not come voluntarily from his gates."

"You demanded his surrender?" The Caronnian looked startled. "When?"

"You misapprehend." Kar Kalim chuckled. "I gave him an order, which he ignored. Now *you* are going to demand his surrender formally; you and the other ambassadors with you."

The spokesmen and their parties muttered in consternation. "Pardon, Lord," spoke up Marius of Egrania, "but that is not our place at all. We are here to show the support of the city-states for what you do—"

"Indeed. And you are going to support me, most unmis-

takeably. I have already told you how. Gentlemen, prepare
yourselves to ride.''

"I think not," challenged Andronicus, scowling. "That is
not why we are here.''

Amrey looked at him cooly. "You will ride, sir," he said.
"You will ride to show that I do not demand Telemar's surrender for my own sake, that there are others here with interest. Now. You will go willingly, or you will go tied to your
horse, but go you will.''

The aristocrats bristled at those words, and their guards
ranged themselves rather more protectively of their charges.
Before the Breo'la could move in threateningly close, I inter-
vened.

"Why *are* you here, then, Andronicus? To sit at a conference table with Valerian for weeks and months more, while
matters stay unresolved? If he would not come to terms with
me at the Autarchs' Council, why would he treat with you?
That is no longer the way the Salt Coast lords wish their
affairs handled. Or did you plan to stand quietly by as witness
while Kar Kalim blusters on your behalf? No. Do you not see:
you show the city-states' position best, by demanding Valerian's surrender. That way his people will have their eyes
opened to all the forces that oppose them." I gestured to the
side and to the camp behind us. "This is not a march under-
taken upon a lark. This army is supported by your masters,
and Telemar must know that. That is why you will speak to
the gate and demand that Valerian come forth.''

It was persuasive enough, and though none of the Arguentans wanted to put themselves so directly into danger, neither
did they wish to defy me openly.

"We will go," Andronicus finally conceded.

"Indeed you will," growled Kar Kalim. "It is only right.''

The two locked eyes for a moment, some angry retort on

the ambassador's lips. "Never fear," Kar Kalim added. "It is a risk my own men share with you. You will be accompanied, and I include my own spokesman." He gestured to a party of horsemen gathered a short distance away; at their head was the dark-browed young man who had won the gruesome prize at Corwin's execution.

Andronicus seemed eased by the fact that Breo'la would also be at risk, and ended the contest with a bow that carried his eyes away from Kar Kalim's. A while later the Arguentans were mounted with a hand each of soldiers from their escorts, and soon formed up with tribesmen from the Kalimat *shivet.*

Shortly before noon, the party left our lines and rode into the shadow of the great gate of Telemar, built of a broad expanse of the heartwood of nigantha, as hard as iron. The gate was tower-guarded on each side, reinforced with iron bands and inscribed with magical wards. The horsemen approached it along the broad cobbled road, dwarfed by the high-walled edifice before them. Countless archers had them in range before they were within hailing distance. Finally the party halted, and an Arguentan called out—Marius of Egrania, I thought. An officer spoke to them from the battlements over the gate.

The words did not carry at this distance, but Amrey listened attentively and leaned forward at one juncture, as if the sounds came to him on the wind. Indeed, that is exactly what happened, for a moment later, I heard his sharp-inhaled breath. In the next instant, archers loosed from the walls, and a cloud of missiles flew true at short range to pierce our riders before the gates. Dead fell the ambassadors, their few guards, the tribesmen of the Breo'la who rode with them. A sally port opened and Telemarans darted forth, dragging the bodies off the injured and squealing horses that had stumbled to the

ground, cutting the throats of the animals to anguished groans
from onlooking Breo'la.

In minutes, the mutilated bodies of our messengers were
strung up by the heels and dangling from the battlements, Salt
Coast envoys hanging beside unkempt horsemen. They were
suspended from tower windows and along walls lined by jeer-
ing archers, a sight that provoked an angry massed outcry of
ululations and war whoops from the Breo'la. In the face of
that fierce noise from the entire encampment, the jubilation
on the walls stuttered to a halt. In that moment, the defenders
seemed to realize they had not cowed with their actions, but
enraged.

No doubt Lord Valerian had been disturbed, even profoundly frightened, by his confrontation with Kar Kalim last
night. Surely he realized that his challenger could have slain
him handily there in his own rooms. But fear, if such he felt,
did not breed caution or wisdom. Instead, that intrusion and
display of power had only vexed him, and caused him to do
this act of murder to spokesmen protected by law and tradition
all along the Salt Coast.

It was a deliberate affront. I had not thought Valerian so
foolish as to provoke so powerful an opponent, but perhaps
he believed he could safeguard his back, or counter Kar
Kalim's notable magicry. Certainly he must look to his Ursbach allies for succor, for he had insufficient force to drive
Kar Kalim's army off his lands by himself. But now he had
stirred the hornet's nest and would pay the price.

Amrey spoke first to the escorts of the men who had died.
"You may join my forces to fight against these craven bas-
tards," he said. "Are you with us?"

There was hesitation among some: they were mere city
guards on escort duty, not soldiers prepared to risk their life

amongst strangers in a war or siege. But Kar Kalim offered no alternative, and the Breo'la camp was no longer a friendly place where Arguentans could come or go at their leisure. Prudence said this was not the time to try to leave this war camp—for with that single volley of arrows, such it had become. With the death of their fellows, the mood had turned aggressive, the horsemen needing an outlet for their rage in vengeance against the city. Her impregnable walls taunted silently, an irresistible draw to the eye of high commander and lowest cook's boy alike, and the horsemen who stalked by wore a dangerous air about them.

To a man, the ambassadorial escorts took Kar Kalim's unsubtle option, and agreed to do what they could in the forthcoming assault. Limited by language barriers, that promised to be little, but Amrey knew, as did I, what witnesses these men would make for the wrong done their masters, and the revenge taken on their behalf by Kar Kalim.

That revenge was not long in coming. The affront given would have been hot spur to any Arguentan lord. To the Breo'la and their overlord, it was as open flame touched to sap pine. Two hours later, Amrey stood upon the hillside facing the northern battlements, his army arrayed in long battle lines to either side of him. I stood at his command post with messengers and karzdagi, and watched him look over the force near twenty thousand strong that he had brought against Telemar. Then he turned his back on his steppe warriors, and faced the city before us.

Low clouds hung in the sky, slow-moving on this late-winter day. The grays and steel blue of the heavens were stark backdrop to Kar Kalim where he stood, his red hair unusual amongst the horse tribes. He threw the cloak back from his shoulders, grasped the wizard-stone with one hand, and began a working that had no visible effect.

I recognized his motions as channeling the Power Without, and cursed the bracelets at my wrist for hindering me from sensing the details of this working. Right now there should be a profound shift in the ether around us, something adept senses could feel like the change of air that heralded a coming storm. I was compelled to watch sense-blind instead, as beclouded as any mundane, unable to guess at his intentions.

Then he threw his hand down, as if casting pebbles to the ground, and stamped upon the hillside.

The quake started as a faint rumble, then a grinding of stone, a mere shudder in the earth that grew stronger as it sped away from Kar Kalim's position. The temblor raced ahead of us in a direct line towards the wall that he faced. Mounts all up and down the battle line danced and reared in place, unsettled by the moving earth but tightly controlled by riders who seemed as prepared as any man could be for this event. I staggered to keep my footing, as did everyone else who was standing; the karzdagi dropped to all fours in doglike crouches and were the most stable of all.

The quake grew in magnitude, plowing the earth into upheaval, shaking dust from the hillside and valley floor like a pall from a carpet. The mighty foundations of Telemar's walls shook, then cracked, then moved.

Ramparts enchanted against physical attack were no stronger than ordinary walls against a shrug of the earth's shoulder. The first cracks appeared and men fled the battlements—or tried to flee, for stonework buckled beneath their feet and chunks of masonry the size of cottages tumbled from the top of the wall. Then in slow-seeming collapse, the formidable battlements of Telemar came crashing to the ground, taking men into oblivion, the end of the quake shaking loose more stone and widening the gap in the wall before the temblor began to subside.

Before the earth had settled, the Breo'la charged forward. Skirling horns and thundering drums urged them to follow the lead of their war chief, Vanye, down the hill, across the valley, through and around the ruins of burned buildings. Horse archers rode in a circular formation past the gaping breech, keeping defenders back with deadly, withering arrow fire. Others took daring dismounts from their cantering mounts and once on foot, dashed for the rubble that had been the thick north wall of Telemar.

Eagle standards met the Breo'la upon the rubble as the Sorex mercenaries responded to this threat. But the horsemen came fast and furious, clambering over debris and swinging vicious curved sabers to fight their way into the city. As defenders reeled from quake-caused injuries and the chaos of disaster, the horsemen fought their way to the gate. A short while later, that great portal was thrown open and their comrades rode to join them. One banner streamed inside the city, then two, and then the battle was carried within Telemar into the city streets.

Screams carried to my hillside vantage long before the first tendrils of smoke did. I heard the distant shrieks of victims falling to Breo'la swords and could imagine all too well what passed within the crumbling city walls. "Spare them!" I appealed to Amrey, half plea, half demand, knowing this destruction was unnecessary, fearing the horsemen would not stop on their own—

He sneered at me. Without a word he mounted his black Guerian and rode into Telemar amidst a guard of Kalimat warriors.

I was kept to his tent, and did not see him again until the city was his own. The sacking of Telemar lasted the day and into the night; the gleeful slaughter a day beyond that. Half the inhabitants were killed outright, for every other person was plucked indiscriminantly from the streets and their hidey-holes, and herded to the city squares where they were methodically decapitated. Pyramids of their heads were stacked outside the entrance to Valerian's palace, just as Kar Kalim had promised he would do.

I was sickened by the carnage. Such cruelty and bloodshed was far beyond the tortures and ill treatment that Arguentan warfare wreaked. The Breo'la glee in it alienated me; Kar Kalim's encouragement of it revolted and dismayed me. I was glad of my confinement in camp, for it kept me far away from the stench of blood rotting in the streets of unfortunate Telemar.

Later, when the family of Lord Valerian was butchered, their death agonies were but the smallest drop added to a great lake of blood. Valerian's public tortures seemed an anticlimax. As promised, he was blinded, chained naked in a cage like an animal, his protests only mewlings, for the tongue had been cut out of his head as last measure of punishment. He was sent on a tour of the northeast with an escort of Kalimat and the Arguentan soldiers who had seen their masters slain. Thus the former lord of Telemar would bear witness in his body to Kar Kalim's terrible revenge, and when he had served his purpose of public display he, too, would be gutted and slain.

Amrey watched the wagon bearing Valerian's cage pull out of camp, and swore it would be so, "`. . . for those who oppose me, die," he said with finality. Then he ordered me to accompany him to the city, and though I dreaded the thought, I did not have the heart to defy him.

The great palace of Telemar was called the Emprelor, an ediface faced with gold-veined marble and paved with red-ochre flagstones. One wing had been laid in rubble when the quake struck, but most of the palace was salvageable. Telemarans were set to cleaning the evidence of battle and looting and bloodshed. I passed women and small children scrubbing floors, men hauling debris, all moving in mincing short steps for the leather hobbles around their ankles, constraining them to a shortened pace.

"Why is that?" I pointed. "To prevent escape?"

Amrey snorted. "To show they are slaves. They are permanently braided on."

"Slaves." My mind reeled with that information. Arguentans did not enslave prisoners, but traded or ransomed them, or eventually let them work or return home. Blood feuds were easily enough engendered without the added aggravation of slavery. But this concept, of entire families taken as chattel . . .

"Surely that does not hold them," I protested. "It is only leather."

"If they cut the hobble and try to flee, their family that remains behind is put to death. Or their tentmates, the other slaves who share sleeping quarters, if they have no family."

"And if the slave is caught?"

He gave me a cold smile, and forebore to answer that question.

We passed the workers in passage and chamber, and came finally into the great hall, the atrium and audience chamber where pillars had cracked but not collapsed. The high-arched galleries were intact and presentable; the mosaic floor chipped in places but soon, Amrey said, to be repaired. He pointed things out with a proprietary air, a man proud of his new home. The long reflection pond in the atrium had been restocked with carp and bluefish from the Sevian; it was an elegant touch, fed by a natural warm spring, decorated by rare black lotus blossoms.

It was jarring to realize Valerian's son had been drowned in it, as he sought to flee his captors after the city's fall . . .

"Would you like to stay here?" Murl asked as we walked the length of the hall. "I believe I will be making my quarters here. I would like you nearby."

He did not speak the invitation exactly like an order, but more as if he were sounding me out, and so I responded in that spirit. "No," I told him. "I would rather stay away from here." He raised an eyebrow. "There is a psychic charge of death and trauma that overlays the palace," I hastened to add, by way of excuse.

He let my opinion pass unchallenged for the nonce and moved to the dais at the other end of the hall, where the blood of Valerian's wife had been scoured from the steps. The coral throne of Telemar was a fanciful work, not as stately as my throne in Moontooth but grand enough. Amrey mounted the dais and placed himself upon it. "Stand here," he said, pointing to his side, "and don your mask."

So. This was a moment of truth for him, I thought. He chose not to put two chairs here, and took the one himself—thus did he unveil the true directorship of power between us for others to see. He held the seat of honor, while I was left standing like an advisor or courtier, at his right hand, dignified only with the mask he had instructed me to bring and the dweomer he had set upon me.

I took that position with what grace I could, and kept my composure while he rattled quick orders to the Breo'la guards nearby. One trotted off, intent about some business; others spoke to karzdagi lurking in the shadows of the gallery. Soon commanders gathered, the Vabronye who lead their clans in battle, some Bronye, sept-leaders, amongst them: they sat in *shivet*-like circles at the sides of the hall near the foot of the dais. It was an informal court, Breo'la style, in this setting wholly unnatural to these people.

When I saw the procession entering the audience hall, I forgot how out of place the horsemen looked amidst marble and cracked mosaic. Men in city finery approached, escorted by soldiers in the bronze-embossed leather armor of the Salt Coast—autarchs' men, all, and not of Telemar, for they had not the fearful, cowed look of the city's survivors.

They came forward, and their spokesman, a short, robust man with curly dark locks, bowed to Amrey upon the throne of Telemar. "We greet you, Kar Kalim, and give you good cheer upon your taking of the city." He removed hand from shoulder and stood upright once more. "I am Cassius, Lord Caethon's ambassador from Stavlia. Allow me to introduce my fellows . . ."

They had met on the road, some of them; others had come together just these past days in the chaos of the taking of Telemar. Finally they had been called to this formal audience with Kar Kalim, a meeting I could have predicted Amrey would rather hold in a great hall than a smokey Breo'la tent, no matter how assimilated he had become among the horse warriors. Here was a grand setting where no nuance would be lost upon the autarchs' representatives.

". . . the ambassador from Singut . . ."

Amrey smiled and nodded, an automatic courtesy that I knew concealed swift calculating thoughts. I had more interest to study his face for his reactions, than the diplomats come before us, but there was no polite way to do so without my attention being noted by all. So I gazed at the ambassadors as introductions droned on.

". . . Clavius of Burris . . ."

My heart paused in my chest for a beat or more, I could swear it, before my mind fully registered those words. I stared hard at the man who had come forward to make his obeisance to Kar Kalim—old and gray now, but unmistakeably he who was once my student, once my lover: Murl Amrey's teacher at the court of the autarch of Burris.

Clavius Mericus rose from his bow and cocked his head to one side, regarding Kar Kalim with a look of recognition and inquiry. Sudden tension electrified the air between the two men, and why that should be, I could not tell. Prodded by this, I glanced at Amrey. He was at the edge of his seat, leaning forward upon his throne, elbow on armrest, one hand fidgeting at his gray-streaked beard. Never had I seen him so unpoised, since his return from Styrcia.

"Clavius of Burris . . ." Kar Kalim repeated the spokesman's name, and Cassius halted his introductions. "Last I heard you were thaumaturge to Lord Pelan. Are you still?"

Silence stretched out until finally Clavius dipped his chin. "Thank you for inquiring. Indeed I am. I am also advisor to his court these last two years."

"Well." For a moment Amrey cast about for words, to my eyes nervous where he sat beneath his old mentor's regard. "We shall have to speak privately, later. I would like to hear more of Burris."

Clavius bowed in acknowledgement, a double reverence to both Amrey and myself.

There was expectancy in the air, a nervous tension that prevailed—and suddenly I put my finger on it. Amrey was concerned that Clavius might say something untoward; might address him as the apprentice he had been so few short years ago on our scale of time. Whether he wielded great magics or no, some part of Amrey recognized the mentor and teacher that Clavius had been to him, and reacted to his authority with the deference of habit from years before. This was one man who could challenge Kar Kalim's abilities in this public forum—and any challenge that disrupted Amrey's calculated show of power would be unwelcome.

He was so different in so many ways, I would not have thought his roots mattered to him any longer. Apparently I was wrong.

"Well, then," he hesitated, eager to move the proceedings along. "Sir Cassius, you were saying?"

My eyes lingered on Clavius as he returned to the rank and file of his fellows. He moved with an air of awkward self-consciousness and I smiled to myself. He had never been so smooth-spoken that he could carry a diplomatic maneuver off effortlessly. His curiousity about us both must be burning bright within him, and no occasion now to pursue his questions in such a public place. As Amrey said, they would talk later.

I resolved that I would, also.

I confess I paid little attention to the niceties that followed. A show of gracious reception was Amrey's game here, nothing more or less. He would have his real interactions with these ambassadors privately, away from the hearing of each other. Here, for now, was a time to impress with his might and the magnificence of his new domain: these men, who thought Kar Kalim would challenge Telemar for a piece of her lands, had never imagined that in one bold stroke the conqueror would reach out and claim the entire city for his own.

Surely they must realize that this man now held a position similar to that of Valerian, so lately abhorred? And what they would make of that in talks with Telemar's new master remained to be seen.

I cared not the least for such machinations. Talk, talk, it was all talk, and me there, bound to Kar Kalim's will, desiring to keep him in check, though I had been powerless to prevent his blithely ordered slaughter of a conquered city, simply to mark his vengeance . . . And now here was come Clavius, like some sign or omen. I doubted Amrey would grant us time together, for he knew of our old association. This man had sent Amrey to me, those years agone—who would have thought he would be the one whom Pelan of Burris would send to Kar Kalim? Or perhaps that was exactly why; perhaps Pelan counted on the old bond between master and apprentice to grant Burris some special consideration beyond what could normally be negotiated . . .

All that would come clear in due time. I watched Clavius and the others, nodded to Amrey's pronouncements when it seemed appropriate, and begged my leave as soon as possible. When the karzdagi walked as if to take me back to the camp, I said no; I would after all take their master up on his offer of lodgings in the Emprelor. Snarling, they showed me to my rooms, adjoining Amrey's own in the topmost habitable floor of the palace—already prepared, I saw, in anticipation of my acceptance of the offer.

Two floors below me, the ambassadors lodged. I spent my evening wondering how I could arrange to meet Clavius and avoid making Murl suspicious of my motives in doing so. No plan came to mind. I slept restlessly, tossing with fitful dreams.

"I am going for a walk," I said to the karzdag outside my door. "I want to become familiar with this place."

My guardian understood me quite well, for over the days of our travels, Amrey had bespelled more of them with the gift of tongues so they could pass my words on to him when needed. Rarely did they converse with me—they had mastered only clipped, growling accents that were difficult to follow— but they herded me less, content to understand my intentions as I stated them, and to follow me about like spies, my constant shadows.

At the door today was a short, black-furred creature I called Sixtoes, for his obvious quirk. He grunted acknowledgement and stood aside as I swept from my room. He padded along a short distance behind; a few other karzdagi ghosted along behind him, escort to my escort, in case of need.

I deigned to ignore them and went my way boldly, as if I had every right to explore each nook and cranny of the Emprelor.

I could not be too obvious in the purpose of my explorations, but the thought was in the back of my mind that at some time here in Telemar, if I needed to, I might be able to slip free of Amrey's scrutiny. Therefore I must discover the layout of this half-ruined ediface, the many passageways and halls and gardens in its orderly tumble . . . the karzdagi I could tolerate, did they but let me walk and wander where I chose. They did, though no doubt report of my meanderings would be given to Amrey in due course. In the meantime, I took advantage of my limited freedom, and began methodically to trace out halls, connecting galleries, the location of small rooms and great chambers and curious cubbyholes.

So it was that I came across an enclosed courtyard, situated between audience hall and the wing that had once housed women's quarters. This was a simple courtyard no more, but a garden—a welter of untidy plants, charming in the verdant abandon with which they crowded the enclosure. It was open to the sky, a maze of untrimmed greenery interspersed with winter-bare branches, overgrown paths, uprooted flagstones— it had been the fancy of Valerian's great-aunt, a slave in the hall explained. She was a god-touched woman who had let nothing be trimmed or transplanted lest its tender plant-self be injured. A woman gutted and slain with the rest of Valerian's family on the palace steps . . .

I was taken with the retreat and immediately desired to

make it my refuge. It seemed a place I could pass the time that lay heavy on my hands, when I tired of walking the endless corridors of the Emprelor, and it had a different ambiance than the rest of the palace where I fancied I heard death cries echoing, or felt the fear and tension of people who had run hopelessly for their lives from saber-armed barbarians.

The next day, trailed distantly by the ever-present dog-men, I found my way there. I thought to compose myself in that living space, to think through my continuing exploration of the palace, wondering if and when I would be summoned to be pawn for more of Amrey's talks with the Arguentans. Such were my thoughts as I left karzdagi at the door—for they had immediately explored the boundaries of the small courtyard, to verify that I was cornered therein. Reassured that I could not leave but through the one exit, they left me to wander its small confines alone.

On this day I entered on the winding path that tucked beneath high walls, blooming succulents crowding its flagstones; walked past fragrant winter peach and sour plum trees that lined the walkways, dwarfed so their fruits in summer would be close at hand and not obscure the sky overhead. One stately nigantha tree rose above the shorter vegetation in the center of the courtyard, its long straight limbs now winter-bare. A silvery fountain splashed nearby, and that was where my steps were headed.

As I drew near, my footsteps faltered. Musical notes blended with the tinkle of waters—not in my imagination, but in reality, a tune plucked hesitantly on the strings of a lyre. And as I walked on, a voice humming a melody, the notes accompanying the hum . . . No Breo'la habit, this, but very Arguentan, and no slave here would dare amuse himself so. I came around a shrub with silvery disks for leaves, and stopped in my tracks.

A man sat upon a bench beneath the black-barked tree, a lyre cradled in one arm, green robe thrown back from shoulder for freedom of movement as he plucked out the melody. His gray head was bent down in concentration, for his playing was not very good, but it was earnest, eked out with the persistence of one who truly loves his music.

I remembered that close-shorn head when it had been black with long curling locks, the nose every bit as hooked then but more tanned, the face not pale with years of indoor studies. He sensed my eyes upon him and looked up, directly at me. We smiled at the same time. Clavius bowed his head, and I came forward, walking around the fountain to stand by his side.

"Will you join me?" he asked, gesturing to the bench.

I was happy that he did not respond to the glamour upon me as if I were superhuman—but then, he had seen it often enough when I had called it forth, of old. It did not bedazzle him as it might another.

"Gladly will I join you, old friend," I replied. My voice dropped into a conspiratorial hush, to keep words from carrying to karzdagi ears. Clavius took my cue and spoke quietly as well.

"It is good to see you." He smiled. "After all this time."

"And you, too. You are in my thoughts often, Clavius. I am glad you have prospered."

"Thanks to your training. You were a fine teacher."

A frown creased my brow. "Too fine perhaps." We both knew who I had in mind, even did I not speak his name.

"Some learn their lessons too well," he said slowly. "He was always canny, was that one. He wanted power."

"He has it, now."

He caught some nuance in my tone and cocked his head.

"You do not support him?" Curious, bird-bright eyes awaited my answer.

Now there was the question I had been dreading, and to hear it from this man's lips, of all people—he was the one person I would be very loathe to lie to. Should I hold up the illusion I was supposed to be keeping for Amrey's sake, that of sponsoring him to the Arguentan lords, of promoting his course of action and endorsing it with my presence? Or should I tell my old lover the truth of the matter?

I realized I was turning the gold band on my left wrist, turning it and staring at it without seeing it.

"You needn't answer," he said quietly.

"No. It is a fair question."

I did not know how to say more and he anticipated my words. "You do not help him of your own free will, do you?"

It was more a statement than a question. I shook my head. The feelings welling up in my breast threatened to overwhelm me—here, the first warm and friendly voice, the first creature sensitive to my situation, since this had begun. I did not trust myself to speak. Intuitively as he always had, Clavius steered the conversation away from the rocks.

"We are dismayed to see what he has done with the city." His tone was as neutral as a chat about the weather. "Innocents were slaughtered. Telemar has less than a third of its inhabitants left to it, and they are enslaved, we are told. Enslaved." I did not comment, and he continued. "Refugees are on the move in the countryside; we saw them as we came here. The carrion . . . he showed us the handiwork of his men."

His tone was no longer so neutral.

"Proud of their work, was he?" I asked.

Clavius shook his head. "No. Not proud. It was a warning, more like. A message for us to take home with us."

"Here is the fate awaits any who defy Kar Kalim," I said under my breath.

"Exactly so." He sat quiet for a moment, and then he spoke with the anguish I felt, and tried to restrain. "What has changed him so?"

I sighed. "Years, Clavius. More than two decades passed on Styrcia—"

"Styrcia?" He inhaled sharply.

"Yes. Murl fled the tower and went there. Stayed there; I thought it would be for the rest of his life. But he came back through. He has been proclaimed overlord of the Breo'la, the horsemen of the steppes, with very different notions of how to conduct himself, how to handle warfare, how to enforce cooperation . . ."

"So I see. And does he coerce you, Inya?"

A bitter smile stretched my lips and I let him take my hand, finger the bracelet at my wrist. "I am nothing, Clavius. Nothing any more. He has chained me as effectively as all these hobbled slaves about this palace."

Tears welled in my eyes. I cursed myself for being so emotional. Was it only because here, at last, was a sympathetic audience? Would it behoove me aught to say more? I would only endanger my old friend, put him in the position of knowing too much, or wanting to help me—and therein lay danger for him, great danger.

One gnarled hand reached out to rest atop my own; his fingers clasped mine in a reassuring squeeze. "We will see if we can remedy this," he said gently. "I'll say we need your council, in Burris—"

I shook my head. "I could get away, I suppose, if I needed to . . . it is more fitting that I stay nearby." I looked him full in the face. "He is sly in his scheming, Clavius, but there is no balance to him. I fear he can fulfill any whim."

A shadow passed over the thaumaturge's face as he considered what that could mean. "Does he . . . is he petulant, then?"

"Not often, or he would be a terrible danger. But he is willful, and only I can leaven that, stop him from the greater extremes."

Clavius frowned. "Tsk. Hear you, now. *You* are the one can control his choices? I think not."

"Not control. Persuade. Influence. For instance: there were places his riders would have foraged, see you, but I persuaded him that their random scavenging would alienate and anger more people, that he could not want to have vengeance-seeking militias rising up in his rear. He heeded that advice, and limited what his outriders did."

"There are still refugees in the countryside."

"There could have been more," I countered. "There are not. Here . . . here I was not able to do much, not during the taking of the city. But now he plans the rebuilding, and how he will continue . . . he discusses these things with me, he wants to secure the city in his grasp. He will do the wise thing—"

His finger came up and touched me on the lips, a terrible intimacy of old that stilled my voice in that same breath.

"It is not necessary to convince me," he said. "If you cannot vie with him power against power, you needs must work more subtly. That I understand."

Power against power! I grasped those words, anxious to change the focus from my boasting of persuasions so hard won, so few and far between . . .

"He has a wizard-stone, Clavius. A Styrcian crystal. Forces that bridge dimensions and alter worlds are at his fingertips."

"Those stories are true then?" His eyes widened.

"True enough. And he exercises great forbearance in its

use.'' My mouth spoke well of him, praised his restraint—and in the back of my mind a voice asked, *why* does he not just magically alter things to suit himself? I doubted he was truly so restrained. Were there consequences instead to the more unfettered use of the *shia*? I did not know the limits to his power, but I sensed that there *were* limits. If only I knew more!

''And what price do you pay, Lady, to stay by his side?'' Clavius' voice was sorrowful. He grasped my hands, his long fingers rubbing the bracelets at my wrists. ''What price do you pay in wearing these?''

His question made me stumble, and I looked searchingly into his eyes. Caring, concern, worry, even, were there. But no knowledge of these bracelets, I thought. He had intuited something about them, from my fidgeting—

''Have you been enjoying your talk?''

Murl spoke from beside a winter peach whose meager frosty buds tinged the air with the mildest of scents. He stared at us accusingly, hands on hips, trousered legs spread in a confrontative stance. He studied Clavius' hands on my wrists, on those cursed bands of gold and iron, and gestured over his shoulder. Karzdagi slinked forward, filling the bushes and garden space around us.

''No need to say farewell,'' he told Clavius. ''Inya will understand you must go, now. It is my turn to have a word or two with you.''

The old man stood and released my hand with a final squeeze. He looked down at me briefly, only concern for my welfare visible in his eyes. I watched him go, worry filling my own.

Amrey caught my gaze as the karzdagi led his mentor past and down the garden path. ''You may go to your rooms, now.''

I stiffened, wanting to protest, but did not dare risk angering him just before he should go on to deal with my old friend. I said nothing, gathered my skirts about me, and edged past him to leave the garden by the same route I had entered it. I heard his feet crunch on gravel as he followed me thence.

Clavius' lyre remained on the bench, forgotten by us all.

CHAPTER 13

M url dined with me that night, but I heard no word from him about his former mentor. He was preoccupied with the business of council with the Vabronye, the clan chiefs whose ignorant parochial opinions I thought he gave far too generous an ear to. In high spirits he related a debate he had had with Elyek about restoring the city—the need for it, or the lack of need as the horsemen saw it—but Kar Kalim would have his way, and the damaged port and trading center would be repaired, he asserted.

"It *must* be restored," he said, "for Telemar to remain an appealing port of call and waystop for caravans. They don't see it yet, of course, but the Breo'la will gain a reputation as peacekeepers, keeping roads free of bandits, assuring that trade is safe—"

He glimpsed the skeptical look on my face. "No, it is true. They will not raid where I tell them not to; they will tend instead to what duties I set them. Besides, they will have plenty of action to keep them satisfied after we have secured the city and set an army of occupation here."

"Occupation?" It was the first I had heard of it. "How so?"

Amrey gave a short laugh. "How do you think I turned the conquering of vills into the building of empire in Styrcia?" he asked. "Occupation. Occupation, and drafting of city

dwellers into a local militia commanded by Breo'la—oh, they
resent it, right enough, when they are drafted, but soon, soon
they come to see it as their home. When they realize they are
part of a glorious thing much greater than themselves, then
they remain in willing service. That and the fostering of their
children persuades them.''

I heard a less innocent meaning in those words. ''You take
hostages from families?'' I asked, shocked.

''We call it foster-adoption: the children go to live with the
family of a clansman of the Breo'la. In either case, it wins
the loyalties of the young and persuades the parents to serve
my rule.''

''How can your warriors possibly adopt children here? You
have no wives or sisters with your men, no families in this
camp. Will you send your young hostages all back to Styrcia?''

Amrey laughed. ''It won't stay this way for long. Women
will come through in time—family camps always follow the
armies. Or horsemen will marry where they are directed to:
Arguentan women, the propertied widows of men who resisted me. They will intermingle our bloodlines. Their children will be clan-raised as if full-blooded Breo'la, of course.''

It took an effort to absorb what I was hearing. This was
not just a plan for laying cities to waste and conquering by
the sword. I began to see the glimmerings of Murl's larger
scheme: a realignment of power, of family ties, of inheritance
and property, changes in governance—all the things that could
wrest the local culture so out of shape that people, reeling
from the upheaval of war, would willingly cleave to his new
regime because it offered each person a niche and reassuring
permanence.

''How do you plan to govern a city-state,'' I asked skeptically, "when your only tool is a collection of wild horse warriors?"

He smiled wryly. "Who do you think has come with me on this venture into Astareth? It is not the men who rule lands for me at home. It is their sons and brothers, those younger tribesmen of promise who look to make their fortune, who want lands and responsibilities even if they must claim them in a new world. I have hundreds of men worth rewarding with overlordship of a town, a city. Some will rule a city-state for me. When the rest of my forces are here, I will have enough to garrison every city we take."

That statement astounded me. "How so? Do you plan to war on all the city-states?"

"That won't be necessary." He laughed. "One at a time, they shall come under my sway. And when all is said and done, I will have gobbled up the Salt Coast autarchs, and turned Arguenta into a domain of my own."

"And then for amusement you'll look farther afield?" It was said half sarcastically, but he did not answer it that way.

"I very well may. The rest of Drakmil awaits, beyond the Salt Coast."

"You will have bitter fighting on your hands if you try to beat the city-states into submission," I cautioned him.

The look in his blue eyes was cold. "You have no idea what conquered men will do when your boot is upon their neck. We keep no prisoners, you see. We ransom no one back to their family. To oppose me is to perish. After a time, people see the truth of this statement, and so come willingly into the fold."

I frowned at his confidence and overstatement. "Not all people are sheep."

"Enough are, that most others follow." His statement was

arrogant; his tone factual. "Those who do not—well, my horsemen need something to sharpen their talons against."

Said with all sincerity, and a light-handed attitude towards the cruelty thus engendered. My appetite fled, and I made do with shallow chat for the rest of our conversation.

As soon as he was done, I pled tiredness and went early to bed, the better to escape his company for a time, and think on what I had just learned this evening.

Kar Kalim did not only have ambition. He had a plan and a method that had been proven to work, and the wherewithal to put it into effect. When would he start to threaten the other city-states of the Coast? How could I possibly sway him from this path? Did I think him a fair and evenhanded ruler, I would not be so concerned for the consequences of his ambition. But I had seen him proven otherwise by his own actions, and despaired of finding a way to steer him from this course.

I realized in a moment of brutal self-honesty that I was failing to do the thing that was my only reason for staying close to him: to mitigate his ambitions, to keep him from running roughshod over the people who could and would be powerless before him, did he choose to wield the force of his *shia*. Now it seemed as if the wizard-stone hardly mattered, for he controlled enough temporal might that he could work his will through flesh and blood, and did not need the power to move worlds in order to effect great change in this one.

Disheartened, I fell into a heavy sleep, dark with mordant spirits and uncomfortable feelings of helplessness. I dreamt of cities burning, sackings, rape, and looting . . . was it precognitive, as my dreams often were, or did I look into another time and place, see a shadow of a possible future or present? I could not tell. In my compelling vision, I was helping to direct the occupation of a city—

"Inya."

I am never called by name in my dreams, and that word intruded greatly.

"Inya." A hand gently shook my shoulder, a shoulder that became present in dream as part of my body image, giving way to body sense where I lay warm beneath the covers, aware of shoulder, of arm. Of a cool hand resting so lightly against my skin.

"Lady."

That voice again, breathing my name, hushed with tension. I recognized it, and forced my eyes open, leaden with the urgency of sleep and the visions that beckoned there.

Lesseth.

I thought the name, not yet returned enough to my body to speak it. I felt his ghostly finger on my lips and then I was fully awake, eyes wide, but heeding his caution not to talk. I felt him slip into mental rapport with me and I followed suit, blending with him into that near dreamlike space where the occasional word was spoken and feelings were shared intuitively from mind to mind.

You came! Joy radiated from my being.

It was difficult. Thankfully the palace wards are incomplete, where the earth energies have damaged them.

There was a quake . . .

I see its traces in the ether. No ordinary earth event, that.

No. But you are here now.

I dare not stay long; there are entities near. Sniffers. Beast-like scavengers that patrol—

I felt his distress. *From Amrey?*

I can't tell. From him, or here from earlier safeguards. Something prowls looking for semimaterial presences like my own. Let me lose no more time, but share what has happened.

We sank deeper into rapport and I saw through his eyes, shared through his mind, what had transpired in his time away.

He had left me on a long journey west that took him over the crumbling hills of the Varia-lun, terrain impossible for men to traverse on foot but of little hazard to Lesseth in his unfleshly state. Thence across the gorges of the Omerian heights, and forging the waters of the Greganios with difficulty—not for the rush of liquid that made passage treacherous, but for the depth and flow of elemental forces that contest a spirit of Lesseth's nature. On to the floating bridge at Benari where it was possible to cross the headwaters of the Nin, thence into the great rainforest of the central valleys, folded ridge upon ridge, each dense with thick undergrowth, finally giving unto the elevated plateaus where Tor Mak nestled high-turreted and serene.

Cendurhil and his kinfolk in Tor Mak were the long-lived, innately magic-wielding descendents of the Derenestu—refugees from ancient, forgotten wars in their long-perished homeland across the sea. Old wisdom and nature magic flourished in that city, an emerald gem ensconced amid trackless forest. Halted at the walls by wardings upon the city, Lesseth had petitioned for audience with Cendurhil. My name secured what he requested, and then words with others who also knew me from our monthly vigils.

Assured of my companion's identity by proofs he could have only from myself, Lesseth conferred with my allies and friends, and told them all that had transpired at Moontooth.

They heard his words grimly. Never had they expected such news: that one came bearing a legendary artifact; that he fancied himself a conqueror and planned to extend his power into our world. It would be a laughable pretension were not the attributes of Styrcian crystals well known to the wizards of

Tor Mak. They knew better than any other in the world, for
they had knowledge spanning eons and dimensions. Once long
ago a founder of Tor Mak had had such a wizard-stone to
use, before she had been lost on journeys between the worlds.

They listened to Lesseth's warnings, and took his words to
heart.

"Here is what we will do," said Cendurhil. "First, you
must give these cautions to R'Inyalushni d'aal . . ." He and
Liuthwe, High Lorekeeper, related what warnings they had to
give about the *shian*.

It was in keeping with what I already knew or surmised:
indeed, the crystals warped the fabric of time and space; they
stressed the elements, and shifted the course of natural forces.
Then Liuthwe's knowledge gave me new insights. Like a
compass needle near a lodestone, a *shia*'s natural attraction
for magical forces directed it towards pockets of mana—the
largest or closest one first—and from there absorbed the energy needed to fuel the causality we call magic.

Mana is not entirely of the physical sphere, although it is
linked to material places and elemental forces. It radiates from
the physical into the dimensions nearby, and thus is suscep-
tible to the nonmaterial influences of a *shia*. A wizard-stone
worked its effects by draining pockets of primal energy from
here and there, randomly—usually someplace close, geo-
graphically speaking, to where the magic is wielded, but no
guarantee or strict necessity for that, either—and therein lay
the rub. Abrupt depletion of mana upset balances of energy,
of nature, of elements, and resulted in unpredictable manifestations and reactions on the physical sphere.

A drought might be spawned somewhere, Liuthwe explained, because elsewhere a wizard-stone was used to create
rainfall. The counterreaction need not be related to the magic
invoked, either: the manifestation of a fortress upon a head-

land could result in a devastating hurricane near or far away, or cause a river to flow with blood instead of water.

Is there no way to correlate use and consequences? I asked Lesseth.

There is not, he replied, *or at least the Derenestu have not found a way.*

This was the genesis of the tales of curses and unforeseen results of using a Styrcian crystal. Its unpredictable side effects were a reality. It was said, too, that one who wielded a wizard-stone risked physical consequences as well: aging, deafness, alteration of physical or mental capabilities . . . Cendurhil related the story of a sorceror said to have gone instantly lame in both legs, withered to the bone when he used a *shia* to raise a famine amongst his enemies.

Styrcian crystals were to be used with the greatest of caution. Even then, it was only a matter of time, it seemed, until some terrible price would be paid by the user.

Perhaps Murl knew this already, I considered. He seemed cautious in his use of the crystal. Or perhaps he saw only the obvious side effects and had not yet faced a true reckoning.

There is more, Lesseth added, *about the stones themselves.* The crystals attuned only to one user, he had been told. It sounded as though my original theory was correct: one fell into accord with the stone in the same meditative manner that one built rapport with elementals or anything one desired attunement with. Thereafter, only one *shia* could be used at a time, and only by the person it was attuned to.

Why only one? I asked.

Derenestu lore records only that it is unsafe to do otherwise. It does not say precisely why. He shrugged, and I felt his wry smile in the dark. *I hope that is helpful enough, Lady. At least now I know more about these crystals than ever I had wanted to!*

I am sure you do. I collected my thoughts for a moment, then asked, *Cendurhil sounded concerned enough about Kar Kalim's ambitions. What do the Derenestu commit to do against him?*

The hesitation in his voice warned me I would not like what I heard. *For now—vigilance only, Lady. The wizards of Tor Mak will watch and observe, see if Murl Amrey's grasp equals his reach. But they will prepare to step into action against him, if it becomes necessary.*

Oh? I scarce credited what I heard. *Were they not alarmed to hear of the fate of Moontooth?*

Greatly so. Still . . . this danger is not on their doorstep.

I snorted. *And what would make engagement seem necessary to them, in their safe and distant haven? Will they wait until Tor Mak itself is threatened?*

He said nothing and I could guess that answer for myself. *True it is that the Derenestu have no responsibility to the Salt Coast,* I admitted, *and it is too late to aid me, a lone ally already come under his apparent control. But if all Arguenta comes under the conqueror's fist, then will Tor Mak have a more difficult time of it if he sets his sights inland. They are the source of much of the wealth that comes down the Nin and the Sevian from the heart of Drakmil. Does Cendurhil think they will be safe from his ambitions?*

Lesseth shrugged. *They do not wish to be overextended, I think. We are after all so far from Tor Mak. For them to go to war against Kar Kalim, or to threaten with a force on his borders, would require a massive arming and calling in of alliances throughout the heartland. And then they would have to wrestle with the logistics of a distant war . . .*

So Cendurhil thought it was not yet time to rattle sword against shield. Surely it was not a move to make in jest or halfheartedly; that much I could agree with. I hoped that when he did see the need, he would not bide until it was too late to mobilize response to Kar Kalim. I had waited with my guard down, and now I was Amrey's pet for all my trouble. The thought turned my stomach sour. Lesseth sensed my disgruntlement and anger.

What will you do now? he asked, a question I was ill prepared to answer.

I sighed and moved restlessly in bed. *I wish I could go to Styrcia . . .*

Why? he asked, gently ribbing me. *Do you hope to meet more of his loyal followers?*

No. I scowled, and punched at him where an arm would be were he more solid. *I wish I could understand better why he acts as he does, what drives him. What he wants. What he knows about the crystal. If he thought it was dangerous, surely he wouldn't use it freely, don't you think?*

Maybe he sees the power of it as worth the risk.

Maybe he doesn't appreciate the risk.

That is all beside the point. You haven't the run of the tower any more, Lady. I went there first, looking for you.

Then I heard of his journey back from Tor Mak. No, he had not met Una along the way; my heart twinged at that, for I had hoped somehow that serendipity would put them in each other's path. He had returned directly to Moontooth and been astonished at the size of the army that had gathered there during his absence. The tower was barred to him, sealed and protected by Amrey's wizard-stone workings. The Breo'la who massed outside were preparing to join Kar Kalim in the southwest, while the garrison force terrorized the surrounding hills and the karzdagi ran amok in upper Caronne.

Moontooth was no longer a place associated with a consort of the night and the heavens, he told me reluctantly. It had become synonymous with fear and terrible things that stalked the daylight hours as boldly as the night. *How so?* I asked. He related how, incorporeal, he had paced dog-men as they hunted deer, then came across the trail of a herd of goats. So easily were they tempted astray, and ran down the scent that promised greater sport. They scattered the animals and then hunted the two youths who had tended their family's herd, harrying them back and forth across mountain meadows like a pack of wolves until exhaustion staggered the boys' steps and they could run no more. The older of the two dropped to his knees pleading for their lives, his arms outstretched in surrender and supplication. Not even slowing to hear his words, the karzdagi were upon him in a flurry of snarls and ripping fangs. His brother met the same fate moments later. The goats and deer were unscathed, for the dog-men hunted as much for bloodlust as for need. This incident was the least of many, many alike. Humans around Moontooth were deserting the area, even as karzdagi ranged ever wider in search of sport and food.

Lesseth had been glad to leave, gladder still I was no longer there—although my absence was barely noted by the countryfolk. People spoke the name Dark Lady with a new meaning, a more sinister inference than before.

I liked that even less, that Amrey's show of me as ally had been so readily accepted by the popular mind that I was now linked to the outrages of his soldiery and his unchecked bestial minions.

I felt Lesseth's hand upon my arm, again, his fingers squeezing there. *The sniffers,* he said. *Something comes. I dare not linger.*

Return tomorrow, I bade him.

I will, he agreed, *if I can*—then he faded beyond reach of my senses.

I lay there, my heart beating fast with sympathetic panic

on his behalf. The room was dark, still. There was no other-worldly tension, no psychic hounds that I could detect, for what little that meant. I huddled beneath the covers, sense-blind and hating my ignorance, praying for the safety of my friend, and thinking of all he had told me. Cendurhil would take no bold action, and my heart was anguished for that, for all my instincts told me that to move too slowly would be to move too late. And from here there was no way to affect his decision in distant Tor Mak. The lore I had been given about the *shian* and their properties and pitfalls seemed like it should be useful, but it swirled in my head as so much disconnected minutia that would not gel into sense or form. This was some-thing to sleep on, to consider with a fresh and rested mind.

I was struggling back towards hard-won sleep when Amrey joined me in bed. His touch on my thigh merely woke me, but his words stabbed me to the heart and brought me fully alert.

"Clavius Mericus is a prideful man," he muttered in a tone half angry, half petulant. "He gives offense too readily."

"What?"

"He has insulted Elyek, who has declared blood feud. They will fight to the death in the morning, to see who has the right of the matter."

As if it were a personal exorcism he must make that con-fession to me, before taking his pleasure. I reeled from his words, and when I did not respond to his touch, he sensed the depth of my disturbance. For once he hesitated and let me be.

Murl's heavy breathing carried me into the dawn, counter-point to plots that would not give me peace. Sleep eluded me, replaced by a slow-simmering anger that heated me with a steady fire deep inside.

*　*　*

By morning I was resolved on what I must do. For the first time since he had persuaded me to bow to his will, I confronted Murl Amrey.

"Call off this farce you have planned for today," I told him. "Clavius' death serves you naught."

He turned to me in the half-light, naked and sitting on the edge of the bed, not yet garbed by the Telemaran body-servants who waited outside our chambers. His form was hard-muscled, more scarred than one would have expected in a student of the arcane arts—the legacy of his decades amongst the horse tribes of Styrcia.

"I cannot stop Elyek," he said. "There is honor to be satisfied. And surely you underestimate Clavius. He is a master thaumaturge; he is not defenseless."

I pulled on a dressing robe of red lambswool, my black hair long and loose about my shoulders, considering how to play this. Surely diplomatic Clavius had given no offense worth blood-feud to a steppes warrior. This was a machination of Amrey's, I had no doubt, and as such, he could halt it if he would.

"He is old and he is not a warrior," I countered. "The Breo'la way of fighting is not one he will be even matched in."

A sound that could have been a snort passed Murl's red-bearded lips. "He should have considered that when he plotted with you in the garden yesterday, Lady."

Ah. There was the truth of it, the thing that rankled. He stood and moved towards the door where the slaves waited beyond.

I saw there was no appealing to fairness with him, who let his rancorous imagination condemn a friend to death. With that observation my last hope for sympathetic compromise died. Let me speak a language then that he *did* understand, if compassion was not in his vocabulary.

"If you kill Clavius," I said flatly, "I will desert you in open council. The Salt Coast emmissaries will see you no longer have my support."

He halted in midstride, right hand curling into a fist, and turned slowly on one heel to face me. "You do not want to defy me, Inya. Others will pay the price."

"Others pay the price regardless. What point do you seek to make with Clavius?" The temper I had felt asimmer all night began to bubble to the surface. "You suspect him of plotting with me? For what? My freedom?"

His brows drew together, giving him a sulky look. "I heard enough of your talk in the garden."

"Then you heard exactly nothing. Or you fancy what you want to hear." I spat the words scornfully and my disdain ignited his anger as well. His other hand clenched and he took a step towards me.

"You touched him in a way he'll never forget." His voice was low, menacing. "Rarely did he speak of you, his well-kept secret clutched close to his heart back in Burris, but I saw that light in his eye and thought him greatly inspired by his master in magic, when I thought you were a 'he.' Later I recognized what it must be. Love." He sneered the word. "Clavius Mericus has loved you all his life, Lady of Moon-tooth. You discarded him and ignored him; he never married, you know, all these years. And now you croon and lament to him, lure him by his feelings to render you aid, though how you think he could really help you is beyond me, or why he even should . . ."

I listened, astonished. His accusations were based only on speculation, but how could he know so much of the intimate life of his mentor? By his own account he had never been

that close to his master in arcane studies, not on a personal
level. And my former lover and I had had our understandings.
I had not shut him out, exactly; it had been mutual agreement
that he leave, but we had remained close in heart across all
these many years.

Then I realized what I was hearing. This was not Clavius
he was speaking of, not entirely: it was himself. And finally
I saw what had pushed Murl into this manner of dealing with
the ambassador from Burris. I recalled the magical exercises
some years before, the visualization of power, of green, an
exercise gone awry that had near drowned me in his posses-
sive jealousy at the same time that part of me enjoyed being
coveted in such a passionate manner . . . It was that same jealousy now, unfettered by wisdom, enabled by the power to
satisfy any whim, that threatened to bereave Clavius of his
life. In some one-sided way Murl loved me, and he was dis-
posing of a rival, a man he knew without a doubt still held
some portion of my affections.

And here I had cast down the gauntlet and made an ultimatum. If he was prepared before to lash out at me because
of my supposed lover and ally, he was ready now to punish
also for the threat of withdrawing my public support. My defiance had compounded my apparent sins in his eyes, those
blue eyes afire now with that dangerous anger I had seen
before. It was a cold rage that let him raise his hand to me or
order the gutting of children in Telemar streets . . . whatever
served his purpose and his lust for vengeance in the moment.

He stepped closer, and I caught myself backing out of his
range. But no: I would not retreat before this onslaught. He
would not find me so easily cowed this time.

"Leave these threats, Murl."

"You think I threaten?" That dangerous glare, torso leaning into a menacing posture—

A doubt stirred about the right tone to take with him. Try again . . .

"I need never see Clavius again," I said. "Send him away. He is no threat to you. I see where my interests lie quite clearly: they are not with a shriveled old man, but with you, by your side. You say you want to build empire—build it, then! Expand your domain, from the Sevian to northernmost Carack, across all of Drakmil! I'll help you where I can, or stay in Moontooth as a Guardian ought. I have no need for petty mages and petty schemes."

I spoke boldly, chin up. The glamour he put on me in public was absent, and I stood before him only as myself, in disarray, shoulders straight and drawn up with all the pride and certainty and regality I could muster before him. I spoke convincingly and I lied. I lied a lie that I made myself believe in that moment, lest he spellcast for truth, lest he quiz me. He must believe. I saw how he perceived me and I spun that image into a gossamer falsehood: the pretense that I scorned Clavius, discarded of old. That I did not care for his fate or the fate of other lesser creatures, but looked instead to my own interests.

In his egotism and power Murl could have no doubt where that interest lay.

He halted before me, lip curled, nostrils flared. His fist hung in the air, arm half extended, forgotten in the midst of its threatening motion. I stared at him steady, our eyes riveted in challenge of wills . . .

I prayed the gods he would believe me.

"Clavius and people like him are worms beneath your feet, Kar Kalim. Spend no energy on them. I will not. You should not."

He bristled at my wording, and a half step put his face into mine. "Don't tell me what to do." His hand lashed out and

a slap left my ears ringing. I dropped my eyes from his, looking more cowed than I felt but taking this moment to soften
the confrontative stance I had assumed. "If I say Clavius dies
today, then it is so."

I blinked, my eyes moist with tears. They came from the
sting of his blow, not from emotions, but I thought he could
not tell the difference to look at me. "Spare him," I said
softly, "and dismiss him. I will do more amongst the Arguentans to further your interests."

He stared at me, then stared me down. Only after I dropped
my eyes again did he relax, stand back a bit. "We'll see. I'll
think what further use you can be to me. Stay here until I
have you fetched."

I ducked my head in acknowledgement and he left me, face
bruised, ears still ringing, confined for the day to the privacy
of my chambers. By time he summoned me to a dinner of
state, and had briefed me on what I would say and how I
would support him, I realized I had won a battle of sorts. He
saw I could work for him aggressively, instead of being only
a silent endorsement. Now, when he wished to widen his
grasp, was the time to use me thus. And so Clavius Mericus
sat with soul and body intact amidst the other ambassadors at
table. I studied him clandestinely from behind my ceremonial
mask, and studied Kar Kalim as well.

I had had long enough to contemplate the right course of
action in this timeless day, when I did not know if my old
lover lived or died, did not know if or how or when Amrey
would use me, or not use me, to further his cause. In all that
time, all that indecision, the necessary thing had come clear
to me.

I had vowed there would be no more Corwins—and now,
no more coercion. I could not stand that Clavius or others
might fall victim to Amrey's malicious demonstrations of

power, and the means he planned to use to achieve his goal
of empire . . . I could not work towards that end, either. Yet
did I not, innocents would perish.

The solution was one that a night and day of soul searching
showed me I had in my heart to effect. Murl Amrey must die,
and I must be the one to kill him.

CHAPTER 14

A tyrant's death is easier conceived of than executed. Plan after plan had gone through my mind, each considered and dismissed: poison—too slow, and me without the wherewithal to secure a certain death in that manner. An attack by night, when he slept in bed—tempting, for I had access, but he had wardings about his person. Should I be caught out and fail, then it would be my own death that I ensured. An ally to attack him unexpectedly—that held a hope of success, but such a creature there was none . . .

Although there was Lesseth. Unexpected, hard to detect, with abilities surpassing that of mortal flesh: he was a likely candidate, but to ask him to undergo such risk on an uncertain venture—that I could not do. As it was we concealed his presence with great difficulty, trusting to his other-senses and intuition to avoid the safeguards that might betray him, constraining his contact with me to times when Murl was distant, or the rare occasions when I was free to wander outside the Emprelor. He remained a friend of my dreams and near-sleep state, much in the way we had first become acquainted, but of this new and morbid ambition of mine I told him nothing. I was left only with the intention, and no certain means to fulfill it. My will, however, did not flag. I grasped that intention close and set about to play my role as consort and aid:

near in person but distant in heart, ever alert to an opportunity to end Amrey's unwanted rule once and for all.

Of necessity I appeared to close ranks with my captor, and turned from Clavius when he would have bespoken me chance-met in the halls. It wrenched my heart to shun him, but fly-spies and other clandestine means were common tools to Amrey, and I could not risk being suspected of duplicity by him.

The last time I heard Clavius call my name, I walked coldly away from him, Sixtoes and other karzdagi in my escort pausing to snarl and posture as if he were a stray dog they could chase back home. His voice was silenced by their threats. The next I heard news of him he had departed Telemar, carrying word of Kar Kalim's victory to the northeastern city-states and relaying formal invitation to a new session of the Autarchs' Council. Amrey's thin pretense to remove the thaumaturge from his presence nevertheless served a purpose: soon he would host his Salt Coast allies in a forum that dangled commerce in their grasp. I saw by the ambassadors' expressions in court that the bait was well received. The Arguentan lords would see this as the opening they had so long sought in Telemar's stranglehold upon trade.

I saw that Amrey's purpose was somewhat other.

The strife between Elyek and Clavius, fabricated and easily diffused by Kar Kalim, had soured the atmosphere between ambassadors and the Breo'la. The men of the Salt Coast were prideful enough, but here at last they were outmatched by a people even more touchy, more haughty, and scornful of ways not their own. Swaggering steppes riders despised the weakness of men who huddled in shelters of stone and terra-cotta tiles, while the urbane townsmen of Arguenta sniffed at their unwashed allies and began to wonder what sort of unruly plague they had invited in among themselves.

There was nothing for it but to use this time to worm closer
to Amrey, to let him see his lust for power reflected in my
own actions and so believe me to be of like mind. It pained
me to behave so before people I had known through generations and aided in my own way for just as long, but my goal
dictated my actions. I moved through those days in Telemar
seemingly swept from one inevitable step to the next. As autarchs from various city-states gathered, I talked and persuaded where I must, cajoled or threatened subtly where it
seemed needful, volunteered helpful advice that furthered Kar
Kalim's negotiations. More and more I was seen to be his
aide—even, Arguentans whispered, his willing puppet. The
Breo'la did not accept me, the Arguentans began to avoid me.
Except for Murl, I was more alone than ever before. And in
the midst of that isolation, his machinations came clear to me.

His game was simple: he brought the autarchs to him and
revealed that he had the wealth of Telemar firmly in his grasp.
That he was, in effect, the new Valerian, just as jealous of the
port city's resources, just as willing to keep the Salt Coast on
a starveling diet of trade, did they not bow to his wishes.

Those wishes were but a few simple things, he claimed,
needful for continuing peace. Payment of tribute was one.
Fostering of noble children, another. The marriage of daughters and widows to his clan chiefs and leading warriors. There
were more such terms, each one equally insulting to free men
of differing allegiances no matter how diplomatically coached.
Though they were not under his physical control, Kar Kalim
made it clear that the city-states must adhere to the same requirements he levied upon Telemar, or they would suffer his
displeasure.

Autarchs who had journied post-haste to Council, eager to
claim their share of trade and riches, heard these demands
with disbelief. The price for Telemar's cooperation was too

high, and they stormed from the marbled halls of the Autarchs' Palace in angry protest. Kar Kalim was an upstart, an arrogant puppy who thought to dictate terms to his allies. The autarchs gathered their escorts to them and prepared to leave the city before Kar Kalim could attempt to compel their obedience.

I, too, wondered at Amrey's extreme demands flamboyantly delivered. Did he truly desire to alienate the city-states who could have been his allies? I asked him.

"Allies!" he exclaimed, astonished. "What need have I of allies? Of course they are offended! Now they have offered me insult and defiance in return, and I have the excuse I need to set myself against them one by one. There will be no autarchs reigning on the Salt Coast, except those who have bowed their head to my yoke."

The pirate navy of Ursbach picked exactly that juncture to fill the harbor with their sails. Until their intentions became clear the city gates were sealed, trapping Arguentan lords and ambassadors within. Amrey and I watched the blood-red sails from the Emprelor's highest tower; from the guarded smile on his face, I would have said that he had much to do with the timing of this arrival. As to the how and when of it, the *shia* about his neck and his own adept powers were all the explanation I needed to imagine how it had come to pass.

The fleet, we would learn, had sailed in response to Valerian's call for aid when Telemar had first been set upon by the Breo'la hordes. As they entered the deep water harbor at the mouth of the Sevian, the foreign ships came in full sight of the silver-shot red-and-black banners that crested the city's high walls. Telemar had a new master, and the Ursbachi vessels stood ready for action in these once-friendly waters. Troop transports were left safely out to sea until the situation

could be assessed, while sea wizards and firecasters and banks
of galley slaves prepared for quick maneuvers that might be
called for inside the harbor breakwater.

Yet they met no unwelcome from the city. The catapults
lay restrained; Breo'la outside the walls rode down to the
waterfront and the black pebbled beaches, not to oppose a
landing but to gain a better view of the novelty of military
ships, far larger than the fishing and coastal traders that
hugged the stone quays. Eventually messengers passed from
Emprelor to flagship and back again, and in due course the
commander of the fleet, Captain-General Mehlimet, agreed to
come ashore.

That evening Kar Kalim held private audience with Mehlimet, a tall, well-fed man with oiled brown curls and beard
in graying ringlets, dressed in the spare dark finery of that
land's seafaring nobility. He was a high lord of the Cerulean
Court, with a cold unblinking gaze that belied his self-
indulgent exterior. He held strategic command over trade and
shipping in the Ursbach alliance with Telemar. It was Lord
Mehlimet who decided if and when Ursbachi hulls would aid
land-based military actions, or engage in sea battles under the
admirals beneath him.

He was met with ceremony and guested in a manner half
Breo'lan, half Arguentan, with a goat's head and best haunch
meat served on a bed of spiced barley, the barbaric feast
washed down with good red Edaeni wine. Afterwards we retired to a private audience chamber where more serious matters could be spoken of. He remarked on the hospitality in his
droll, lilting accent. "I had not expected a warm welcome
from Valerian's . . . successor." The word was weighted and
carefully chosen. Kar Kalim smiled, savoring the term before
repeating it himself.

"Successor, indeed." He lounged in the coral- and gold-bossed autarch's chair, one step higher than where I stood waiting court upon him. "I see no reason why things need change in our partnership with Ursbach. I've read the agreements, and will renew them with you this very night if you like, signed by my own hand."

The offer took the captain-general by surprise, but he did not pause long. "Assurances of good faith are welcome. However . . . It could be that our alliance with Telemar has outgrown its usefulness."

"Because you see little evidence of trade at dockside, except for the minimum to feed the city?" Kar Kalim laughed. "Or because the city is ragged and looks like a refugee camp?" Mehlimet blinked; the statements were unvarnished truths, not the diplomatic euphemisms he was used to hearing. "Or do you think you stand to gain more profit by open raiding along our coast?" That was the Ursbach tactic of old, and we all knew it.

The Ursbach lord shuffled, and patted the lace at his wrist affectedly upon his lips. "We are not at war with Arguenta—"

"You have never needed that excuse before." Kar Kalim leaned forward, his tunic of silver-threaded black velvet stark against the salmon red of the coral. "I give you a simple offer, Lord Mehlimet. Continue in trade alliance with Telemar, carry our goods, and aid us in war. You'll be paid outright for your trouble, and your men keep half the booty from the cities they help take."

The Ursbachi cocked his head, ringlets shaking, as if he had heard amiss. He repeated more slowly, "We are not at war with Arguenta . . ."

Kar Kalim quirked a lip. "Nor am I. Yet. But I have made certain demands, and those who resist—well, a lesson will need to be brought home to them. You have troops to hand."

"Ursbachi soldiery serves the Cerulean Court. They have no loyalty to outlanders."

"Other than what you command, my lord. I mentioned compensation for your trouble." He waved a hand; two beast-men came hunched to the foot of the dais, carrying a weighty chest between them. Crookfang stepped forward and opened the lid. I did not need to see the riches therein; the greed that lit in Mehlimet's eyes was mirror enough. He looked up at Kar Kalim, for all his own worldly wealth yet agog at the treasure before him. "That is yours now," Amrey said, "in earnest of good faith. More will come later, according to the terms you had stipulated with my predecessor. I will need your transports to stand ready off the coast of Mardevis a few days hence. Are you agreed?"

Crookfang shut the lid, and the Ursbachi commander looked contentedly at the chest before his expression became veiled once again. "We were able to come to an understanding with Telemar before," he said. "I am gladdened to see such a thing is possible under her new sovereign as well. I see no reason to alter the terms of our agreement and naturally, if Telemar has need of military support, we stand ready to offer it. In exchange for certain considerations, of course."

"Of course." Kar Kalim stood; I followed his lead down the steps of the dais. "Then let us confer, and we shall see how Ursbach may be of assistance."

The captain-general returned to his flagship, and Kar Kalim ordered the gates of Telemar cast open. Ships were permitted into the inner harbor, and the penned autarchs allowed to depart if they desired.

"Why let these lordlings go from the city," I asked, "if you plan to set yourself upon them anyway? Those who would oppose you are all gathered here conveniently within your reach.'' Not that I wished to urge him to such extremes, but I wanted to understand his reasoning in releasing the very men who defied him and soon, no doubt, would openly challenge him.

"They will not all oppose me," he said confidently. "The weak ones will look to the stronger to set the tone. I need only take those stronger ones down, in order to bring the rest into line. It is worth my while to let them all return home. Let them live anxious about my intentions and poised for disaster; let them remember the deaths of innocents here because I was defied. The Breo'la will welcome open conflict with the more belligerent of these autarchs. The others who concede in the end will have their resources and their emotions strained, in waiting to see what fate I mete out to them. They will come all the more readily to hand when the time is right.''

As he spoke, so it proved to be. Mardevis was the first to fall to Kar Kalim's grasp, the closest northeastern neighbor, most jealous of the trade once shared, now monopolized by Telemar. Leodoric of Mardevis was the first to leave the Autarchs' Palace, but even in his haste to strike homewards, he could not surpass the speed of the seaborne Ursbachi. No sooner did he arrive than he found his city invested by Telemar's allies, himself denied access to his stronghold by the foreign troops that had landed outside his walls. Behind him, a swift-riding vanguard of the Breo'la came to reinforce the siege and caught Leodoric not far from the coast road when he attempted to flee across marshlands with his loyal retainers.

Kar Kalim joined them through a *shia*-forged rift, appearing in his horsemen's encampment as Leodoric absorbed the grim truth that his city was besieged and himself prisoner of his enemies.

I remembered him from the Council, a dark-browed man, broad of shoulder, loud in conversation, ready to fight. He was one who would be quite ready to fling imprudent challenges in the teeth of the Lord of Telemar.

"He was an obstreperous little man," Amrey told me later, "given to bluster. 'Combined, we are your match.' He threatened me, as if the city-states would fall so readily to arms behind him! So I held him with a spell and spoke reason to him. I would annex Mardevis, marry his daughter to Perevya, a noble Vabron amongst the horse tribes. He protested that she is already married; I assured him she would be a widow soon enough, did she not immediately divorce. Then he whined about their sovereignty, how no outsider had ever held the throne of Mardevis, how such a disgrace would not happen in his time. He did not wish to compromise, that was clear."

"But now you are in possession of the city. How did you convince him—?"

"I had him killed and sent his head to his son, who led the city's defense in his absence. That disheartened them, and when I threatened to level the walls as I had at Telemar, they surrendered." He smirked. "The boy is no leader of men, but he did not defy me either and so he kept his head. Leodoric's family is out of the palace now, and their children held in Telemar as surety for their good behavior. Perevya is installed as governor with his new wife by his side."

I wondered at his tactics. Was it all to be so simple, then? Would there be no battle, no resistance, but one city-state after another falling into his hands like overripe fruit from the vine?

"Men who are surprised lose their will to fight, do you see," he told me. "We invested their city by sea and land in the night, so they awoke to the enemy outside their walls. We took their leader on the road. They would have engaged, but leadership in the city was indecisive and inexperienced—they had not expected any real conflict to come knocking upon their doors, even though they were ready to challenge me in any number of ways elsewhere. It won't always be so easy, but that is well, too: the Breo'la are eager for a better test of their battle prowess than Mardevis proved to be.''

So kindled a fire that grew into an inferno, and threatened to sweep all before it. Surprise had carried the day in Mardevis. Others were more prepared to defend themselves, but my presence at Kar Kalim's side offered the hope of peaceful compromise. This empty promise held reluctant combatants in check long enough for the Breo'la to gain the upper hand. Amrey's tactics ranged from kind and cajoling to brutal and destructive: one city-state was approached as earnest ally, told how wise it would be to cede their territories to Kar Kalim's protection. Another city-state he would threaten, letting his horsemen ravage the countryside before marshaling their barbaric forces on the doorstep of the place he wished to subdue. To each alike, Kar Kalim would sooner or later deliver his ultimatum: surrender and keep your lives, or defy me and die.

For numbers and mobility and fierceness in battle, the Breo'la horde was unsurpassed. Militia that was prepared to face other foot-soldiers in regimented battle lines were overawed by the wild, daredevil horsemen of Styrcia. City walls were little protection, for Kar Kalim's magic cracked their defenses with brute force if Breo'la failed to take the gates by stealth and surprise. Aided by the transports of the Ursbachi navy, landing at unpredictable times and places and reinforced by seaborne infantry as well, steppe riders proved their superiority against the sturdy but outmatched soldiery of Arguenta.

Egrania did not take the conqueror to heart, and was razed to the ground. Singut remained intact but not a living soul was left in her streets—just heaps of skulls on every street corner and corpses left for scavengers outside the gates. The rest of Kar Kalim's army marched from Moontooth, taking Caronne with a small party that seized the gates, backed by the persuasive argument of thirty-thousand horsetroops poised to enter the city. City-states once neutral in the disagreement with Telemar stirred uneasily at the pleadings of their neighbors, then succumbed one by one to Kar Kalim's barbarian hordes and seafaring allies. Ambassadors who had spoken openly of their cities' defenses now rued that they had embraced the Styrcians, fearing—rightly so—that they had said too much that was too revealing in moments of erstwhile friendship.

Belatedly the more distant city-states mustered in their own defense, going beyond the levy of militia to the mobilization of aristocrats and their retainers and the hiring of mercenary forces. It was too little, too late: Rajpor and Gervaes surrendered, were garrisoned, were governed by Breo'la in the same week. Caethon of Stavlia raised the greatest resistance, marching into the field with an army of volunteers and mountain levies, only to be crushed by a hurricane loosed magically over land. The storm destroyed their encampment and swept men and horses away with flood waters until the sodden wreck that was left of Caethon's army was easily slaughtered by the sabers of the Styrcians.

When it seemed I could awe, persuade or intimidate, Kar Kalim brought me forth, made me a part of negotiations or ultimatums, or even the centerpiece of a court reception, where my presence would affect the attitudes of locals. Otherwise I was left behind, in his tent or in Telemar, for my scruples would come to the fore now and then and needle him so that he would want me out of sight for a time.

The longer I saw him wage war, the more outraged I became, and finally dared to revile his actions. The worst was his treatment of cities that had resisted him, where he squelched future resistance by killing all the men and any boys too tall to walk upright beneath a table. Bereft of their men and breadwinners, left with small children and hungry mouths to feed and the importunements of the wild Breo'la on their doorsteps, women did what they must to keep body and soul together, and all hope of defiance in conquered territories faded like smoke upon the wind.

When I protested this brutal excess he exploded in fury, stopped himself just short of striking me for my challenge. "I like it not, but they leave me no choice!" he cried. "Where there is one youth, where there are two, there is a rebellion born. Our numbers are too few to risk it! It must never be possible for these people to rise up against us, so any who do resist are killed, and any who *could* resist are not given the chance to try. These widowed women will work themselves ragged in the fields and the shops, then when they are lonely enough they will gather in Breo'la tents, or take horsemen for their husbands. And one man takes many wives, if he desires to. In a few years, when Arguentans are raising children fathered by their conquerors, their hearts will turn our way!"

He had much more to say in that vein, all well practiced, as if he spoke to convince himself. Or maybe he did believe these things, for the cold effectiveness of these tactics was indisputable. I saw that Murl's Arguentan sensibilities had perished beneath a Styrcian outlook, the result of harsh years on the freezing steppes and the cruel customs of nomad warriors. Kar Kalim had chosen to become a product of his adopted people's culture. Whatever qualms he might once have had, he had uprooted and destroyed them as methodically as he reduced the resistance of a city. All that was left in this man was righteousness, and an unshakeable belief that his ends justified any means.

I was not immune to the shadow he cast, either. My heart was pained to see that Arguentans once awed by my presence and respectful of my wisdom now skulked and scurried from my path as if I were a monster. I had become Kar Kalim's lap dog. It was I who had purportedly summoned the hurricane that had destroyed Caethon, Lesseth whispered to me; it was I, supposedly, who encouraged the karzdagi to run unleashed through the Caronne hills, and killed on sight any native who came within viewing distance of Moontooth. But the truth of it was something else again. I had seen enough blood and grieving families aplenty; heard the cries of frightened children, witnessed coffles of slaves taken from devastated towns, and listened to Murl's rationale that made these things all right. I had seen enough, all around, and could bear it no more.

In a fit of anger over my protests, he banished me to Telemar. When next he summoned me thence, I was resolved to move against him.

I have killed in the heated moment of self-defense—karzdagi on my first foray to Styrcia; the lizard folk of Zila; a man, once, who tried to waylay me on an incognito night-prowling in Nimm. I value life but see how it can lay with different weight in the scales, and have never scrupled overmuch about how and where one's allotted fate comes home to rest.

This changed when I contemplated the cold-blooded murder of Murl Amrey.

It was necessary. It was calculated. And it was a thing difficult to confront, to admit that the only way to stop his wrong-doing was in a sly, clandestine manner that would coldly take his life from him. Imprisonment or disablement would not serve, for either his magic or the Breo'la would wreak a terrible vengeance should he continue to live. Even were he dead, the horse tribes' vengeance might be terrible enough but they, at least, were only mundane opponents without Kar Kalim's special powers to back them.

In spite of what lofty goals might be served by eliminating him, my conscience twisted and squirmed in this light, for I knew that I resented him. Nay, worse: a part of me had grown to hate him with a burning passion, and that part lusted for his death, an end to his malignancy. I asked myself if I wanted to put a halt to his doings for the evil they imposed on others, or for the bane they were to me. That question had no simple answer, and for weeks of his excesses I hesitated, unwilling to raise hand against Murl to serve a selfish personal end. The optimist in me had not yet quite given up on his redemption, and thought there was something still lovable in his heart of hearts . . .

That foolish optimism did not want to listen to hard-headed reason, yet reason ultimately prevailed. Or reason and resentment. The day the Styrcians took Burris—full of defenders as pugnacious as their Lord Pelan—that day the city was laid waste and ashes, the autarch and his court slain in public display. I stood by Kar Kalim's side as he oversaw that event, a grand exhibition to impress the rebellious with his indomitability.

In the last moments of that display, one man dared to defy the conqueror. Clavius Mericus emerged from the crowd, a magical globe of protection flaring to life about him, also enveloping Pelan's family whom the thaumaturge hoped to save. Surely he knew he was doomed to failure, but try he must, and so he attempted to protect his lord's family from an ugly death in the public square.

I heard the breath hiss from between Amrey's lips as he recognized his antagonist. One hand moved to the crystal at his throat; his other hand extended, one finger pointing towards Clavius and the handful of people he had gathered within his sphere of protection. Something like lightning blasted soundlessly from his hand, shattering Clavius' spell like a burst globe of glass. Onlookers cried out as the backwash of energies singed hair and heated metal items amongst the crowd. Breo'la stood back as if at some unspoken order from their lord. Clavius placed himself defiantly in front of the children and broken adults he sought to rescue, and faced his opponent and me.

Amrey gestured again, and though Clavius tried to ward himself, his efforts availed naught. His magic was but the weak flailing of a child in contrast to Kar Kalim's *shia*-fed powers. Pelan's thaumaturge was raised into the air above the crowd of captive citizens and bloodthirsty tribesmen. His clothing sifted to the ground, a sudden shred of rags, and his skin began to peel slowly back from his flesh, flaying from his body one long, slow strip at a time.

His screams carried over the crowd for an endless time. Then inhuman pressures twisted his agonized form, somehow still conscious, until organs burst and his skull was crushed.

It was the last I needed to witness of Murl's callous atrocities. Justify it how he would, I knew that satisfying the battle-thirst of the steppe riders did not require cruelty in such measure. It was jealousy that drove his spiteful, cruel demonstration, but even taking the personal element out of this, I knew him fully capable of doing the same again and again if it suited him. It was his nature to find the point of weakness and push against it until the victim winced in pain, and dared not face him down again. It was his nature to make a cruel travesty into a demonstration that left an indelible impression. It was the same bent of character that had run amok in my tower those years agone, his workings that I thought were merely overenthusiastic spellcraft, but matured now into a corrupt and self-serving power. I could countenance it no more.

I returned to Telemar at my first opportunity, and stayed there in a black study for days.

Lesseth became my privy council, fellow confessor to the dire thing I envisioned. I met him in the garden court in Telemar with the buds of early spring blushing green and pink on bushes roundabout. I sat on the bench beneath the nigantha tree, small leaves in tight-furled spikes of yellow-green set close against its branches. I did not trust to spoken word where Kar Kalim had set his wards and so I let the water of the splashing fountain lull me, sinking into that drowsy rapport that links with earth and sky, the nature force vibrant in the awakening tree. Then I slipped deeper, past those earthly energies to connect to a place beyond, where Lesseth awaited. My friend was present in spirit; I heard him like a voice from my dreams in my gentle garden repose.

He heard me out, and let me talk until I had no more to say. "I did not want to suggest this course," he agreed, "but I have thought about it ere now. It is one obvious way to end Kar Kalim's reign of terror. Unless you want him to rule?"

"He will not change the tenor of his conduct," I replied. "Why would I want him to continue to gather power to himself?"

"You told him it was all the same to you."

"Of course I told him that. You know why, Lesseth: so he would continue to keep me close. And he has, for the most part, except for those times I speak too hastily and provoke him."

"You provoke him easily, it seems."

"He is angered by anyone he believes is set against him." I shrugged and took time to calm my breathing, become more rapid with the anger I felt towards Murl. "He has tossed all order upon its head, destroyed whole cities, set the countryside in upheaval as people flee his army, or look for new homes where they have been burned out. This cannot go on.''

Lesseth paused, then played the countermelody to my argument. ''This situation too will stabilize,'' he ventured. ''Wars eventually give way to peace. If Styrcia has prospered under his rule, he might in the end be a beneficial change.''

''Do not speak foolishness, my friend. There is no end in sight. He has told me of his plans: after Arguenta, the inland courses will be his, the Rajpor hill roads, the Sevian and its upper waterways . . . He will bring more Breo'la through from Styrcia, set up family camps, turn half the population of the Salt Coast into a drafted militia, and march them with horsemen at their back, to conquer yet more lands in the heart of Drakmil. He would halt short of Tor Mak, perhaps, but there is no certainty of that. He commands the magic that could sorely test Cendurhil and the Derenestu. Half the continent could fall under his sway, more if he uses the wizardstone to bring in fighting forces from other spheres.''

I felt the shock in Lesseth's tone. ''He would do that? Isn't that hazardous?''

''Very. There are terrible things in other places, martial and eager to kill, and not nearly as biddable as Amrey likes to think. He fancies he can summon up great horrors and control them. I am certain he cannot. You've seen . . .''

''Yes.'' We were quiet for a moment in shared consideration of the grotesqueries so near to this sphere. Many lay beyond the rifts guarded by Moontooth, but could be accessed from anywhere by the brute force of a *shia*. Did Kar Kalim wish to augment his forces so he could extend his realm yet farther, he would have to tap into lands and resources that gave even a seasoned dimensional traveler pause. Yet blinded by his ambition, I was certain he would not pause at all.

"There is no point in contemplating the possibilities," Lesseth finally said. "They are as endless as the rifts and spheres themselves."

"I know." I let myself be guided back to the heart of our dialogue. "You realize that I am not asking for your help? It is far too dangerous, should you be caught."

If a rude noise can be communicated via thought alone, Lesseth succeeded in doing it. "I will not let you attempt this thing by yourself, and you have no means to prevent me. I will be there to render aid; that is a certainty. And so, Lady, you had best plan how to use my services."

I sighed, and slumped more against the tree trunk at my back. Tears welled beneath the lids of my closed eyes; one drop ran free down my cheek. Lesseth is not mortal as we understand it but he could be hurt and injured and constrained. If he were caught, his agonies could last lifetimes longer than any human frame would ever support. For me the penalty for failure could be—likely would be—death. For Lesseth, the possibilities were much worse. It was a brave thing he did, in insisting to help. His gifts were priceless, and could well make the difference between success and failure. But they were nothing I could demand of him, in good conscience. I had taught Murl Amrey and helped create Kar Kalim, in a way. It fell to me to deal with this disaster once and for all. Yet I would not say no to my friend's aid.

I opened my eyes, took in the glory of the light blue sky, frosted with high white clouds that moved on a brisk spring breeze. "Stay as close to me, then, as you dare, Lesseth. The next time we are in his camp, it will be the best time to make our move."

"Amidst all the tribesmen? You will have no hope of escape!"

I dismissed his protest. "His wards are weakest there. He

relies upon the Breo'la for protection and thinks himself safe
from attack in the midst of their camp. He is more on guard
on the road, and best-protected in the Emprelor, as you have
seen. You speak from the ethereal right now for that very
reason. No, it must be in Kar Kalim's own tent.''

"You think he will summon you there again soon?"

"Of course. It has been more than a week since he's seen
me, since he began this rampage against Burris and the northeast. Like every soldier he will visit his doxies, but sooner or
later he comes to stud with the one whose taking means most
to him.'' The thought was bitter. "He will recall me to his
side again. It is only a matter of time.''

I heard Crookfang's summons with the least equanimity of
any I had ever received. Not in his rage or his pride or even
in his cups had I ever quailed so at the prospect of being with
Murl Amrey. I feared the consequences of my imminent actions: what the Breo'la would do to me, if I were unable to
slip their grasp before they found Kar Kalim dead. Murl
would fetch me to him with the *shia,* but upon his death the
crystal could not serve me as transport again and I would be
stranded in the middle of the Breo'la war camp. It would be
difficult simply to ride free from there, though this were the
same problem I would face in one guise or another no matter
where we took action against Amrey. I hoped to escape the
wrath of his followers, should a way offer itself to me, but
knowing there was no certain out made it very difficult to set
my plans in motion. I dared not dwell on grim possibilities
lest my courage fail me.

Thought of Lesseth was comforting, and I was glad I had
conspired with him. I felt committed to that friend of my heart
and my mind, who would undergo risk greater, even, than my
own. Because he was dedicated to seeing this through it was

easier to cleave to my own purpose, and with that in mind, I tore my thoughts from such morbid turn as the deaths of Corwin and Clavius. I donned the gown of brocade blue that Kar Kalim preferred on me at such reunions, and followed Crookfang from the room.

Steeling myself for what lay ahead, I watched the star-splashed velvet of the *shia* rift open before me. Lesseth's distant ghostly presence reassured me, and then I stepped through the portal on Crookfang's heels. Immediately on the other side, my spirit friend again brushed the edges of my consciousness. I relaxed, relieved that he had made the transit disincarnate, inhabiting a body of vibrational frequencies native to the ethereal sphere. This had been our first, most vital moment of truth: could Lesseth move through the rift in this state? Obviously so. And as long as he stayed in that elevated sphere, he was beyond the range of detection of the spells and wards that guarded Kar Kalim from physical threat. With my secret ally nearby, I turned to Amrey and went to his side.

The atmosphere in his tent was, as always, dark and a little dank, the felt tenting hanging low overhead as it did in all Breo'la shelters. It was lamp-lit, one brazier burning to drive off the damp; it smelled of rain-wet furs and the smoke of an old cooking fire, masked with sweet cedar incense and the musk oil Amrey sometimes perfumed himself with. His battle garb left him looking half warrior, half wizard, his tunic as scarlet as the blood that Clavius had dripped in his torment. Silver bracers cuffed his wrists and a breastplate of silver scales covered his upper chest. The *shia* glowed muffled blue from the filigreed ball at his throat. His trousers were black felt, his boots of black horsehide set with silver spurs—an Arguentan affectation unknown to the steppe nomads, but worn comfortably by this man once of Burris. He was bathed and scented, his red-gray hair damp and curling more than ordinary: the picture of commanding manhood, with just the right touch of vulnerable humanity. I reminded myself again how his actions were so different than his noble posturings, and then I stepped forward to greet him.

Long-bearded Kalimat guards watched me materialize from the blackness of the rift, then bowed, hands to scale-armored breasts. Upon my arrival, they backed out through the inner tent to the outer one and beyond. Kar Kalim did not leave eavesdroppers in earshot of his conversations with me, much less his lovemaking. Or his rutting, when the mood was on him. I put loathing aside, turned that well-practiced smile upon him, and swept close, hands outstretched to take his own.

"Murl," I acknowledged him with the name I reserved for moments of apparent closeness between us, and bussed him on the cheek. It was an informal greeting, yet impromptu enough to show affection, as if I had missed him and was glad to see him again. It was something I thought he would take for granted, and so he did.

"I'm glad you're here," he said, gesturing me to a stool beside his own. "We have made great inroads." He began to describe the advances of his troops and their newest conquests. Though reports and rumors came naturally to the Emprelor he was proud of his accomplishments and liked to boast of them. I could not quite tell if he meant to impress me or anger me with such revelations, or was simply moved to share his progress with someone who knew him from before, who would be perhaps more impressed with what a thaumaturge's student had achieved. Whatever motivated him, I listened and nodded and praised as he talked. He bid me serve us Egranian wine and as the bottle emptied, he told of his horsemen, their

sieges and village raids, of bloody battles won and foolish
city-dwellers duped. Finally he ran out of words, and fell silent, looking at me across the glow of the brazier.

"I've missed you," he said, studying my face in the soft
light. I looked down in what I hoped was a nearly coy manner,
to hide the spark of anger in my eyes. Missed me by his side,
I thought, where I could help win the trust and then effect the
betrayal of more hapless Arguentans?

"I hate it when you anger me," he continued. "I fear sometime I may do more than banish you from my sight, and I
think I would regret that."

His voice was languid, but coldly thoughtful . . . he was not
voicing any deep regrets, but musing about a possibility that
might be bothersome—or might not. He did not want to hurt
his pet but might be driven to it out of rage at her behavior.
I bristled at the threat, glad again that I had resolved upon the
only right course of action left to me.

"Let us not talk of this," I said, looking up into his eyes.
"Surely there are better things that can occupy us at this
hour."

It had been twilight in Telemar; here in the northeast, it
was full dark with little moon. The remains of dinner had been
taken away by the departing Kalimat; this should be a time
when Amrey was inclined to feed other appetites. My look
was inviting, and the hour and the wine had put him in the
right mood. He leaned back in his chair and beckoned me to
remove his boots. I knelt gracefully and did the task, his willing servant, it seemed, in all things great or small.

My heart raced in my chest as I did so, for the moment of
truth would soon be upon us. The ploy Lesseth and I had
discussed would take full advantage of Murl's inclinations to
relax into the moment with me, and attack him unawares in
the one place it was most difficult to ward: the vital energy

fields of his body. That energy extended beyond the physical sphere, radiating in a coherent body of light into the astral and beyond—exactly those places Lesseth was so free to move. My spirit companion touched my thoughts, reassuring that Amrey's energy form was accessible to him, and reminding me to center, to stay in the moment so that I could distract our target as needed while Lesseth did his work.

Murl took the flush upon my face for excitement, for no sooner were his boots off than he pulled me tumbling into bed with him, one hand in my hair so he could bare my neck and sink his teeth into the base of my shoulder. It was a love bite that had fired my passion at other times, foreshadowing the kind of rough encounter that he liked best.

Lesseth caressed my thoughts again, affirming that he had attuned himself to Amrey's body of light and was in synch with those higher vibrational frequencies. Murl put his hands upon my body and started to have his way with me, while Lesseth twined as yet unsensed about the chords of power that knit that man's body and soul together.

Throughout the human form there run nerves and nexi, centers of power that affect not only the physical body, but channel vital forces into the corpus from higher spheres. Through such means is the soul and spirit bound to the earth-plane body. Just as a finger jabbed into a nexus of nerves could paralyze the physical body, so too could energy, thrust into a center of the light body, have devastating effects on the motive force of the corpus. This was the tactic we had resolved to employ: that Lesseth would assault his heart center at the same time that I kept him preoccupied, distracted from this untoward psychic and physical assault. By time he could pinpoint where the attack was coming from it would already be too late. He would be lying dead at my feet then, his heart stopped, for the disruption of the vital link between energy body and physical body would rock his system in a way no other blow could.

This was a rare and difficult technique, something I would hesitate to attempt even were I in discorporate form. But it was well suited to Lesseth, who worked so instinctively with such forces, and it was necessary to the precautions and magical guardings Amrey had about himself. Any physical attack or overt spell would meet with swift and sudden failure, and alarm the camp to boot. This approach was the only one that could avoid those pitfalls.

As Murl moved atop me and pinioned my wrists, Lesseth twined his ghostly fingers and thoughts into the web of energy that vitalized this man. He groped for the flows that coursed energy through Amrey's heart—then cooly interfered with their natural current and rhythm.

Murl's back arched. I knew it was not the arousal of lust that had taken him, but Lesseth's extension of force into cortex and energy nexi. My companion probed for those power centers where higher energies are funneled into the corpus, visible in auric colors and pulsing like colored threads throughout the physical form. Amrey convulsed again.

Thankfully, sounds of a struggle in this tent would go unheeded by the guards outside, given Kar Kalim's behavior with me when the mood was upon him. They would not disturb his pleasure; when he thrashed and kicked over the goblets, I paid no heed to the clatter. The next probe struck him in the spine, but not yet directly to the internal heart—the target that not only vitalized the body, but was wellspring of emotions and storehouse of spirit-level memories. Tears sprang to his eyes, the result of heart-level emotions stirred up by Lesseth's intrusion. More interference in that energy center should jar Amrey's spirit loose from the force that anchored it to the body, like a barnacle scrapped free from the hull of a ship . . .

The next blow from Lesseth struck true: Murl forgot to pin me to the bed as his eyes glazed over and he looked beyond, or inside, sensing something dreadfully wrong, something he was unprepared for. He released one of my hands to grab for the *shia* around his neck.

I grabbed his wrist to prevent him, and held on with all my might.

He struggled against me, releasing my other hand. I gripped both his wrists then, desperate to stop him from touching the wizard-stone. Again he tried. Pain or anger convulsed his face as more heart-energies were disrupted in his light body. He was distracted from his struggle against me and seemed to curl up, his chest bending around the center of his being as he fought instinctively to keep heart and spirit intact. But he could only respond on this most primal level, without the wherewithal to do more, uncertain, surely, of how he was really being attacked.

I kept my deathgrip on his wrists as he toppled to one side off me, off the pallet onto the floor. Still I clung to him so he could not grasp the stone. And I saw his chest heave as if air pulled into the lungs could hope to keep vital force and life energy trapped inside as well. His eyes grew yet more distant, started to roll up in his head, the automatic response of the corpus as the soul departs the body. I could almost see the silver chord and the light body lifting free, would have seen it, I knew, did I have my other-senses freed of this burden he had chained me with upon my wrists.

In that moment the Styrcian crystal flared blue, and I cried out, blinded by its brilliance. He had not touched the stone, but still it had reacted! It flashed again and I felt enervated, unable to hold him any longer. In the next moment I was flung to the furry carpets and watched in horrified disbelief as Murl Amrey stirred back to life.

He sat up fiercely, revitalized and strong as if he had never been touched. With a *word* of power the air crackled with tension that brought every hair standing upright on my body. Lesseth appeared in the air and plummeted down to crash against Amrey's torso, whence he was thrown and kicked to the ground beside me. Lesseth was semimaterial as once before, when karzdagi had first taken him in my tower. He whimpered in shock and looked bruised or charred in a place or two.

Somehow the wizard-stone had responded to its master's need. Whether Amrey had detected what was amiss, or the crystal had done it for him, made no difference to us in the end. His assailants were before him now, helpless before his vengeance. He reeled still from the onslaught, tears streaking his face, his muscles held stiff in a rictus of anger.

He glared at me, betrayal and inexpressible rage upon his face. He stood and I shrank back, certain he would start his revenge on me right there, but I was wrong. He left for a moment, then returned with guards behind him. "Take them," he gritted out. "Tie them. Then wait for me."

I was stripped and bound naked; Lesseth was secured with physical bonds, as well as energy bands provided by Amrey with a spell. Then Kar Kalim left the tent, and left us under the ruthless watchdog eyes of his guardsmen.

CHAPTER 15

We had not long to wait before orders were passed and the guards hauled us out of the command tent. Before us shimmered a rift. The Kalimat pushed us unceremoniously through it, staying close by our side. I staggered to keep my footing, then looked up in surprise. We stood before Moontooth.

I inhaled sharply, astounded at the squalor that sprawled before the noble white granite tower. A massive camp of Breo'la was here—partly the military garrison I had seen before, but now grown to include family encampments and all their wagons, baggage, women, children, and dogs come direct from Styrcia.

Here at last I glimpsed the domestic side of the horse tribes, not that it looked much different from the rough garb and custom of the warriors themselves. Their women wore trousers and longer dresslike tunics, the braid of their waist-length hair the greatest difference between them and their men at a glance. The children were dirty, barefoot, dressed in short leather dresses like their mothers' tunics. They seemed a capable, tough people, the women as well as the men able to ride or set hand to hunting knife and campfire, and none too fastidious for all that.

The door to Moontooth gaped wide, framing horse manure and debris tracked through the tower and down the terraced steps. Even at this late hour, men and a few women walked in and out of the door; two children herded several goatlike creatures out and down into the camp as I watched. Clearly this was the only route to the portal to their homeworld, and they used it readily.

But for Kar Kalim who awaited us there, they cleared a path. Towering in his rage, Amrey strode through the door and up the muck-stained stairs; Lesseth and I were prodded and shoved along in his wake. Breo'la stood out of our way as we went, staring frankly as we passed. Murl stopped at the open portal I recognized, where the doorway had been blasted off by his first forceful entry into the stronghold.

He turned on his heel, looked from me to Lesseth. "Say farewell. This one goes to that abyss you mark the top of the tower steps with." He barked some orders in Styrcian, and horsemen took Lesseth away, to await their leader's pleasure farther up the stairs.

In spite of my own danger, I was appalled at what I heard. "No!" I cried. "You haven't opened it?"

His hand lashed out, striking me hard and splitting my lip. "Don't speak to me. I will hear no more from you unless I ask it." He looked through the portal into another encampment nearby, the counterpart to the one outside the tower, the source of these people coming through from Styrcia.

"I have opened that gate," he said, preoccupied, "and care not for what lies beyond. Your demon-lover will find it . . . challenging, no doubt, especially in this state he visits so rarely, that of having a body." He turned his baleful glare on me. "As for you, come."

He grasped me by the nape of the neck and pushed me through the gate into Styrcia. The cold wind bit through me instantly. I was naked but for the bracelets on my wrists, bound, fearful of his unstated intentions. I hated shivering by his side, for it showed vulnerability. Habit made me wish to seem untouchable even in these circumstances, and I stifled an hysterical laugh at the thought.

Another nomad camp sprawled on this side of the gate, a well-trodden path from here to the distant alabaster hills showing the way the Breo'la had come, bringing their families and oxcarts and all they would care to take into Astareth with them. Behind me the portal opened into Moontooth but I had no chance to study it; onlookers jeered, but they too became small distractions. I had eyes only for Kar Kalim, who reached once again to the Styrcian crystal at his neck, and conjured yet another rift with the stroke of one hand. He took my arm in an iron grip and pulled me through the blackness with him, stumbling on hobbled feet.

We emerged on a barren snow-dusted plain, spires of crystal-jagged mountains rimming half the horizon as if we stood near one edge of a giant bowl. The grass here was short and brown, tufted above the snow that covered the ground in thin patches. The terrain was uneven, broken by gullies and slicks of ice, a wintry wasteland all around.

"Welcome to the Prebia ruins in high summer," he said. "A vill of some importance was once here, but it was laid waste when they coveted a *shia* stone too greatly. It is a place that had meaning for me once, and now is a forbidden land where no one lives or dares to tread." He smiled grimly. "Here I leave you, Inya."

I licked blood from my lip, reluctant to ask why, but wanting to know more. He anticipated me. "You exiled me in Styrcia," he said. "Now I return the favor."

I could not believe he meant it, and blurted, "You left on your own! You never tried to return!"

Anger flared in his eyes. "I tried. You had the gate closed and sealed against me."

"I heard no alarms set off by your attempted return!"

"Why attempt a return when the way was so thoroughly barred? I could see that from this side of the gate." His tone was bitter. "You left me to fend for myself in this godforsaken hostile land. I made the best of it that I could." He looked me over critically and a cruel smile stretched his lips. "Though you, I think, will fare somewhat worse."

I was astounded that he planned to let me live. "Why leave me here like this? You condemn me to death. You could just as well end it now."

He curled a lip. "Because it is a long, slow, lingering death here, alone. The cold will get you, or thirst, or starvation. Or the untamed karzdagi, who roam here in small hunting packs, and rend their victims alive. I will not have your blood on my hands, Inya. Yes! Laugh not. I have a scruple or two left. I want you to suffer as I suffered, knowing that death awaits you slow and torturous, or fast with your throat ripped out and your limbs gnawed from your torso before your soul has left your body. Welcome to Styrcia, the icy hell you condemned me to. You marvel at my ways, and they are harsh, yes, born of a harsh land. Without them, here one dies. As you will discover yourself soon enough. Here."

He gestured and a vulture-headed bird manifested, hopping with awkward wing flaps a short distance away before turning to regard me with its bald red head turned sideways in the cold wind.

"A silent observer of mine, who will record and bring the tale of your passing back to me. Or of your pitiful attempts to escape. You can try if you like. There is no where to go and it will tire you out, but it would be amusing to watch."

His taunting angered me. "I won't curl up and wait to die," I said defiantly.

"You had just as well try it. It would be a mercy, to fall

asleep in the cold and not wake up, rather than be hunted
down or starve, knowing you are perishing but unable to halt
it.''

He snorted. ''You have no idea how I passed those early
years in this idyllic place. It is a fitting punishment I give you,
I think. I need the Midnight Rider no longer, and will not
nurse a snake at my breast. You have signed your death warrant this day, along with your helpful demon. Fare well.''

He spat at my feet, then turned and walked back through
the rift. A moment later, the blackness vanished and the air
was transparent to the empty horizon.

I was alone on a snow-drifted plain, with nary a settlement
in sight. The conjure bird watched, unperturbed as cold sank
through to my senses and I began to shiver. To shiver and
curse, for my hands were bound behind my back and I had
nothing on me, no clothes, no weapon, no way to kindle a
fire, no means to work magic.

Amrey had left me to a slow and miserable doom indeed.
I stood in shock and disbelief, my mind racing for solutions
to my dilemma, coming up with exactly nothing that could
save my life. I would have stayed there in contemplation but
the cold made it unbearable and soon I was forced to move,
putting one bare foot in front of the other to the limit of the
hobbles which bound my ankles. With short hurried steps, I
moved as rapidly as I could simply to keep warmth in my
body. I struck out towards the distant mountains, thinking perhaps to find water at their bases, wondering how far I might
get before the westering sun left the sky and the land was
cloaked in darkness. Broken ground and jagged rocks made
going difficult; the sun set and a brisk wind came off the
distant crystal peaks, setting my teeth to chattering violently.

I trudged across the twilight steppes, tripping and stumbling
on sharp-edged stones, moving in a futile effort to stay warm

and cursing the spy bird that flapped always just out of reach of a kick. So I continued into the night, and somehow, staggering like a dying creature, into the light of dawn.

The sun was a too-bright point of light spearing through fog on the ice-clad horizon. I saw by its position that I had gotten turned around in the night, no longer heading towards the mountains but directly across the rolling plain towards the rising orb that teared my eyes with its brilliance. Yet I had been so certain of my course. I thought Styrcia had only one moon, though last night I had seen two: one high overhead, three-quarters full, and its twin just above the glacier-crested peaks before me. That second moon had not moved, holding its place just above the mountain tops. After studying it for a time I saw it was stationary, and so used it to guide my steps and direction. It had held a strange fascination for me, what I thought was an illusion but did not fade. It was steadily present all through my wandering, and only sank beneath the horizon near dawn.

It should not matter yet somehow it did: what course I followed, how true to my path I had stayed. Was I so befuddled with cold and exhaustion I could not even steer by a moon that remained so kindly still for me? I wondered if it had been a simple trick of the atmosphere that had fooled my eyes and guided my footsteps wrong, away from water and a chance of survival . . .

I followed that thought with the rambling pointless obsession of one suffering from shock or exposure, fixating on the need to get to water or its likely source, to find the base of the mountains although they appeared no closer than the evening before, and me dry mouthed after this mind-numbing, body-numbing night. The biting wind blurred the moisture in my eyes and near froze the tears that ran onto my cheeks,

moisture I begrudged to lose this way. I turned away from the
sun and blinked, looking for the jagged peaks I had sought in
the distance.

I blinked again and my eyes did not clear. I wondered for
a moment how much worse my chances would be if I could
no longer see to navigate across the steppes. The gullies I
risked falling into; the sharp stones that could cut my damaged
feet far worse than they were already; the possibility of wandering in endless circles, lost, until I dropped of exhaustion . . .

Despair mounted. I was worse off now in the light of day.
It seemed I had made no progress and I felt myself weakening,
unable to pick a path across the ice-brilliant ground, unsure
of footing or direction. My shoulders were aching and my
arms were numb, my hands long senseless. I yearned to lie
down and rest but knew that sleep could claim me even in
this cold, and then I would be lost beyond recall.

As I stood there swaying and bedazzled, it seemed the
morning sun reflected off the ice in pinpricks of warmth. I
felt for a moment as if I could stand there and be warmed
through by the vast reflection off the ice all around. This, too,
my brain dismissed as illusion, but the feeling of heat continued. Even the spy bird that dogged me seemed to fluff its
feathers and relax in this odd oasis. I wondered if I had stumbled across some strange natural phenomenon like hot springs
or a geyser. The wind had died in this place I had come to,
and from that quietude of air alone I felt ten times warmer.
And then there was this comforting temperature that I swore
was real, and made me reluctant to move from this spot. Now
if only I had water to soothe my thirst—

"There is water nearby, sister. Come there and drink with
us."

I laughed at the obliging voices in my head in this barren

place, but blinked moisture from my eyes and tried to focus
on my surroundings. No doubt this was another hallucination
like the stationary moon and the warmth, but I could not stand
the heartbreak of thinking I had bypassed aid because I had
not the eyes to see it.

I looked around, clear-sighted. There was only reddish soil
and rock beneath my feet, dusted with powder snow and slick
with patchy ice. I stood on a flat stretch of ground, the tufted
brown grass pricking my feet, but that more pleasant than the
flint-sharp edges some of the rocks bore. The vulture bird
preened atop a large stone that gave it footing above the snow,
and watched me with one round black eye to see what I was
going to do.

I looked around wondering that selfsame thing. I was certain now the heat I perceived was no illusion, although the
ice had not melted from the ground in consequence. It was a
conundrum I was incapable of applying logical thought to.

"Drink with us," came those insistent voices again.

One older voice countered the others. "Beware the *hegye,*"
it said critically.

In the next moment the vulturous spy bird exploded, literally burst asunder in a flurry of feathers but—unlike a real
bird—no guts or meat or warm blood. A breeze stirred and
the construct was gone, blown magically to oblivion, its pieces
scattered across the plain.

Then I saw who had called to me as illusion dropped from
their forms. Six women drew near, emerging from the refrac-
tions of the ice-bright landscape to stand before me in needle-
sharp clarity. I wondered how I could have overlooked them,
even against this too-bright background. And such women
they were . . . nothing like the nomads I had glimpsed in the
Breo'la encampments. They were older, and heavier set, their
waist-long hair worn loose about their shoulders. They wore

tunics wrapped close to their many skirts with colorful sashes, and upon their horse-hide vests a myriad of small amulets were secured, winking reflected sun like so many pieces of bright glasswork. But glass they were not: they were silver and polished stone, bronze and leather and beadwork. Ornate beadwork such as they wore draped around neck and wrist; amulets and talismans and round discs of unfired clay and dyed cloth . . . a varicolored hodgepodge so that when they moved there was a faint clink and rustle of the oddments upon their clothes. It nearly distracted from the two long knives each wore in her sash, a handy dagger to the left in utilitarian sheath, a longer curve-bladed thing with hilt of bronze to the right, for who knew what purpose? But the blade was the length of a forearm, and each wore hers with a sense of purpose.

They were barefooted, I noticed, and seemed unperturbed by jagged rock or freezing ice. They walked as comfortably as if on smooth carpet.

This was more unbelievable than the illusions that had lured me so far, but nothing was left of Kar Kalim's vulture spy but feathers and so I must believe this much evidence of my eyes, at least. I was trying to make sense of what I saw, when the first spoke to me.

"I am Magya, teller of this *esh 'tek,* this group of Workers." She said that word, "workers," with a special weight that implied the working of power to me. I trembled, a reflex of fatigue and stress, and listened further.

Magya's face was weathered and her hair graying, but she was not much older than her companions. She studied me soberly, and another of the *esh 'tek* spoke, a woman with several black bird feathers tied over her heart.

"Today is Suntide, midsummer. Telling-songs sang your journey here long before you contemplated it. We have awaited you since before midsummer's eve, during the days of the reflected moon.''

"The night mirage that sits upon the brow of the glacier we call White Mother,'' explained Magya.

"She is exhausted,'' said the shortest woman, coming from the back of the group to stand closer by my side.

"I understand you!'' I answered stupidly, for the sense of their words meant less than the fact that I grasped what surely must be the Styrcian tongue.

"There is a kenning upon you,'' said Magya, "for it was needful to meet you. We cannot aid you yet.''

I stood within arm's reach, naked and mostly freezing, exhausted to the verge of collapse, and could not believe my ears. "I—''

"Hush,'' said another. "You have not decided yet what road you walk, sister.''

Magya nodded in agreement. "Become clear on that, and if it chances that your way lies with ours, we will be by your side when you need us.''

"I need you now!'' I exclaimed. "Surely you cannot stand by and leave me like this?''

"Can, and will.''

I thought I had found succor; rage and then chill despair washed over me. No doubt these people were allied in some way with Kar Kalim, too, had no need or wish to aid me, and risked his wrath did they do so . . .

"We do not heed the conqueror's will,'' the short woman said. "He is no friend to us. He came and lured many but we would not tread his path. The way-chiefs and their folk came with us as well.''

"Way-chiefs?'' I looked at her uncomprehending, weaving where I stood, as if some revelation would make all come clear to me. Why would they not help me?

"We are the Duryevu," she said. "We are tellers and dream-workers and wielders of what little mana remains on this broken world. Way-chiefs are those sept-leaders who are initiates into some mysteries, those who sense the greater whole that we work to achieve. A wholeness shattered by Kar Kalim."

The faces of these women went grim and distant. I sensed they did not speak of his temporal exertions only. "Why do you not help me?" I asked, a pleading tone in my voice. I was tired, so tired . . .

"Way-chiefs seek a path," said one, her left eye clouded with blindness. "They do not favor emek vill, nor karzdag, nor yet Breo'la war camps. They seek equilibrium in between. It is necessary to live in balance, to restore the balance that has been lost to this world."

The words were plain but their meaning cryptic. Yet the gaze of the Duryevu was so intense and unwavering, I knew there was something here I must grasp. I struggled to comprehend their meaning. "How so?" I asked.

"Child," Magya quirked a half-smile, "do you think the *shian* that Kar Kalim uses is a novelty of this time and place? There have been others who used *shian* in the past, and wreaked havoc with them. They turned a fair garden world into a cold and shriveled ball trapped in endless winter."

I remembered the mana-fueled quirks in nature in Astareth, saw how catastrophe could easily follow abuse of a Styrcian crystal. "Mana . . ." I breathed.

"*Shian* have a life of their own," the blind one said, "though not one we would recognize. Some dream-singers connect with the stones in dream-time."

To hear this now, as I struggled to keep my eyes open in the warmth and respite from movement, was beyond comprehension. I fear I looked every bit as witless as I felt.

"Enough," said Magya. "She does not perceive our meaning."

"Nor will she," said the short one, "so long as she stands here."

"Then we must let her choose her path." The eldest of the Duryevu said it with finality and took a step back from me. The others followed suit.

"Find your way, friend of the white tower," one said.

"Choose your road," urged another. Then they turned as one and walked towards the sun. My eyes bleared in the light and they seemed to vanish into the ice-bound landscape. "Wait!" I called. "Help me!"

"Pick your path," I heard in the distance.

Then they were gone.

I cried out and nearly fell to my knees in frustration. Surely they saw the state I was in? Surely they could help me! Were they so cruel, or did they not dare? What was this path they spoke of? What was there to choose?

With their absence the wind intruded into that becalmed place and the cold returned, as frost-born as ever before. I did the only thing I could: I trudged on, in the footsteps of the women who had been here, this time walking directly towards the sun. I marked the place where it rose on the horizon by a distant outcrop, then dropped my eyes to the ground ahead, to place my tender feet with care as I tottered along. I saw no footprints on the snow, no scuff on the ice before me and wondered if my visitors had been real or a fever dream. I stumbled on in the direction they had disappeared. I wondered if I should have stayed where they found me . . . was that what they had meant by choosing a path?

I walked in delirium, thinking now and then to check for the outcrop on the horizon and correcting my path accordingly, but eventually, not thinking about it at all. My world shrank down to the ground just ahead, to the next safe place to plant a foot, to the effort of staying upright when all of me wanted to collapse to the ground and lie there in deep, cold slumber. My strange encounter with the Duryevu took on a dreamlike quality and like a dream, it haunted my waking steps. Their words bothered me and soon were going through my mind like a chant . . . *Way-chiefs seek a path . . . equilibrium in between . . . we must let her choose her path . . .*

What path? What choices were there to make that I needed to make? A choice to survive? That choice had already been made; I was engaged in that struggle this very moment: I wondered if my commitment to destroy Kar Kalim was what they meant, for I had failed in that. For lack of resolution, perhaps, for I had quailed as we fought, and relied on Lesseth to complete my work for me. Was I not dedicated enough to deserve their aid? They had spoken ill of Kar Kalim and clearly were no friends to the conqueror of Styrcia . . .

Insight eluded me. I plodded and stumbled as the sun rose higher until every step took such effort it nearly toppled me onto my face. I was oblivious to the cold for it had frozen me so thoroughly that I was numb, no longer feeling extremities, barely aware of legs that felt like tree trunks. My vision narrowed to the patch of ground a handspan ahead, where I could next step with feet now swollen to something twice their size. If I could feel them I knew I would be in agony, but why wish for sensation? I was on an aimless hike across a timeless space to a certain doom. No doubt I had imagined the encounter with the women, some part of my brain anxious to pose a riddle to the other part.

What path remained for me to take? The choices I had made had set me here, but if I had handled things differently with Murl would it really have mattered in the end? To defy him early on would have resulted in my death or confinement to the tower. I was not proud in hindsight, though, to have been out and by his side, for I had compromised too much of myself to play that role. I had aided him, furthered his plans, tarnished my reputation and my good will with people who had trusted and looked up to me . . .

I had sold my integrity, and asked none too dear a price for it. I had thought him redeemable, but I was wrong, and others had suffered as I discovered the truth of that. Hoping against hope that I could make a difference, when in fact I could not. Had I deluded myself or had there ever really been a chance? Even now my instincts whispered that he would never change for me, or anyone else. No one ever did. They changed only to suit themselves, and Kar Kalim was content with the person he had grown to be.

Anger stirred in me at that thought, jarring me out of my haze a bit. Even at this juncture, I still wanted to end his abuses, right the wrongs I had contributed to, unwittingly or no.

Choose my path. I had chosen wrong at every juncture. Chosen to compromise; chosen to plead and cajole, to keep myself safe at Kar Kalim's side while others suffered all around. I had opted to live a lie as if I had cared for him, could be an intimate to him, when I reviled myself now for all the intimate time that had passed between us. Even when I had resolved to put an end to it, even then, I had looked to a friend to share the risk, been unprepared for the reality that the wizard-stone could preserve his life in extremis. Was he then virtually immortal? I asked myself. And shuddered at the answer.

Yes he is.

I heard them in my thoughts, those women's voices. Relief at hearing them flooded through me. I knew then that I was not abandoned, and gave over to the emotions of that moment with a sob.

We dare not help her if she remains his mirror, someone said as my knees grew weak. *She acts as he does.*

Shh, someone replied. *This has touched her deeper than that . . .*

I sank to the ground, somehow trusting they would not let me die out here.

Knowing when to trust, and when not to. Knowing where to gauge the line in my own actions. I had thought nothing of using power to awe and overawe, to sway people in their decisions so they would bend to my will. The only difference between Murl and me was that I was less ambitious, had never used that leverage to my own aggrandizement, at least not on the scale that appealed to Kar Kalim. He had used me and other means to very great purpose, but in the end our tactics had been the same. I had scruples that I had rearranged as conveniently as he to serve my own ends. There was a time when I thought such use of power acceptable, enjoyable, even; wielding such a force was always a challenge, with the rewards accruing to the one who played the game best. It had been a game to me. Kar Kalim took that game and played it in adult wise: in intimate relationships that hinged on control, or with armies and cities and innocents dying by his swords in consequence. But the game was the same.

It was one I could no longer play. I succumbed to exhaustion with that thought in my mind.

A long time I was swaddled in darkness, the deep sleep of utter weariness, until my spirit edged closer to awareness and dream images came into my mind's eye.

A young woman dressed in the colored skirts and many

sparkling talismans of a Duryev approached me upon the same plain I had struggled across all night and day. I recognized the place only with the knowing familiarity of dreams, for the plain did not look the same at all: in my dreamscape it was clad in meadow grasses and wildflowers in summer bloom, here and there a copse of trees growing along the edges of green watercourses—the gullies that had been so treacherous in their bone-dry version on my trek.

"R'Inyalushni d'aal." She greeted me, and reached for my hand. I felt glad to see her but hesitated to take the out-stretched hand, knowing that to do so was some kind of ir-revocable step.

When I finally brought myself to grasp it, the plain dropped away beneath our feet until I saw a world entire, the globe that was Styrcia, mountains and small inland seas and verdant land stretching beneath cloud cover. It was far unlike the gla-cier-ridden barrens I knew of: too alive, and too warm, too densely populated with men and wildlife. Then there was a spark far below, the blue flash I had come to recognize as the greater working of a wizard-stone. In consequence, a string of mountains erupted into fire as long-dormant volcanoes blew into violent life.

"Jeraganovi, a traveler from elsewhen, appropriated a *shia* and used it much as Kar Kalim uses his," my companion said. "He started a string of natural disasters with terrible conse-quence for Styrcia." I watched as ashfall blackened the atmo-sphere in accelerated time flow, and winter sank its chill claws into the globe. "One of our own, a way-chief who knew the secrets of the crystals, set out to counter the disaster and to stop Jeraganovi from further workings of power."

Hurricanes rose into being over the inland seas. Fed by their limited waters, they all but drained the shallow oceans of their liquid and blasted the land with what turned to freezing snow by time it hit the ground. "It was the start of irreversible disaster. The wizards warred until they destroyed each other, and nearly took our world along with them." The globe beneath our feet flared blue as *shia* stones came in proximity, then the planet seemed to die. Lakes and watercourses dried up, green turned to brown and then to sere stone. Glaciers crept over the earth till only grasslands were left in a temperate equatorial region, and little else seemed habitable.

The Duryev turned to me, dark eyes bright in somber, unlined face. "*Shia* lore became a secret knowledge, entrusted only to the rare few, the dream-tellers who could pass on such knowing without needing to speak of it. Way-chiefs were denied that initiation; Bronye and Vabronye who survived the Dying Times thought most of the stories legend and later generations forgot the truth of the stones they prized as they would diamonds. We guard against their discovery and exploitation by others. We assured that Kar Kalim's first attempt for a stone netted him only a *fe'shia*, a flawed one incapable of real function."

"I tried to use that crystal."

She nodded. "We intended you no harm. We sent the way-chiefs of Lodanya to watch his path and deal with him should he return, though we had little expectation of it. But he did, to our surprise. He lured the way-chiefs and the Bronye with promises of power, showing them enough of his magic that they made him welcome in their vills. Magic like his had not been seen here for eons, for there is little enough mana left and no one to teach the craft to natural adepts.

"We have watched him from that time on, for it became clear that this man had an inkling of the *shia* lore and was powerful enough to work a wizard-stone on his own. He desired a true *shia*, and spent some years finding one."

A crude stone hall in a mountainous emek settlement took

shape before us. The grizzled, fur-robed Vabronye of the Lodanya vill sat at table, the *shia* about his neck wire-wrapped and tied to a thong. A younger Murl Amrey sat nearby; now and then his glance would stray to the item worn merely as jewelry by the Vabronye. "He coveted it, and tried one night to steal it," my guide told me. "The Lodanya chased him forth and he barely escaped with his life and the clothes upon his back. Styrcia is hostile to the stranger without food or heat or clothes, more hostile still to one without friends or clan. Kar Kalim lacked nearly all those things. He wandered and starved until he fell in with the karzdagi."

I watched his acts of desperation to hunt and kill food, his despair when he failed; gnawing at tree bark to keep alive, nearly being taken by karzdagi as he slept. He was less likely prey than they thought, though, turning the tables with a spell or two sufficient to cow his hunters, and gain him time. Time to talk and work his persuasive charm upon the beast-men.

He got them to shelter him and once he was recovered from his travails, his magic helped them to feast better that winter than ever before. He gained influence with the scavenging karzdagi, and when he was ready to assert himself, he killed three chieftains and had the rest licking his boots in no time at all. The beast-men were in awe of him and he acted brutally, mirroring their tactics and customs, to speak in a language they would recognize and respect. And they were not all that intelligent either, readier than men, perhaps, to see him as something more than human, even god-sent to give them aid.

When next the karzdagi traded with the horse nomads, Amrey was there, curious about these tribesmen, a conglomeration of outlaws and malcontents from the emek way of life who since the Dying Time had grown into their own ho-

mogenous population with customs long divergent from those
of the vill dwellers. Murl saw his interests would be better
served by living in human community. He worked his way
into the intimate circle of the Vabronye of the Kroi Breo'la,
a far-ranging clan known for their touchy pride and fierce
loyalties.

Murl became a right-hand man, then wizard to the clan, a
unique find in a culture that did not practice any but shaman-
istic magic. That stroke promised to bring much recognition
and power to the Kroi clan chief, who adopted Amrey into
his family. Shortly thereafter, Amrey killed him and took his
wife. It was Breo'la tradition that let him do such things: fight
and kill a rival—or what looked to be a rival, for what purpose
it served; take his wife as booty; make blade-claim to the
Vabroncy in his place. His magic did not make him proof
against attack, but it was the decisive edge he needed to face
down all challengers. Adopted into the clan and married to a
matriarch of the Kroi, Amrey was acknowledged as one of
their own.

"It was appealing bait he put forth," the Duryev remarked
to me. " 'Follow me and I shall make you invincible' was his
promise. 'The vills that have withstood your grasp because of
their fortifications, I can tear asunder.' He demonstrated the
truth of this, too, and warriors flocked to his banner.

"The irregularity of his leadership position tore the clan,
though: the ambitious and violent favored him, the cautious
and more reasonably inclined hesitated to agree that he had
right to the Vabroncy at all. We were asked for our opinions,
and offered the truth: there were prophecies about this time,
and the wars he would bring could bring vast dominion to the
sons and daughters of the Breo'la, or could obliterate them
entirely.

"He scoffed at such dire predictions, and led a raid against

Lodanya that turned into a successful conquest, breaking the richest of their vills and bringing new Breo'la from far-flung septs flocking to his banner.''

In my vision I witnessed the gathering of the tribes. Amidst this influx stood firm the Duryevu who were not cajoled by Amrey's promises or fired by his plan for ever-expanding conquest. They opposed his search for a *shia* to use in battle, and saw no reason why the Breo'la should wage concerted war against vills when isolated raids had served their purposes in the past. Their resistance to the upstart chief of the Kroi was noted by all.

The controversy sundered the tribes, with some following the guidance of their dream-walkers. The tribes who heeded the Duryevu split from the rest, moving into the colder steppes where only the hunt and the herds of wild grell would feed them. There were no emek to raid, no vills to conquer, only karzdagi for occasional trade, and little traffic with their kinsmen who rallied around Amrey's banner.

Around that time Amrey learned of a *shia* unearthed from the Gorsek mine, and reduced Eshmiak vill to make the wizard-stone his own. It was one of the most powerful resonant crystals ever unearthed. What to most Styrcians was simply a decorative if very precious and valuable stone, was to him a tool of power. When he laid hand to it, a storm-tossed month of havoc resulted as he learned to harness its properties.

When he had done so, he enthralled what was left of the Eshmiak, and began to be known as Kalim, the Conqueror.

His conquests continued, from one end of habitable Styrcia to another. A decade later, he finally demanded that the Prebia kneel to him. They defied and he destroyed them, not least of all because of the newest *shia* in their keeping, said to be more powerful than the Gorsek stone. The Prebia crystal was all that it was rumored to be. He put the Gorsek *shia* from him, mastered the new stone, and expanded his campaign of annexation until he ruled all that he surveyed.

Kar Kalim, he was called then, conqueror of all, when he had mastered the world of nomad and vill and karzdag.

It was not quite all in a literal sense: the Duryevu septs roamed in an icy wasteland and were not of interest to Kar Kalim. Some few small mountain vills evaded his grasp also, too inconsequential to be annexed into the system of governorships he established. The Breo'la swept invincibly over the rest of the land, a warrior caste proud to rule, but growing restless without a goal and outside enemy to reckon with. Disputes began to break out amongst clans and Kar Kalim saw rightly that his horse tribes needed a focus, something new to crush between their teeth . . .

Kar Kalim looked where no amount of brutality could create vendetta amongst the tribes, to a place where he knew there was richness and plenty and a country conducive to the resettlement and growth of Breo'la and land-hungry emek. Astareth, his homeworld, would serve. The place he had been barred from by my magic, the portal he could not cross unaided.

Now master of the Prebia *shia*, he had all the power of the multiverse at his command. He staged his warriors and blasted his way through the rift between the worlds, and in the doing left mighty chaos to sweep Styrcia in the form of quakes and hurricanes, torrential floods, volcanoes burst into fiery new life and extreme blizzards that dropped a year's worth of snow in one season's fall. Glaciers crept forward measurably with his agitation of natural forces. The great elemental paroxysms came and only gradually faded. They were impetus to the Breo'la to follow their leader through the rift and into a new world. Only the Duryevu understood all too well exactly what was happening, and were concerned. Kar Kalim's use of brute force had shifted the weather patterns of battered Styrcia, and precipitated another cycle of deepening cold and hardship for the beings that lingered on that globe.

"His *shia* is linked to this world," my guide said, "for it is part of the substance of this place. The open portal between our spheres allows that link to continue to function. Each use of the stone resonates across the dimensions like a bell ringing through the rooms of a house. It stresses the fabric of Styrcia's energy weave."

Her voice saddened. "We weep to feel the distress of Styrcia, the contrary energies that pull her this way and that. I dream her as an old woman, her back twisted out of true by torque upon her limbs . . . she aches. She rebels at this ache. We do not wish to see things worsened."

"Does he know?" I asked.

"He cannot help but know, for the wizard-stone makes it clear to its user what price is paid. He does not care about the fate of Styrcia. On Astareth he uses more restraint, thinking perhaps to prevent repeating this problem . . ."

I saw this world again, had a sense of something out of balance, a balance that mana-working Duryevu might hope to effect—

"As long as a portal links us and a *shia* is used, there is resonance between the stone and its homeworld pulling energies askew. While this persists we cannot hope to effect change at all."

I saw the rift moved, severing Styrcia from Moontooth portal entirely, and my heart dropped as I recognized the kind of displacement the Duryevu hoped for.

"That is what created the abyss at the top of the tower," I said. "A severed link."

My guide nodded. "We would rather risk whatever might

wander through that rift, than stay bound to certain doom in
the form of the Prebia crystal.''

I shook my head. ''Moontooth is like a knitting needle,
spearing through the fabric of space and time. In each layer
or level that it intersects, there is a rift—a gap in the weave,
held secure by Moontooth's placement in it. The abyss—that
was an accident, where the substance of a dimension ripped
as it tore away from Moontooth as anchorpoint. If we did the
same with Styrcia, there is no telling how wide that rift will
become, or what treacherous dimensions you would invite to
overrun you. Besides—'' I cleared my throat—''I haven't the
means to sever the link, once it is in place.''

It was the working of many Guardians, to make or break
such a link, and that craft was beyond me. My Duryev companion seemed to age in that moment, her face becoming
older, more like Magya, who had spoken with me on the
plains. ''There is another way,'' she said, sitting cross-legged
on air to speak with me. ''Destroy the crystal. The hazard is
that there will be backlash of power: how great, we cannot
say.''

''And will that restore balance to Styrcia?''

''Not by itself, no. But it will mean we are free to work as
we must to counter the damage Kar Kalim has already done.''

Then words came to my lips that I dreaded to speak, but
knew I must. ''How does one destroy the crystal?''

The woman in my dreams studied me with the deep, dark
eyes of Magya, the Duryevu spokeswoman. ''There is only
one way. To bring it into proximity with another crystal also
attuned to its wearer.''

''Is there such a thing?''

''Oh, yes.'' She sounded cynical. ''As soon as he began to
link with the new crystal, he put the Gorsek *shia* far away.

He could not destroy it without injuring himself, so he hid it in a place forbidden to all. Prebia.''

Prebia! The wasteland of my exile and my intended death. I considered her words carefully. ''Why could he not destroy the crystal without hurting himself?'' I asked.

''The stone is like a tuning fork keyed to his personal frequency. Destroying the *shia* disrupts that resonance.'' I had a vision of a sound at a certain frequency causing a glass to shatter. ''That is why he hid the one stone: if two attuned crystals come together, there is a feedback effect that destroys them both, and devastates the surroundings in proportion to the strength of the *shian*. He would be killed in the process.''

I took in her words. ''You are saying that to have a chance of undoing the damage here, the *shia* that created it must be destroyed. And with it, its wielder, and the innocents who are around him at the time.''

''Yes. Unless you think he will forbear ever using that power again?''

I looked away from her piercing eyes. ''No,'' I whispered.

''Then the decision is yours, R'Inyalushni d'aal. Choose your path.''

That was a name that signified Guardian of Moontooth, a position that held responsibility to the rift-places the tower anchored. How was I to turn my back on that vow now? The well-being of Styrcia and the fate of Astareth lay in the balance. As abstract as that sounded in thought, I knew it boiled down to the lives of emek in their vills, the children of the Breo'la, the Arguentans who were harried through Caronne by karzdagi on the hunt: the people that Kar Kalim crushed blindly underfoot as he grasped for power.

The Duryev bowed to me and faded from my dream, the rest of the vision swept away in her wake as well. I came to my senses knowing that piece of wisdom I had brought from my dreamstate was real and solid.

There was a way to stop Kar Kalim and counter the tool he used so blithely as weapon. I knew I had to do exactly that.

I awoke in a frozen grotto, with glassy walls and blue-green sheet ice underfoot. Magya and the other wise-women sat around my pallet. As before, the frozen water held no cold and I lay comfortably at rest.

"Are you ready, sister?"

I nodded and sat up, glad for the tunic they had given me in my sleep. A healing had occurred, for my body felt whole and well, no longer suffering from the rigors of my ordeal on the plains. I threw back the covers with one hand, and the gold bracelet there slid down my wrist. I frowned at it out of habit.

Magya's gaze followed mine. "Do you wish to be rid of those, then?" she asked.

My eyes darted to hers, filled with sudden hope. "Can you remove them?" Even I heard the pleading in my voice.

"Not directly," she said. "That is a binding on you of ancient force, of the type way-chiefs once knew to make. How came you by it?"

"That must be a piece of arcane lore Kar Kalim gathered to himself, then. He put these on me when he surprised me in my tower, and I've had no spellcraft since."

"Ah." She smiled sadly. "We can not free you of that binding ourselves."

"You cannot?" My heart fell. Not until that moment did I realize how hopeful I had been of aid from these women, adversaries of Kar Kalim's power. Magya sensed my distress and rested one hand atop mine.

"We can show you the way, though. Set your feet upon the trail. But the challenge is yours alone to master, if you can."

Her words encouraged hope. "How so?" I asked eagerly. "Is there something I must do, some skill I must learn—?"

She inclined her head. "Oh, there is a learning involved, right enough, but it is nothing we can explain, or put in your hands like a Name-Day gift. It is an evolution from within, that only you can nurture."

I frowned and pursed my lips. She spoke of an inner quest, like that which had directed my steps here and opened my eyes to the matter of choosing the right path. . . .

"I am willing," I said, putting all the intensity of my months of frustrated captivity into that statement. "I cannot exist in this manner." I raised my wrists by way of illustration.

She made a wry face. "I can imagine you think not. But try you ever so hard, we cannot guarantee that you will ever be free of that burden."

"You can show me how to try, you said."

She nodded. "But there is a price to pay. You must make an exploration of self, in a way that is not common to your ordinary mental state. This is something we can introduce you to only in dream-time. Only there can you gain what you will need to free yourself of that hardship." She emphasized her words with a glower at those cold bracelets of gold.

They had spoken to me already of dream-time. Clearly they worked in an overworld of sorts, probably the lower or higher astral, it seemed to me, a place where thought became manifest form, and consciousness traveled outside the body. Well, that was a place I was familiar with from my own long time of arcane workings. "So help me into dream-time," I urged her, "and I will learn whatever I must, to break these bonds."

She studied my face as if searching out signs of weakness or indecision there. Of that, there was none. I wanted to get

on with this, to return to Astareth as soon as possible and deal
with Kar Kalim when he should least expect me.

"You can do this only in dream-time," she stressed again,
driving home the point she seemed to think I would balk at.
I met her gaze with just as stern and earnest an eye as she
had turned on me. These shackles had hindered me for far too
long and I chafed to be rid of them.

"As you say. I am ready when you are," I assured her.

She acceded with the merest shift of posture, a relaxation
of her shoulders. "Very well, then. Come with us."

I rose and followed Magya and her kin through a series of
icy caverns, neither too cold nor melting from the unwintry
warmth. Most were habited with chests and pallets and oddments of magical craft: pots, braziers, and such. Along down-
sloping passageways of ice we walked, into and beyond the
heart of that frozen complex, until we had left the dwelling
places behind and trod corridors more rough, where the breath
of natural chill began to pervade the air.

Heir to a magical tradition of ceremony and cantrip, visualization and shorthand word of power, I expected something . . .
well, magical, to aid and instruct me. Instead, the women led
me to a remote grotto, smaller, this one, with walls of clouded
black ice that did not reflect the light, but trapped it and surrounded this cool space with translucent dark. A smudge pot lit
the corner with sullen glimmer. The shortest of the six tossed
leaves on the coals, so that pungent smoke filled the air; two
others together laid out furs and blankets in the center of the
floor. Magya motioned me to lie down upon the bed that was so
made. As I did, the women sat in a circle crowding in around
me, sitting so close their knees nearly touched.

The blind one leaned forward and gave me to drink of a
flask she carried that contained a bitter beverage, tchai-like
but acrid and strongly medicinal. When I tried to hand it back

after a short quaff, she motioned me to drain the potion. I did, then settled down upon the pallet, the shadow-dark forms of the Duryevu surrounding me where I lay.

The women began a hum that turned into a low subvocalized chant. No one offered me a word of explanation; I thought I should join in the sound that was so compelling, but I did not. I found myself breathing in time to the droning of their voices. One by one they closed their eyes and continued the chant, and I realized that a trance state was talking these women away and out of their bodies.

Magya watched me through half-lidded eyes. She reached out to take the hands of women to either side. I did not do so, but the knees and clasped hands of the close-gathered chanters touched me too. I felt the electricity of the circle thrill through me, and my eyelids fluttered shut. There was no need to see with the physical eye, when so much was present here and perceivable only with the other senses.

The senses I would normally use were numb, but there are primal centers that function even in the most primitive and mundane human. On those levels—subconscious, superconscious—I had a sense of the strong energies flowing in this circle around me, and soon found myself humming a counterpart to their wordless chant.

I heard Magya speaking, whether in ear or mind I could not quite tell. *Listen to yourself. Your answers lie within. Look there now for what binds you. . . .*

What binds me? I frowned at the non sequitur; obviously Amrey's crafting bound me, visible on my wrists. This was nothing that lay within, nothing I had done to myself. Except for leaving myself less well-guarded than I should have been. If I had not permitted him to bind me in the first place—

That thought suggested others. On the one hand, I could

not have prevented his overpowering me, not given the great
forces at his command with the wizard stone. Then again, it
seemed that I *could* have resisted somehow, since I was on
many levels the source of my own power. I had not given it
away to him, not that personal power, but I had . . . directed
it wrongly? Used it incorrectly? There were wheels within
wheels here.

"Aum mjo na haa lo kwan riiii" droned through the air
around me, long, drawn-out, sonorous tones replacing the
wordless hum of earlier. I felt my consciousness become dis-
jointed from my body, lifting free to another state of being,
something transcendent of the physical, and I noted with surprise that I had, after all, never been in such a state before.

There was a realm here, the Duryevu were showing me this
instant, a place of the mind that freed one of the body. This
was different from magical visualization, this: this was a
whole flight of the soul, a journey beyond. I perceived with
a start that *this* was "dream-time." This was a place alien to
me, in all my out-of-body sojourns and occult travels.

It was like that place between waking and sleeping, a state
where my thoughts wandered at seeming random, nudged by
conscious mind but not directly controlled, skipping from the
Duryevu to their chants to a vision of Amrey in the staircase
of Moontooth, clamping these bonds upon my wrists . . .

I shrank from the memory, for it angered and frustrated
me—and here, I sensed, such response also threatened to
plunge me back into the body and disrupt this altered state I
had entered. *Do not shy from such thoughts.* Magya cautioned
me before I could react in full. *That which makes you most
uncomfortable is what you must face down and walk through.
No matter how long the seeking takes. . . .*

The Duryevu were with me here, their presence light but

tangible. Yet they stayed silent, except for Magya's warning. They would not coach me along the way, I saw. Still, her brief encouragement helped me to focus, to direct my musings differently, for left to itself my mind had wandered as blithely away from Murl Amrey as it had towards him. With renewed effort I forced my thoughts back down that well-traveled road, resisting the temptation to stray from what discomfited me.

I experienced that moment again, when Amrey had muzzled my power, his harsh grip and the chill that ran through me when the bracelet snapped closed around my wrist. Such a turmoil it put me into, all that could have been avoided, had I not succumbed to his machinations.

For once, that turmoil found release. In dream-time, I could rant and rail against that fate in a way I had been forbidden in the flesh-and-blood world. At some point as I did so, I because aware that but one guardian presence remained near, one Duryev in place of her many sisters. The others had dropped out of dream-time, unnoticed by myself, but still through their sister they kept a watchful eye on me.

I turned from that recognition to the free associating thoughts that fueled disturbing visions in that strange space.

It is not an easy thing to review one's life critically, to see oneself with unjaundiced eye; dispassionately, honestly. It is harder still to probe at weak points of character: to question motivations, reviewing choices not made and actions not taken, and the reasons why. In dream-time such introspection became a waking vision, an otherworld experience where I moved in the likeness of a body from thought to scene to relived encounter. It was a semblance of reality, enlightened by sudden insights and the abrupt leaps of intuition that are the product of dream-state explorations.

And eventually in that place, when I recalled all that had bound me, and explored all that lay hidden in my heart about it, I came to see that no one could fetter me or control my actions unless I acquiesced to such limitation.

It was not what Amrey had done to me, I knew in that moment, but what I had done to myself. I had not tested my bonds thoroughly in an energy sense, but only physically. Told that I was limited, I had agreed to be.

The truth of that flooded through me in a realization that brought a cold chill in its wake. Rapidly that chill spread over my body, counterpoint to the sensation that washed from those accursed bands whenever I had tried to use my powers. This was an energy flow from the light body to the physical. It shattered my rapport with dream-time, drained that vision landscape of life and immediacy, and pulled me down, down and back into the body. As it did so, it imbued me with something, in that moment of self-revelation, that transcended what mere flesh should be able to encompass.

I heard the snick as the bracelets clicked open on my wrists. Relief flooded through me, and I willed my eyes to open—

And they would not. I tried to move my arm—and could not. Brief panic came over me, for my body felt like a prison unresponsive to my will.

"Shhh," a woman's voice spoke in comforting tones. "Lie easy, child. It will be a time before your body revives."

Revives? I had been in deep trance before, but never like this. I felt hands upon me, distant; warmth and massage and the aromatic scent of some unguent rubbed into my skin. And gradually, slowly, I felt myself inhabit my body again.

A weak and enervated body. My eyes opened and I lifted one hand, trembling, to my face. The bracelet dangled open, but I froze in shock at the feebleness I perceived in my person. Shriveled, my arm seemed, muscles loose from lack of use, like an invalid who has been too long abed. Something was very wrong with me.

Magya was by my side, others behind her, but my eyes struggled to focus that far. "How long—?" The words croaked forth, my throat hoarse from disuse.

She put a finger on my lips. "Don't tire yourself. It will be a time before you are in vibrant health again."

Someone gave me water to drink and I tried again. "How long have I lain here?" I asked.

Magya's brow furrowed. "Time passes differently in dreamscape."

She spoke as if stating the obvious, and so I suppose she was. Slowly I began to understand. My awakening body screamed protest at me from every limb.

"Magya—" I began again.

"Two years and six months," she forestalled my question.

"What?" I could not believe what I heard, though my body said otherwise.

"We could not foresee how long you would be in dream-time," she explained. "It varies from seeker to seeker. Always the body is in a coma; add to that, that you are not adept in that realm. We cared for you as we do the other sleepers, and kept watch with you in dream-time. You were in no danger, but for the passage of time."

So this was the price I paid: time lost from my life and from my body. So natural an experience to the Duryevu, perhaps, they had not thought to explain in any greater detail. Two years and six months had passed, and left me weak as a babe! And what had Kar Kalim wreaked in all that time? A sudden urgency gripped me and I struggled to sit up, moved abruptly to action. Magya put out one hand and easily shoved me flat again.

"No, child. Remember that time also flows differently between Astareth and here. You may have been long absent from your body, but not half a year has passed in Kar Kalim's new domain.''

Ah. That was so. I calculated swiftly in my head. . . . Four months and some weeks had gone by in Astareth. Surely not long enough, yet, for Kar Kalim to crush all of Drakmil beneath his heel. Or so I hoped. There was still time for me to halt his transgressions, now that I was free to use my powers.

My fingers strayed to the bands hanging loose about my wrists. They were simple golden bracelets now, seemingly devoid of magic.

"How is this possible?" I wondered. "Anything I tried—"

"You did not try certainty," Magya said gruffly. "You were not certain of yourself or your abilities or your desire to resist. You let yourself be muffled, on some deep level."

I blushed and knew that was true, for I had discovered those certitudes in my vision quest. Before, in Moontooth, I had simply flown into a rage that merely engaged my captor more. I had never stopped to explore this external problem by delving inside, not even in the way I made a student do in an elementary exercise of manifestation! I had grappled with the form, not the substance of this binding.

"I thought it so secure," I said with chagrin. "Could I have done this myself at any time?"

"Can a child run before it can walk?" Magya smiled gently. "I think not. To see this self-limitation takes a different perspective than you had at the time. You might have stumbled into it on your own, but it was not likely. We in our numbers could help to lift you out of yourself, to a place where you saw things differently. And saw what to focus on. Once you did, you could work that knot loose for yourself."

Ah. And that was an unusual concept, for me who works always alone. A group permits a different viewpoint to be achieved, a different kind of work to be done, indeed. I had never thought to ask anyone for help.

"And well it could be there was none to help you, R'inyalushni. Perhaps you will alter that in the future. You are welcome here, if you should wish to study or work with us."

I slid the bracelets from my wrists and dropped them to the blanket that covered me. I relished the upwelling sense of connectedness as long-unused occult reflexes engaged. Helpless though my body might be, my other-senses functioned no less well for their long disuse. In moments I was detecting auras, the tension of magic in the air, stray thoughts. . . . I thought to manifest a cantrip effect and felt the old familiar flow of powers moving in their long-practiced courses. I snuffed the faery fire before it could bloom fully, lest I drain myself of physical reserves I could not spare, then gave a tired laugh. In the ways that truly mattered, I was restored.

"I owe you all a great debt," I said to Magya.

"We shall see what you owe us, after you use this."

She stretched forth her hand, and in the palm, a blue-glowing crystal rested. I inhaled sharply. Had this been here all along?

"We have watched Kar Kalim for years, through persons and through craft," she answered my thought. "His hiding of the Gorsek *shia* was not so sly as he likes to think, though his forbiddance of the Prebia ruins keeps such trinkets safe from anyone but us. We have had this in our safekeeping nearly since he put it away, against the day when there would be a use for it. It is purposeless for magical workings, since it is already attuned to an owner. But as we have said, there are other uses for the stone even still."

My desire to destroy Amrey's power was unabated, regardless how much time had or had not passed outside my subjective viewpoint. I took the crystal from her hand, a wrap of silver wire and a silver chain attached. Hands reached to help me slip the chain over my head, and the Styrcian crystal nestled into the hollow of my throat.

I felt like I carried a deadly thing there, and so I did. Nursing a snake at my breast, to use Amrey's expression; one I hoped would not bite me before its time.

I rested my head back upon the bed, and sighed as a wave a tiredness made my eyelids heavy. "Then if it pleases you," I told my allies, "let us see how best to return me to health. And then, to Astareth."

CHAPTER 16

Willpower, food, and the discipline of enforced exercise did much to restore me to myself over the next many weeks. I begrudged the delay, imagining what evils Kar Kalim must be up to in the place I had made my home. Yet when the Deryevu agreed that I was fit enough to leave, the six weeks I had spent amongst them amounted to only six days in Astareth—a translation in time that I was glad for. Rumors reached even the remote Deryevu of the conqueror's unqualififed successes in Astareth. I was glad when I was finally on the road with my companions and journeying out of the Prebia wastelands.

Our journey across the snowy steppes was far slower than pleased me, but alternatives there were none. Magya and the others accompanied me to the gate between our worlds, to see me safely through the Breo'la and the portal they guarded. They, too, had something to accomplish regarding Kar Kalim and their people and I could not gainsay them on that point. But our travel was slow, confined to the pace of horses, and I fretted at the delay. I had no mist-dragon to command here, and though my powers were restored, I now understood the state of weakened energies on this world, and felt the truth of what they said about the fitfulness of magic here. I did not want to strain my resources or theirs, and so left magic aside to travel in the mundane manner they insisted upon.

The time would have weighed heavy on me, but for the exercises Magya set me. Her instruction gave me a mental focus that carried me out of the body for long periods in our travels, so that from sunup to sunset I could scarce say what had transpired on the earth, so engaged was I on other, higher levels. There were meetings, lessons, explorations—all happening on a plane and a place hitherto unknown to me. I tested this new facet of self and learned to relish the difference it made in body energies. Awareness on new levels began to permeate my consciousness. This was not awareness of simple things like auras and thoughts. Rather, I had a new sense of the wholeness of everything around me, of how things were interconnected and aspired to fulfill their natural potentials. It was an education I was loath to break off by time the sprawling Breo'la encampment came into sight.

With my hair long and black like their own and wearing the garb of the Duryevu, the tribesmen we passed took me for one of my companions without a second glance. I wore a talisman-shirt, less bedecked than the others, and though I knew not how to tap its powers, I now felt the energy with which it was imbued. With a calmness and surety whose source mystified me, I rode with the wisewomen to the gate that interrupted the open air of the steppes.

Our progress had an effect I recognized from my own grand entrances in the past: heads turned and tongues whispered, an expanding reverent hush falling over the crowd. People nearby stood back respectfully, while those at a distance pressed forward to see—for the Duryevu, I understood from Magya, were no longer a common sight amongst the nomads, and their presence was most remarkable and unsettling. They were the soothsayers and dream-tellers, and most clansmen had a healthy respect for their fabled abilities, even if they had never experienced them firsthand. So we rode at the apex of a widening pool of silent attentiveness, until we came face to face with the Kalimat guards who stood around the portal.

Magya led our way, myself at her right hand. The guard captain looked unsettled, confronted by this bevy of dream-tellers. He inclined his head respectfully but did not leave his position where his fellows barred the approaches to the gate. Behind him I glimpsed the hallway of Moontooth, and a family leading packhorses out of sight down that hall. Still their exodus trickled through . . .

"We are come to end this," Magya said in a voice that carried far beyond the Kalimat guard. The silence that had been polite grew tense, as folk strained to catch her words. "As was foretold, the end of Kar Kalim's exploits are near. If you stay here, you will likely die when the source of his power is reft from him." She turned her back to the guards-men, and looked at the Breo'la gathered around. "If you would save your families and kin, we urge you to leave this place and not"—she extended an arm—"through that gate-way. Seek the safety of the steppes, as far distant from here as your mounts can carry you."

Sounds of consternation murmured through the crowd as she turned back to the guards. "We send our sister through, with word for Kar Kalim." She pushed me forward with a shove on the arm. "She speaks with our authority."

The guardsman looked uncertain. "You are not authorized to pass. I cannot allow—"

"Kar Kalim has not the Dreaming. He could not foresee our need to be here. Yet here we are. Let her pass, Jegar, son of Vanye, or you contribute to your lord's downfall."

The man was nonplussed to hear his name from the lips of this old woman he had never met. The Duryevu could command by willpower alone, it was said, and so it seemed in this instance. Magya's unbending stance and riveting eyes compelled in a way no other approach would have. Uncertainty gave way to resolve, and he sketched a quick bow to the cluster of wisewomen before him. "Come, Duryev." He gestured to me. "I will give you an escort to Kar Kalim, though he is a long journey from the tower."

"No need," I said, the gift of tongues magically upon me and my Styrcian as flawless as any native's. "I can be by his side with the speed of an arrow. But I have no time to lose."

I gathered my skirts and pushed past him to the threshold of Moontooth.

None opposed me. I paused there, looked over my shoulder at Magya and the rest. They underwent great risk, for in the next moments my perfidy would be revealed, and how they would choose to explain that to their distant kinsmen, I had no idea. The older woman nodded at me once, and closed her eyes for a moment—in the next breath I heard her words in my head. "Go, child. You are right, you have no time to lose."

I turned my back upon them, and stepped through the doorway into Astareth.

For a heartbeat or two my stomach reacted to the transition. I seemed sensitive in a new way, on different levels than before: now the contrast between magical potential here and where I had just been was physically tangible in the air. I smiled to myself. Unfettered at last, with freedom of action in my own home, it was time to put a stop to this business of invaders and misuse of the tower's gates.

There was no longer a door to shut the portal with. Hinges twisted and broken remained affixed to the wall. In the next moments I conjured a door that was a seeming made solid, set it on magically straightened hinges, and slammed that new door shut in the Styrcia gateway. For a moment I heard surprised outcries on the other side, and then silence, for the portal had vanished from sight from their viewpoint, and the rift—to human senses—had been shut.

Not on an energy level, though. I had that yet to tend to where Murl Amrey was concerned, but first I would set my house to rights.

When one commands unearthly powers against the mundane, it is like an adult chastising very small children. It is easily done; they are easily overpowered, and it is easy to ignore their railings afterwards. I had come here already with protections set about myself, and next, took time to unwork and dispel the wardings that Kar Kalim had set about my home. They were few, thankfully, for my own spells of before prevented unwanted exploration and he had been content to let those stand.

Magic that warned him of intrusion, or barred access to Lesseth and other spirit friends of mine—it was suchlike that I dispelled, or redirected so that he was not alerted to their disabling. With that safeguard out of the way, I swept the tower, from topmost chamber to entrance hall, binding karz-dagi and Breo'la and wandering goat-thing alike, and chased them all out of Moontooth, down the terraced steps and out into the mud-churned assembly field, now part of a family camp before the tower. That disgrace I would deal with later, but for now, intruders were out of Moontooth—and the tower properly warded is a bastion proof to any force that might clamor at the outside walls.

I shut and sealed the front entrance as well, and dismissed the Breo'la hordes from my mind.

Back into clothes more of the kind I was used to, a gown and robe and soft half-boots, and then up the stairs once more. There at the top, that gateway into nothingness loomed. It was a place I had feared and abhorred and never cared to look into, but the place, last I knew, that Lesseth had been exiled to.

I braced myself for that exploration but took time also to center in a way new to me, using Duryevu techniques and a mental chant. Tied to higher forces, different perceptions than were my usual, I dared to unlock that gate, and stood on the threshold peering within.

It was a black and howling void, with winds that plucked at clothes and hair and threatened to suck the soul from my body, so terrible and ominous it felt.

It was an unbearable place to look upon, much less be trapped within. By my reckoning I had been in Styrcia twenty days. In that case, twenty weeks had passed here, and how much time had passed for Lesseth in that hellish realm? Would he retain his sanity? That I could not guess, but I had to find out.

I spun a magical traceline, a tether that gave me an anchor point to Moontooth's solid reality. Leaving that secured at the door, I braced myself, and took a step into the blackness before me.

There was nothingness beneath my feet, and vertigo swept away my sense of orientation at once. Was I falling, floating, drifting on that abyssal wind? I had no idea. All was dark, except for the golden line that strung out from my solar plexus to someplace distant in the darkness—but it was not yet time to trace that path back to reality. I must discover if Lesseth was here.

Something cautioned me against simply calling out his name. Those words would be torn from my mouth on that hot dry wind and blow my intention who knew whither? There were dangers lurking in the dark here that would be quick to pounce on one who drew their attention. Instead, I tried a new-learned trick, and concentrated instead on Lesseth's *essence,* on the sense of his personhood and soul and vibration, as it were. I knew well the feel of what I sought, and expanded my senses in search of it.

It worked, for I felt a tugging in a certain direction and followed it, eyes straining at endless gloom to make out a form or shape. No such luck, but there was a stirring before me, something that was the source of distress and agony, a resolution to endure . . . against what?

No sooner wondered, than sensed. There was a nightmarish quality here, the suggestion of things unseen but ready to grab one with a terrifying touch. For me it was yet a small discomfort, a niggling that threatened to grow large. How would I feel if I had spent twenty weeks as the subject of such attention? Did night-fears grow larger the more one gave themself to them? I thought so, for here was Lesseth, semisolid in the dark, and terrors hung around him like a black cloud, the stuff of dream and nightmare, of fear and guilt and self-hatred. Something tugged at his soul, wanting him to depart the body—but he could not leave, for he had no body at all, really, and so he was trapped beneath the attack of a thing that would have caused a dreaming man's heart to stop. In the body one would force oneself screaming awake from such night-terrors, but here, there was no escape.

I touched him, and he fought against me, certain I was yet one more element of the endless nightmare that tormented him.

"It is I," I said, but the dry wind whipped the words from my lips and he struggled harder, sensing deception.

Nothing for it but to take him, struggling, from this place. Outside he would be freed of this insanity, I hoped.

Returning was not so easy. There was the path marked with that golden chord of energy, but the things that held Lesseth in their grip did not want to let him go, and so swarmed over me as well. Self-doubt, sadness, waves of emotion crashed upon me, and then paranoia. Why did I care to rescue him? He would only hinder me as he had before, betray me to Kar Kalim, probably, given the chance—

I kept on out of habit and dogged persistence. Winds like cyclones swept across our path and I knew that if one caught us we would be whipped away from this marker chord, thrown into the abyss forever—

Somehow, we evaded the storms of oblivion, and straggled to the door and out again.

I collapsed on the floor, Lesseth half-materialized and moaning in my arms on the floor beside me. With the last of my will, I closed and sealed that treacherous gateway behind us. To be lost in the nothingness between nothing, where nightmares live and oblivion awaits. . . . It was not a fate I would wish on anyone, perhaps not even Kar Kalim. Better the clean end I brought him, with the cool stone at my breast. Glad I had secured the tower, I took Lesseth to my rooms, and there dreamless sleep embraced us both.

"I am not well," my friend told me, "nor am I unwell. I am . . . drained."

He could not explain it better, for the experience that would have exhausted a human physically and mentally had sucked him dry in another way, tapping into his resilience of self. If a ghost can seem wan, he was so. His physical capabilities had recovered quickly enough, but I was not so certain he was really whole again. He was uncertain, also. "But we have no time to wait on me, if as much time is agone as you say."

Twenty weeks, and who knew what havoc Kar Kalim had wreaked in this interim? Our next step was obvious, to me at least: we must go where there were allies and intelligence, where we could quickly gain an overview of Amrey's actions, and I could determine precisely where to find him, and take him by surprise. For it must be surprise that put us face to face. If ever he suspected what deadly gift I bore him, he would do his utmost to prevent our ever meeting. And that simply could not be.

"Tor Mak," I said. "You are coming there with me."

"What about the horse tribes outside?" Lesseth asked.

I waved a hand dismissively. "They can do nothing against the tower. They are a mess, the backwash of migration that can be cleaned up later, but no immediate threat to us. As long as they are barred from Moontooth's portals, they can do no real harm."

"They will overrun the countryside for food."

"As they have been doing. That can be dealt with later. Kar Kalim is more important, Lesseth, and to get to him, we must journey to Tor Mak first."

He could not argue with my logic. By sunset, we were atop the tower, and Reydjik came to my open-armed summons, boiling out of cloud and mist and night sky to greet us with enthusiastic billows of fog and damp. Soon enough we approached the high-walled city of the Derenestu, where a messenger-spell I sent ahead had forewarned Cendurhil of our coming. The wards were down, the central tower lit, and the wizards assembled there to greet us.

"R'Inyalushni d'aal!" Cendurhil came forward, took my hands as I dismounted. "Kar Kalim has told the world of your defiance and defeat. How glad we are to see that he has not the right of it!"

I did not bother to cloak myself in dweomer, not this time, but looked into Cendurhil's eyes with my own undisguised visage. "His telling is not so far off the mark as all that, Magemaster. But we have much to discuss. The council is here, I see?" I glanced beyond his shoulder at the others as he nodded agreement.

"And anxious to meet with you as well, Lady. Morigaz is half destroyed, for Father of Ashes has erupted after all and threatens the coast and hinterland alike. Ri'ush, Lord of Fire, ignores our entreaties, and quakes and whirlwinds have threatened our city more than once. We see Kar Kalim's hand in all this. He is turning his attentions our way, now that the Salt Coast has fallen beneath his sway. We are as eager as you to stop him, but our martial preparations serve naught against this kind of elemental onslaught."

"Indeed." My tone was grim. "There is more afoot here than you know. Shall we meet now?"

Cendurhil gestured me ahead of him with a wide-flung arm. I swept past, nearly as regal as in the olden days, and it gladdened my heart that I was treated as respectfully without being dweomer-clad, as ever I had been in it.

The wizards of Tor Mak showed us what Kar Kalim did, as much as could be gleaned from their scrying tools versus Amrey's protections from divination. Sickened, I watched him march the hostage citizens of Selenius before his army to Veredux, where they were so much fodder for the archery that the besieged defenders aimed against the foe. More slaughter, more intimidation, until populations revered him in fear and rulers put their necks beneath his boot in ceremony of allegiance, so that their people would be spared Kar Kalim's infamous retributions.

He deployed his continuing influx of Styrcians to various garrison points and governorships and was well on his way to consolidating the east. Now, ignoring the near-wilderness of the south, he prepared to embark his forces on Ursbachi hulls. His horse army would be delivered to Morigaz's doorstep, most prosperous port in the west. There would be no real defense in that city, caught reeling from natural disaster. The militias that Tor Mak had rallied might serve to hold that particular stronghold, but men in this part of Drakmil had felt unthreatened by Kar Kalim in the east, and had not taken seriously his potential threat to them. They were unprepared to repel a concerted invasion, much less one spearheaded by magic that could destroy their cities as easily as I conjured faeryfire. If Kar Kalim landed on their doorstep, I thought certain doom awaited them.

Lesseth, restored to his immaterial state, agreed with me. "The only way to halt this is to deal with Kar Kalim now, before he departs Telemar."

Cendurhil and others exchanged glances. "Certainly we wish that we could," Gaelis said. "We can gain access to the Emprelor, but what to do once there . . . ?"

I smiled without humor. "That, honored adepts, is what this is for." I pulled the Styrcian crystal out from about my neck, and set it on the table before them. "A wizard-stone," I said to their sharp intakes of breath. "But not just any stone. This is a *shia* Kar Kalim once used, and so it is attuned to him. When it is in proximity with his present *shia*, they will destroy each other and all that is around them."

The silence was abrupt and strained. "You cannot mean to take that yourself," Lesseth said quietly.

I looked at him, startled. Why, certainly I did. Who else would or could or should take it, but me? Then I realized what he was saying, what the others were saying with their silence also. For the bearer of the stone to bring it close to Kar Kalim, meant death to both.

I looked down at the blue-glowing crystal. Of course. Somehow that conclusion had not come cogent into my thoughts. Some part of me avoiding thinking out the natural consequences, I supposed . . . And yet. It was what I must do. I could not ask another to do it for me.

"Kar Kalim threatens the well-being of two worlds," I said.

"This is the only way to put a stop to it. I know how he thinks, what he is likely to do. I have fought him before and know what to expect from him again. It must be me, and it will be."

My tone of finality did not invite argument, and yet Liuthwe spoke up. "We could send a seeming in your place—"

"No. A seeming would be defenseless, should magic be called for. I will do it, and that is the end of that discussion."

They resisted me yet a while, but my will was adamant. No one could propose a way to get the *shia* close to Kar Kalim with complete certainty short of a person carrying it, and to that task I alone was suited.

So we forged our plans in the night, and I was left to sleep through most of the next day. By sunset the wizards of Tor Mak had gathered in high conclave, and I joined them in their workings that would, we hoped, bring an end to Kar Kalim.

We spied him out, as close we might. There was no way to see Kar Kalim direct, but while his person was obscured from such spying, his surroundings were not. I recognized the room in the vision Liuthwe manifested for us. It was a long chamber in the palace where Amrey had started to study text and lore plundered from the libraries of Telemar. Now, to judge by artifacts lying about, it was a workroom as much as a study room. Whatever he might be engaged in there could surely lead to no good. I would be happy to disrupt it with my unexpected arrival.

Teleportation was never a spell I had mastered, and it takes a special sensibility to make it work across long distances, to a place never seen or seen only in vision. Gaelis was long and careful in the preparation of that spell, never faltering, speaking to me in a distracted aside when finally she had something to say.

"Stand you ready over there, Lady. This is a variation on the basic . . . it will not simply displace you. This will open a tunnel for you, rather than a doorway, and we will keep the passage open for a time here, as long as we are able.''

Her words confused me; I thought such transference was a quick dislocation in space, nothing more. Cendurhil caught the look upon my face and explained. ''We are making, in a manner of speaking, a little rift. We will be able to see through, as long as it is open, though we cannot join you. You who have stepped through can come back the same way.''

His meaning sank in, hastened by Lesseth's whispered comment. ''So you can return, if there is time.''

Ah. So that was the purpose of this fancy work. We did not know how long it would take for the *shian* to interact, for the Duryevu could not say. Whether instantaneous, or a process that built up over time—they were allowing me a chance to get away, did the opportunity present itself. And did it not, if the interaction of the stones had a rapidly destructive effect, then surely they were leaving themselves open to disaster as well, in Tor Mak.

Cendurhil squelched my protests with a look. ''We have talked this out amongst us. It is not for you to say what risk we may undergo or not. You have chosen yours, and we, ours. Leave it at that, Lady.''

I bowed to the inevitable, and hoped that their foolish generosity did not earn them death as well. I said good-bye to Lesseth in my thoughts, where we spoke most confidentially. I felt his spirit embrace me, and then felt him fade from the physical sphere.

The wizards of Tor Mak worked their magic, and the dimensional doorway opened in the center of the circle of power they had drawn. Firelight shimmered through the gap. I clasped the wizard-stone tight in my hand for this journey— a little more comfortable, that, than carrying certain death around my neck—and stepped through the portal before a moment longer had passed.

His back was to me at the end of the room, his figure outlined by fire, and I thought in that moment of Amrey's visit to Valerian, once lord of this palace. A similar surprise, then, approaching an unguarded back. He did not stay ignorant for long, for some spell or second sense warned him of intrusion. He turned to face me, stepping to one side as he did, and I gasped at what I saw there.

What I had thought to be flames in an open fireplace were not. Ri'ush, lord of fire elementals, stood as a body of flames upon the floor, in converse with Kar Kalim. It was his fire and smoke that lightened that end of the room.

"You!" Amrey was astonished to see me walking towards him. This was Murl as I had never seen him before: dressed in velvets and silks, the garb of an Arguentan nobleman. His fortunes and position had changed since last we'd met, and it showed in his stance and commanding air. He raised one bejeweled hand to gesture, to put me in a binding spell, but this time I was prepared for him—not only with my own magics, but reinforced with protections bestowed by the wizards of Tor Mak. I felt those protections give, one after the other, like shells of nested eggs being cracked, yet at the core of them I remained as yet safe, unhindered by my enemy's first spell casting. I quirked a lip—the look on his face told me as clearly as words that this was the first time his casual binding had not held or stopped its target. Before he could redouble his efforts, I cast a spell of my own that I had had readied and waiting.

A sphere of rainbow-swirling light flew towards him, and he was occupied for precious moments in fending it off and neutralizing it. It was a globe of entrapment that, had it settled about him, would have thoroughly isolated him from his surroundings. I did not really expect it to ensnare him, but it served its true purpose—delay and distraction. I was much

closer by time the globe vanished, and felt the Styrcian crystal
in my hand warming with internal heat.

He felt the same from the stone at his throat, glowing suddenly brighter. "What—?" He touched it with his fingers, a
look of confusion on his face. He spotted the bluish light
leaking from between my fingers, and realization of his danger
dawned upon him.

"Lord of Fire!" he said over his shoulder. "You always
said that you would give the Dark Lady a warm reception,
did you ever have the chance to host her." He backed away
from me as I came more near. "Then do you have at her now.
Take her to your home this instant, and I will cede you Morigaz, complete!"

A grin and a booming laugh split the avatar's fire-formed
face. "Done!" he agreed, and stepped between Kar Kalim
and me.

I faltered, uncertain how to proceed.

The *shia* in my hand began to resonate, a subtle vibration
that grew stronger with each passing heartbeat. Ri'ush loomed
in his elemental form, some attribute of the summoning spell
insulating the air of this room from his furnacelike heat, but
fire roared and the radiance of him was a palpable wall of
force as he studied me.

And then he dashed, with all the speed of a wildfire, straight
towards me.

Retreat would save my skin but would not harm Amrey,
and now that he was forewarned, we would never have as
good a chance again. Yet I dared not let the fire lord set hand
to me. My protections would last me some little while, but
they were not intended for assault by an elemental of his stature, nor for a sojourn on the elemental sphere. If he laid hand
to me and took me there, it would mean my death, and that
to no purpose.

I feinted to the right, then ran to the other side, hoping against hope to skirt his mad rushing charge and win close enough to Amrey for the wizard-stones to do their work. Even as I darted, I saw Ri'ush change his course, saw he would intercept me, that my effort would fail—

I heard his words before I saw his shape. "Inya, no!" Lesseth near shouted in my ear. He materialized before me, scrabbling at my hand. Foolish, foolish spirit! Come through the rift with me in that trick he had honed at Kar Kalim's expense . . . His hand became more manifest and pried my fingers open.

"Go! Flee!" he commanded, "before he is upon you! I'll gift this to Amrey!"

Protest died on my lips as Ri'ush closed with me. Out of self-preservation I fell back, away from his awesome heat, slipping away from grasping fingers of flame that singed my hair and set my gown to smoking. At the same moment Lesseth pulled the *shia* from my unresisting fingers. He was our best hope, now, immaterial, swift moving, airborne, while all eyes were upon me—

The avatar of the Lord of Fire did set hand to me then, in that last moment where I stumbled back through the rift, and I cried out as his elemental heat singed through warding spells and crisped my shoulder beneath his touch. But then it was too late and I tumbled back into the warm night air of Tor Mak, cooler still than that workroom in Telemar. Through the rift that linked us I saw a wall of flames, stymied in its advance by this spellgate that retrieved only what it sent. And there, beyond and through those flames, a man's figure moving.

A blue glow heightened, then went incandescent, and a flash blinded us even as Gaelis collapsed the rift, severing us from the destruction of Telemar half a continent away that lit the night sky with a sickly blue glow far, far over the horizon.

* * *

The Wastes of Kar Kalim stretch from what was once Veredux to the ruins of Mardevis, and inland past the headwaters
of the Sevian. Telemar has vanished with its fabled wealth
and most of the Ursbach navy. It is just as well that Arguentan
enemies are fewer in number, for the folk of the Salt Coast,
also, are fewer, and struggle to assimilate the Breo'la who
were stranded here when dimensional gates rent by force cast
our two worlds out of juncture with each other.

Moontooth was not damaged on the physical sphere, although now there is a second gateway into a haunting abyss
where once I could view a cold and grassy plain. The debate
about the Breo'la resettlement continues; Halvericus leads a
new council of autarchs, and I have much to say to that
body—not as a fabled near-deity, but as the woman who has
taken responsibility for the families and foreign clans en-
camped upon her land and their refugee cousins leaving
once-conquered autarchies and hoping fruitlessly to return
home. I have prevented some warfare where Breo'la thought
themselves in rulership, and though Singfa remains in horse
tribe hands, the nomads are hard put to fit comfortably into
the depopulated mountain lands they claim for their own. For
them, it seems aid will be needful, the humane thing to do.
There is much work needed to restore the Salt Coast to a
state of peace, and I fear at times that the feuds and blood-
hatred engendered by Kar Kalim's war of conquest will mar
the Arguentans—and the Breo'la—for many generations to
come.

It can be hoped that I am wrong. The karzdagi, for one,
have transferred their loyalties to me, for with the restoration
of my powers I soon learned how easy it was to steer those
simple, animalistic minds. It is far harder to curb their beastly
natures, and all I can do for now is keep them away from
humans, allow them to prowl the far hills of Caronne, where

they hold themselves ready for some future service not yet defined. Crookfang does not seem to believe my ruse, but his fellows do. I keep a close eye on the dog-men, until I can see what best to do with them.

For the friends who perished in the wizard war against Kar Kalim I have long since grieved; the scars of my burns remind me what price is paid by proud and self-serving leadership. No more do I hold audience in disguising glamour and mask; no longer do I work on purpose to feed the mystique that has insulated me from this world and its people all these years. The illusion that hid the road to Moontooth has been dispelled, for there is much work to do, and much coming and going to accomplish it. I had never wanted such responsibilities as autarch, but there is no way around it now. Kar Kalim left his mark on the land, and on me as well. And who else has seen Styrcia and understands what drives these people from a near-dying world, who will fight against any odds just to survive? I do not like the Breo'la, but I respect them, and that is the basis for something good to grow between us.

I think of that when Halvericus tries to shout me down in council meetings. I have ever been one to enjoy a man who is a challenge. Sometime soon, I will have to invite him to Moontooth as friend, not as fellow autarch, and we shall see what kind of alliance can grow from that beginning.

Meanwhile, Kar Kalim no longer overshadows the land, and though the Wastes are avoided by all, grudging trade has started between Breo'la and Arguentans elsewhere on the Coast. I am at peace, most nights, when I sleep.

Wherever a spirit goes when it has passed beyond, I hope Lesseth thinks it was worth the price.